CRAVE

The Blood Secrets Series

A.K. ROSE

To the ones who were told to behave,

who bit their tongues until they tasted blood,

and still wondered what it would feel like

to be ruined by someone who whispered,

"Be good for me."

This is for the ache you buried beneath your ribs.

The hunger you tried to silence.

The craving that never left.

This story is a dark romance.

Crave contains content intended for mature audiences only. It explores the psychological, emotional, and erotic boundaries of obsession, power, and control. The following themes may be distressing to some readers:

Content Warnings:

• Non-consensual and dubiously consensual sexual situations

• Psychological manipulation and gaslighting

• Erotic coercion and control

• Stalking and obsessive behavior

• Possessive and controlling love interests

• Blood play and knife play

• Breath play and impact play

• Sexual degradation and praise kink

• Power imbalances and forced proximity

• Public and semi-public sexual scenes

• Religious trauma themes

• Parental neglect and emotional abuse

• PTSD and trauma flashbacks

• Scenes of violence, including torture

• Death of secondary characters

• Graphic sexual content throughout

This book is not intended for all readers. It contains intense **emotional triggers** and scenes of **extreme psychological descent.** Please read with care.

vi

Unlock Porcelain Girl. Your descent begins here

Porcelain Girl is a standalone Blood Secrets teaser — a dark, brutal descent into shame, obedience, and hunger.
Angelica Ares smiled for the cameras. She knelt for them. She wasn't born to rule — she was raised to be obedient. In the end, it's not the name that saves her. It's the brothers who break her.
This isn't a full book.
It's a sharp taste of everything Blood Secrets promises — raw, twisted, and unforgettable.
One-click now. If you dare.

Chapter One

ANGELICA

"HE MURDERED HER, CAN YOU BELIEVE THAT?" THE woman's whisper drifted from the back of the crowd. "He killed his own wife in cold blood before he turned the gun on himself."

"Dear Heavenly Father," the Priest called a little louder. "We ask you to heal the broken in heart and bind up their wounds. Mercifully look upon those who are bereaved here today and take them into your arms."

"They say the study was a mess, blood splatter all over the walls and the floor."

I stared at the casket in front of me as it was lowered into the earth.

THUD.

Cold dirt hit the shimmering oak as it sank deeper.

"Can you imagine that? Imagine the kind of man who'd take a gun and—"

Movement came further up the line of men beside me. Silas wrenched his head around and the vile whispering ended instantly. No words were needed...not when you felt the choke-hold of his wrath.

THUD.

I flinched hard.

Promise me. My mom's faint words resounded in my head. *Promise me on your life, Angel.*

THUD.

Swear. Mom's voice pushed in. *I need you to swear to me.*

That ache in the back of my throat clenched. I need you to—

I closed my eyes as that desperation grew louder and that same panic returned.

I NEED YOU TO SWEAR.

THUD.

Jolt. My body jerked and trembled. Fingers clenched tight around the icy ache.

The piercing squeal of tires followed in my head. The memory more vibrant than the plague of blood red roses covering the two caskets in front of us.

I need you to swear on your life. SWEAR TO ME ON YOUR LIFE. SWEAR IT. SWEAR IT!

"I promise," the words were nothing more than the movement of my lips, uttering the words she desperately needed to hear. "On my life, I swear."

THUD.

The soft smack against my arm made me open my eyes. I glanced at Gabe. Red-rimmed eyes shimmered with tears, pleading for someone to ease his pain. I couldn't ease his pain, no more than I could ease my own. Still, I took his hand, my knuckles aching and throbbing, finding the warmth of his. His soft, sad smile made my chest hurt even more.

Theo never moved beside him, hiding pin-prick pupils behind dark sunglasses, staring at nothing. Jude was next, his head dropped, his shoulders curling under the weight of not one casket in front of us, but the two of them. He shoved his hands into his pockets, his grief all consuming.

But not Silas. There was no bowing from the man who stood at the head of our line. No, there was no sign of emotion at all. Not until he slowly turned his head and that hateful bottomless glare settled on mine.

My pulse quickened.

They can never know. Mom's plea resounded. *Angel, they can never know.*

"That concludes this morning's sermon. The family has asked that you respect them in their hour of need. Any form of well wishing may be directed at the small and intimate gathering we have provided. If you want, linger for a moment and express your love for Dante and Meredith, then please feel free to—"

Silas turned away, moving first as he cut across the front of the gathering and barged past the Priest. The old man of the cloth stumbled sideways, his eyes widening with fear. His assistant lunged, grabbing hold of him to keep the old man upright as all heads tracked my brother.

"Jesus." Gabe muttered as he shook his head.

Lincoln Ares stepped forward. Grabbing the Priest's hand. "I'm sorry, Father. Please accept my apologies on behalf of my nephew. He's in a lot of pain."

The Priest nodded as everyone moved. Those behind us stepped around us, casting roses into the holes in the earth, moving from one, then to the other.

"Are you coming?" Gabe asked.

I turned my head, my thoughts achingly slow. The others were already gone. Theo, Jude...leaving Gabe as he waited for me. I gave a slow nod and followed, my heels sinking into the soft grass as we made our way to the reception.

This wasn't for us.

This was for them.

For all the whispers and all the lies.

For the eyes that saw everything, drinking in our pain as though they were dying of thirst. I stepped up the stairs of the sprawling building, dark brown wood matched with black stone and steel made this place feel somber and empty.

The conversion burst into life as I stepped inside. All those fake tears that'd been holding back while the sermon was given now flowed freely and loudly. I followed the rest of my family, heading to a small room at the rear of the building. Platters of food lay spread out on tables, water and juice in full glass carafes that beaded on the outside.

Gabe grabbed a glass and poured, splashing apple juice into the depths before he grabbed them and headed back to me.

"How long do we have to stay here?" He asked.

I shook my head. "I don't know, until we're told we can leave, I guess." I took the glass from him although I didn't lift it to my lips.

I ached as I stood there. My ribs were painful, clenched tight around a heart full of lies. Others came and went. I lost track of their faces. Some blubbered, grabbing hold of me in a panic, their long nails clawing my arms as they slammed me against their chest.

I never fought, never pulled away, just emptied myself a little more, bit by bit until only the flesh remained. Until, finally... there was no more. I glanced around the small room, finding Jude at the doorway.

"Thank you for coming. Thank you...thank you so much for coming. Yes, we appreciate all your concern. We will reach out if we need anything. Thank you. Thank you for coming. Thank you."

Over and over and *over*.

"Let's get out of here." Gabe whispered.

I gave a nod as he took the empty glass from my hand. I stared at it for a second, unable to remember when I drank the contents before he placed it down and motioned me forward. I followed him, slipping behind Jude and headed for the rear of the building where a car for us waited.

Silence lasted all the way home. Once we were inside Gabe turned around and gently pulled me close. "You can come to me anytime." Thick, husky words filled my ears as I nodded.

I shifted against him feeling his hard chest pressed against mine. He'd become too big lately, too hard, too...masculine. Thank God he stayed sweet, unlike his brothers.

I wrapped my arms around him, gripped him tight and then pulled away. "I will, and you too. If you ever want to talk, or..."

"Sisterly advice." He joked with a smile.

It was a joke, although none of it was funny. I winced, then gave a huff. "That's it, sisterly advice, you know where to find me."

"I do." That sad smile grew only sadder as it stretched. "In the bedroom next to mine."

I shook my head and stepped away, watching him turn around, taking long strides to head for the kitchen at the rear of the house. He was always headed there. I turned around, listening to the utter silence. There were no staff today. No house cleaner to dust or vacuum, adjusting the vases perfectly in place. No chef on standby to cook my brothers whatever they wanted. Just us. Just silence.

I glanced along the hall, catching Gabe disappearing before I headed for the front of the house. They say the study was a mess, blood splatter all over the walls and the floors. My steps were soundless on the thick runner along the hall, until I stepped onto the wooden floor and turned left toward the study.

The place where it happened.

Mom.

Dad...

And death.

I stopped at the closed door, my heart pounding. That uncontrollable urge to look over my shoulder reared its head. I spent my whole life in this house doing just that. Watching out for them, always ready for their cruel words and their hateful stare.

They didn't want me before, and they sure as Hell won't want me now.

A name meant nothing.

I wasn't a true Ares.

I was a fake...*and a liar*.

My fingers shook as I grabbed the round, ornate brass handle, turned then pushed. Flashes of images assuaged me. Then and now. Then...with the blood sprayed across the room and my mother's dead body sprawled out in front of the desk and now with the desk clean and uncluttered. Not a book was out of place. Not a pen on the desk. Nothing but cleanness...and the faint scent of alcohol.

Then...

I took a step, my pulse thundering in my ears as I settled on the brand new chair pushed into place. But that wasn't the chair that'd been here. That wasn't the chair in my head. No, the soft brown leather of that chair was darkened with splatters of blood, just like the arc of spray that cut across the books behind him. The ones now removed.

I took a step deeper inside, moving around the edge of the desk and lifted my hand to the bookshelf. That throbbing, growing thing crawled up my chest and into the base of my throat. My fault...my—fault.

"What are *you* doing here?"

I spun around and stumbled backwards, finding Silas standing in the doorway.

"Well?" He stepped inside, scanned the desk and the computer and anything else I might've touched.

"Nothing." I murmured, lowered my head and made for the door.

He grabbed my arm, jerked me around until he pushed me hard against the desk. *GET THE FUCK OUT OF MY HOUSE!* The words burned in his stare. Even if they didn't reach his lips. It didn't matter that this house was all I remembered. That this family was the only family I knew.

"They..." I whispered. "Were my family too."

His lips curled before he pushed me away like he was revolted by the touch of me. His hard chest rose with a breath. He didn't wear a tie now, in the corner of my eye I saw it clenched in his grip. But I stared at the tattoos that now peeked out from his open shirt.

"Don't come in here again." He snarled, staring at the desk instead of me. *"Now, get the fuck out."*

I moved as fast as my trembling legs would carry me, lunging around him and scurrying for the door. I didn't stop, not until I raced along the hallway and turned down to the small wing of our rooms.

Gabriel's music slipped out from under his closed bedroom door. His words still hovered in the back of my mind. But I didn't stop as I hurried past, yanked the handle of my bedroom door and stumbled inside.

Soft, pale pink greeted me. I closed the door behind me and leaned back against the frame as tears welled in my eyes. We don't want you...we don't want you. We don't...

Warmth spilled, raining down my cheeks. I had to get out now. I had to find a way to leave. I pushed off the door and stumbled to my bed, my mind racing with just how to do that. This wasn't about their outright hatred of my existence. No, this vein of betrayal flowed deeper.

The police ruled it as a murder suicide, even my parents own friends whispered as such standing behind us at the funeral. As cruel as that was...it was better than the truth. Better than knowing what happened.

Better for them.

And for me.

I grabbed my cell from the bedside cupboard, finding the only person who could help me now.

I'm ready to leave here now. Can you help?

I hit send and waited, lifting my gaze to the bedroom door. It was weeks since my parent's deaths, weeks while I waited for the truth to come out. It hadn't. But that didn't mean it wasn't going to. I knew only too well what would happen then.

They'd come for me.

I lowered my gaze to my cell. I had to make a plan, gather what money I had in my account. It wasn't much. Fifty thousand maybe. It'd get me a plane ticket to the middle of nowhere, that's all I cared about. If I laid low, changed my hair...and my name it might stop them.

Jesus, please let it stop them.

Beep.

I looked down, through the washed out blur and found my boyfriend's message.

Penn: Tell me what you need and it's yours.

A sob tore free. Penn was the only one I could trust. The only one who knew how cruel these men had been to me and the only one who knew how dangerous they were. His father was a lawyer, maybe he could help me get a new ID and smuggle me out of the country somehow?

I didn't know.

But at least I had a plan.

I gripped my cell, staring at the beautiful, pink room built for a daughter my mother wanted...and one the rest of my family tolerated. A daughter who was ready to leave this house and the Ares name behind.

A daughter who was desperate to survive.

Chapter Two

SILAS

Two weeks later.

THE CLUB WAS FUCKING PACKED. Women jostled for prime spots on the dance floor while the guys crowded darkened corners where they drank and had lap dances in front of us. As entertaining as it was watching some asshole finger a bitch for the third time, I'd had enough. I rose from my seat, earning a glance from one of my boys, Jamison. "You out of here?"

"Nah," I shook my head. "Just to the bar."

I didn't want to go home to the hollow fucking rooms of our home. I sure as Hell didn't want to go home to her—*Mom's fucking angel.*

I leaned both elbows on the bar and pushed the empty glass forward. Heads turned my way, eyes widened a second later when they recognised who I was. It didn't take long with our faces plastered all over the goddamn media. Who else's father murdered their mother, then blew out his fucking brains dressed in Armani?

My father, that's *who*.

"This doesn't look like your scene either."

I turned my head finding a blonde next to me. "Oh yeah?" I muttered. "And what exactly do you think is my scene?"

She gave a soft shrug, those brown eyes roaming my body. "Oh, I dunno. An illegal street race perhaps?"

The corners of my mouth tugged a little. I scanned the crowd, hating this goddamn place. I'd give anything to be outside, to feel the cold air biting my face and the searing scent of gasoline in my lungs. But I wasn't out there with the guys pushing my bike as fast as it'd go, because right now I didn't belong there either.

The weight of my own goddamn legacy weighed me down.

The glass slid toward me. I grabbed it, downing the contents until that burn moved through me. Laughter pushed in and whispers followed as the blonde moved closer. I could see her friends urging her on, daring her to approach the hard Ares bastard who was looking desperate as fuck.

That's because I was.

I nodded to the bartender. "Leave the bottle."

He knew better than to argue. I downed the next glass and poured as the blonde moved closer. Was she still here?

"You're beautiful, you know that?" She shifted while her

girlfriends jabbed her in the side. "Yeah," she added. "I'm pretty sure you know that."

I turned, giving her my full attention. "Beautiful, huh?" My words slurred as I grabbed her, sliding my hand around to the back of her neck.

Long waves of her hair slipped over my fingers. She reminded me of someone. Someone who nagged at the back of my mind, along with the empty fucking tomb we called home. My focus shifted to the crowd, gravitating to a group of suited up coke-sniffing chumps and found my brother smack bang in the middle. He laughed and drank, one arm wrapped around some random bitch. His attention shifted, finding me instantly before he drunkenly lifted a glass in fucking salute. Even from here I could see he was fucking wasted.

What a goddamn bloodline our parents left behind.

He murdered her, can you believe that?

The words pushed in, leaving me to look away. But the blonde found him. "You know him or something?"

"Yeah." I slid my hand from her neck and grabbed my glass. "Or something."

The bottle in front of me didn't last for some reason. Inch by inch, pour by pour it dwindled until I didn't see one empty bottle, I saw two.

"You want to get out of here?" She slid her hand along my arm. "You can take me to your place."

I laughed and shook my head. "You don't want to go there."

She gripped my jaw, forcing my gaze to hers. "But I do."

Her brown eyes shimmered. No, that voice whispered. She didn't really want to go to the murder house. But the thought didn't take hold. Instead, I drained the last dregs and reached into my pocket, pulling out my black Amex. "You know what? *Fuck it.* Let's go."

The card was swiped in a heartbeat. I grabbed the thing, then her hand and headed for the front. Doors opened.

"Mr. Ares, enjoy your evening" The bouncer called.

I barely heard him, sucking in the cold night air as I scanned the cars. Headlights flared as a sleek black BMW pulled around and parked in front. The driver was out in an instant, rounding the front to open the rear door. I climbed in, dragging her with me.

The door didn't even close before she was on top of me. The sequins on her fucking dress scratched my face as she pushed her tits against my mouth. I didn't have the goddamn strength to fight. Just take it. Take what you fucking want from me. I'm done.

We made it home. I couldn't remember much, stumbling in through the rear of the house. My clothes dragged from my body as I found my room and stumbled inside.

"I'm gonna fuck you so well, you'll never want me to leave."

I doubted that.

I doubted that very much.

I gave a nod and a slur, saying something. Her hands were all over my cock, yanking open my jeans. Sharp nails stung the head.

"Watch it!" I hissed.

"Sorry." She murmured, grabbing the back of my neck to drag my mouth to hers.

Jesus Christ. It was like getting mauled by a bear. All nails and fucking desperation. I stumbled backwards, hit the side of the bed and fell...and the bitch fell with me.

Lips, tongue.

Her mouth was on my cock, taking it all the way inside. How the fuck I was hard, I didn't know. Still, I closed my eyes, fighting the muted wave of pain in my chest and the alcohol, trying my best to focus.

He murdered her, can you believe that?

That ravenous abyss in my chest grew larger as someone climbed on top of me. I didn't even remember who. All I remembered was the image of that study the moment I opened the door and saw what waited for me.

Mom.

Dad.

And all the goddamn blood.

"That's it, baby."

I bounced and bounced and fucking bounced. My stomach rolled until the burn of alcohol splashed into the back of my throat.

"Oh *GOD* that's it."

What the fuck?

I looked down as she flung her hair back, grinding and riding, her dress now gone. When the fuck did that happen? Who the fuck was she? I had no idea and it was far too late to find out. My balls tightened as she rode my cock like a goddamn mechanical bull.

Her moans were grating, her face nothing more than a haze. One I was already desperate to forget. I closed my eyes, unleashing a moan that was part desperation and a whole lot of agony. But she unleashed a cry of release and my cock did its own thing, twitching and jerking as I came hard.

A second was all it took to understand exactly what I'd done. I looked down as those violent thrusts slowed and she slid off me, falling to the bed like a rag doll.

"Oh my God, that was so good." She moaned.

I looked at the mess she left behind. "Condom." I managed.

She lifted her head, cracking one eye open. "It's a little late for that, wouldn't you say?"

A little late?

I had no idea what the fuck just happened.

"Besides." She pushed up, kissing me on the lips before she snuggled right in against me. "I'm on the pill. We don't want kids just yet, do we? I plan on getting to know you real well first, Silas." Her nails dug into my side as she pressed harder against me. "And I want you to get to know me as well."

No.

Fuck no.

I opened my mouth to say just that, but it was no use...she was passed the fuck out. Her heavy breaths turned into a snore. I unleashed a moan and lifted my arm, shoving her aside. "Get the fuck off me."

My cum cooled against my thighs, leaving me to swipe my hand through the mess and slowly drag my ass up from the bed before I stumbled for the bathroom.

I didn't even reach for the light, just took a piss, then used the hand towel to clean myself. Shadows blurred. Fuck, how smashed was I? I didn't have the answer for that, just shoved out my hand, bracing on the door as I made for the bed once more and fell, hitting it hard.

A moan came from someone beside me. There was a panicked moment that rose from the dark, before in an instant, it was snatched away...and everything else with it.

Beep.

I surfaced for a second, then plunged back down.

Beep.

I flailed, my face buried into the pillow and somehow found my phone. One eye cracked open to find the blurry caller ID. Motherfucker. My finger pressed the button before I pulled it close to my ear. "St. James. I told you to never call me again."

"You'll want this one." His deep growl echoed, reminding me of my father. An ache flared instantly in my chest. "I have information about your mother."

My mother?

The words were icy water in my veins pushing the drunken haze further away. I shifted in bed. "What kind of information?"

"The kind of information that will rock your world."

I glanced over my shoulder to the shadowed figure under the sheets and rose. Faint memories came back to me. Some fucking club where I was smashed off my face. Claw marks that still stung across my body. A woman who was very available. I didn't even remember her name.

Fear pushed deeper. That knowing hovered just out of reach and my pulse sped. Still, I rose and made my way out of my bedroom, closing the door behind me. "Speak."

There was a heartbeat of silence. London St. James, like my father, wasn't used to others speaking to him like that. In fact I doubt anyone did...or saw daylight after. I licked my lips, tasting the bitter tang of regret. Right now I didn't give a fuck what St. James liked or didn't like.

"You didn't want to be involved in the war with Hale and the Order." I walked along the hallway where our bedrooms were, stopping outside Theo's open door. His bedroom was still dark, his bed still made. "I think that was a mistake," St. James chided.

"Oh yeah?" This asshole was starting to piss me off.

I kept walking, stopping at the small alcove and the bedroom door at the end of the hall, my sister's Angelica's. "How's that?"

"Because I have in my possession a recording...of your mother... on the date of her death...having sex with a man who's not your father."

I froze staring at her door.

My pulse thundered.

My world darkened.

"You want to say that again?"

Fucking bullshit.

Fucking BULLSHIT.

This motherfucker was going to say anything. He was going to say—

"I'm watching the recording right now. It's her, your mother and another man...and not only that...your sister, Angelica...she knows the truth."

That brutal rage plummeted inside me, carving all the way through the pain and the loss. "Send me the recording, London...no more lies. No more secrets. I want the truth."

"I agree." He said and started typing. "It's time you get to the bottom of this. I'm sending it now. If you want more...I have it. Find out who did this, Silas and protect your family."

"I will." I stared at my sister's door, then hung up the call.

My breaths were heavy, staring at the darkness of her door. Fingers clenched around the cell. I took a step as a beast inside me howled for vengeance. I shook, desperate for the need to go in there, to tear her from her fucking bed and scream in lying goddamn face.

She knew.

She fucking knew.

That goddamn bitch stood next to us as we buried our parents and still she said nothing. It took all my goddamn strength to move backwards, but I did, turning around and headed for my bedroom. One click and the glare was instant, flooding the room. A low moan came from the woman in my bed. I bend down, picking up her dress and her purse and threw it toward her. "Get dressed, then get out."

She opened her eyes. Black mascara a damn mess. "What?"

"I said." I leaned on the bed, seeing her clearly now. *"Get dressed, then get the fuck out."*

Her lip trembled as she shook her head. Stupid whore didn't know when she was used. Only...it seemed like she was the one who did all the using. I rose, waiting for the realization to hit.

It did...

And it was messy.

Tears came as she crawled from the bed, and then came the screaming. I stood there, taking her blows and slaps, all the while my mind replaying St. James's words. *My mother... fucking another man?* There was no way it was her. It couldn't be...my parents had their fucking faults. But they were in love.

"I thought we had something!" The bitch in front of me screamed.

"We did," I answered coldly. "A mistake."

She dressed and I walked her out, messaging for an Uber before leaving her outside the house.

"You're a bastard, you know that?" Her words stopped me.

I gave a nod. "I know," then walked back in, closing the door behind me.

I had a video to watch.

A sister to interrogate.

One way or another, I was finding out what happened. I headed back to my room, finding Theo leaning against the doorway to his bedroom. "That was entertaining."

My lip curled. "Where the fuck were you?"

He gave a shrug, not answering. I glanced at his pupils and shook my head. "You're a fucking disgrace."

He turned as I made for my bedroom. *"And you're the fucking pride of the Ares name!"* He called. "It's only a matter of time, Silas before good 'ol Uncle Linc comes calling, and tears our entire business apart!"

I slammed the door behind me.

Goddamn asshole!

He was right. I winced as that agony grew claws in my chest. My breaths were tight, that ache moving deeper. As much as I hated that druggy sonovabitch I called a brother, he was right. Lincoln was breathing down our goddamn neck, just waiting for the opportunity to take the Ares business for himself. After all, it was all he ever wanted right? Take my legacy. Take my life.

My cell came alight with a message.

Inbox: Video you asked for—London.

I made for my desk, yanking out the chair and hit the mouse of my computer, bringing the screen to life. There it was...waiting for me in my inbox. I clicked the link, opening the video and stopped with the mouse hovering over the play.

I didn't know what I was in for...but I had a feeling it wasn't good.

Chapter Three

ANGELICA

Goosebumps raced along my arms. I shivered, rubbing them. I wanted to blame it on the cool aircon air billowing out of the vents overhead, but it wasn't. I risked a glance across the expansive room drowned in everything red cedar to him. My brother, Silas.

My chill was because of him.

Any other day he refused to acknowledge me, going out of his way to pretend I didn't exist in his life. Today I would've preferred that to the chilling glare he directed my way. Our gaze met, my pulse skipped in response. His dark brown eyes never moved from mine, searching for something. But there was a twitch at the edge of his lips...a sneer. Panic pushed in and my thoughts raced.

What did I do now?

The door opened abruptly and a frantic, balding man awkwardly dressed in an expensive suit rushed in. "Right, sorry about that folks," he looked down as he spoke, flopping into his

22

chair and spun.

A thick, leather-bound folder impacted the desk with a *slap*. I jumped, hating how Silas still stared at me. What was his problem? I risked a glance as the lawyer started.

"As you can understand with the many holdings and private equities your father had, it's caused me a great deal of time to go through it all.

"And?" Theo snapped.

Jude cut him a look. "Theo, *enough*."

But the lawyer kept going. "Some portions of your father's business have been updated to obey his latest wishes, but there was a large portion which wasn't...and that's that older portion of the business and the income derived from that portion we're having a discussion about today."

Silas pushed forward. "What do you mean the older portion of the business?"

The lawyer's cheeks went red. That wasn't a good sign.

"There's a rather large portfolio here. This," he motioned to the thick folder. "Is basically a list of names that your father has, the..." he cleared his throat. "The ones on paper anyway."

"And the ones which aren't?" Silas cut across the room.

The lawyer scanned the room, seeking help or something. But no one was moving, not even Jude.

"All of the casino's, the restaurants and other properties including all the houses are yours. That's all water tight. But there were portions of the financial strategist holdings that weren't updated. Those parts were rather difficult for your father as you well know to...um, update."

Silas slammed his hands down on the end of the desk. *"What the fuck are you trying to say here?"*

The door opened and in walked a man I barely knew. A man who looked very much like his brother, Dante Ares.

"He's saying it comes to me." Lincoln answered as he stepped inside and closed the door.

Silas just glared at his uncle as he moved inside the room.

"No." Silas shook his head, then stabbed his finger in the air at his uncle. *"Fuck no."*

"Sil." Jude stepped forward, heading for his brother's side and put his hand on his shoulder.

Silas shrugged it off hard and pushed away.

"There's large portions of the...dealings listed in the will that automatically goes to your Uncle, things like...the risk team and negotiators."

"What the fuck?" Silas shook his head. "This isn't happening."

"It's not the end of the world, Silas." Lincoln chuckled, shaking his head. "After all, we *are* family."

I didn't think anyone could earn more hatred than Silas harbored for me, but as he shifted that barely-controlled look of rage at his uncle, I realized I was wrong.

"Think about it this way." Lincoln smiled. "We get to finally work together. Your father's talked about you non-stop, says you're quite the negotiator. I'm looking forward to seeing you in action."

Silas took a step closer, meeting Lincoln eye to eye. "You and I don't work together, not now...not *ever*."

Lincoln's smile grew wider before he nodded to the thick folder on the desk. "I think you'll find that it does. I own half the holdings and half the teams. You and your...family, the other."

Family?

What did he mean by the word family?

What he should've said was brothers. Heat rushed through me as the lawyer pulled the file closer. "The business is one large part of your parent's legacy, but there are others. More personal ones...that involve everyone here today."

Silas went grey, the color drained out of his face. Gabe glanced my way and reached for my hand. I couldn't stop from shaking, leaving him to grip me even tighter.

"Your parents have expressed their very strong desire to keep you all together as a family."

I flinched as the lawyer lifted his gaze to me. "This includes you, Angelica. You'll all stay in the house and be awarded financial security as a family until such times as all five of you agree to leave. This decision has to be unanimous."

"What the fuck are you saying?" Theo barked. "We have to stay *together*?"

"If you want your money, then yes." The lawyer answered.

Theo spun, throwing his hands in the air. *"What the fuck?"*

Then they all looked at me. One by one. Silas wrenched that glare my way, baring his nostrils flared before he muttered. "We'll just see about that." He turned away from everyone and strode to the door, yanking it open so hard it hit the wall with a crack, before he was gone.

That burn filled my cheeks as I trembled.

Then Theo glared my way, only he didn't leave. Gabe gripped me tighter, shifting protectively against me.

"It's not her fault." He urged.

"Of course it's not." Jude shook his head. "No one's saying that?"

"It sure seems that way." Gabe muttered.

"This is a lot for everyone to come to terms with." The lawyer rose, giving a pathetic smile that was more than a wince. "Maybe take some time, talk amongst yourselves and then we can make time to discuss the specifics?"

He was done, that was easy to see and couldn't wait to be rid of us.

"Thank you, Marvin. I think we all need to take some time." Lincoln strode forward and grabbed the lawyer's hand and my brothers saw it all.

I knew them well enough to know when the lines of war were drawn.

"How about a shake?" Jude tried to ease the tension. "Let's get out of here and head to Monicas, we can talk about this all later, okay?"

I didn't nod, nor did I fight when Gabe smiled, then turned to me. "Yeah, that sounds good."

As always I went along when Jude jerked his gaze to Theo who glared at Lincoln. "Theo, now."

A huff came from Theo followed by a snarl before he strode for the door. This was going to be bad. I knew it in my bones, but as I headed for the door Lincoln turned around and took a step toward me, giving me a smile. "Angelica."

I stopped, freezing as he grabbed me and pressed me against his chest. "I know it'll be hard now without your mom." He eased away, staring into my eyes. "I just want you to know I'm here for you, day or night. I want you to call me for anything, I truly mean it. Day or night for whatever you need. I know how much Meredith loved you."

"Thank you." I murmured as Gabe gave a yank, pulling me toward the door and my brothers waiting.

"Didn't know you two were chummy." He muttered coldly as we headed along the hall.

I grabbed the door as he pushed open, stepping out into the morning sun to find our limousine waiting for us. "We aren't." I answered.

He gave me a look and climbed in after Theo and Jude, taking a seat with his back to the driver, leaving me to do the same. My brothers stared at me, not saying a word. Normally this didn't bother me, but it did today.

The door closed with a thud.

"This changes everything." Theo muttered.

"It changes nothing." Jude shook his head. "It's not about money and the business. It's about us and how we stick together."

"I wouldn't say that around Silas if I were you." Theo finished as the driver climbed in, started the car and pulled out.

Silas. He was going to be even more pissed off than usual. Better to stay in my room, at least until I could get away from them. I didn't care about the money, didn't care about the cars or the business I was never involved in. I cared about survival, especially now.

Heat moved through my cheeks with the weight of his stare. I met Theo's glare with my own. "What?"

"Nothing." He shrugged. "Just trying to work out how a nobody like you wormed your way into our family."

"Wormed." I snapped. "The only worm I see around here, Theo...is *you*."

He moved fast, lunging across the interior of the car. But Jude was there, grabbing him around his waist and driving him backwards. *"Enough! For fucks sake you two, get it together! Our parents just fucking DIED!"*

Theo shoved his brother away, adjusting his shirt. That cruel fucking glare aimed at me. *"Our* parents! Not *hers!"*

"Oh give it a rest." Jude shook his head. "You've played that same fucking song all your goddamn life." He glanced my way. "Angelica is as much a part of our family as Gabe. You want to bitch about him too?"

I swallowed the pain.

"Well?" Gabe snapped, staring at his brother. "Are *you?"*

"Of course not!" Theo glared. "You're our fucking blood."

Gabe puffed his chest out and jerked his head my way. "And *so* is she."

Theo pushed back in his seat, dragging his hand through perfect dirty blond hair, sulking and seething like he always did. But that glare didn't last long as it drifted down my body. I shifted against the seat, tucking my dress in around my thighs. I hated it when he looked at me like that. Like he'd enjoy hurting me given the chance.

Only I wasn't about to let that happen.

Family or not, I was a ghost. They just didn't know it.

The limousine pulled into a private driveway, heading to the rear of the packed restaurant. Monica opened the rear door as we climbed out, giving us a sad, awkward smile that rang false.

"Mon." Jude called, giving her a hug.

She hugged him back then more, before touching Theo's arm and ruffling Gabe's hair. But for me she just nodded. I followed my brothers inside to our table and at the rear of the expansive diner and took a seat.

"Whatever you want is yours." She said, "Juan's even got your special pepper poppers you love so much Theo."

He just nodded and leaned back.

"Thanks Mon." Jude started. "Maybe give us a minute?"

"Of course." She smiled. "I'll send Stacey over when you're ready."

Theo was already looking at Stacey, his ravenous gaze undressing her where she stood serving other customers. Disgusted, I looked away staring at words that were a blur. My thoughts raced through my head. The reading of the wills was not what I expected.

I prepared myself for Silas to take over their holdings and to run the business whatever they were. I expected to be given a modest sum of money, nothing extravagant. A hundred thousand would've been more than enough before they sent me on my way and asked me to never come back here again.

I would've.

Without a glance over my shoulder.

"So we all have to live in the house. None of us can leave?" Gabe asked.

"Looks like it." Theo muttered under his breath.

Gabe glanced my way as though somehow he knew what I had planned. But he couldn't possibly have any idea, because I never told him.

Beep.

My cell vibrated. I lifted it, staring at the message.

Penn: are you rich now?

I focused on typing: *Not anywhere near it.*

"Something funny?" Theo snapped.

I lifted my gaze. "You mean *apart* from your face?"

"Jesus." Jude rolled his eyes.

I just looked away, replying to Penn instead: *I'll tell you later.*

Beep.

Penn: *good, cause I'm coming to yours.*

I stared at the message as the waitress neared. I pretended not to hear the sleezy tone from Theo as he ordered his stuffed peppers. Jude was next, then Gabe.

"I'll just have a shake, vanilla. Thank you."

She gave me a sympathetic smile, glared at Theo and walked away. The food came out fast as it always did. I once heard Jude say that the Ares Holdings owned Monica's Diner. Dante revived it when the money ran dry and the place closed down. He sank a lot of money into it, rebuilding the place and with a fresh wave of advertising, he built it to where it was now.

Apparently he did a lot of that. Spent more and more and more from Casino's to car washes, diners and a thousand other places I didn't care enough about to listen to. Because the only question that remained was...where was he getting the money?

It never ran dry, that's for sure...no matter how much of it Theo shoved up his nose. I lifted my gaze watching him shove forkfuls of bacon wrapped chicken into his mouth and chew. He saw me and grinned.

"I think I'll head home." I said, rising.

"What?" Theo called, his mouth open full of food. "You're not gonna stay for dessert?"

Christ he disgusted me.

"I'll send the car back." I muttered and pushed my chair back in.

"Want me to come?" Gabe asked, almost panicked.

"Chill little brother." Theo chided. "Don't chase bitches, unless you want to fuck them. You don't want to fuck her, do you? I mean, apart from being our sister and all..."

"Adopted sister." Gabe muttered his cheeks red. "And don't be disgusting."

"It's okay." I gave his shoulder a squeeze. "I'll see you back at the house."

I couldn't get out of there fast enough, slipped out the rear door and climbed in the limousine.

"Just you, Ms. Ares?" The driver asked as he started the engine.

I gave a nod, leaving silence to fill the space.

I couldn't leave, not yet at least. But if I did, what then? Would they hunt me down and drag me back? If there was money or power involved, then absolutely. I lifted my gaze to the view through the tinted windows as we turned into our estate, then our street, finally pulling up outside the house.

The driver climbed out and opened my door.

"Will you go back and wait for the others?"

"Absolutely." He answered. "Would you like me to escort you inside?"

I shook my head and headed for the front door. "Thank you, but that won't be necessary."

*Promise me...*Mom's voice came out of nowhere as I pressed my thumb against the scanner. I half expected the locks to not open. But they did, leaving me to push inside.

I was a stranger in this house. In this name and this future. The events of the last few weeks cemented that. My chest ached as I made my way through the foyer and along the hallway. My steps slowed at the doorway to the living room and my father's study, but I forced myself to keep going, heading deeper until I turned toward my room.

You don't want to fuck her, do you? Theo's foul words resounded. *I mean, apart from being our sister and all.*

God, he was vile.

The moment I gripped the handle to my bedroom door I knew something was wrong. The sense of another was so innate it was gripping. I stopped, stared at the door, then slowly pushed it open...staring into what was left of my bedroom.

It was trashed.

My bed shoved aside. My bedroom drawers pulled out. My underwear strewn all over the room. We've been robbed. *WE'VE BEEN—*

I spun around and lunged, tearing past Gabe's room and spun along the hallway like my life depended on it...until Silas stepped out of his bedroom. I slammed into him, grabbing his arm. "We've been." I gasped sucking in hard breaths. *"We've been ROBBED!"*

He said nothing, just stood there. That stony, hateful stare fixed on mine.

"Well, don't just stand there!" I yelled. *"Call the police!"*

Only then did I look past him into his bedroom. His desk was there, his ten thousand dollar computer lit up like it always was. Rolex watches. Gold chains. It was all there. So how come they robbed my room...and not his?

Because it wasn't a robbery, *was it?*

The words hit me. I tried to think, but the agony plunged deeper.

I lifted my gaze to his. "Why?"

He said nothing. Just like he always said nothing.

He did this. He fucking did this. Why? Because of the will? Because he couldn't get rid of me? "Fuck you, Silas." I spat and leaned closer, meeting that glare with my own. "Fuck. You."

I spun around and strode away, my knees shaking. I barely made it back to my room before the tears came. My room blurred until I swiped it away and moved. The drawers were first, I righted them, sliding the drawers back in and gathering my underwear. This wasn't just anger...or frustration.

This was blind rage.

The kind that wasn't just dangerous.

But lethal too.

I was going to need to be careful around them now. More than I was ever before.

Chapter Four

SILAS

I looked away as revulsion burned in my gut. Her pleas echoing through the speaker, leaving me to hit the volume and turn it low. The last thing I needed was my brother's stumbling in to find this.

"Please, my mother begged," stepping backwards until she sank to the bed. *"Don't make me do this."*

But she did...didn't she?

She did and then she ruined our goddamn family.

"You want your husband to know about us?" The bastard she was cheating with asked.

Tears slid down her face as she shook her head. The sight of them made me sick.

"Then take off your blouse, Meredith. It's either you or your daughter and both you and I don't want that, do you?"

Her or her daughter?

They were both in this?

I shifted my gaze from the screen. This bastard was threatening to fuck my sister instead? Then why the fuck didn't she let him? This asshole could've whored her out for her entire life, for all I cared.

It would've been better than this...

Jesus fucking Christ. *Was this why dad killed her?* Because he somehow found out my mother was having an affair? I put myself in his shoes. Our family lived, breathed and consumed money and connections. That afforded us many things. Protection was one of them.

The blood-spattered study filled my mind. The choking scent of gunpowder forever etched into my memories, mingled with the sight of my parent's dead bodies.

I turned back to the screen as she unbuttoned her blouse with trembling fingers. "How many more times must we do this? You've got what you wanted. I've told you everything I know about my husband's dealings. You have enough to wipe us all out." Her blouse dropped, leaving her in a black, lace bra.

I nodded my head slowly, that cold, hearted bastard inside growing cold with the realization of just the kind of women my mother and sister were.

"I'm begging you, please don't make me do this."

This woman begged. She wasn't my mother anymore. Not one I ever wanted in my life. She was a cheater. A fucking...whore.

"Clothes...off. I want you to lay back and spread your legs. I want us to record just how perfect your cunt is before I fuck you so hard I destroy it. Then, when you're full of my cum you can get dressed, get your daughter and go home. I'm sure her training will be done by then. It sounds like Angelica is quite the natural when it comes to giving head."

I pushed up from the seat at my desk and looked down at the screen.

My mother shook her head, her blubbering words useless as she slid her bra down, revealing sagging breasts and dark, pinched nipples. I'd never looked at my mother like this before. Like she was no different to the bitches I used every other night. Never saw her as anything other than a dutiful wife and an attentive mother. But that...*that woman was a lie.*

She slid her slacks down, taking her panties with them. I reached up, hitting stop the moment her legs rose and her knees parted. I sure as fuck didn't need to see that.

I looked at the email again. The one with London St. James personal email address, it took all of me not to hit reply and ask to meet him.

That man is dangerous.

My father's words resounded from the day St. James and his Sons came to see us. It wasn't that dad didn't trust him...more like wary. The guy as resourceful and just as fucking ruthless as we were...as was his sons.

I remembered that night at the fight. The one where Carven killed a man...

He'd been thrown out.

But fuck he was terrifying.

I shook my head and clicked out of the email. St. James and his weird ass fucking offspring wasn't someone I wanted to associate with. The Order.

The browser was still up, the expensive looking building ominous on the webpage. I turned around, glancing at the rumpled sheets. There was no more sleep for me tonight. Not now. Probably not ever. I strode to the bathroom, hit the light and yanked my shirt over my head, wincing at the sting. In the mirror I saw all the claw marks.

Jesus.

I shoved my jeans down low, hit the taps and stepped into the shower. The sting was instant, leaving me to drop my head under the hot spray. The recording played in my mind as I washed. The longer it did, the angrier I became.

I washed and stepped out, wrapping a towel around my dripping body and headed back into my bedroom. *The Order.* That place lingered as I pulled on jeans, a t-shirt and then my boots before I grabbed my black helmet and strode out, heading for the rear of the house.

The sun was slowly rising, lightening the night sky at the edge of the horizon. I made for my bike, pulled on my helmet and climbed on. The engine started instantly, vibrating between my thighs. Lights were bright, spilling along the driveway before I kicked it into gear and surged forward, driving along the house, then turned, making my way toward the freeway, heading out of the city.

My mom...

My fucking sister.

All those fucking times she could've said something, not even to the cops...but to me. She stood at that doorway seeing their bodies. She saw what my father did...and yet, she said nothing.

I clenched my jaw and pushed the bike harder, pulling onto the on-ramp. I moved around those heading to work, carving in and out, pushing to make the amber street lights until I pulled off the freeway and was out of the city.

I didn't come out here, not where the mountains waited and the trees grew close to the road. I stayed in the city, hiding away in underground street racing and illegal fights. I stayed in the dark, coming out into the light when my father needed me.

Now, he needed me more than ever.

I pulled out my cell, glanced at the GPS and slowed the bike, taking a turn up ahead and headed for the thick forest. The sun glinted off steel in the distance, drawing my focus to the ten-foot high fence that was topped with razor wire.

Razor wire for a religious organization seemed a little... excessive. A gnawing in my gut grew as I slowed the bike, coasting past where the wire had been cut. Up ahead the guard hut was destroyed and the chain around the gates were cut and open. Someone had been here...I scanned the dirt and the washed out tire tracks—although not recently.

I edged the bike close, yanked the gate, widening it enough for me to slip through. All I saw were trees as I drove closer until I turned and found the sprawling brick building.

It didn't look like the photographs now. The windows were smashed and it looked like someone had forced entrance, leaving the door wide open. I pulled the bike up and killed the engine before climbing off. The place didn't look any better when I removed my helmet, in fact it looked worse.

Dirty and ruined. The place felt abandoned. I climbed the steps and pushed open the front door, listening for any sounds. But there was none, leaving me to step in. I had no idea what I was looking for...but the moment I stepped through the foyer leaving the false pretense of the church behind I knew this was the place from the video.

It had that sinister feel.

My boots resounded against the empty hallways. Locked double doors were now wide open. I glanced at the dead access points then pushed though to find the empty rooms, stopping at the doorway to peer inside. An empty cot was shoved in the corner, the bedding still rumpled. I scanned the rest of this tiny, soulless room. This place wasn't a church...it was a goddamn prison.

I kept walking, making my way along the halls to a cafeteria, then headed toward the back. There was blood splatter on the walls...and a darkened patch on the floor. "What the fuck happened here?"

There were no reports on the web. Nothing apart from the dead asshole who founded this place. The guy St. James had been convinced was alive. But as I walked along the hallway and stopped at some kind of medical wing I realised maybe St. James was telling the truth.

I moved on, pushing through unlocked doors to a wing that looked like offices...and amongst them rooms large enough for a group. Three doors down I glanced into the glass to freeze. There was a bed there. The same, generic type that was in the video. Was this it? Was this the place?

My knuckles ached as I gripped the handle and pushed it open.

It was there, in the middle of the room, just like it'd been in the recording. I stepped inside, glancing at the tripod set up for recording. "Motherfucker."

Beep.

My cell chimed making me jump. I grabbed it from my jacket and glanced at the message.

Unknown: *Enjoying the Order?*

What. The. Fuck?

My pulse kicked, then raced as I spun around, strode back into the hallway and scanned the empty hallway. That eerie feeling in the pit of my stomach grew colder. I looked down, punching out a reply.

Who the fuck is this?

Send.

Beep.

Unknown: *You'll find out.*

"Fuck you." I spat, rage moving in to replace fear.

I needed to get out of here...and now. I started walking back the way I came...until I stopped at that larger room. *I'm sure her training will be done by then. Those words from the video surfaced. It sounds like Angelica is quite the natural when it comes to giving head.*

The cells.

The doors.

The blood...and this room, big enough for training. This place made me want to run from here and never look back. My boots ricocheted as I hurried, fighting the urge to fucking flee. The moment I slammed out of the front I sucked in hard breaths. I'd been so thankful to see my bike.

I yanked on my hemet, started the machine and took off, punching it hard until I slowed at the gate. The moment I was through I was out of there...desperate to get back to the blaring, rush of the city.

But I didn't go home. I couldn't...instead I headed for the Lair, slowing the bike as I cruised into the side street and turned, catching sight of the boys sitting in parked hard. One leaned out of the open driver's door, nodding at me as I passed.

He'd call in, letting them know it was me. Couldn't be too careful lately. There was some strange shit going down, even here. I slowed the bike, pulling into the derelict compound, past the smashed down brick wall, and parked.

Illegal fights.

Street racing.

Raves.

We had it all.

I parked the bike between a cherry red Lamborghini Huracán and a lime green Nissan GT-R, switching off the Ducati and climbed off. Iron's men patrolled the grounds and crowded the doorway. I stepped up, raising my arms. The pat down was fast, swiping the wand before the big guy ran his hands over me.

"Silas." Iron called as the thud...thud...thud of his cane echoed before the old guy stepped out from around the ruins. "What do I owe this pleasure?"

I gave a shrug. "Who's fighting?"

Iron squinted. "A couple of punks from out of town, mostly foreplay really."

"So not like Carven St. James."

Iron grew cold suddenly. "No. Not like Carven."

I gave a nod and stepped past, heading to the right where their homies gathered around. I was here, but I wasn't here.

"Something you need?" Iron asked.

I shook my head. Yes, that voice whispered. I glanced at him sideways. He waited, not pushing.

"What do you know about the Order?"

"I know enough to stay the fuck away and if you were smart you'd steer clear as well." Iron turned toward me. "Or you *will* end up like Carven St. James."

What was that supposed to mean?

Humm...Humm...Humm.

I froze, staring at the fight master as my cell vibrated in my pocket. Iron slowly glanced down. "You going to answer that?"

I reached into my pocket and pulled out my cell. Dragomir. "Shit." I pressed answer and turned around. "Alexi."

"Silas." The thick Russian accent echoed through the line. "How are you, Son?"

"Good, Sir. I'm good."

"Excellent. I'm sorry I haven't been in touch since...since the terrible tragedy. You know how fond I was of your father."

"I understand." I kept my voice low. "Is there something I can do for you?"

"Yes." He sighed. "I was wondering if we could meet. I'd like to discuss with you any potential issues with our current arrangement."

I swallowed hard, feeling the weight of my legacy. This was what my father and I had been working toward, me taking over the business...and making sure the millions of dollars a day was washed clean. Alexi Dragomir was one of those clients. "Of course. Whatever makes you feel more comfortable."

"Excellent. Tonight at ten?"

"I'll see you then." I finished, but he was already gone, leaving me to listen to the heavy thud of a fist.

Alexi Dragomir, the king of the cocaine trade in the southwest wanted to see what kind of business man he was dealing with... one who'd better get his shit together...that was who.

I PULLED into the parking lot behind SudzandCycle Laundromat, taking the midnight BMW M5 instead of the bike and parked. It was five minutes to ten, because the last thing I needed was to be late, especially for Alexi Dragomir. I'd spent the day in a haze, locking myself in my room to stare at that email from London St. James.

The longer I looked, the more savage I became and my rage

centred around the one person alive to earn my wrath...my unwanted adopted sister, Angelica.

She knew...she fucking knew and said nothing. I shook my head staring at the brightly lit coin-operated business as people came and went carrying in their dirty laundry.

Yeah, well...she was ours, wasn't she?

Unwanted.

Dirty laundry.

The day mom bought that skinny, timid little bitch home I knew she was trouble. But that's all Mom ever talked about, having a daughter. Because having four sons wasn't enough for her.

No, she wanted more.

Now look at her.

The betraying, fucking traitor. I wanted to do more than tear her room apart. I wanted to confront her in front of all my brothers and force the truth from those tight fucking lips.

Then Gabe would see her for who she was...and he'd hate her for it.

Beep.

My cell chimed making me jump.

Unknown: *Did you find what you were looking for?*

I stared at the message, and that same fear came rushing back. My pulse raced, the thudding ache like a fist in the middle of my chest.

Beep.

Unknown: *Maybe, I can help?*

Video incoming....

"What the fuck." I whispered as headlights flared in the distance, filling the interior of the car.

My hand shook as I pressed the button.

"You will be on your knees. Do you understand?"

"Yes."

"Yes, what?"

"Yes, Sir."

A jolt raced through my body at the sound of her voice. I shifted against my seat as the sleek black limousine pulled into the dirty parking lot at the back of the laundromat.

"Open." The man on the video commanded.

I tried to see her, to catch a glimpse of something. All I saw was that same fucking room, until the camera shifted, the blur cutting across her. Her big green eyes looked up at me before they were gone. My breaths raced, my pulse frantic...sending a shockwave all the way to my cock. It was her...it was her. My thumb hovered over the rewind, to find those lying eyes once more.

"That's it." He groaned. "Jesus, that's it."

The sound stopped me.

The slick sucking sounds were faint. Fuck me. I jerked my panicked gaze up as the driver climbed out of the car and headed around for Alexi's door. I needed to be out there. To be the one he saw when he climbed out. But this video...this fucking video gripped me like a vice. I licked my lips, sucked in heavy breaths and looked down.

"Deeper." He groaned, the guttural sound animalistic. "Just like you've been trained."

Trained?

Christ. Outside Alexi climbed out of the car and looked around. I couldn't fuck this up...everything was riding on this.

"Fuck!" I cast my cell across the seat. It took everything in me not to grab it and slide it into my pocket. But it bounced against the seat, coming to a rest as I shoved open the door and climbed out.

There was a look of disappointment on Alexi's face as I strode forward.

"Silas."

"Alexi." I forced a smile, stepping close to hug him.

"I thought you weren't coming." He murmured. "No one makes me wait."

Liar, he knew I was here. I forced a smile. "Sorry."

"Another reason why I'm...shall we say, concerned."

"I have never faltered, not once." Anger rippled through my voice. "Not even when you called in the middle of my parents funeral. The moment you sent a message to say your money was late. I called my men, personally taking care of it. Has there been a problem since? Has there been any kind of hint that business isn't as usual?"

He shook his head. Thick grey hair caught the shine of the streetlights. "No."

"Then how can you doubt me?"

Alexi shifted awkwardly, glancing at the open door of the limousine. It was then I saw the shadow shift inside and someone slowly slid across the seat and climbed out.

I clenched my jaw. "You?"

Lincoln straightened, adjusting the open collar of his white shirt. "Nephew."

"I should've known." Disgust rolled through my voice.

"You misjudge." Alexi shook his head. "Lincoln is here to ease my fears, to show me you can be trusted."

I didn't believe him.

"We're family." Lincoln stepped closer, grabbing my arm gently. "I want us to be family."

That distrust wavered as Alexi urged. "Lincoln told me about your father's wishes. That you two should work together, building something more powerful and bigger than your father dreamed. You know how I feel about family. I want this for you. Clean the money and work together. You do that and you'll have my support."

The sonofabitch railroaded me...

I stared at Lincoln, even as Alexi nodded, glanced at the both of us, then gave a nod before he climbed back into the limousine. The rear door closed with a thud. Still, I never looked away, not even when Alexi's car rolled forward, turning sharply before it headed back out into the parking lot, leaving us behind.

"This is my legacy."

"It's *your* legacy." Lincoln repeated.

"You don't own the majority."

He shook his head.

"Nor do *you* go behind my fucking back."

He stilled.

"I don't like you." I snarled. "I never have. But it seems as though I'm forced to work with you, to keep what my family has. What little I have left."

"What is that supposed to mean?"

I shook my head and turned away, staring at my car.

"I haven't been around a lot, I get that. But I've always been here, working in whatever capacity your father allowed. But if you or the others are in trouble, Silas...I want you to know you can come to me."

"Did you know?" The words slipped out before I knew.

"Did I know what?"

I turned around. "Did...you know my mother was having an affair, and whoring out my goddamn sister?"

He froze, his eyes widening. I knew surprise when I saw it. Maybe some part of me deep down suspected he was in on this. But this look said the opposite.

He shook his head instantly. "That's a lie."

"No, it isn't."

The muscles of his jaw flexed as he strode close and grabbed my arm, hissing. "Your mother loved Dante. *You know that!* There's no way in Hell she'd even look at another man. I should fucking know. God knows I tried my best to get her to notice me when she first started dating your father. She was the most beautiful, dynamic woman I'd ever met in my life. But she never even gave me a second look. Her eyes were for Dante. She fucking worshiped him and there is no way she'd throw that away."

"But she did." I answered coldly. "And I have the recordings to prove it."

Lincoln unleashed a low tortured moan and turned away, running his fingers through his hair. But then he stilled as slow resignation overtook his anger. But he didn't believe me completely. Instead, he turned, met my gaze with that pain filled stare and said. "Show me...show me and we'll find this bastard and murder him in his sleep."

Chapter Five

ANGELICA

I NEEDED TO GET OUT OF HERE. NOW THAT IT WAS LATE I'D slip away and no one would know until at least morning. By then I'd be long gone. I punched my duffle jacket into my pack, pushing it down as hard as I could. It was the largest bag I could find, still it barely held the essentials: a pair of jeans, three pairs of clean underwear, socks, t-shirts and what jewelry I had after Silas destroyed my room.

The necklaces and rings I'd pawn to get out of here. The thought of that hurt, especially parting with the tiny gold angel pendant on the expensive chain mom gave me for my eighteenth birthday. You're my angel, her words still rang in my head. The daughter I was meant to save.

But she didn't save me and now the only way for me to save her was to get out of here and run as far and as fast as I could. The fur-lined hood peeked out. I folded it now and yanked the tie before flipping the weatherproof flap over and lifted my gaze.

That was it.

The last thing I needed.

I looked around to the room that's become my sanctuary in a volatile, treacherous place. I heaved my pack up, my chest aching as I strode for the door, eased it open and slipped out.

"Are you going somewhere?"

I froze, my hand on the handle, then slowly turned. Gabe stood there in the space between our rooms, his careful gaze taking in my jeans, boots and cashmere top before he moved to the pack on my back. Pain flared in his soft, kind eyes. Cutting, cruel pain that hurt to see.

"Gabe, I have to."

"Why?" His voice was wounded and husky, sounding cruelly young in that moment.

But he wasn't young. I took a step and reached up, cupping the cheek of a man. "I have to."

We never spoke about his brother's hateful tone toward me. It was more from Theo and now from Silas, but there was a vein of indifference from Jude, one that ran from the patriarch of this family. The man who didn't even know his wife adopted a daughter. One he tolerated.

"They don't want me here." I whispered.

"Fuck them. *I* want you. Doesn't that count for something?" He searched my eyes.

I shook my head.

"Please," he begged. "Please, don't leave me."

I didn't have time to argue as he wrapped his arms around me, slamming me against his hard, trembling chest. Tears welled in my eyes as I wrapped my arms around his waist. It'd been weeks since I had any kind of affection. Weeks since I'd had any kind of comfort at all.

"It's okay." I forced the words around the ache in my throat. "Come on. I'll stay.'

He clung tighter. "You're...you're the only one who gets me."

I looked over his shoulder as he curled his body, pressing against every inch of me. The agony of betrayal cut deep as I shook my head, gripping his shirt at the small of his back. I became aware of him, very aware. The way his arms were a vice. The way he turned his head, drawing in my scent with deep draws of breath.

Heat moved through me, finding my cheeks and my belly, then moved lower.

No.

I shifted against him, brushing against the bulge at the front of his jeans before he pulled away. He looked embarrassed, instantly turning his body away.

"Hey." I said suddenly. "How about we make some of that microwave popcorn and watch a movie."

"As long as it's not Sleepless in Seattle again." He mumbled. "I swear I can recite that movie in my sleep."

A hard bark of laughter tore free. I shook my head, playfully punching his arm. "Deal. You can pick this time, but if it's Fast and The Furious I get to make all the car sounds."

He grinned, meeting my gaze. "Deal."

"You go start the popcorn and I'll put this away."

One nod and he was striding away, leaving me to head back into my room. The moment I closed the door the gravity of this hit me. How could I leave him...and now of all times? I stared at my room and that sinking feeling swept through me.

I couldn't...that's how.

The straps of my pack dug in as I pulled it free and tossed it on the end of the bed. But I didn't unpack, not yet. That same fear only grew bolder. I had to be careful now. I had to play it safe. Keep my head down, say nothing even when Theo is a bastard.

I had to be invisible.

But I guess, I'd spent most of my life being that to this family... what was a few more months?

I headed back out, glancing along the quiet hallways as I made for the kitchen. The *pop...pop...poppoppop* sound of popcorn greeted me before that delicious buttery scent flooded my senses. I stepped in, folded my arms and found Gabe grabbing a large bowl.

We were more alike than the others. He was blood but he was softer than they were, kinder and sweet. I hoped he always stayed like that. He lifted his gaze, catching me staring and grinned. "What?"

I shook my head. "Nothing, just trying to work out why we're so different."

He laughed, but I could tell he wondered about it too. "'Cause not everyone can be strong and protective like Silas, or smart like Jude, or even outgoing like Theo. Sometimes there needs to be space for the quiet ones like us." He gave a shrug. "We have our own place here, they just need to be reminded of that." He jerked his head toward his brother's rooms as the sound of the popping corn slowed."

That same agony inside me roared to the surface. He always saw the best in people like that, especially his brothers...and me. My pulse raced, that panicked flighty feeling took hold. There was no way out of this for me. Keeping quiet until I could escape was one thing, but now after the reading of the will and being forced to stay here it meant I had to be more than quiet—I had to not exist at all.

"Oh, *ouch* that's hot." Gabe shuffled the bag from hand to hand, tugging at the opening until he upended the contents into the bowl and handed to me proudly like he was the one who tilled the soil and grew the damn thing. I grinned, grabbing it while he made for the refrigerator and grabbed two colas following me into the living room.

He flopped down hard, in my head I could hear mom chiding him. Gabe, *really?* Can't you just sit like a normal person?

For a moment. One perfect moment...life was normal.

He hit the button, scrolled through the movies finding some mind-numbing action movie for me to get lost in. I did, shaking my head at the ridiculousness of it, until the rear door closed with a thud and the sound of footsteps echoed, heading our way.

Gabe glanced at his watch. "Huh, looks like an early night for a change."

I peered at the time. "By early you mean eleven o'clock."

He smiled, then hurtled a piece of popcorn into his mouth. "Early for them at least."

I was already yawning, waiting for the movie to end, but as I caught Silas turning the corner and headed toward the study I knew that'd changed.

Gabe laughed and looked my way. I tried to pretend I was still watching, but I wasn't. Instead I focused on the study door as it opened...until the rear door opened again minutes later. But it didn't sound like Theo. The steps were slower and heavier, drawing both our gazes.

Silas stepped out of the study door as Lincoln stepped around, meeting our gaze and nodded. Only it lingered on mine, searching my eyes before taking in my body.

"Lincoln." Silas called. "Over here."

Gabe's uncle turned away from us, we both found each other, surprised as Hell.

"What the fuck is he doing here?" Gabe murmured as Lincoln made for the study and disappeared with Silas behind the closed door.

"I have no idea." I answered as that cornered feeling pushed in. "Maybe it's business?"

"Maybe," Gabe repeated. "And maybe not."

It had to be. That's all I knew. Because there was no way they'd know any different. Gabe turned back, yawning as the movie ended. "Ready for bed?"

I shook my head as tired as I was. "Another one?"

He looked exhausted, still he nodded and scrolled, finding something else to play. But I didn't care about the movie, not anymore. I cared about one thing and one thing alone...them never finding out the truth.

They were in there for what felt like forever.

I waited...and waited...and waited.

Until finally the door to the study opened and they both stepped out.

But Lincoln didn't head for the door, not right away. Instead they stared across the hallway at me. I tried not to notice, to keep my focus on the movie instead. But the weight of their focus grew so heavy it weighed me down.

"Tomorrow night." I faintly caught the words from Silas.

"Until then," Lincoln headed our way, stopping long enough to glance at the screen. "Nice to see you Gabe...and you... Angelica."

My cheeks burned. All I managed was a weak smile and a nod before he left.

But Silas remained, standing outside the study...that hateful stare locked on me.

Chapter Six

SILAS

Clothes off. I want you to lay back and spread your legs. I want us to record just how perfect your cunt is before I fuck you so hard I destroy it. Then, when you're full of my cum you can get dressed, get your daughter and go home. I'm sure her training will be done by then—

"That's enough." Lincoln looked away.

I never moved so fast in all my life. Hitting the stop button and exiting out of the video.

"That," my uncle shook his head and ran his fingers through his hair. "I can't believe it. I can't believe she'd do something like that."

"Well, she did." My voice was stony.

"Who is this bastard, do you know?"

I shook my head. "Not yet, I don't. But you can be damn sure I will."

"He's dead," his voice darkened. "Whoever it is, he's a fucking dead man, right after we find out exactly what information she gave him. We can't let this slide. We have to be on top of this. Christ, if Alexi knew."

"He doesn't."

My uncle swung around, his eyes glistening with fear and rage. "Are you willing to stake our business on that?"

I stilled, my resolve waning.

"That's what I thought. And training...what the fuck was he talking about her daughter's training?"

Something clenched inside me. Closing tight around that information, guarding it as though it staked a claim. But it wasn't mine to keep. I turned my head as though I could look through the walls to that traitorous little bitch playing house with my family. "There's another recording."

"With your mom?"

I shook my head.

"Then who?"

"My sister."

"Jesus fucking Christ." Lincoln groaned before he stopped. "Show me."

No.

I don't know where that controlling need came from...or why it was here. But as I reached into my pocket for my cell I felt a darkness rise with it. "There's not a lot to see," I said.

"Doesn't matter. I need to understand exactly how deep we're in here. What kinds of things your mother and your sister has told them."

I swiped my thumb across the screen, opened the message and stopped. But she didn't know anything. Not about the business anyway.

"Is that it?" I gave a slow nod, my grip tightening as Lincoln reached for my phone. "Can I see it?"

I had no choice but to release my hold, to let my cell slip away. He pressed play. I closed my eyes to the slick sounds that came from the speaker.

Christ that's so good, open...that's it. Your mouth is the best I've ever felt. I cannot wait to push inside that sweet cunt. You will be a good girl for me, won't you Angel? My sweet...sweet angel.

He let it play all the way through, this time not saying a word. Rage rippled deep as I forced my eyes open. My uncle's lips were parted, his eyes fixed on the screen until he flinched and jerked his gaze to me.

I saw it. *Hunger.*

"We need to know." His voice was deep and husky. Eyes flicked back to the cell in my hand. One lick of his lips and he murmured. "Maybe there's information embedded on the video somewhere. My guys can find it. Send the recording to me."

I swallowed hard. No. Not this one. "The one from my mom..."

"No." He shook his head. "That one is best."

Why? So you can watch it again?

I didn't need to look to see if he was hard. I knew he was.

"The last thing we need is for this to get out. It'll...it'll ruin us, Silas. You get that, right?" Lincoln stared at me until I slowly gave in and nodded.

"Good." He stepped closer and squeezed my shoulder. "Send me the video, son and leave it to me."

"We need to confront her." I met his stare. God, I didn't realize how much he looked like dad. "We need to demand the truth."

"And we will." He urged. "Give me the day, okay? Then we'll do whatever you want."

That clenched grip inside refused to release. Some part of me didn't want to send it. But Lincoln looked at me like he was kin. Even if he hadn't been around, he was...blood kin and now controlling half the business he had just as much at stake here as I did.

Whatever belonged to me now belonged to him also.

Lying adopted sister and all.

I lifted my cell and started typing, adding in his email. "Do you want the other one as well...the one of my mother?"

"No. Just your sister. That's the one I want."

I lifted my gaze, meeting his stare before he turned around and headed for the door.

Woosh.

The sending email finished as he opened the door and stepped out. I followed him to stare across the living room to where she sat watching movies with Gabe like she hadn't just conspired to destroy our entire legacy on her fucking knees.

I'll find out the truth.

Then, I'll make you pay.

"I'll be in touch." Lincoln murmured and headed toward them, stopping to say something before he was gone.

The moment he was gone I knew sending the video was a mistake. I opened my messages. But it was far too late. Whether we wanted this or not we were on a collision course. One I thought started the morning I found my parents dead. Angelica turned her gaze to mine—but it looked like I was wrong...

The destruction of our family started long before that.

Beginning and ending with my mother and my sister.

All we needed to find out now...was to whom...and why.

I closed the study door behind me and headed for my room, forcing myself not to launch across the room and strangle the bitch where she sat.

"Night, Silas." She called and a nerve twitched in the corner of my eye.

How fucking dare she. I yanked open my bedroom door, closing it hard behind me. "Fucking bitch...you goddamn fucking bitch."

I headed straight for the bed, kicked off my boots and fell to the mattress, burying my face deep into my pillow and unleashed a primal roar. I punched the mattress, fighting everything in me not to tear her apart. My breath was warm, billowing back against my face before I lifted my head, looking to the door.

The sound of their steps grew closer.

"Night." Gabe's faint voice echoed.

Hers was indistinguishable...but I knew it was there.

Their doors closed with a soft thud. I lay there knowing right now Lincoln would be watching her. I licked my lips and reached for my cell, opening my messages to find the video.

Christ that's so good, open...that's it. That deep voice echoed. I shifted on the bed, searching the camera. *Who the fuck are you?* The camera shifted, blurring until it panned left catching her kneeling, her eyes wide. I stopped the replay, pulling the recording back and stopped with her face in full view.

She was in her underwear, some kind of white lace thing, the tops of her breasts spilling out. But it was her mouth I stared at. Lips parted, just like he instructed.

My cock hardened and my breaths deepened. She was my fucking sister...but she wasn't was she?

No.

She was a stray.

A liar.

A fucking whore dressed in white.

Mom's beautiful angel. I could still hear mom calling her.

"Mom's angel." I lowered my head, my hips slowly thrusting into the bed. "Mom's lying goddamn angel. I bet you liked being on your knees, didn't you? I bet you give head real fucking good"

Jesus I was rock hard, moaning with the ache as I fucked nothing but air. With a groan I shoved away from the bed, driving myself to the bathroom. I slapped on the light, tore my clothes free and stepped into the shower, hissing at the sting on my ribs. I looked down, finding the red claw marks on my side.

I'd forgotten about them.

Forgotten about her too. The crazy bitch who rode the Hell outta me.

I'd forgotten everything...but these videos.

I stayed there, lathering myself and winced at my stiff cock. I wanted to fist myself. It wouldn't take long, a couple of thrusts with the image of her in my head and I'd be all over.

No.

No fucking way.

I pulled my hand away. There'd be no relief, not for me...or for her.

I switched off the taps and climbed out. Water beaded along my shoulders as I dried, then walked into my room. It was almost three am...no wonder I was beat. I pulled on boxers and climbed back into bed, smacking into my cell as my eyes closed.

Still, I saw her.

Those green eyes.

I'm sure her training will be done by then...I hear Angelica is quite the natural at giving head.

I moaned and turned over.

*I'm sure her training will be done...I'm sure her...*I opened my eyes. She just wasn't going to let me rest, was she? My body was heavy as I pushed upwards and stumbled from my bed. I don't why I walked out...don't know why I made it to her room. I don't know why I turned the handle to her bedroom and stepped inside.

But I did.

Darkness greeted me. The scent of her room soft and clean. The opposite of a whore like her. I neared her bed, my eyes adjusting to the gloom, finding the outline of her body. Soft, deep breaths rose and fell. How does a liar like her sleep? Well, apparently. Real fucking well.

"No." She mumbled and tossed, thrashing her head. I stepped closer, staring down at her. She was always a stuck up bitch, never going out to the clubs. Never going anywhere that I knew...except for that boyfriend. How did she meet him anyway?

Your mouth is the best I've ever felt.

Does she use those skills on that weedy bastard? I bet she did. I grazed my teeth over my lip as my gaze drifted down. I bet she sucked him real fucking good.

I want that.

The thought gripped my balls making them tighten.

I want that mouth.

Those eyes.

I shook my head. Blood or not she was still family. What would mom think? My cock twitched, warmth at the front of my boxers cooled, the wetness rubbing against me. I was going to come just thinking about how I'd ruin her fucking angel.

I took a step and reached out, grasping the sheets and lifted. My thoughts filled with madness. The kind I knew I'd never come back from. Soft, white cotton peeked out from under the sheets. Her nightie was perfect and pure. It didn't belong on a body like hers.

Her chest rose with a breath. "Momma." She called in her sleep. "I promise. I promise." The last was breath, falling deeper into the dream which gripped her.

I dropped the sheet and stepped away, before I headed back out and to my own room. I needed to think about this. To plan...and find a way to tell my brothers. Yeah, that's going to be a whole conversation I don't want to have.

Still...it had to be done.

I headed back to my room and crawled back into my bed. My sleep was fitful and restless, dreaming of snakes. Ones who licked at me with poisoned, forked tongues.

"GO AWAY." Theo mumbled, ignoring my presence as he stared at the latest trading information on Yahoo.

I glanced at the still neatly made bed. I swore my brother never fucking slept. "Where were you last night?"

"Why? You going to handcuff me to the house, maybe force us to stay here forever?"

I strode forward, shoving him hard. "Hey, that wasn't my goddamn call here. You know that."

He gave me a glare, straightening the collar on his deep blue polo shirt.

"It wasn't *my* call. You think I want to stay here...especially now that I...now that I know just how fucked up our family really was...and still is."

He sneered, eyes blazing with anger. "Maybe you just didn't look hard enough."

"Did you know...did you know about mom?"

He scowled. "Did I know about mom what?"

"That she was having an affair."

That scowled deepened before he looked away. "You're lying."

I knew Theo wouldn't believe a word I said. Not without hard evidence. I had that in spades. I lifted my cell...and our mother's pleading voice filled the room.

Theo shoved up from his chair so hard it toppled backwards. "What the fuck is that?" His cheeks burned. "Switch it off," He demanded. *"Switch that fucking thing off."*

I did, hitting the button and ending that tortured sound. I didn't look at it anymore, only listened. But part of me still really didn't believe it. It was that part of me who still loved her, who saw her as the dutiful wife and the caring mother. Each time I heard this, that part of me died, leaving behind the man who saw her for what she was.

"That's a fucking lie." Theo croaked and turned around, pacing the floor. *"That's a goddamn lie.* Someone is playing with us, someone is using our parents death to bring us down."

"No." I shook my head. "It's her. Because I found the place where this was taken...and that's not all."

"That's not all?" His eyes flew wide. "'Cause that's not enough?"

"Angelica was in on this as well."

He froze, his eyes widening. "What...what did you say?"

I stopped mom's recording too early. "Listen." I said and pressed play once more. *Then, when you're full of my cum you can get dressed, get your daughter and go home. I'm sure her training will be done by then. It sounds like Angelica is quite the natural when it comes to giving head...*

"That little fucking bitch." He said slowly. "That stuck-up, prissy fucking bitch."

"There's a recording." My voice was husky, fixed on my brother's reaction.

Part of me knew this was wrong, that the addiction I felt for this was dangerous.

"Show me." He said instantly, his eyes sparkling. "I want to see it."

I looked at my cell. "It's not much, just—"

"Is it her?"

I slowly nodded.

"Then, I want to see our lying little bitch of a sister."

Hate seethed in his voice. Out of all of us, he resented her the most, taking our mom's attention drew his cruelty out into the open. It wasn't just rivalry between them, it was a visceral hate, a rage that came from somewhere I didn't know...and if I was honest, I didn't want to know. I lifted the cell and pressed play knowing with a few blurred seconds of a recording his rage was about to get a whole lot worse.

You will be on your knees. Do you understand?

Yes.

Yes, what?

Yes, Sir.

Theo's gaze was riveted.

Open.

That's it. Jesus, that's it. Deeper…just like you've been trained.

"Trained," my brother's voice was a husky whisper. He jerked his gaze to mine. "What does he mean by trained?"

I stilled, time to take a steep dive off a cliff. "It seems like mom and our sister were involved in the Order."

"That stupid cult St. James wanted us to fight? What the fuck does a bunch of rich old fucks have to do with us?"

I looked back at my cell. "I have no idea. But I have a feeling we're about to find out."

"Is there more…" he licked his lips, finding my cell. "Maybe we'd understand if there was more footage."

Jesus, he liked this. First Lincoln, now Theo…and me, *don't forget me.*

The idea of our holier than thou sister being forced to her knees made me feel a hunger I'd never felt before. I was savage in the way I wanted to see that, to watch the fear and the pain in her eyes as she was forced to kneel. "No." I whispered. "I don't have anymore, but you know this means we have to confront her."

His long strides made for the door. "Then let's do it."

He was so keen, so desperate. I lunged, grabbing his arm and earned a glare.

"Not yet," I shook my head. "When we confront her it has to be in a way she can't get away. We'll force the truth from her one way or another, but we need everyone on board."

"You mean Jude?"

"Yeah," I nodded. "Jude."

"What about Gabe?"

I shook my head. Our little brother loved her, there was no denying that. He was old enough to defend as well. The moment he heard the recording he'd go to her. That was a fact. We couldn't have that, not until we found out the truth. "We say nothing to him. Not until she's told us everything."

"I fucking knew she was poison." Theo growled. *"I fucking knew it."*

"I need you to come with me to Jude. He won't listen if it's just me."

"That's because he thinks you hate him."

I flinched. "I don't hate him."

"Then stop forcing him to be part of the business. You know he wants nothing to do with it."

Anger flared. This was so Theo and Jude. I leaned closer. "Then maybe he needs to stop driving around in his fucking BMW and spending the money this business creates. Just like you, Theo...you're either in and part of it, or get the fuck out... and find a job." I searched his eyes, remembering all the times I watched him shove a line of coke up his nose. "And stop taking from our clients."

"Hey." He grinned. "If they want to take care of my needs, who am I to say no?"

"You're a fucking Ares." I answered. "It's about time you all start acting like one. Now, are you going to help me with our brother, or do I have to do this like I have to everything...on my fucking own?"

"Lead the way." Theo motioned toward the door like an asshole. "Daddy."

Motherfucker. I ground my jaw and walked out, heading across the hallway to the south wing...and where Jude's bedroom sat separate from the rest of us.

My brother wasn't like me. In fact he wasn't like any of us, spending his time with his nose deep in books, preferring the company of his yuppy, snobby friends to his own blood. But he was blood, and it was about time he started acting like it.

I didn't even knock, just bore down on the handle of his bedroom door and pushed in. He was there, huddled over a mess of open books, turning to peer at me over a set of glasses. I stopped and stared. "I didn't know you wore glasses."

"I didn't know you were so fucking rude barging into someone else's bedroom, although I should have." He muttered, pulling his glasses free. "You never did respect anyone's privacy." He looked past me to Theo. "What now?"

He sat in silence as we closed the door, then proceeded to tell him everything. I showed him mom's video, some of it at least until he looked away. But when we showed him Angelica he went silent. "That's not her. It can't be."

"It is," I countered. "You heard it yourself in mom's video and you can clearly see her."

"How do we know we're just not falling into a trap?"

"A trap of what?" Theo snapped. "They already betrayed us. This is the reason why dad died, for all we knowing they could've murdered him."

"Then who murdered mom, Einstein?" Jude muttered.

Theo thought about it as my mind raced trying to make it all fit.

"Maybe Angelica murdered them both." He said finally.

We all looked at each other. Could a hundred and thirty pound woman kill two people bigger than her? Drugged and tied up, it was possible, except there were no drugs found in their system. Did Angelica have a gun?

No.

I tossed her room, trashing it and there was no evidence of any weapon at all. It didn't seem plausible. "All I know is she is hiding all of this. Even if it has no connection to their deaths, which I highly doubt it's still a reason to investigate.

"And exploit." Theo murmured.

"Come on." Jude winced. "She's our sister."

"Adopted sister." Theo added. "She was forced on us, remember? Now it's time to do a little forcing of our own."

"When?"

Give me the day, okay...then we can do whatever you want. "Tonight," I answered, slowly meeting their gaze. "We do it tonight."

Chapter Seven

ANGELICA

I NEEDED TO GET OUT OF HERE.

And I needed to get out *now*.

I sat on the edge of my bed, my mind racing as I dragged the soft bristled brush through my hair, trying to work out what exactly changed in the hours since the reading of the will. What should've happened was rage, and retribution. For Silas to go on the warpath he always did and shut everyone out... especially his uncle, Lincoln.

But that's not what happened.

Not at all.

Instead, it was the opposite. Secret meetings in our father's study. Dark, ravenous stares across the living room, directed at me. It was enough to give me nightmares.

Did Silas want me out? Even if the will told me I had to stay. I hoped so...it'd give me an excuse to leave. He might even give me money...then, I'd be gone for good.

Gabe's pain would be solely directed at Silas. They'd all fight. Which was exactly what I needed. That'd give me the time to get as far away as possible and try to forget what happened.

I dropped the brush, grabbing my cell instead and stared at the empty screen. Penn hadn't returned my call. In fact he hadn't returned any of them, which freaked me out even more.

I pressed the button, waiting for the message bank to pick up. "Penn, it's me. I'm starting to worry. I need to get out of here and I need to do it now. Please, call me back as soon as you can. I'm worried."

Terrified more like it.

Still, I couldn't wait. I swept my hand over my dress, grabbed my purse from my ruined bedside drawer and quietly hurried out of my room. The house was quiet, my brothers were probably still asleep. I glanced at Gabe's door as I passed, fighting a pang of regret and kept walking.

My heels hit lightly. I lifted them, muffling the sound as I reached for the rear door and fumbled for the lock. It gave a clunk making me wince as I yanked open the door. One panicked glance over my shoulder and I opened the door wider and stepped outside.

"Going somewhere?"

"Jesus!" I screamed and stumbled sideways, finding Silas leaning against the wall outside. "You scared me half to death."

I glanced at the town car where the driver stood, his sleeves rolled up as he cleaned the windows.

"Well?" Silas pushed.

"Nothing...I mean nowhere. I was just heading to the mall." I rushed, panic setting in.

"The mall." He pushed off the wall. "Right, let's go."

"With you?"

He stopped and slowly turned. "Sure, why not."

Fear nailed me to the spot. I glanced at the driver as he finally straightened, noticing us. My pulse raced, I wanted to do more than just go to the mall. I wanted a backup plan to escape this city given the chance. I met Silas's scowl. I couldn't do that with him looking over my shoulder.

"There a problem?"

"No."

"Then by all means." He swept his hand toward the gleaming black BMW. "Consider me your private chauffeur."

I swallowed hard as he turned, made for the passenger's door and opened it. Tattoos peeked out from the sleeves of his leather jacket. I stared at them, trying to quell my racing pulse and headed for the open door before I slipped inside.

The scent of leather and that new car smell filled my nose. I breathed deep, watching Silas skirt the front of the car and climb in behind the wheel. The door closed with a soft thud behind him. He glanced my way and pressed the button starting the engine with a growl.

Silas pushed the car into gear and punched the accelerator, leaving the powerful beast to respond. I clawed for my seatbelt, staring at the Ares's family driver still standing behind the car as we tore past.

"The mall, huh? You sure you don't want to go anywhere else?"

Click. I couldn't get it closed fast enough. "No, where else do you think I want to go?"

"I dunno...somewhere out of the city maybe?"

Out of the city? The Order rose before I pushed it away. He couldn't possibly know about that. It had to be something else. Maybe it was Penn? Did he think I wanted to visit my boyfriend? My cheeks burned. "No, not out of the city."

"Suit yourself." He muttered, sounding instantly pissed off.

He pushed the car harder, forcing me to slam back against the seat. I cut him a glare. One I knew he saw because the corner of his mouth twitched in amusement. Everyone stared as he hurled past, hugging the hard corners and swung the car into the parking lot of the mall.

Heads turned when we pulled in. He was used to that. He even enjoyed it. But I didn't. Heat rose as I scanned the area and pulled my belt free before opening the door. He was always so in your face, climbing out like he was royalty. I hated that. Hated the pretence and the lies. More than that I hated the attention...I received enough of that as it was.

I lowered my gaze, closed the door and hurried around the car. "Thank you, Silas. I can find my own way from here."

"Stop."

I froze, finding his stare.

He scowled. "We're family," then stepped closer. "I can't leave you here." He scanned the crowd obliviously heading in and out of the mall. "Don't want you in danger now, do we?"

Rage simmered in his stare. My lips parted, the words on the tip of my tongue. *Right now the only danger to me...is you.*

"Do we?" He took a step forward and I fought the urge to move back.

I swallowed and shook my head. Gotta get away from him. Gotta get away from all of them. That urgency rose as he motioned toward the entrance. I turned away, hurrying along the parked cars to the crossing as my mind raced.

They barely acknowledged me before. Pretending as hard as they could I didn't exist...until now. Now they knew I existed a lot, and I didn't like it. I hurried through the doors. My panicked plan slipped through my fingers.

I pulled my cell out of my purse, glancing at the empty screen. Where the Hell are you, Penn? Not here, that's where. Not anywhere I needed him. Silas was a dark blur at the edge of my focus, bearing down on me. I scanned the stores and made for the first place I could get away from him...Honey Birdette.

Bras that weren't even bras greeted me. They were nothing but black straps designed to cover your nipple, because they wouldn't cover anything else. My cheeks burned hard, memories pushed in. *You're to wear white for now. Red is for training...black is sold, do you understand?*

Black.

Black was sold.

"You like that?" His deep voice was at my back.

I spun around, knowing I still stood in front of the mannequin wearing the kind of lingerie I was sure Silas was used to. "What?"

He glanced at the barely there bra. "Do you like that?"

"No." I shook my head and looked away, praying to God no one heard us. "No, I don't *like* that."

He gave a huh, and pushed past me. "Maybe this is more your taste." He picked up a black lace thong.

I looked away, mortified.

"Or this?" He pulled up a soft apricot color. His thumb sliding back and forth over the thin strap as he settled that dark stare on me.

I swallowed hard, shaking my head as my core clenched. Still, his thumb never stopped rubbing, rubbing...rubbing.

A pang ripped across my chest, burning as I released my breath and stumbled away.

"What?" He called out. *"I'm just trying to help you."*

But he wasn't. He wasn't helping me at all. Just go away! Go away and leave me the hell alone. Panicked, I grabbed the first thing I liked. White, lace and not a thong and hurried to the register.

The young woman stared, watching us intently. Had she heard him?

"Looks like your boyfriend knows his way around a thong." She murmured, staring at him as she rang the purchase up.

I pressed my card against the machine, waited for the beep before I snatched the bag and hurried out of there, mortified. "He's *not* my boyfriend." I murmured.

He never left me alone, crowding my steps as I raced from store to store. I didn't even know which ones I went into. All I cared about was getting away from him. He strolled casually, his long, predatory strides eating the distance while I scurried, hiding around towering clothes racks and ducking between shelves until for a second I lost him.

I stopped at the end of an Asian grocery aisle and glanced around searching for him, the pungent scent of salty and sweet filling my nostrils. But he wasn't there. He wasn't anywhere.

"Thank God."

But then there he was, trailed by some woman outside the store. He turned around, grabbed her wrists, pinning them together as she stared up at him with desire and hope in her eyes.

He said something to her. Whatever it was, she didn't want to hear it. She shook her head, but he was cold and cruel, pushing her away and turned his back. He turned his head, that callous glare finding me. The woman followed his focus and stopped. Rage burned in her eyes. She said something that made Silas flinch before she turned and stormed away.

I didn't stick around to see the fallout, slipping out of the grocery store and kept walking toward the food court. The crowd grew thicker, pushing against me. I spied a woman standing on the outer edges, trying her best to hand out flyers and headed her way.

"Charlie Hunter Women's Shelter needs your help." She called those walking past. Her smile, hopeful, but they ignored her, striding past.

"I'll take one." I pushed through them toward her.

Her eyes lit up. "Really? Oh, great. Charlie Hunger Women's Shelter is a non-for-profit organization..."

I shook my head, glancing over my shoulder. My mind was already racing as I turned back to the number in bold, trying to fit it all together.

Escape. The word filled me. I could slip out tonight, then call for help. They'd come and pick me up, and wouldn't even ask any questions. It's what they do. "It's okay. Thank you."

Her smile turned to confusion as I shoved the flyer into my purse. I felt him before I saw, like a hunter searching for his panicked prey. That's exactly how I felt. Panicked and prey. I slammed my purse closed, squashing down the pamphlet and ran hurrying toward the bathroom.

Free.

That feeling raced as I hurried along the hallway, looking over my shoulder before I plunged into the ladies restroom. I needed an escape, to find some kind of way out of here...without my so-called brother watching my every move.

The hand dryer howled, making me jump. I jerked my gaze to a woman watching me with curiosity before she strode my way. I stepped out of her path. "Sorry."

Others glanced my way, coming out of the stalls. I spun around, hoping with all I had Silas was gone. But the moment I stepped into the hall he was there, leaning against the wall, watching the women who walked past.

"You know this is the perfect pickup place." He murmured, staring at a cute brunette as she almost skipped past. She gave him a smile, turning her head to watch him as he pushed off the wall and turned to me.

I was mortified. "How...why..."

"How, why what, sister?" He gave a shrug.

My whole face felt like it was on fire. "Never mind."

I gripped my bags and strode out, my focus on him behind me. He was a dark blur never more than a step behind me as though he was letting me know I wasn't getting away again. Only I had to...now more than ever.

I made my way into Luxe and picked up their soaps, smelling them before I grabbed summer breeze and made for the counter. He said nothing, but he didn't have to. Women stared at him walking past, it didn't matter their age. All they saw was a six foot two muscled bad boy, heavily tatted with gorgeous dark eyes and perfect lashes. Silas was more than handsome, he was beautiful.

If only they knew the real him.

I walked out of Peter Alexander, sick of the attention he was getting and turned around. "I'm done."

"Are you?" He searched my eyes. "Going to come clean, are you?"

"What?"

He lowered his gaze to the Luxe bag. "The soap."

I just shook my head and strode away heading for the mall doors. Sun hit me the moment I stepped out, moving with the crowd and across the crossing to his car. The boot clicked, opening instantly as I neared. I dumped my purchases in and headed for the passenger's door, yanking it open and climbed inside.

Slam. I jolted with the sound as Silas closed the boot a little too hard, rounded the car and climbed in, closing the door behind him. I fought the urge to look at him and stared straight ahead instead, until he leaned over and between my legs.

"What are you doing?" I screeched.

But he grabbed my bag, yanking the top of the pamphlet that stuck out free.

"Charlie Hunter Women's Shelter." He read slowly. "Now why would you have something like this, little sister. You're not in need of saving are you?"

My heart slammed against my chest as I stared at the paper in his hand.

"Well?" He asked, turning toward me.

"That's not your business." I mumbled and snatched it free.

He let me take it. Eyeing me before he turned and started the engine. I thought he was going to demand a response, even as he backed out of the car space and headed for home. The hair on my arms rose with every minute I waited for his wrath. But it never came, even when he pulled into our driveway and headed along the side of the house to the external garages at the back.

Armed guards patrolled the grounds, nodding at Silas as we passed. I couldn't wait to get away from him. This whole thing was a wasted trip. I stabbed the belt, and shoved the door open the moment we were stopped.

The growl of the engine died a second later the driver's door opened and closed.

"Don't you want these?" He called as I almost reached the rear door.

The click of the boot sounded, stopping me cold. No, the whisper raced as I slowly turned, watching him reach into the boot for my bags. The urge to flee was overwhelming. Still, I forced every step back to him, reaching for the bags in his hand.

But the moment I did, he pulled back, making me stumble to grab them, until we were that close we almost touched.

"Last chance, Angelica. Are you sure you have nothing you want to say to me?"

"There's a lot I want to say to you, Silas." I yanked my bags hard and he let them go. "Starting with the fact you're an asshole for trashing my room. I know you hate me, but even that was an all time low."

The corner of his lip rose as he slowly nodded. "Just remember *I* gave you a chance."

"You gave me nothing." I responded and stepped backwards, not taking my eyes off him.

The door opened behind me.

"Angel?" Gabe called.

I all but ran for him, clutching my bags in my hand, cutting him a panicked look before I raced inside.

"What did you say to her?" Gabe called.

I didn't stay long enough to hear Silas' response. Just raced for my bedroom and barrelled through the door, slamming it shut behind me.

Just remember I gave you a chance.

I closed my eyes and tried to ease my booming pulse. A chance. That's the one thing he never gave me.

No.

I've had to claw and beg and plead for those all on my own.

Daughter.

The neon word flashed in my head. My breath caught as those murky memories pushed to the surface. "No." I whispered. "Please, no. Not now, not here."

But still, they persisted.

Daughter.

Owned.

Liar...

Chapter Eight

SILAS

She scurried past Gabe like a goddamn mouse and disappeared inside. All I wanted to do was to go after her, to grab her and her fucking bags, and drive her against the wall. I wanted answers. But it wasn't just answers I wanted now. I wanted that look...that piercing goddamn stare from the recording as she looked up at me on her knees...the one now etched into my head.

"Hey." Gabe called, striding toward me ever the white fucking knight when it came to his sister.

Our sister remember?

I strode around the car, but he was in front of me blocking my way. I stopped, lifting my gaze to him. Jesus, how the fuck did he get so tall all of a sudden? He was supposed to be my little brother. But the pissed off male scowling in front of me wasn't so little not anymore. But he didn't understand what was going on here...and he needed to stay the fuck out of it.

"Leave it, Gabe." I moved around him.

"No." He stepped at the same time, stopping me.

"I said *leave it.*" I forced the words through clenched teeth.

"If you *think* she had anything to do with any of this, then you're an even bigger asshole than I already thought."

His words hit me hard. "What did you say to me?"

He sucked in a hard breath, his eyes widening with a flare of panic. Still he stood his ground. "She didn't write the will. She asked for nothing, only to ever be included in the family. But you and the others have never wanted that, and now you're making that clearer than ever."

The will?

That's what he thought this was all about?

The lying bitch could stay here all she wanted. In fact, I wanted her here...right where I could control her.

I shook my head. "Think what you want."

"Then tell me otherwise. What *is* your problem with her?"

He wasn't going to leave it, was he? I met that flicker of panic. Maybe I should tell him what he wanted to hear. I saw it in my head. I'd get my phone out, replay the recording. Let's see what he thinks of his innocent little sister when he watches her sucking some motherfucker off.

My pulse raced at the thought. What *would* he think of her?

Not what I was thinking that was for sure.

"Maybe she didn't have a hand in the will, but that doesn't mean she's entitled to a goddamn thing."

"She is our sister by law. That means she does. It's about time you and the others realised that. Maybe you think the same about me?"

"What? No." I barked, running my fingers through my hair. *"Of course not!"*

He gave a slow nod as Theo strode out of the rear door and headed for us. But Gabe was done, that panic now turned to pain. "You know one day you might not have all of us around, maybe then you might appreciate those we have left."

He turned and strode away, passing Theo as he headed back inside.

"What was that about?"

"The same thing as always." I murmured watching Gabe stride after her. *"Her."*

"Speaking of. Are we doing this tonight?"

I glanced his way, scowled then remembered Lincoln. "Give me a second." I grabbed my cell, typed out a message.

Are we on for tonight?

I hadn't heard from him all morning. Sending him the recording still didn't sit right. The second he had it he was gone, what the fuck was he doing with it anyway? Those thoughts crowded in and a flicker of anger followed. I bet I knew what the bastard was doing with it...the same thing I was.

Beep.

I looked down.

Lincoln: *No. Not yet.*

"What the fuck do you mean, not yet?" I snarled, finding Theo. "Who does this motherfucker think he is?"

He gave a shrug. "The one calling the shots by the sounds of it."

"The fuck he is." I typed back a response.

This is happening tonight, be here or don't be here. I don't give a fuck.

Send.

Rage moved deeper. First it was him pushing into the business, now he wanted to push into our life. He was trying to take it all. That's what he was doing. I glanced toward the house. I wasn't waiting anymore. I wanted the truth about what happened to our parents...and I wanted it tonight.

"It's happening tonight."

"Good." Theo nodded. "Then the little bitch is ours. I'm going to make her life a living hell."

"You do anyway." The last words were a murmur. I didn't mean to say them out loud.

Theo cut me a glare. "You're one to talk," he snapped before he walked toward his grey Audi RS7, hit the button and climbed in.

I didn't wait for him to leave, just strode toward the house. I wasn't waiting for anyone when it came to the truth about what happened to my parents. My father was the one I focused on, how he must've felt finding out just how our mother betrayed him.

Did he find the recording?

How far did he realise their betrayal went?

Who the fuck killed him?

I strode along the hallway and turned into my room. There was no way he killed himself, not after finding out what mom did and there's no way in Hell he killed her. I closed the bedroom door and turned, dragging my fingers through my hair. He'd be enraged, there was no doubt about that. He'd be dangerous. But not to her.

No.

Never to her.

Only for everyone else.

"He would've found out the truth. That's what he would've done. He would've found out who this guy was and he would've killed him." That was my father. Not a man missing the entire side of his face by a shotgun blast to his head.

I didn't even think we owned a shotgun.

I spent the rest of the day researching, finding out as much as I could about Hale Halestrom and the Order. But there was very little to find and by the time Theo strode in later that day I was done waiting. I pushed up from my chair and walked into his room. "Get the others together."

One brow rose. "Is it time?"

"I'm not waiting any longer."

"You letting Lincoln know?"

I held Theo's stare. "No. I don't think I will."

Beep.

I grabbed my cell and looked down.

Lincoln: *Don't approach her. Wait until I get there.* "Speak of the Devil. He wants me to hold off."

"I say go for it." He pushed up. "Corner her, force her to tell us the truth. This has got nothing to do with Lincoln, he can fuck off."

The truth, that's all we ever wanted. One slow nod and I turned. Theo was right behind me as we made for her room. I didn't knock. I didn't need to. This was my goddamn house, wasn't it? Anyone who wanted to live here was under my goddamn rule. I owned her...and it was about time she realised that fact.

I pushed her door inward, glanced at the shopping still unpacked on the end of her bed, but she wasn't here.

"The kitchen." Theo turned around and strode away.

We hunted like a pack, making our way into the kitchen. Victor, the cook lifted his head from packing pans away. "Can I get you anything?"

I shook my head and scowled. "Angelica?"

"I saw her earlier, made her a sandwich and wrapped it up for her trip."

"Trip?" My blood ran cold.

"Yeah." Victor looked from Theo to me. "She was leaving for a while. She said you guys knew..."

But we didn't know, did we? I spun around and raced for her bedroom once more and barked. "Check the garage!"

Shit!

SHIT!

Did Lincoln tip her off? Did that motherfucker stab me in the goddamn back? Rage rippled through me as I stride back along the hallway and into her room, throwing her door open with a bang!

Where the fuck was she? I scanned her bedroom once more and lunged into her walk in robe, finding a small gap in her clothes. She was gone. I strode forward, throwing her nun-like dresses aside. *FUCK!*

Then I spied the bag at the bottom of the cupboard. It looked like a hiking bag, stuffed to the brim. I bent down, flicked open the flap and opened it. The tuff of fur from her jacket sprang free. I pulled it aside and rummaged through the rest of her belongings.

It was a go bag, that was easy to see. That meant she hadn't left...yet.

"What are you doing?"

I lifted my head to Gabe standing in the doorway.

"Where is she?" I rose.

He scowled. "Why, so you can make her feel like shit even more?"

I strode toward my little brother who wasn't so little anymore. "I said, where is she?"

He scowled. "She's gone to the cemetery."

I stilled. "Why?'

"Why do you think?" He snapped.

To say goodbye, that's why...

Theo strode in. "She's not here and the driver is gone."

I held Gabe's stare. "It's okay. I know exactly where she is."

Gabe looked from me to Theo and back again. "Does someone want to tell me what the fuck is going on?"

I didn't want to, not yet at least. But if I didn't give our brother something, then this was going to get out of hand. "She lied." I said carefully. "About mom and dad. She knows more than she's told us and the police."

He shook his head, scowling.

"It's true, little brother." Theo urged softly. "She isn't who you thought she was. She's a liar and she knows what happened to mom and dad."

"No." Gabe croaked, but he looked desperate.

"It's true." I said carefully as the faint sound of tires crunching on the asphalt sounded. I lifted my gaze and turned my head.

"What is it?" Theo asked.

"Not sure." I made for the door.

The engine didn't sound like the town car, maybe I hoped it was. I strode along the hallway and pushed through the rear door. Lincoln climbed out of the backseat of his Audi, his driver rounding the rear of the car to hold the door. It was later than I thought. The sun was sinking fast, casting deep pinks and sultry blues across the evening sky.

Tailored suit and a sleek ride. My uncle looked like a very different man than I saw in the lawyers office. He was stepping up in the world by the looks of it, and using our backs to get himself there.

"Silas." He called and strode forward, casting a glance at my brothers behind me.

"Why are you here?" I cut his driver a glare.

There was a careful smile. "Now, how is that anyway to greet family?"

"If it's what they deserved." Theo snapped behind me.

Lincoln's smile faltered until the flare of headlights cut across all of us. Slowly the town car drew closer, blinding us. In the piercing glare I remembered her backpack tucked away in the corner of her wardrobe. The one where she hid her fur-lined jacket and all her things. She was running, desperate to get as far away from us as possible.

Not a goddamn chance, not while she held the truth of what happened to my parents and as the car pulled up to a stop in front of us, Lincoln moved striding toward the rear door before the rest of us. Theo cut me a savage glare, his lips curled, rage detonating in his eyes.

I strode forward as Lincoln opened the rear door and reached out his hand. "It's okay." He said quietly. "We were just worried, that's all."

Just worried?

No, I was fucking furious.

I stepped around Lincoln, grabbed her arm as she stepped out and pulled her against me. "Inside." It wasn't a request.

"Stop." Angelica pulled against me. "Silas *stop*, you're *hurting* me."

I didn't care. I couldn't care. Even as Jude pushed through the rear door of the house, watching me drag her toward him, then pushed her inside.

"Get off me!" She screamed.

"Move." I wasn't nice, pushing her through the door and inside. "The den *now.*"

She spun and stumbled backwards. "No. Not until you tell me what the *hell* is going on."

"You know you lying little bitch." Theo snarled behind me.

The color drained instantly out of her face, leaving her pale and ashen. Her eyes widened as her steps stuttered, sending her crashing against the wall.

"What did you say?" She pushed back against the wall, looking up as Theo flanked me and pushed in.

"You heard me, you're a fucking liar and we know it."

There was a tiny shake of her head as though she didn't believe what we were saying. But she would...soon enough.

"Now move." Theo dragged her from the wall and shoved her hard.

She stumbled sideways, frantically scanning my brothers behind me. "Gabe...please."

"He's not going to help you." I stepped into her line of sight and jerked my gaze toward the den. "Not anymore."

Chapter Nine

ANGELICA

SILAS JERKED HIS HEAD TOWARD THE DEN. "YOU CAN WALK on your own, or I can drag you. It's up to you."

No.

No. No. No.

This wasn't happening.

I caught Gabe's wide eyes behind him. "I don't understand what's happening."

There was pain in his stare. Desperate, cutting pain. Still, he didn't come to my defense, staying silent as Silas stepped closer, driving me along the hallway, but as I turned I caught Lincoln at the rear of them, those dark eyes fixed on mine.

I only wanted to say goodbye. Tears welled in my eyes, until I bit down on the inside of my cheeks, stopping the ache in the back of my throat. I should've left when I had the chance. I should've grabbed my bag and called the shelter. I could've been miles from here by now. I could've been...no one and lost in a sea of those desperate to escape.

My back skimmed the wall before I turned and scanned the hallway, desperately seeking a way out.

"You run and you won't get far." Silas warned. "You don't want me tackling you to the ground now, do you?"

The thought of him crashing into me was terrifying. He'd be cruel...because that's who he was when it came to me. My chest tightened with the thought, almost feeling the weight of him on top of me. My gaze went to the doorway of the den as my knees trembled.

Don't let them see you're scared. Mom's words suddenly rose inside me. *You're an Ares, Angel. That's who you are and Ares don't break for anyone, just remember that.* I stopped walking, dragging in a hard breath and straightened my spine.

No.

We don't break...not even when it comes to our own.

I fixed my gaze on that doorway and forced myself to move. My knees stopped trembling as I walked in and stopped in the middle of the room before I turned to face my accusers. Silas eyes shone in the murky amber light. This wasn't a room I came to often. It was a masculine room, dark, gloomy, the air tinged with the faint scent of expensive cigars. Deals were made in this room, secrets too...

"We want the truth and we want it now." Silas strode closer, bearing down on me.

The others flanked each side of him and stood there staring at me silently. Even Lincoln. My face grew hot as I glanced at him.

"We know you're lying." He held my stare. "Where were you on the day of the attack?"

I shook my head. "What?" I glanced at my brothers. "I told you and the police. I was here."

He took a step. "Doing what?"

My cheeks grew hotter. "I was...I was with mom."

*Promise me...*Mom's faint voice tried to push it. But I kept it at bay, focusing on the men in front of me. Men who were once family.

"And what were you doing?"

He thought we were scheming, was that it? Scheming the murder of our father. "Nothing."

"Nothing? You have to be doing something."

"I wasn't planning murder, if that's what you're asking."

"How do we know that?" He spat, his lips curling. "I don't trust a single thing that comes out of your mouth."

Promise me.

I pushed that voice back. "I could ask you the same thing."

He scowled, his voice growing dangerous. "What did you say to me?"

"I said," I met that stare, holding it. "I could ask you the same thing. Any of you." I scanned every gaze in that room. "I did nothing. I *know* nothing."

Silas reached into his pocket and pulled out his cell. "Where do you and mom go when you go out?"

"Where we go?" My mind raced. "Functions, fundraisers... shopping. I don't know, where do you go?"

He clenched his cell in a fist and strode forward, towering over me. "This isn't about me, is it?"

I searched his eyes finding the glint of rage. "Then why is it about me?"

"What is the Order?"

I froze. My breaths racing.

Promise me on your life you'll never tell them. That whispered plea grew louder. Only I didn't know what I was supposed to keep secret. I...didn't remember. The dark patches in my memory were far to frequent for me to piece together. Vague words flashing behind my eyes. *Daughter. Owned. Control.* The moment I tried to remember more a heavy weight smothered my mind, suffocating every memory I'd ever had of that place.

I closed my eyes as that weight descended. Fragments flickered and my senses sharpened. The hard floor against my knees as I knelt. Someone's heavy breath against my ear. A sudden stretch between my legs, my body trembling.

"Tell me what you do there?"

That's the girl, now open your mouth.

Heat moved, spreading through my belly and plunged down. The pressure between my thighs grew bolder.

That's it...Jesus Christ, Angel, that's it. The man's grunt filled me.

Panic flared as I opened my eyes, finding that hateful glare from my brother.

"What is the Order?" He demanded.

My pulse was dull and booming in my ears. I shook my head, my voice croaky and distant. "Nothing."

"Liar."

"Silas." Lincoln warned.

But Silas didn't care about his uncle. Instead he lifted his cell and swiped his thumb across the screen. Theo, Jude and Lincoln stood mesmerized as he opened some kind of message. But Gabe never looked at them, he looked at me.

"It's...it's an orphanage." I whispered.

"Liar." Silas barked and pressed play on the video.

"You will be on your knees. Do you understand?"

I jolted with the sound of that voice. The same one from my mind. No...no...

"Yes." My own voice echoed through his cell.

"Yes, what?"

"Yes, Sir."

"No." I whispered and took a step backwards. *"No!"*

Theo looked smug. Jude was riveted. But it was Gabe who jerked his gaze to Silas. "What the fuck is going on, Silas?"

"That's something you need to ask your sister about." He jerked that glare over his shoulder. "There's more. Do you want to hear it, little brother?"

His lips curled into a cruel smirk as he turned back to me. He was enjoying this, reveling in my destruction. But none of this had anything to do with the murders now, did it?

No.

This was personal.

He pressed his thumb against the screen.

"Open." The voice commanded and that pressure built in my head. I couldn't remember any of this and yet...yet it felt as though I should. Black holes lingered in my memory.

"That's it. Jesus, that's it." The guttural growl filled the air.

"Turn it off." The words were a whisper. *"I said TURN IT OFF."*

Silas hit the video and moved, lunging toward me so fast I barely had a chance to move. But I did, throwing myself backwards until I hit the wall in the den so hard the painting above me rattled.

"What do you do there?"

NO!

Nonono...please...

I slipped away from his reach, moving deeper in the room. "I...I don't know what you're talking about." His face blurred as my voice thickened.

"Show me." He snapped. *"Show me what you do there!"*

Show him?

My stomach sank. The icy touch of terror plunged deep, carving through the last traces of heat. "No."

Those dark eyes blazed. "No?"

"No." The word was a husky whimper.

He didn't look at the others anymore. No, his rage was all for me. "You will show me, or I'll hand you over to the police and tell them you conspired with our mother for murder."

The floor seemed to fall out from under me. "No...you *wouldn't.*"

"Wouldn't I?" He pushed. *"Dare me."*

Dare him? No...no...this wasn't happening. I shook my head as my throat tightened and that memory surged even bolder than it had before.

The hard floor.

The weight of *someone* against me.

The warmth of his skin.

And that husky, deep voice in my ear, open your mouth, *Angel. You're going to suck what I give you, do you understand? You're going to suck and lick and you're going to be good at it.* His hand fisted my hair. The sudden jolt as he jerked my gaze up to his, and yet all I saw were those eyes... those dark eyes. *You're going to be my good whore and if you're behaved I might even let you come. How does that sound? So open your mouth, take it all inside, just like you've been trained...*

"Show me."

I was wrenched back to that den in my house...and the row of men in front of me. Gabe's eyes were impossibly wide as his brother lifted his cell. "Or do I keep playing the recording?"

Tears blurred his face, just like the man in my memory. Slowly I shook my head.

"Show me what you do there."

"You don't," I whispered. "You don't understand what you're asking me to do."

"I have a fair idea. But I want you to show me...I want you to show us all, just what a lying fucking traitor you are, Angelica. Now, walk over here and show me before I drag you from this house and have the cops throw you into a cell where you belong."

But I didn't do it.

I had nothing to do with our parents murder.

I had nothing to do with any of this.

"It's your decision. Stay here and tell us the truth of it all...or..."

I took a step, then another moving to him. "You're asking me... no, you're forcing me to."

He lifted his cell. "On your knees...*sister.*"

On your knees...on your knees...ON YOUR KNEES. *Just like you've been trained.* That husky voice urged in my head. Neon words flickered.

OWNED.

CONTROL.

DAUGHTER.

No...no...no...no. My mind said one thing, but my body did the opposite, knees buckled as I slowly sank in front of him.

"Now, show us what you do at the Order." Silas growled.

I lowered my gaze, my body trembling out of fear, until those blinding words collided inside my head. Then something inside me took over. I lifted my gaze to his. *Just like you've been trained.* I wasn't this person, not the one who reached up, sliding her hands over his thighs and squeezed, staring into those rage filled eyes and leaned in. No, I wasn't the woman who turned her head, rubbing my cheek against the denim of his jeans and slowly rose upwards.

"What the fuck is she doing?" Gabe croaked.

"Shut the fuck up." Theo snapped. "This is happening."

"Show us." Silas savage tone was husky now. "Show us what you and our mother did there."

On your knees. Those words echoed as I opened my mouth. My breath warming the fabric against my cheek as the outline of his cock hardened.

"Do what you've been trained to do. That's what he said, right? *What you've been trained.*"

His husky words made no impact. Because I was someone else now. I was...her. The woman mom needed me to be.

Keep our secret, Angel. Whatever happens. Keep our secret. The hard metal edge of his zipper pressed against my mouth. I gripped the tongue and dragged it all the way down. A low, desperate sound echoed in his belly and spread outwards and a tremble followed. He was hard, so very hard.

Open your mouth.

The man in my head commanded. I did, leaving my tongue to

lick against the warmth, leaving a slick trail against his skin as he finally sprang free.

"That's it, show us what a whore really does." Silas growled.

He wanted to hurt me, to punish me. I looked up and opened my mouth wider, hovering over the head of his cock. A clear bead welled in the eye, desperate to be licked. But the second I moved so did he, grabbing me around the throat.

"Stop this!" Gabe roared. *"Stop this now!*

"You...fucking disgust me." Silas hissed, then shoved me backwards.

I hit the ground hard and lay there. The impact was brutal, agony tore through my thigh, shattering that grip over my mind. As I lifted my gaze that sickening wave of horror plunged deep inside. Silas stood in front of me, his hard cock encased in his fist and I knew...

It's happened again.

Oh, Jesus...it's happened again.

They all stared, even Gabe. But he didn't see me...only her. Disgust flickered in his eyes, before he looked away.

"No." The cry burned as I shoved forward, desperately reaching for the only ally I had left in this house. But he wouldn't look at me.

Silas fought his body, trying to shove his cock back inside his zipper, but it wouldn't stay, springing free, desperate to be taken care of...

"You're nothing but a whore, aren't you?" Theo snarled. "You and our mother. Did you think we wouldn't find out? Did you think you could get away with it?"

"That's why he killed her, isn't it?" Jude asked. "Because she was having an affair."

"*NO!*" The scream tore from me, burning deeper now, carving all the way into the pit of my belly. Rage and desperation erupted. "*She wasn't having an affair.*"

"Then *TELL US!*" Theo strode forward until he stood over me. "Tell us what happened!"

"*I DON'T KNOW!*" I fisted my hands as desperation filled me. "I don't know, don't *you* get that? I don't remember! *I don't remember anything!*"

"Why should we believe you?" He stared down at me.

I'd never felt so pathetically low. "I...don't know." I sobbed. "I just don't know."

"That's enough." Lincoln demanded, his tone thick and husky. "Go to your room, Angel. You're to stay there, do you understand?"

"You try to run and we'll catch you." Silas added. "So you can put your things back."

"I'll have a man stationed outside her door." Lincoln grabbed his cell.

"The Hell you will." Silas yanked his zipper up and turned to face him. "She is *our* problem. *We* will be the one to stand guard."

Lincoln shook his head. "But..."

Silas strode forward, facing his uncle. "We don't really need *you* here. This..." He glanced over his shoulder at me. "Has no bearing on the business, so it doesn't involve you."

"Dante was my goddamn brother." Lincoln snarled.

"One, you decided to walk out on." Silas responded and glanced at Theo, then Jude.

They both moved, Theo first, turning on his uncle...then Jude.

"It's a family issue moving forward." Silas sided with his brothers. "We'll handle it."

Lincoln clenched his jaw, the muscles bulging as he held Silas's glare. "You're making a big mistake."

"Then I guess we'll find out. Goodnight uncle, don't let the door hit you on the way out."

One desperate glance my way and Lincoln slowly shook his head. My arms trembled, leaving me to push upwards. He knew now. He knew what I did...and what they did to me.

But as he stood there a new fear pushed in. He was the only one who could get me out of here. The only one standing in the way of my brothers...and me.

"Good luck, sweetheart. I think you're going to need it" He said to me, before he turned to the others, fixing his stare on Gabe. "You know where to find me." Then he left, striding out of the den...and headed along the hallway.

"You heard me." Silas turned on me. "Your room. You even make a goddamn peep and I'll make you regret it."

I scurried forward, skimming my back along the wall and raced out of there. I couldn't run fast enough, plunging along the hallway and yanked open my bedroom door and threw myself inside. The flimsy lock was useless. Still I slammed the door closed and in the dark, leaned against it.

Oh, God…

Oh. GOD.

But I knew it wasn't over. They'd never stop, not now they knew what happened in that place. Still, they didn't know it all…not yet. I closed my eyes as a shudder tore through me. It was fear that waited…fear and the whisper of my mom's voice. *Promise me, Angel. Promise me they'll never know.*

I opened my eyes and stared into the dark. I had to find a way to get out of here. If I didn't, my days in this house would be terrifying.

Chapter Ten

THEO

Her bedroom door slammed with a *bang*. Outside, a car's engine started. Still, we never moved, all four of us frozen, staring at the spot on the floor where she'd fallen. "What the fuck was that?" I slowly shifted my gaze to Silas finding his pinched brows and his hardened stare.

His chest moved with a hard breath.

None of that was supposed to happen.

Not forcing her to her knees...or what she'd almost done after.

But it did, didn't it?

It did happen and now there was no turning back.

Not for her or for us.

I reached down, tugging the front of my trousers to ease the tension.

"You...bastard." Gabe slowly lifted his gaze turning to Silas. "You *goddamn fucking bastard!*"

He lunged before we realized, flying across the room to land a blow on Silas' cheek with a crack. I moved fast, but Jude was closer, wrapping his arm around Gabe trying to haul him away. But the kid wasn't going easy, fighting like a goddamn demon, thrashing in Jude's arms.

"Gabe!" Our brother barked, wrestling him.

I stepped between them, finding the shattering look of pain in our youngest brother's stare. "Easy." I urged.

"Fuck you, Theo!" He raged, throwing Jude off.

But Silas' never defended himself. He turned his head back, his cheek reddening with the blow.

"Why the fuck did you do that?"

"Because." Silas answered coldly. "She's a liar."

"She's our goddamn sister!"

But she wasn't...not anymore. To me she'd never been to begin with. Her haughty fucking stare and perfect flowery fucking dresses, always hanging on mom's every move.

Now we knew why.

I glanced back at that place on the floor where she knelt looking up at Silas with tears in her eyes. Do what you've been trained to do. I licked my lips and forced myself to step away.

"Where are you going?" Silas wrenched that glare my way. "I need you to watch her."

I shook my head and dragged my fingers through my hair. "No fucking way. You want the bitch here, then you're on your own." I needed out of here, away from the image of her on her knees and the scent of fucking hunger in the air.

"Do you think about anyone else other than yourself?" Silas strode toward me, his cheek blazing and his eyes full of rage.

"Leave it." Jude answered. "I'll do it. I'll watch her door."

I gave Silas a shrug and turned away, leaving them all behind.

Beep.

My cell vibrated. I grabbed it out as I headed for my bedroom and stepped through, flicking on the light and closed the door. I stared at the screen but saw nothing, just the image of her tears falling down her cheeks. *I don't know! Don't you get that? I don't remember anything.*

I leaned against the door shifting my weight. Still my fucking erection didn't ease, aching all the way to my goddamn balls. I need to get out of here. A line or two of coke and I'd get my stuck-up fucking sister out of my head. I licked my lips and pushed off, finding the message once more on my cell.

Stevie: *We're waiting for you at Jacks.*

"On my fucking way." I strode into my wardrobe, grabbed my jacket then turned around and left.

The streets blurred behind the wheel of the Audi RS-7. I shifted gears, hugging the corners and pushed it harder on the straight, pulling in behind the steady stream of traffic heading downtown.

That's why he killed her, isn't it? Because she was having an affair.

NO!

I drove my foot harder against the accelerator as Angelica's scream ripped through my head. Headlights blinding me.

Horns blared. I wrenched the wheel, pulling back onto the right lane and barked. *"Fuck!"*

My pulse was booming.

The sound, thunderous in my head.

I couldn't shake that goddamn image of her on her fucking knees, rubbing her face against Silas's cock like a cat drunk on milk. She fucking loved it...No, she needed it.

Christ, I'd never seen a woman so fucking obsessed with being on her knees like that before. It was like she was possessed or something...our goddamn sister, adopted or not. She'd lived with us for long enough to know what we did was wrong.

Very fucking wrong.

My fist clenched around the wheel. Now Lincoln knew what we'd done. He was going to use it against us. That was only a matter of time. "Fuck." I grunted and yanked the wheel, pulling into the back street and pulled into a parking lot marked No Entry.

Signs like that weren't meant for people like me. I pulled the Audi into the parking lot and killed the engine before climbing out and locked the car behind me. The dull throb of music spilled from inside. Looked like the party had already started. I stopped at the rear door, wrapped my knuckles on the damn thing and waited. Heavy footsteps sounded before the door was wrenched open. I stared into the savage glare from the six-foot four bouncer on the other side and muttered "It's me, open up."

He did.

Of course he did.

I pushed past and walked along the hallway until it spilled out into the back area. Black and chrome filled the space, glinting from low lights at my feet. Glasses clinked. Girls laughed and guys chatted. They all turned my way as I walked in and stopped at the back bar.

I didn't even have to speak. The bartender turned and grabbed a bottle from the top shelf before pouring it neat.

"There you are, it's about time you got here."

I turned at the husky female tone. Stevie sauntered her way toward me, wearing a pantsuit that was split to her thigh, leaving very little to the imagination. She grabbed me, pressing her body against mine and kissed me...hard.

We'd fucked.

Once.

That was all it took for her to brand me as one of her playthings. A name I didn't care about. Not that it stopped me from getting as much cunt as I wanted. She broke the kiss, but instead of pulling away she leaned in close to whisper in my ear. "I have some of the purest shit you've ever tasted in your life."

A glass slid my way. "How pure?"

She eased backwards, meeting my stare. "As the driven snow."

I grabbed my glass and followed her to the back room of this small and exclusive club. Only the wealthy came here, billionaires with their Maserati's and two hundred and fifty k Rolexes with their weekend houses in Malibu which they never visited. No, they stayed here....because in this city was where the fun was.

I nodded as I passed, catching each ravenous stare aimed at Stevie. She was beautiful and fun, shoving as much coke up her nose as I did and yet there was some reason I wasn't into her. Some hollow part of me that felt nothing when she kissed me.

On your knees.

The words tore through me as we stepped into the back room. Three guys lifted their heads from a countertop and turned my way, the remnant of a line dusted one nostril until they snorted hard, wiping it away with a thumb. One cleared their throat and downed the rest of his glass.

"Here." She squeezed something from a dropper into a full shot glass sitting on a tray with a heap of other ones and handed it to me.

"Really? We're starting the night off with acid?"

Get...on...your...knees.

"And a line of coke." Stevie opened the small bag and tipped out some of the contents. "Just how you like it."

I opened my wallet and pulled out a hundred dollar bill, rolling it as she laid it all out into two neat lines.

Open your mouth, just like you've been trained to do.

I shook my head, desperately trying to shake her from my mind.

"What is it?"

I lifted my gaze finding a scowl. "Nothing."

"Then what the fuck are you waiting for?"

What the fuck was I waiting for? I snatched the shot and downed the alcohol and acid into my mouth, swallowing hard before I leaned down. One hard inhale and the burn cut all the way, blinding me. "Jesus fucking Christ." I croaked as that blazing neon burn ignited into white hot sparks.

"I told you." Stevie answered.

But I couldn't see her anymore.

I couldn't see anything.

The world faded away. All the rush and the chatter and the sounds grew dull and hollow, like it now lived in a drum. Or maybe I was the one in the drum? One filled with blissful silence.

Show us what you do at the Order.

The words slowly slipped in. I couldn't fight them this time. I couldn't do a damn thing as the memory of her returned, falling to her knees in slow motion in front of my brother, with that empty, vacant stare. It was that look which got to me. The one so unlike the haughty fucking glare she always gave me.

In my head she was falling to her knees and I couldn't fucking look away.

I didn't want to.

Christ, I didn't want to.

"Are you with me?"

The moment was achingly slow, still I turned toward Stevie. But I couldn't see her. All I saw was my fucking sister. One nod and she glanced behind her to the group of assholes who just strode through the door. I scanned their faces finding the bland goddamn face of Penn Hargreaves...my sister's so-called boyfriend.

He walked behind the others, out of place in a room like this. Nervously glancing around until he caught sight of me. I was moving before I realized, leaving the table and Stevie behind.

"What the fuck are you doing?" Stevie slurred.

I stumbled sideways, latching hold of a table and righted myself. I didn't know myself. But what I did know was that feral fucking wave of anger that rippled through me, aimed at him.

"You?" I slurred, bearing down on him.

The others he was with moved out of my way, leaving the pathetic bastard behind. I grabbed his shirt, pushing him backwards until he hit the wall.

"What the Hell?" He barked, looking down at my grip around his perfectly buttoned shirt. In fact everything about this asshole was neat and goddamn square. So, what the fuck was he doing here? It didn't matter, the only thing I cared about was the scene replaying in my head. The one where we found out our mom and our sister were straight up fucking whores. "Did you know what she did there?"

He stilled as his eyes widened. But was it out of fear...or did he know the truth?

"Did...where?" He croaked, then looked to the guys he came with. They never fucking moved.

I yanked him harder, driving him against the wall once more. "At that fucking place...the goddamn Order."

Movement came from behind me. But I didn't care what schmuck started. I was beyond that now.

"What...*Order?*" He whispered and shook his head. "I don't know what the *Hell* you're talking about."

I dragged him forward, ready to slam him back against the wall over and over until he told me the truth, until that sickening wave eased and I saw the terrified, stupid fucking look on his face.

He looked desperately at the others behind us, then turned back to me. "I-I have n-no idea what you're talking about."

He didn't. I could see that now...and in the blinding moment of clarity I saw him...the man. His dweeby fucking shirt and scrawny frame underneath it. Jesus Christ, was this the kind of man who did it for my sister? Weak and pathetic?

Get on your knees.

No, a command like that came from someone strong and powerful. There wasn't a goddamn thing about this asshole that was powerful, not like she needed. Silas flashed in my head standing over her like he fucking owned her. My cock twitched at the memory. To own a woman like her needed a special ruthless sonovabitch. My pulse sped as that image in my head shifted...and it was me looking down at her as she whimpered and begged.

Goddamn...

Heat raced through me, clenching around my balls and driving that sick fucking need all the way from my cock into my goddamn soul. My body shook, consumed with the kind of hunger I'd only had for the neat white lines I shoved up my nose on a daily basis.

"You fucking disgust me." I croaked and shoved him backwards.

"A lovers quarrel, I see." The baritone rumble came from behind me.

I knew better than to turn as Nathaniel Wolf and his gang of ass-lickers walked in. I stiffened instantly, looking down and behind me as a shadow spilled across my feet.

"Although not the type I took you for, Theodore. This one is too pretty, and thin." Nathaniel gave a shrug as he stepped closer, staring into Penn Hargreaves's eyes. "But easy to dominate, so maybe he is your type after all?"

"Fuck you, Wolfe." I forced the words through my teeth, earning a chilling fucking grin.

I'll punch those perfect fucking teeth into the back of your throat. Let's see how well you'll smirk then, motherfucker. I hated the Wolfe's...no, we hated the Wolfe's. My father's goddamn rival was always slinking in the shadows trying to undermine us. But we'd risen above the petty bullshit, well dad and Silas had.

The hold of the drugs inside me eased, leaving me to glance around at everyone watching. "Better watch your mouth, Wolfe."

"Or what?" He grinned. "No daddy around to protect you anymore."

I stilled, the chilling grip of rage clenching tight until I lunged, swinging my fist. Only his buddies were there, stopping my fist in mid-air.

"I don't need him!" I screamed as they pulled me backwards. *"I can take you on just fine on my own!"*

The bastard just smiled, then glanced at his guys who had my arms on either side. "I think he's had enough boys, let's help him outside."

I bucked, fighting against their hold. Still, it made no difference. They dragged me from that room and out into the open bar area before driving me forward along the hallway. The bouncer was waiting, opening the door for them to shove me out and into the night.

I stumbled, righting myself and rose.

"Get the fuck out of here, Theo." Nathaniel stepped up behind them. "No one wants you around."

"Oh, yeah?" I turned around, shaking with rage. "You better watch yourself, Wolfe. There's no one around to stop me coming after you."

"Get a hold of yourself." Nathaniel stopped in the doorway. "I'd say get yourself into rehab but I doubt even that will help you. Some people are just born to destroy themselves and Theo, you're one of them."

I unleashed a roar and lunged, but it was too late. Nathanial Wolf stepped backwards, grabbed the door and slammed it closed with a boom locking it in my face.

"Fuck you!" I screamed and slammed my fist on the door. "Do you hear me? *FUCK YOU!*"

The faint sound of the music throbbed, echoing through the door.

I spun around, my vision blurring before it sharpened...fixing on my black Audi.

"Fuck you." I croaked and made my way forward. 'Fuck you all."

I wanted out of this fucking dump anyway.

I had better places to be.

Places where I could drink the memory of my goddamn adopted sister out of my head.

Or try to at least.

Chapter Eleven

ANGELICA

THERE WAS ONLY SILENCE OUTSIDE MY DOOR. I STRAINED to listen for any hint anyone was out there at all. But there was nothing. Just an emptiness. A hollow void where salvation lay in wait. Would I dare make a run for it? I'd be out of the rear door in an instant. Forget about the shelter, I'd just run and I'd keep on running. The only question was, did I dare do it now?

Open the door. Find out for sure. My hand trembled as I twisted the handle and cracked open the door, finding only darkness.

My pulse pounded as I opened it wider and stepped out, rolling my feet as I crept along the hallway.

"Need something?" Jude lifted his gaze from the end of the corridor, then pushed against the floor and rose.

I froze, glancing at Gabe's closed door just in front of me and turned back to him. "No...I, ah."

But he kept coming, heading along the hallway toward me.

Fear kicked inside me, leaving me scrambling back to the safety of my room once more. I grabbed the handle, pushing the door closed before Jude stopped it with his hand.

I jerked my gaze to his hand and moved backwards, as he entered. He looked around, his eyes adjusted to the gloom as he looked at my room like it was the first time he'd ever been in here. Who knew, maybe it was.

"We went too far last night." He said carefully and looked my way. "I want to make sure you're not about to run screaming to the authorities."

I said nothing, my senses screaming at the careful, dangerous tone he was giving.

"Are you?"

I swallowed hard. "Am I what?"

He narrowed in on me and strode forward, pushing me backwards until I hit the far wall and stopped. In the faint spill of moonlight his eyes looked demonic black as he lifted a hand placing it against the wall, blocking me in. "Going to cry rape and run to the police."

I did that and I was over. I knew that without hesitation.

Jude was the quiet one. The Ares son who wanted nothing to do with the business.

"Because if you did, that would cause problems for my family. In particular Silas who is under a great deal of pressure right now. We don't want that now, do we?"

His black eyes sparkled. I understood at that moment just how dangerous this family had become for me. At first it was my salvation from the cruel orphanage where I was raised. A beacon of hope and love, especially in the arms of the woman who became my mother. But now she was gone…and that light of hope was now gone, leaving something dark and hostile to move amongst the shadows.

"No." I whispered. "We don't want that."

"Jude?" I turned my head as Gabe stood in the doorway. He looked at his brother, then me. "What's going on?"

"Nothing little brother." Jude pushed off the wall and took a step backwards. "Just making sure our sister here was on the same page."

He turned around then and left, striding past Gabe. "I'll be just out here in case you need anything, Angel."

My stomach tightened at the name mom gave me. She was the only one who'd ever used it and now so did Jude.

"You okay?" Gabe asked when his brother left. But there wasn't a trace of concern in his tone. He might as well have asked me if I was a murderer.

I crossed my arms over my chest remembering the look of disgust on his face from before. An image that was now burned in my mind. "Do you really care?"

Silence.

I guess that was an answer in itself. I turned my head, unable to look at the detached, stoney stare anymore.

"It's not safe here for you anymore. Maybe it is best for you to leave."

My knees buckled, leaving me to slide down the wall. Gabe was the only one left who cared about me. Agony tore across my chest and tears followed, blurring the darkened outline of him.

"I thought you were better than what you did tonight. I thought you were...special. I guess now I know you're not. You're just like the rest of them."

A sob ripped free, searing like fire in the back of my throat. I closed my eyes as the memory came, tearing me apart with talons. *OWNED. DAUGHTER. MINE. MINE. MINE.* I was back there, at that place. With that man. He stood over me, looming in the shadows. His face was nothing more than a blur.

That's the way. He gasped, breathing hard. *Just like that, Angelica. Just. Like. That.*

My body reacted, throbbing and warming. I opened my eyes staring through the blur at an empty room. Gabe had left me, just like he had last night. I was alone now. Maybe I always had.

Beep.

Through the watery glare I caught the screen light up from my cell phone. The one I had in my purse that Silas stole from me. I stopped crying, and looked at the empty door knowing it was Gabe who left it. Gabe who didn't quite turn his back on me after all. Gabe, who gave me a way out of here.

I lunged, scurrying forward across the floor and grabbed my cell.

Penn: *Your goddamn brother just attacked me at a party. What the fuck is happening and where are you?*

I sniffed, my hands shaking as I unlocked my cell and pulled up his message. He hadn't responded to the last five of my calls and messages...until now. I typed a reply.

Penn, I need your help. I need to get out of here. My brothers...I stopped, my mind racing before I started again. *My brothers think I had something to do with our parents' deaths. I need you to come and get me. Can you do that?*

Send.

I waited with my heart in the back of my throat.

Beep.

Hurriedly, I turned the volume down, pushing the cell hard against my chest as I shoved up from the floor and moved to the door, closing it as gently as I could before turning to the reply Penn sent me.

Penn: *what the actual fuck, I'm sorry I missed your calls. My stupid brother broke my cell and then dragged me to this goddamn place with his friends. I can't get you tonight, but I promise to come tomorrow, unless you're in actual danger. Are you in danger?*

Am I in danger? I weighed up the question. Yes. No. *Maybe,* I didn't know. I was in my room, guarded by my damn brothers who were planning what I didn't know. But I had time, didn't I? I had time to figure out how to get away from here. I glanced down at my cell.

No. I typed. *I'm not in danger. I'll see you tomorrow and Penn. I'm glad you're okay.*

Send.

I made my way to my bed, slipped under the covers and pushed my cell under the pillow. It was the only weapon I had now.

One which might get me out of here...but it did nothing to ward off the nightmares of that place.

The moment I closed my eyes they swept in, almost like they were waiting for me.

Promise me, mom barked, her eyes wide as she wrenched her gaze from the road to me. *Promise me you'll never tell them*. I looked down at the buttons on her blouse and fear gripped me.

Mom. I lifted my gaze to hers. *Mom, your buttons aren't right.*

Terror filled her stare as she looked down.

The car swerved, pulling over hard on the shoulder. Her fingers shook, fixing the buttons before she stopped and burst into tears.

Mom. I reached forward, pulling her against me. My body ached, my jaw the worst, tender as I held her.

He will kill me if he ever finds out, you know that right, Angel. She lifted my gaze, staring into my eyes. *No*, she said. *He will kill us.*

He will kill us.

Those words echoed over and over again.

He. Will. Kill. Us.

Chapter Twelve

SILAS

THAT BITCH...THAT *LITTLE FUCKING BITCH*. I DRAGGED MY fingers through my hair, pacing my darkened bedroom. The pit of my stomach gnawed and seethed, like a goddamn beast. That's exactly how I felt at this moment. A fucking beast.

My cock throbbed and pulsed, barely contained by the zipper of my goddamn jeans, and a vein throbbed at the side of my temple, driving me insane. I didn't dare risk going near the bulge at the front of my trousers. I doubt I'd last a fucking second before I came.

Maybe that's what I needed? Just something to take the edge off, and get my goddamn sister out of my head. I licked my lips and stopped pacing. I needed to get myself in control. Stunts like the one I did tonight was dangerous...for me and her and in front of my goddamn brothers and Lincoln for Christ's sake?

What the fuck was I thinking?

I wasn't. That's what.

Not when it came to her.

I reached into my pocket before I knew. My breaths were heavy and thick as I swiped my thumb across the screen and bought the recording up. But I hovered over it for a second, knowing deep down I was sliding into an abyss I'd never crawl out of.

I had to stop this now. Turn her over to someone else and she can become their problem. But the moment I thought about that, about handing her over that emptiness inside howled with rage.

She knew what happened that night.

I knew that for a fact.

But she wasn't saying.

I needed to get the truth out of her and until I did that she'd stay...right....here where I could watch her. I looked down at the cell in my hand, my thumb poised over the play button on the screen, before I pressed down and watched the recording play out.

My other hand went to the button of my jeans, one hard tug and the zipper spilled open, releasing me in a rush. A sickening, guttural sound came from the pit of my chest as I wrapped my fist around my cock. The goddamn thing trembled.

"Open your mouth." The asshole on the screen commanded.

But in my head it was me.

Open your mouth, Angel. That fantasy bloomed. She did, parting those tight lips. Anger sparkled in her eyes. But she was unable to fight it, doing anything I said. *Now suck.*

My breaths raced as the heat of my fist became her mouth, swallowing the twitching head of my cock as she drew me deep inside her. I wanted more...so much more. My hips bucked forward, thrusting deep against my palm.

"Oh, fuuuccckkk."

Warmth spurted across my fingers. I closed my eyes, those heavy breaths slowing. Still the ache was there. I opened my eyes while still seeing her. The goddamn lying bitch who dared share my last name. This wasn't just a physical reaction, not just some need that once sated drifted away. There was something deeper at play here. Some primal hunger I couldn't get rid of with a fucking tug of my cock.

I wanted her.

On her knees.

Staring up at me like she did that motherfucker in the camera.

I wanted her naked, spread out in front of me. I wanted her...I wanted her *begging*.

"Jesus." A shudder ripped through me.

Begging and desperate. Familiar. That's what I wanted. I wanted something I could use whenever I wanted. Another image carved into my mind. A memory. Theo stared at her with a look of cruel hunger. He felt it too, that need to bring this stuck-up little bitch to her knees.

The idea of that didn't repulse me, not like it should.

I released my hold making my way into the bathroom and hit the taps, washing my hands. Because she's a liar. The thought came to me. I lifted my head, finding my darkened stare. She needs to be taught a lesson. One we were obligated to teach her. There's nowhere she can run, no one who can save her. She wants to be family. Then she will be, she'll be family now whether she wants it or not.

I hit the taps, letting my fingers drip before I reached for the towel and wiped before casting it aside and fixed up my jeans. At least I wasn't stiff as a board. Not yet at least. It was time to think, time to plan. I wanted to go back out to that place, to the ruin that was the Order and search the hallways more.

There had to be things I was missing. Who was the man behind the camera? Who was the bastard responsible for my parent's death? Someone had to know. I needed to find that someone.

I snatched my keys and headed out, making sure I didn't look toward her room, knowing damn well that aching void inside would bellow and howl.

I headed out of the rear of the house, climbing onto the Ducati before I started the engine, bringing the engine to life. The heavy throb was what I needed. I yanked on my black helmet, pulled the tinted visor down and pulled out of the garage and left the house behind.

A house I'd never really felt part of.

It was an art gallery for my mother. A talking point between her and her stuffy goddamn friends as they sat at their fundraisers and a house that held secrets with my father. Murmured conversations were held behind closed doors. Shady deals which he kept from me.

But not anymore.

My father demanded we stay there, then stay there we would. All of us.

I gunned the engine, pushing the bike harder as I headed for the city. That nagging desire to go back out to that empty building filled me. But not under the cover of darkness. In the light, where I could get a better look.

Incoming call, Sloane Brooks.

"Answer." I commanded.

"Silas." Our head of operations called. "I'm sorry to disturb, but we have a situation here."

I scowled, pulling in around a line of cars. "What kind of situation?"

"A breech of epic proportions."

My hand slipped on the throttle. Fear plunged deep before I turned the wheel taking the closest off-ramp. "I'm on my way."

I made the trip in record time, pulling into the driveway of the inconspicuous accountant building and parked the bike near the rear entrance. There was no buzzer on the door, no way to get in at all unless you had an access card. But you can bet your life you were being watched. I lifted my gaze to the cameras and hit my card against the scanner.

Buzz

Click.

I pushed open the door and strode in, heading for the elevators. The building was three stories high. But it wasn't what I wanted. I stepped into the elevators and pressed the button marked no access, then I went down, stopping at a level very few people visited.

The dark room was alight with monitors. I strode along the floor between the row of desks that sat a number of high-level operators who ran the backbone of the Ares empire. This wasn't just a building, equipped with state-of-the-art protection, encryption technology and the kind of detection systems the FBI or CIA could only dream of.

Lights flickered in the bank of servers behind the glass wall. I turned right at the end and headed to the only brightly lit office in this place and slowed at the door.

The man sitting behind the desk lifted his head, a scowl etched deep between his brows. "This is bad, Silas."

What, no hello?

"You said that. How bad?"

"Like breech of security and data."

I froze. "Who's data?"

He shook his head. "It's widespread, a bit here and there, concentrating on two main areas."

I rounded the desk seeing a jumbled bunch of information flying across the screen. "Which areas?"

"The Cartel del Diablo portfolio was copied. It was brutal and swift, happening before I was even alerted to someone trying to hack the system."

"How the *fuck* does something like that even happen?" I barked.

"I don't know. I swear to God every barrier and failsafe is in place. I've run countless diagnostics, nothing is showing that it's broken. I'm at a loss."

"So one of the most dangerous Mexican cartel's in existence has had their data stolen by who the fuck knows and we don't know who's done it?"

Sloane looked fucking grey, his blue eyes were sullen and sunken in his skull. His hands shook as he typed. I'd never seen the guy rocked like this before. He was the one who was steady. The quiet, dependable person. No one knew money laundering and cybersecurity like this man. No one.

"You need to find them." I said carefully. "Until then we keep this quiet. No one knows." I glanced around the quiet office. My staff might not be here, but this was only one of many interconnected locations. "Not even the other offices, do you understand that? We need to hide this."

"You're making a bad decision." Sloane shook his head. "If they find out we knew about the breach and didn't tell them, it'll be bad."

I leaned down, placing my hands on the desk. "That's why we're finding out who did this now? I want an IP address and a location by morning, Sloane. Give me that and I'll take care of the rest...personally."

But he wasn't convinced. "I said there were two main accounts that were hit, the Cartel was only one of them."

I said nothing, waiting.

"The Ares file was hit the most." Sloane said carefully. "Personal information, especially that pertaining to the investigation the private investigator sent in."

I winced. "And the police reports?"

He nodded. "All of it."

Rage plunged deep.

"Background checks, crime scene photos, even the ones kept out of the standard police file. The ones only a certain number of high-ranking officials had seen. The ones where my father's hand was wrapped around the trigger of the shotgun."

A wave of nausea hit me. I'd tried my best to keep the information out of the media. The last thing my family needed was more lies and allegations. My fingers curled into fists. "They're fucking dead." I lifted my gaze. "Messing with business is one thing, but messing with my family is a whole other thing."

"I'll find out who this is." Sloane straightened his spine. "Believe me, I won't rest until I have a name for you."

"I'll be waiting." I straightened and turned. "And Sloane."

"Yes, Silas?"

"Thank you."

I left the office, walking back along the empty workstations and headed back up and out of the building. By the time I climbed back onto my bike I was shaking with rage. Motherfuckers! I started the engine, and kicked the bike into gear, tearing out of the parking lot.

Gabe's sweet face filled me as I turned back for home and punched the throttle hard. The last thing I needed was him seeing his father's dead body plastered over every vile dark corner of the fucking internet. I needed to get home before it got out. I needed to protect them...because that's what I did.

"Siri, call Theo."

A second later my brother's cell rang, before it was answered. "Yeah, what?" He snapped.

"Where are you?"

"Why?"

"Answer the goddamn question, Theo. Where are you?"

Now he sounded concerned. "I'm just pulling up at home."

"Good, stay there. I'm on my way home."

"What's going on?"

I wanted to tell him, but it wasn't something he needed to hear over the phone. "I'll explain as soon as I'm there."

I pulled in around cars and trucks, pushing the bike hard. Red and blue lights illuminated as cop cars headed the other way. Still, I didn't slow, tearing past the traffic as though it stood still until I finally hit the off-ramp and sped along the quiet, upper class residential streets. I lifted my head, searching the streets ahead through my visor. A memory nagged me. St. James turned up on our doorstep the day he moved into the neighborhood.

Dad didn't trust him.

Going so far as to get Sloane to add him to the watch list. Which made him a target. Was he behind this attack? I didn't know. Right now, everyone was a goddamn suspect. I pulled the bike into the cul-de-sac and slowed at the entrance to the driveway. An armed guard stepped aside, nodding as I passed.

I pulled in, killed the engine, glancing at Theo's Audi parked almost sideways and shook my head. Cool air rushed in as I pulled my helmet off and placed it on the bike. It was time for a lot of things. For them to know the truth...and for me to get answers. One way or another.

I strode in, locking the door behind me and headed for my room, the musky scent of desire still lingered. I ignored it, tossing my keys onto my desk and walked out, striding to Theo's room.

One hard knock and I pushed the door open finding him tugging on a cotton t-shirt with what looked like the beginning of a bruise on his cheek. I pointed to my own. "What happened there?"

"Nothing." He muttered sullenly. "Going to tell me what the fuck is going on?"

I jerked my head. "In a minute, come with me."

I headed along the hallway finding Jude sitting against the wall, his head leaning back and his eyes closed. I kicked his foot gently. "In the study, now."

He opened his eyes, finding mine a second before I left him behind and made for the study. They needed to know, but not Gabe...not yet.

The moment Jude stepped inside he closed the door.

"We have a problem." I said carefully. "There was a breach at the office. A rather large one. But the most important thing for us is that the police and the investigators reports were taken. Now, it could be anyone. Sloane is working on an ID now. I plan on having a name by morning. You can bet blood will be spilled. But we need to keep Gabe off the internet. The things in that report no one wants to see, let alone our goddamn brother."

"And Angelica." Theo asked instantly. "What are we going to do with her?"

"I have an idea." I answered, and that slow heavy thud in my chest hit a little harder. "But, I'm pretty sure she's not going to like it. In fact...she's going to fight me all the way." Thud. Thud. Thud. That deafening boom filled my head. "Either way, we're going to find out exactly what she knows."

"When?" Theo urged.

"Tomorrow." I answered coldly. "Then, this will all be over."

Chapter Thirteen

ANGELICA

"WAKE UP."

The snarl came before a weight pressed over my face. I jerked my eyes open, finding the darkened blur looming over me. A blur that looked a lot like my brother.

"No." I shoved backwards as shadows moved in behind him. Still I knew it was Silas as he reached for me. His heavy hand pushed harder, smashing my lips against my teeth.

"Quiet." He commanded, then. "Get her arms."

The others kicked into action, yanking me from the bed and forced me to my feet. I fought them, wrenching my arms from their hold and dug my feet hard against the floor. But my pathetic attempts at fighting were useless against their strength. They dragged me toward the door before one turned and picked me up, throwing me over his shoulder with a low snarl.

It was Theo.

I knew him anywhere.

My nightdress rode high, revealing my bare thighs. Still, I didn't stop, beating his muscled back with my fists. *"Put me down!"*

It was useless...no, I was useless, slamming my pathetic blows into the side of his head, until I earned a savage glare. "Do that again," he growled. "And see what happens."

I froze, my blooming pulse all I could hear as they carried me toward the front of the house. There was no salvation of sleep anymore. No, that was ripped further away as all three carried me to the brightly lit study and stepped inside.

"What are you doing?" I bucked in Theo's arms until I fell, hitting the floor instantly.

My knees buckled before I landed on my ass, staring up at them. Jude closed the study door and turned to me, leaving all three of them staring down at me.

"What the Hell do you want from me?" I dragged my knees closer and pushed backwards.

"You will tell us what you know." Silas' voice was colder and deeper. "You're not leaving this room until you do."

I glanced from him to the only other brother who might've helped me...Jude. But one glance his way and I knew it was over. *Are you going to cry rape and run to the police?* His warning from earlier rose. *Because if you did, that would cause problems for my family. We don't want that now, do we?*

I found Silas' cruel stare once more. He licked his lips, his chest rising hard. "Don't make me hurt you, *Angelica*."

The way he said my name sent a cold shiver along my spine.

"I don't know anything—" I started...until he clenched his jaw, the muscles bulging.

There was an edge to him now, a dangerous edge. One that hadn't been there last night. Something had changed. My mind raced, sending that icy wave of panic deeper.

"Tell us and we'll let you go." Jude added slowly. "You can leave today if you want. We'll even give you money and you won't ever have to see us again."

Theo shifted with that, clenching his fists. Deep down I knew it was a lie, still that thrum of desperation took hold.

Jude leaned down, bracing his hands on his knees. "You're our sister and I know you'd want to help us. You want to tell us the truth, because hiding something like that must be tearing you apart."

Silas and Theo just glared at me.

"I told you before." I whispered, carefully. "I had nothing to do with what happened."

"But you know things we don't." Jude urged. "Tell us what you know about the Order."

I shook my head, memories collided, fragments of them so clear...the click of the locks on the door. The shiver that raced as that voice came. You know what to do, Angelica. On your knees. But the rest of the memory was nothing more than a darkened blur. I just...didn't remember.

"Tell us again where you were that day?"

I lifted my head, my mind trapped on the hazy blur inside my head. "What?"

Jude stared into my eyes, searching for something. "Tell us where you were *that* day."

"Shopping." I murmured without thinking.

"Lie." Silas snarled, those dark, unforgiving eyes fixed on me.

I gave a tiny shake of my head. But he wasn't having it. He strode forward, then lunged, grabbing me from the floor and dragged me to stand. Cruel fingers dug into my arms, bruising as he drove me backwards until I hit the wall. He was everywhere, crowding in until his body blocked out the others.

"Don't make me hurt you," he shook me so hard my teeth gnashed. *"TELL ME WHAT WERE YOU DOING THE DAY OUR PARENTS WERE MURDERED?"*

"Shopping!" I screamed. *"I was shopping!"*

"STOP LYING TO ME!" He released my arm and grabbed my throat instead, clenching tight enough for me to feel his strength.

"I'm not lying," I gasped.

"You told us you were at a fundraiser." His thumb pressed down against my throat. "So, which one is it? Were you shopping, or partying?"

His face blurred through the sheen of tears.

"See, this is how I know you're lying, little sister. You've done everything but tell us the truth from the day you came here. You've lied. You've manipulated," his grip clenched until I couldn't draw breath. "And now it's time..." His jaw clenched so hard the muscles bulged. "It's time for you to feel the consequences."

I opened my mouth, my lips moved even though there was no sound.

"She's trying to speak." Jude said.

But Silas never looked away. Instead, his lips mashed together, turning bloodless with the effort. Stars danced behind my eyes as I tried again, my lips moving.

"*Silas!*" Jude barked, grabbing his arm and broke the hold.

My knees buckled, sending me crashing back against the wall as I sucked in hard, consuming breaths.

"For fucks sake!" Jude roared. *"You could've killed her!"* He grabbed me, lifting my chin to stare into my eyes. "Are you okay?"

I couldn't even nod, just dragged in enough air to drive the darkness from eating the edges of my vision.

"What were you saying?"

Tears slipped free as I blinked and lifted my gaze to Jude. His hazel eyes darker under the dull overhead lights.

"Angelica." He urged. "This is important now. What were you trying to say."

My throat burned, still I forced sound into that hiss of air. *"I. Don't. Remember."*

He scowled, then slowly rose to his full height. The glint of hope dying in his eyes. He dropped his hand and took a slow step backwards. "Okay. If that's how you want to play this."

The door opened to my right and Gabe stepped inside, blinked his sleepy stare away and mumbled. "What the Hell is going on?"

Theo strode forward, trying to shove him back out and started to close the door. "Nothing."

Gabe saw me. He stopped, then glanced and panicked at Silas and Jude before he looked at me once more.

I fought weakly, clawing at the hands that pinned me.

"I don't know!" I screamed. "Don't you get that? I. Don't. Know. I can't REMEMBER!"

They all froze. "What do you mean you can't remember?" Silas snarled.

"Just that, *genius*. I can't remember what happened in that place. Not completely. Only fragments." Through the blur of tears I found his cell in his hand. "That video was the only proof I've ever seen that this really happened."

He looked down, scowled, then it was his time to shake his head. "You lie." He growled, then met her stare. "That's what you do. You lied to get into our family and now you're lying about this."

His words hit me harder than any blow he could deliver. "*No...I never lied.*"

"You were abandoned, right?" He took a step closer. "That's what our mother was told. That you were some sad fucking abandoned kid right on the cops doorstep. Only that never happened, right? Just one more lie. But it was that lie that got you in here, where you could dig your claws into our family."

Our family.

But not mine, *right?*

No, because someone like me could never be wanted. Not like they were.

Agony plunged through me, thickening the back of my throat as they moved in closer.

"Well?' Silas leaned down, those harrowing dark eyes fixed on mine. "Admit it. You lied from the moment you saw our mother. She was so fucking desperate to have the one thing she didn't already have...a mini version of herself that she swallowed them too."

"F-fuck you." My whisper trembled. But I refused to look away...I wouldn't give them the satisfaction of seeing me broken. Still, their faces blurred. "Fuck all of you."

I looked for the doorway, desperate to run, but they blocked my way.

"I think that's enough." Gabe said slowly.

"No," Silas rose to his full height, looking down at me. "She's not leaving until she tells us the truth about what happened."

Tears slid down my cheeks as I stared up at him. It didn't matter what I said to him, the truth, a lie. He'd believe what he wanted to believe. I saw that now as I stared into the empty depths of his stare, and he stared into mine.

"I have no memory." I whispered, trying one last time to get him to understand. "Don't you get that."

"Maybe...she's telling the truth?" Jude glanced at Silas.

But our brother wasn't interested in the truth, was he?

No.

He wasn't interested in that at all.

He wanted to hurt me. I could see that now. He wanted me exactly where I was, on the ground at his feet. I don't remember what I ever did to make Silas hate me the way he did. But I don't think that mattered one little bit.

Because he was made for hate. I lowered my gaze from his eyes to the heavy tattoos around his neck, to the ones peeking out from under the sleeves of his shirt that ran all the way down to his hands.

He was hatred coiled up in the body of a man...and now I saw him for what he was.

I lifted my gaze once more.

"Believe me or not. I don't care anymore."

"Were you drugged?" His voice was husky.

That's the way, on your knees and open your mouth. That voice echoed back as perfectly clear. I shook my head.

He leaned down again. "Then how can you not remember?"

Mine.

Owned.

DAUGHTER.

"Maybe she's telling the truth?" Jude said louder, inching closer to stand in front of Silas.

"This is bullshit." Theo barked, pushing Jude out of the way.

He came for me faster than I could move, lunging to grab my arms and lift me.

"No! Let me go!" I screamed, thrashing and fighting, until he drove me backwards and against the wall.

"You need to tell us the truth." He bellowed. *"DO YOU HEAR ME? TELL US THE GODDAMN TRUTH!"*

I tried to fight him but Theo was cruel, wrenching me forward until I slammed into him. The strap on my nightdress slipped falling down my shoulder. He was like a shark scenting blood in the water, narrowing in on the movement and yanking me forward.

Cool night air caressed the tops of my breast. The white lace one he liked me to wear.

OWNED.

OWNED.

OWNED.

"Things could get really ugly for you," Theo's tone was dangerous as he lifted his gaze to mine. Hunger moved behind them, like the predator he was. Still, he pulled the strap lower, until the satin strained as he murmured. "Tell us what happened. Tell us now and this can all stop."

For a moment I couldn't breathe. Memories collided, the way Theo caressed my nightdress was exactly like him, the man in my dreams.

"No." I shook my head, trying to force away the memory, but when I looked at Theo...all I saw was him.

It was his hand that dragged my nightdress lower. His big, powerful hand cupping my breast. His fingers exploring. I stood there, trapped by my brother's wrist around mine and the memories of that place. Memories that lulled me. There was no panic here, no sadness or hate.

That's the way, listen to the sound of my voice. Let me in, Angelica. Let. Me. In.

"We don't want to hurt you." Theo's voice sounded dull now, and so far away. "But we will."

I couldn't fight him even if I wanted to. My face went slack, my own need passive and robotic. "Okay." My whisper was so faint I barely heard it. "Whatever you want."

"Whatever I want?" Theo repeated, his chest heaving with a hard breath. There was a flicker of panic, of hunger and excitement as he slid his finger under the thin strap until he brushed the top of my breast. He wanted this...no, he craved it.

"What I want..." He started, then stopped before slowly lowering his gaze. "Is the truth. Tell us." His nail dug into my flesh, inciting panic inside me. "Tell us and this can all end here."

Do what I tell you to do, that deep throbbing voice echoed from a memory. *That's a good girl, just like you've been trained. Now, on your knees.*

My knees trembled. I was moving before I knew it, looking up at him as I sank lower until I hit the floor. This was where they wanted me to be. Where I needed to be. On my knees with my hands behind my back.

That's it, now open your mouth. That hypnotic command resounded in my head and every cell inside me wanted to *obey.* My lips trembled, slowly parting.

"What the fuck is she doing?" Jude stepped forward, reaching out to grab me.

"Don't you fucking touch her." Theo growled, his dark hazel eyes fixed on mine as he licked his lips.

"That's enough." Jude pushed past, grabbed me and dragged me forward along the floor.

Like a sudden screech of tires, Jude jolted me from that hypnotic hold and slammed me into the present. "Don't you... *don't you dare do that to me again!"*

Only Theo and Silas both stared at me.

"Both of you need to calm the fuck down." Jude barked. "This is the second goddamn time this has happened. We're supposed to stick together, not fucking attack each other. What the Hell has gotten into both of you?"

They never answered as Jude yanked open the study door, steadied me, then pushed me out the door.

"Go to your room." He commanded. "Don't come out until I figure out what to do. It's not safe for you here anymore." His voice lowered. "Not even amongst family."

I didn't wait for him to say more, just tore away from him as I raced back to my room and slammed the door behind me. Warmth slipped from my eyes and raced down the side of my nose. Jude had finally realized what I'd known all along. This place wasn't home for me...not then...and not now.

No, this was a war zone.

And I was the enemy.

Chapter Fourteen

SILAS

Jude didn't close the study door, leaving me to track the soft thud of her bare feet on against the floor as she fled from us. I took a step, then stopped, fighting that howling need to go after her. Heat raced along the back of my neck as I turned my head finding the disgust in Gabe's stare.

"Who the fuck are you?" He whispered quietly, then looked at Theo. "It's like I don't know you anymore."

I clenched my fists and bit down on all the things I wanted to say to him. Because the truth was, I didn't know who I was myself.

Beep.

My cell chimed as Gabe strode out of the study after them, leaving Theo and me behind. I reached into my pocket, pulling my phone free.

Lincoln: *We need to talk, in the office...now.*

"What's that about?" Theo asked, peering over my shoulder.

The heat that lingered on the back of my neck grew hotter. "Nothing." I answered, pocketing my cell. "I've got it handled."

Theo dragged his fingers through his hair. "I thought she'd tell us."

"Yeah," I swallowed down the desperate need to go after her. "Me too."

I did leave, making sure she was behind her locked bedroom door before I headed to mine. Lincoln no doubt had been informed of the breach of our systems. That didn't take long. I grabbed the keys to the Maserati and headed out the back door.

Headlights flared as the engine started. I pulled out of the garage, leaving the house behind and headed back to the office. I was tired, maybe more than I'd been in my entire life, but the worst thing was I couldn't sleep. Every time I closed my eyes I saw that blood-splattered study, the cloying stench of my parent's blood clinging to my nostrils as I woke.

I met my own gaze in the rearview mirror, finding the harrowing empty stare as I took the backstreets and pulled into the almost empty carpark...apart from Lincoln's Mercedes. Even the sight of his car pissed me the Hell off. I climbed out, slammed the door closed and locked the car.

Thumb against the scanner and the locks disengaged.

I was pushing through, heading to the elevators before I released a pent-up breath.

I don't remember!

Her scream resounded as I pressed the button and the doors closed.

I have no memory. Don't you get that?

She lied. That's all she did. I couldn't trust a thing that came out of that mouth of hers. I licked my lips, picturing the bloodless slash of her mouth. A mouth she parted for the bastard on the video. A mouth that would part for me.

Thud.

The elevator shuddered to a stop, wrenching me out of the thought. I inhaled hard, straightened my spine and walked out as the doors opened. A few of the guys sat around monitors. But I never looked at them. Just at the brightly illuminated office at the end of the room. The one where my uncle stood there waiting.

I stepped in, then closed the door behind me, rendering the room soundproof.

"I'm sorry, Silas." Sloane said carefully. "He already knew."

"It's okay." I met Lincoln's blazing stare.

"You want to explain why the fuck I wasn't told about this?"

No wonder my father wanted his brother out of the business. Because he was a giant pain in the ass. "I didn't think you needed to know."

"You didn't think I needed to know? And why is that, Silas?"

I clenched my jaw as he paced the floor in front of me. "Because I'm handling it."

One glance at Sloane as he rose from behind his desk and I could see the man hadn't stopped searching for the leak. His shirt was creased, sleeves unbuttoned. There were two empty coffee cups on an otherwise spotless desk. No, the man had barely moved since I'd left.

"You're going to ruin this company." Lincoln warned.

I wrenched my gaze upwards, rage seething inside me.

Lincoln saw it, stopping suddenly as I took a step forward. "You wanna say that again?"

"You're making bad decisions." My uncle continued, looking me up and down. "Look at you. You look like you haven't slept in a week and you reek of desperation." He searched my eyes. "It's her, isn't it? It's Ang—"

I lashed out, grabbing his shirt. "Say her goddamn name and I'll put my fist through your fucking teeth. Family or not."

His eyes widened. "Y-you're fucking unhinged." He stuttered. "You know that?

Okay.

Her voice moved inside me.

Whatever you want.

My pulse boomed at that dull, empty tone.

"What we did was wrong. No, what you did was wrong." Lincoln pulled me back. "You need to stop this mindless pursuit of revenge before it gets out of hand. Give her to me. She can stay at my home. She'll be under my guard. I won't let her escape."

I flinched, scowling. I saw the way he looked at her in that den, and the way he was acting now made it all too fucking obvious. He wanted her. Wanted my sister under his roof and in his bed. I could see it now, she'd be on her knees for him and he'd fucking love it. Just one more piece of our family and our legacy he could steal from me. I lifted my gaze meeting his stare. The idea of that made me feel dangerous. "No." I answered. "I'm taking care of that too."

"How?" Lincoln barked, anger flaring, before he got a hold of himself and adjusted his tone. "She's a problem to you, let me take care of it. I'll find out what she knows about your parent's deaths. If she knows anything at all."

I saw it now. Saw just how much he wanted her. That's what this whole thing was for, wasn't it? It wasn't about the breach of security. He wanted to use that to make me hand her over. To give him...the one person who could tell me the truth about that night.

I didn't think so.

I shook my head and stepped away. "She stays with us...her family."

"Silas." My uncle growled my name, stopping me as I headed for the door. "You're making a big mistake."

"It's not the first time though, is it? Sloane," I glanced behind me. "I'll be waiting for your call."

I didn't wait for him to answer, instead I grabbed the door handle and yanked, getting out of there as fast as I could. By the time I slid back behind the wheel I knew this wasn't over, not by a long shot. Lincoln wanted her bad enough to make out it was about the business. If he couldn't get her away from me, then there was no doubt he'd go after Jude next, or Theo. Hell, Gabe might even be in his sights. My little brother was soft enough to fall for his lies too.

No. She stays where she is.

Somewhere I can watch her.

Somewhere I can control her.

And make her talk.

Don't you get that? I can't REMEMBER! Her screams echoed.

I reached into my pocket and pulled out my cell as the rear door of the office opened and Lincoln strode out. He saw me and stopped. That same desperation still in his eyes, like I was the only thing standing in between him and his brand new fucking toy.

He wanted her...that was obvious. It was only a matter of time he'd try to get her again. The only question was, why?

That image of her on her knees rose. She looked so peaceful there, so...empty. Like she was born to be right there. Her knees parted, breasts straining against that satin nightdress with every breath.

"Yeah well, let's see about that."

Across the street my uncle took a step toward my car until my cell vibrated in my hand. I scowled, looked down and stilled at Jude's number splayed across the screen. My younger brother rarely called me. I pressed the button, answering instantly. "Yeah."

"What the fuck did you do?" Gabe screamed in the background.

"Silas," Jude said, his voice strained. "You need to get home right away."

"Why?"

"Look at her!" Gabe sounded hysterical. "Angelica...*please,* look at me."

"She's having some kind of episode." Jude snapped. "It's like she's catatonic. I think we broke her, Silas. *I think we fucking broke her!"*

I stabbed the button, starting the car. "I'm on my way...and Jude? Don't call anyone else until I get there."

"Okay...but hurry."

I shoved the car into gear, swinging out of the car park in a screech of tires and hauled ass back home. With every corner my mind plunged deeper into the abyss of panic. I think we broke her...

"Jesus." I gripped the wheel and pushed the sports car harder, hurtling along the city streets as the sun started to rise.

By the time I pulled into the drive Jude was already standing outside waiting for me. The biting smell of the hot engine hit me as I climbed out.

"She won't stop murmuring, won't look at anyone, just stares at the wall."

I slammed the door closed. "What the fuck happened?"

"I don't know. I just came in to check on her and found her like that."

"Christ." I followed him through the rear door and into the house.

We did this.

They were the words unsaid. Still, they stayed with me as I followed Jude to her bedroom. Gabe paced the room, wrenching a desperate, savage stare my way as I entered. "Look!" He stabbed the air desperately. "Look at what you've done."

I stepped around the door and stopped instantly. She sat in the corner of the room, her feet curled under her, eyes wide, staring at the wall.

Jude stared at me, waiting for me to do something. Only, I didn't know what to do.

"Daughter. Owned. Order. The Order. I belong...I belong to the Order." She murmured, still the words were clear.

They hit me hard.

"On your knees." She whispered. *"Owned. Daughter. The Order. The Order. The Order..."*

The Order?

My pulse thundered. That place? That's what she talked about?

"Don't just stand there." Gabe strode closer, pushing me toward her with a shove. "Do something!"

I jerked my gaze to him. "What the fuck do you suggest I do?"

"Owned. Controlled. No...no, Order. I obey, Order."

I did this.

I fucking *DID THIS.*

I gripped the back of my neck, squeezing the muscles as I stared at her all curled up in the corner of her damn room. I'm sorry. The words lingered on my tongue as everything and everyone else in the room faded. I winced at the sight of her, that menacing hunger inside me battling a new opponent, one that wanted desperately to protect her.

"Please..." she whispered and closed her eyes. *"Someone help me."*

I took a step forward before I knew. Her body trembled, her skin pebbled with goosebumps. I spun around, searching her room and strode toward her bed, tearing the comforter free.

"Easy." I murmured moving toward her. "I'm not going to hurt you."

She looked so fucking small like that. Her legs curled up, her thin arms limp and lifeless at her side. I bent down, wrapping the blanket around her. "Angelica. Can you hear me?"

Her eyes stayed closed, but her lips moved. *"Owned. Daughter. The Order...the Order."*

There was that goddamn place again. I wrapped my arm around her shoulders, pulling her against me for warmth. Yes, that's all this was...for warmth. Her boney body pressed against my chest, quaking as she shivered.

"We need to get you warm." I murmured, glancing at the thin satin nightdress she wore. "Do you understand me? You need to come out of this now, you need to wake the Hell up."

"He wants me here." She whispered. "He likes it when I..."

I clenched my jaw. *When you what?* I didn't want to think about it. Not about the way she looked in that video on her knees, or the other things this sick fuck forced her to do.

But there was a part of me that wanted to know. That lethal part of me that craved that tortured emotion.

"Someone needs to help her get dressed." I forced the words through clenched teeth and looked behind me at my brothers.

"Don't look at me." Jude shook his head.

Gabe looked utterly horrified, his face as pale. Eyes wide and transfixed on her.

Fuck.

Hard gnashes of her teeth sealed the deal. I shoved upwards and spun around before I stopped. "Well, are you two going to just stand there and watch? Get the fuck out.

They did, Jude moved first before he stopped. "Gabe... come on."

My little brother didn't want to go. But he did, finally tearing that fixed stare from her to me. "Fix this, Silas. Fix this or else."

Or else what? That panicked flutter in my chest knew all too well. Fix this or live with the fact we broke her tonight. No...I broke her. It was my idea right? Push her til she cracks. Use that stupid hazing mentality to break her.

Well, we fucking succeeded.

Only this wasn't what I had in mind when I decided it.

"Order...the Order." She murmured behind me as Gabe left the room and closed the door behind him.

Yeah, the Order, I got it the first fucking time.

I strode to her walk-in robe and switched on the light, before I looked at her clothes and stopped. "Jesus." I didn't know what to get, where were her fucking sweats for God sake? There was nothing but dresses and slacks and...I grabbed an almost sheer cream colored blouse with long ruffled sleeves. What the fuck was this?

I couldn't figure out what to put on her. I turned, finding her in the same spot, her eyes still closed. She sure as Hell couldn't stay like that. With a snarl I strode out, turned the handle and walked out of her room.

"Where the fuck are you going?" Gabe barked as I strode past. "Silas...where are you going?

Bang!

I slammed my bedroom door closed, then stood there, staring at my room but not really seeing anything. I did this....I did this...I closed my eyes. *I did this.*

She was in there, wrapped in a fucking blanket, cold and shivering and goddamn catatonic. I shouldn't care. I shouldn't give a goddamn fuck about that lying, treacherous little fucking bitch...so why did I? Why did I feel this fucking hole inside me? Why did I want to tear something apart in one second and go to her in the next.

Why did I torture myself?

And why the fuck was I standing here?

I waited for a sign, for a clear decision, to either leave her there and walk away or return to her. But no thought came so in the end I opened my eyes, stared at the poem drawers of my cupboard and the soft, warm fleece that peeked out, waiting for me to tug them on and start running.

I headed for them, pulled out sweat pants, and a t-shirt as well as a sweater and thick, warm socks before I slowly headed for the door once more. Gabe was still in the same spot when I passed. Only this time he never said a word.

I closed her bedroom door behind me and moved closer. "I brought you something warm." I said and winced. Christ I sounded pathetic. "I'm going to need you to wake up now. You can put these on for now. It's not the best, but it's the best I can do."

Only she never turned her head, never looked my way. Never obeyed my command.

"Daughter." She murmured, staring at the fucking wall.

"For fucks sake." I dropped the pile of clothes beside her and knelt, grabbing the shirt first. "You're going to make me dress you like a goddamn baby."

I yanked the shirt up, stretched out the neckline and eased it over her head and her nightdress, only when I tugged it down and reached for her arm I stopped. I couldn't pull it over the goddamn thing. What was I going to do with the skirt, tuck it in?

I had to take it off.

Didn't she need some kind of bra?

I stopped, closed my eyes and sank a little deeper into that endless pit inside me. No matter how hard I tried to fight it, this was my doing...so I needed to undo it. I opened my eyes and pushed up, striding to the beside drawers and opened the top one.

Neatly folded white panties sat on one side, a few lacy black and red one peeked out from the rear. But she didn't wear those, did she? No, she wore white. I reached down, grabbed the top ones. The sheer white lace so goddamn soft to the touch. I never took any notice before. Then again I was rarely putting these things on. I was more focused on taking them off.

I fisted her panties, then reached for the matching bra. No wire, soft cups, they were smaller than I expected. What did I expect? Flashes of images assaulted me. The glimpse of the side of her breast as that bastard said, *on your knees.*

I turned around and strode back to her as she sat there with my shirt hanging from her neck. "Believe me, this is going to be more traumatic for me than it is for you." I said, dropping her underwear beside me and set to the task easing the t-shirt back over her head and pushed the comforter aside.

The satin nightdress slipped out from under her easily. I tugged it upwards, over her thighs and hips before I eased one arm upwards, then the other and finally tugged it free.

Her body quaked, dusky, pink nipples puckering hard. I tried to look away, grabbing her bra instead. But the moment I looked back I was mesmerized. "You're so cold." My words were husky and raw as I reached out, dragging the back of my finger along her arm, watching for any sign she felt me at all.

She didn't move. Didn't register, not even when I reached higher, tracing over her collarbone and lower to the top of her breast. She didn't flinch, not until I opened my hand and covered her breast with the heat of my palm. Only then did she stiffen.

"On my knees." She whispered, echoing his demands. "Owned. Owned....contract."

Contract?

My mind raced, still I didn't move, only rubbed my hand over that hard nub in the middle of my palm. "I'll warm you." I eased closer, drawing in the faint, sweet scent of her. Christ she smelled good. I didn't realise that before as I gently rubbed, sweet and faintly floral. I licked my lips. "You can wear my clothes, the t-shirt is warm, but I'm afraid it'll smell like me."

My cock twitched, hardening at the idea of that as I looked down. Her breast was warming, that puckered flesh smoothing out underneath me. I wonder if I put her in my mouth would I warm her more? The resounding answer was *yes*.

But that would cross the line. A line I was already rubbing away with every gentle knead of my hand. I pulled away instantly, watching her small breast cool and her nipple grow tight once more. I needed to stop this. Just fucking stop it. So I forced myself to ease her bra over her arms, then slowly tugged it into place and hooked it together at her back...before I lowered my gaze to her panties.

A moan ripped free. Seeing her breast was one thing...but down there...

"You can leave those on, I think." I croaked and grabbed the t-shirt, pulling it back on over her head and eased it over her arms. My sweats were next, I looked everywhere else but between her thighs as I worked them higher. By the time I was done my clothes swarmed her, but at least her teeth stopped chattering...and her murmured words slowed.

All she said now was *the Order. The Order.*

As I picked her nightdress up and tossed it toward her bed I realised maybe that was the one place she needed to be. "Is that it? Will that bring you out of this?" Maybe it was what we both needed. I get the answers I wanted...and she...she can find her way free.

I nodded, then glanced toward her closed bedroom door.

I'd need help...they were just as responsible as I was...and I'd be damned if I was going back into that place alone. No, this time, they'd all come with me.

I looked back at her. No, with us. They'd all come with us.

Chapter Fifteen

ANGELICA

"Order." I whispered, as the memory of that heavy, air-conditioned air filled my mind and the loud click of the double doors followed. I was caught between the past and the present. Trapped by teasing, flickers of what happened to me there and the neon white words that ignited behind my eyes.

DAUGHTER.

OWNED.

THE ORDER.

"The Order." I whispered. "The Order."

"You want to go there so bad?" Silas's deep, guttural snarl fought to pierce the hold. "Then why don't I just take you?"

I tried to shake my head, tried to reach through that smothering hold to plead. You don't understand...you don't know what they did in that place. But if I did hear me, he never listened.

Instead his hand slipped under my knees and lifted. Warmth pressed against my side. Part of me was aware of him carrying me, but I couldn't get free of the hold as in my head the door opened and his heavy steps came behind me.

"Angelica." He murmured.

The sound of my name on his lips sent shivers along my spine. He stepped around me and waited for me to meet his stare, commanding my attention. "Owned." I whispered. "Daughter."

That's right. The man in my nightmares murmured. He stepped away, heading to the door of that room. *You are owned.*

I was fixed on the moment, reliving the way my pulse thundered and my breath caught.

Inside my head, hinges squealed as the door swung inward. Goosebumps raced, leaving me to shiver and wrap my arms around myself. My fingers touched bare flesh. I looked down, seeing the white lace bodysuit I was forced to change into.

He wanted me in white.

The faint crunch of boots drew me away from that memory. I shivered but I wasn't cold. Not anymore. Soft warmth covered me.

"Get the door." Silas commanded.

The sound of a car door opening followed and the heady scent of rich leather filled my nose. I closed my eyes and lowered until I hit the seat. I wanted to climb back out of that car and race back inside to the safety of my room. But I couldn't move. Even if I did, my room was no longer the salvation it was before.

I couldn't escape the demons in my head...or the ones I lived with.

I'm not going to force you, Angelica. He said in my head, drawing me back to that first moment I stepped into that room. But you want to obey me, don't you?

OBEY.

OWNED.

Thud!

I jumped, knowing it was the car door that closed. Still, I couldn't pull out of the illusion of that place in my head. No matter how hard I fought, I couldn't shake the memory of that place free. It was always in the back of my mind, just one whisper away.

The faint sound of a car's engine rose. I could hear my brothers talking, their raised voices making me panicked. But I wasn't invested in what they had to say. How could I be?

Angelica. That look, throbbing murmur drew me back to him as he stood outside the open door. Are you going to obey?

OBEY.

The word made me shudder. I couldn't fight him. Not that deep throbbing command. My feet were moving before I knew my movements took me closer to that room. I lifted my head as I slowly passed. Still, I couldn't see him. His features were nothing but a blur. A monster without a face.

Inside. He commanded.

I turned my focus to that room and stepped inside.

The door closed softly. But I held my breath.

You know what happens now? His voice resounded all around me.

We begin training?

Good...good girl. And what is the first thing we do when we train?

Establish the balance of power.

Yes. Very good. Tell me, Angelica. Who has the upper hand here?

A shiver coursed through me. *You do.*

You will obey my every command, won't you? He stepped closer, stopping at my back. *Even if it causes you pain and it will cause you pain.*

I swallowed hard, trying to fight that clenched ache in the pit of my stomach. It would cause me pain. I knew that. Because this betrayal wasn't just mine, was it?

No.

It wasn't only one trapped in this Hell.

Won't. You?

I jerked my gaze up to him in that room and a wave of deja vu hit me. He slid his finger under the strap of my bodysuit.

Yes. I murmured. *Yes, I'll obey.*

"Theo." Silas' threatening tone pushed into the nightmare. "You'd better get your ass to this fucking place, or so help me God, you'd better not come back home. Do you hear me? Theo...Theo..."

"Is he gone?" Jude asked.

"Yeah." Silas' tone was graveled.

I blinked, slowly coming back into my body. Warmth pressed against my back. I lifted my head, looking behind me to Gabe.

"You're okay." He said, his words slow and warped. "We're not going to let anything happen to you."

I stilled, what? Then, slowly the blurred view of where we were heading sharpened.

My breath caught. My stomach dropped.

The imposing front of the Order seemed to shimmer in the morning sun. Glaring rays bounced off broken panes of glass, flooding the interior of the car.

"No..." I shoved backwards as Silas pulled the car up in front of the place.

He met my stare in the rear view mirror. "It might help you remember."

But he didn't understand. He didn't realize how dangerous this was.

On your knees, Angelica. I want you on all fours.

My body trembled in that car as Silas pulled up and killed the engine. For a second I was frozen, unable to move as the rest of my brothers climbed out of the car, then opened the door in front of me.

"I'll get her." Silas murmured and stepped closer.

"No." I shook my head and kicked out my feet, driving myself backwards.

But he wasn't stopping, reaching in through the open door to grasp my ankle and yank me toward him.

"You don't *UNDERSTAND!*" I screamed as he grasped me around the waist and lifted. "You don't understand."

"Maybe we should think about this for a moment." Gabe said carefully.

Silas heaved me higher, lifting me over his shoulder. "I want answers. If this goddamn place is going to get her to talk, then I'm okay with that."

I lifted my head as he walked. My vision blurring with every thud and Gabe's wide stare only grew wider.

"Please." I whispered. "Please, you don't know what you're doing."

They didn't.

How could they?

On your knees, Angelica. That man in my nightmares commanded.

I bit down hard on my lip, stifling a moan. Still, it reverberated like a wounded thing in the middle of my chest.

On your knees and let's see if your mother is ready to talk.

Silas stopped at the front door. I thought for a second he came to his senses before a thud and the door crashed inwards. The bright sunlight slipped away as he carried me inside. I was back there, to those endless hallways and the locked double doors that were everywhere you turn.

He won't find it.

It was my last hope. That no matter what, Silas wouldn't find that room where they ruined me. But he turned right and strode along the hallway, pushing through the now busted open doors without a second of hesitation. My stomach clenched, fear plunged deep.

"No...NO!" I bucked and kicked, punching his back and shoulders. "Let me go...*SILAS, LET ME GO!"*

Smile for your mother. The past reached out and with it, that memory came flooding back. I was on all fours, the bastard's phone shoved in front of my face as he fisted my hair and yanked backwards. *Let's see if she's ready to talk now.*

"No." I moaned, but the sound slipped from my lips in the present. Silas dragged me with him forcing me to turn along the smaller hallway to another wing...a more private area, hidden from the rest of the others. One I knew was kept especially for me.

"I must admit it took me a while to find it."

Thud. Thud. *Thud.*

"And I almost gave up. But there was one thing driving me. One burning desire." He turned his head, those dark brown eyes piercing. "To destroy you."

My entire world went gray.

There was no air.

No warmth.

No...protection.

He turned again, finding another hallway...one that was sickeningly familiar and stopped. One hard yank and I slid down his chest. Those cruel hands grabbed me before I hit the floor.

Tears blurred his handsome face. "You're a bastard."

He leaned down lower. "And you, sweet sister, are a goddamn liar."

I shook my head and shifted my gaze to the doorway behind him.

"Are you going to play nice, Angelica?" That monster's voice resounded in my head and I took a step backwards.

He was in that room, still waiting for me. My head burned with the memory of his strong fingers entwined in the strands.

"You remember, don't you?" Silas stepped closer.

Movement came behind him as Gabe and Jude moved closer.

"What the fuck is this?" Jude snapped. "We need to get out of here. It's not safe...it's—"

"We're staying." Silas's focus never left me. "Until she tells us the truth."

I shook my head. Tears slipped down my cheeks.

"Tell her...tell your mother what I'll do to you if she doesn't give us what we want."

My pulse thundered as I stared at that room.

"You want to go in there?" Silas stepped closer and grabbed my arm.

OWNED.

DAUGHTER.

THE ORDER.

"The Order." I whispered.

"That's right." Silas pulled me closer. "That's exactly where you are, and you're going to tell us what happened here, aren't you? You're going to tell us what happened every goddamn time you came here. Because, we're not leaving until you do."

No mom, My own plea echoed. *Don't tell them...don't tell them anything.*

I could still see her face on the cell he shoved in front of me. Her wide, terrified eyes and the way she shook her head. *Angel.* She cried. *I'm so sorry.*

Tell me what we want to know, Meredith. Tell me and I'll let your daughter go.

YOU. BASTARD. Slap!

I flinched with the brutal sound as Silas shoved me through that open door. In an instant I was back there, kneeling on the ground in that room on my hands and knees. The terror. The need slammed into me. I couldn't stop it. My knees buckled, sending me crashing to the floor.

"Silas for fucks sake!" Gabe yelled as he followed us inside.

"We shouldn't be here." Jude repeated. "Silas we need to leave now."

"What happened?" Silas growled above me. "Tell me and I'll let you go. Tell me and I'll."

"Order." I whispered, my mind blurring.

I was slipping...falling away.

"You will do exactly as I tell you, do you understand?"

OBEY.

OBEY.

OBEY.

My hair was grabbed and yanked backwards. "Who is he?" Silas demanded, rage seething in his eyes. "Who is the bastard who killed my father?"

"What the fuck..."

A shadow spilled in through the doorway. Silas had my head yanked upwards and to him, so I saw him. Arctic blue eyes pierced mine, before the blond male scanned the room. Silas released me, straightening instantly. "Carven, what the fuck are you doing here?"

Only Carven didn't answer him. He stared at me...no, he stared through me. I knew him. My memory blurred and sharpened. A room, our room. Him, and another...a mute, Theo called him and a man...a man my father called London St. James.

A hum came from deep inside. A trembling. A knowing. It was deeper than an introduction...a calling.

He took a step closer. "Daughter?" He whispered, his eyes widening. "You're a Daughter."

DAUGHTER.

OBEY.

THE ORDER.

"I said," Silas repeated. "What the fuck are you doing h—"

He never finished as the blond male lunged from the doorway, grabbing his shirt and drove him across the room to slam against the wall.

"I'm going to ask you one last time." He growled. "Or I'm going to treat you like my goddamn enemy. Trust me, Silas, you don't want that. What the fuck are you doing here...and what do you want with her."

The male was cold, chilling, mechanical. Dangerous. Yes, that's what he was...he was dangerous.

Silas lifted his hand stopping Gabe and Jude as they lunged. "No." He sucked in a hard breath. "He'll only hurt you." Before he leveled his stare on the man in front of him. "You wouldn't understand."

Carven eased his hold and straightened. "Try me."

Chapter Sixteen

SILAS

"Don't mom." She moaned. "Don't tell them."

I jerked my gaze toward her. "What the Hell did you say?"

Carven was fucking dangerous, but in this moment I didn't care. I pushed past him, heading for her, then stopped staring at her. She had that glazed goddamn stare once more. Where she was here in body, but not in her head. I knew she saw him...the bastard responsible for my parents murder.

Sweat beaded across her forehead as she unleashed a moan and rocked forwards.

"Don't." She shook her head, then slammed her fists against the side of her head with a thud. *Don't tell them anything!"*

I stood over her, watching her beat herself senseless. I shouldn't care...I didn't care. A pang of agony tore across my chest with the thought, until Gabe strode forward and dropped to his knees beside her.

"Hey." He grabbed her fist as she swung once more. "Stop, Angel. *Please!*"

She looked up as he pulled her against him and that unfocused stare fixed on me. Terror found her at that moment. Her eyes widened as she shook her head. "Don't make me do this. They'll never understand. They'll never."

My gut clenched with her pleas.

She saw him in me.

Whoever this bastard was.

Never understand what?

"We need to get her to the shrink." Carven murmured.

I turned as he strode toward my brother. Fear punched through me. I'd seen this bastard take on two men three times his size... and leave their dead bodies behind. Killing machines, someone once called him and his brother. Cold, detached killing machines.

Seeing them then and now here, I was inclined to agree.

But he never even noticed Gabe sitting there, just knelt, slid one hand under my sister's knees and wrapped the other around her back before rising with her in his arms.

I was moving before I knew it, striding forward to bend down and grab his arm, stilling him cold. "Don't."

Carven slowly shifted his gaze, first to my hand clenched around his arm, then to meet my stare. "If you don't move your fucking hand I'll tear it from your goddamn body. You have no idea what shit you've waded into here."

My pulse boomed with fear and it had little to do with the threat of maiming me...but of what this goddamn place was.

My hold eased, then fell away. He carried her with the utmost respect as he headed for the doorway.

"Where the Hell is he taking her?" Gabe scurried to stand, jerking that panicked glare my way.

"Hell if I know." I made for the door and headed after him, leaving my brothers to follow.

We made it back out of the front door where my car was parked. But Carven didn't even look that way, just headed for the far end of the building and around the ruins of what looked like the aftermath of an explosion.

I followed until I saw the black Explorer. The locks disengaged with a thud. He was shifting Angelica in his arms, yanking open the rear door before he gently eased her inside.

"Owned. I'm owned." She murmured.

Carven froze with her words, before he gently eased her legs inside and closed the door.

"Wait." Gabe charged forward as Carven started to turn. "I'm going with you."

"Gabe." I snarled through clenched teeth.

But my little brother didn't hesitate, just yanked open the passenger's door and climbed inside.

I glared at Carven.

Motherfucker.

"I don't think this is a good idea." Jude muttered as I turned.

"And what part of any of this is?" I strode to my car, yanked open the door and climbed inside.

My damn hands were shaking as dust kicked up in a cloud in my rearview mirror as Jude climbed in. I started the engine, backed out and accelerated, catching up to the four-wheel drive before he made it out of the gate.

"What shrink is he talking about? And can we even trust him? I thought dad said London St. James was a man he didn't like?"

I clenched my fist around the wheel and pushed the accelerator harder as the Explorer picked up pace, taking us back toward the city.

"This isn't good." Jude murmured in the start next to me.

I didn't look his way. Just kept on driving as we headed onto the on-ramp and headed toward home. But we weren't going home, instead we tore past our street and pulled into a cul-de-sac about four streets down, leaving the Explorer to pull up outside the house.

The front door opened and London St. James strode out, glancing my way instantly.

Don't trust him. My father's words resonated in my head. That man and his sons are dangerous.

He looked every bit as dangerous now as he rounded the car and opened the rear door. My gut clenched in warning as he leaned inside.

Don't you dare touch her. I clenched my jaw and stabbed the button, killing the engine before climbing out. It was barely seconds, still it was long enough for London to pull my sister from the car and head inside.

"Hey!" I called out.

But St. James never stopped, just strode inside, leaving Carven to cut me a glare and follow along with Gabe. Sonovabitch. I slammed the car door behind me and headed for the house, taking the two steps before I entered the open door and headed inside the one house I never expected to step a foot inside.

"London?" A female called out.

"In here." He answered, striding along the hall.

From the left a woman came rushing toward me, casting me a glare before following London to what looked like a study. Gabe stood against the desk, his eyes wide as he watched them.

"Is she conscious?" The woman asked as London lowered her to the sofa in the middle of the room.

"Owned. Daughter." Angelica murmured. "No, please mom. Don't tell them."

I stepped inside watching the woman bend down, brush her hair away and lift her gaze to London. "We need Kane."

"I already called him." London took a step backwards, leaving the woman who was his wife to tend to her. "He's on his way. Do you know her?"

She shook her head, then jerked a glare at me. "What did you do?"

"Nothing." I snarled.

"Don't fucking lie." Gabe croaked. His stare shell-shocked as he looked my way.

"What did you do to her?" London's wife snarled and rounded the sofa.

"Vivienne." He warned.

But she came for me, striding across the study to stop in front of me. "What the fuck did you do?"

I looked at her. At her rage and her beauty, I saw something unattainable—loyalty.

"I'd be careful if I were you." Carven warned as he pushed past and stepped into the study. "This one's likely to tear you a new ass."

"She can tr—" I started as Colt followed his brother inside, meeting my stare as he went.

"When did this start?"

I looked back at her.

"Time, day. Was it today?"

I shook my head.

"Then when?"

I tried to think. "Yesterday, the day before...I don't remember." I answered.

But I knew exactly when it was. The night of the attack, when she dropped to her knees in front of all of us.

"She could be broken, do you get that?"

I stared through the woman, watching in the corner of my eye as Carven neared my sister.

"What's happened to her?" Gabe asked. "Why is she like this?"

"Because, her mind has been manipulated to obey.' Vivienne snapped.

Jude jerked his gaze toward her. "You mean like mind control?"

"*Exactly* like mind control." She stared at him, then Gabe. "You have no idea what she is, *do you?*"

What she is.

Not, who she was.

Vivienne swung that deadly glare my way.

"She's *our* sister."

If looks could kill I'd be a dead man. "Really?" She muttered. "I'm just loving your sense of loyalty here."

What the fuck? How in the world is this woman judging me?

Beep.

London grabbed his cell, reading the message. "They're here."

Who's here?

Murmured voices came from the front of the house barely a second later. I stepped backwards into the middle of the hallway and turned watching a woman and four guys head toward me. She looked just like the one staring daggers at me inside the study. But this one stopped in front of me, searched my eyes silently, then slowly shifted that piercing stare to the study.

"Where is she?" The male behind her pushed through, dressed in a goddamn suit looking all fucking business.

Only then did it hit me. They were serious, weren't they? I jerked my gaze to the sofa as the guy in the suit rounded the end and knelt down in front of her. *They were serious and this was real.*

My fists clenched as this asshole reached for her, murmuring. "Angelica, my name is Doctor Kane Cruz. Can you hear me?"

I wanted to step inside that room. I wanted to round the end of the sofa and stand in between him and her. Who the fuck was this guy touching my sister? *Back the fuck off her.* Jealousy hit me like a ton of bricks. I took a step, moving inside the doorway as he kept speaking.

"My friends tell me you were in the Order."

"Order." She whispered.

"That's right." He urged. "We're going to do our best to get you out of there, okay?"

I stepped closer, watching him gently lift the lids of her eyes and reach for her wrist, checking her pulse.

"I'm going to ask you to do something for me, do you think you can do that?"

There was a tiny nod of her head.

"Good. I'm going to help you to sit upright, and then I'm going to ask you to close your eyes for me and listen to the sound of my voice. Can you do that? I know you feel trapped right now. But we're going to get you out of that place. Can you do that? Can you follow my voice?"

Another small nod. I caught my breath, watching this so-called doctor lean close, grip her arms and help her to sit. I didn't like that. Not one goddamn bit.

"I want you to listen to the sound of my voice, find it, Angelica. Can you do that?"

She slowly nodded.

"Look around," he said. "Tell me where you are."

"In that room." She whispered. "With him."

"Can you describe him? Can you tell me what he looks like?"

She waited for a second, then shook her head. "I can't...I can't see his face."

"That's okay. Can you see the door?"

A shiver raced across my skin. Drawn by the sound of the doctor's voice and her tiny whispers I stepped around the edge of the sofa. Her brow pinched as she slowly shook her head. The doctor glanced at London, then spoke.

"So can you tell me where you are?"

"My...my bedroom."

It was the doctor's turn to scowl. "And what are you feeling right now? Can you tell me the words running through your head?"

"Desperate," she whispered. "Need them to want me...to use me...to tell me things. Things he wants to know."

I flinched, that savage, hateful feeling rippling from deep inside me.

"What the fuck?" The mutter came from one of the men standing at the rear of the room. "That's not part of the programming."

"No," the doctor standing in front of my sister said. "It's not." He moved closer, searching her closed eyes. "Now this is very important, Angelica. I want to know what you need them to tell you."

"Everything."

The word was a gut punch. Rage unleashed, making me jerk my gaze to my brothers. "I fucking told you, didn't I? She's a goddamn mole living right under our fucking roof."

"No." Vivienne shook her head and stepped forward, barely a second later the other one who had to be her sister did. "Not a mole..."

"Programmed," the doctor lifted his gaze to me. "Her thoughts have been altered."

"By who?" I forced the words through clenched teeth.

"Now *that* is a very good question." London murmured and pushed off the edge of the desk where he stood beside his wife. "It's not like you don't have a whole list of enemies just desperate to take out the Ares family."

I clenched my jaw and breathed deep.

"But the real question remains, who had access to the Order to program your sister in the first place...and why?"

I stared at the side of her face and the way her brow was pinched, like she was fighting whatever demons were inside her...but she wasn't was she? No, because she wanted this. She wanted our ruin, it was what she'd been programmed to want. I dragged my gaze down to the sweater I put on her, my hand clenched remembering the warmth and softness of her breast against my palm. The nipple puckering under the brush of my fingers. The more I thought of it, the more I wanted it. I wanted her writhing under my hand. I wanted her tortured.

"Can you fix her?" I asked, not even caring about the answer.

"I can try," the shrink answered. "But in doing so I could put her mind at risk. She's in a very fragile state right now, any kind of force could do more damage than good."

I gave a slow nod then strode forward, stopping in front of her and bent down. One heave and I lifted her from the sofa and into my arms.

"What the Hell are you doing?" The doctor snapped.

"Handing it the only way I know how." I growled and lifted my gaze to London. "Privately."

Vivienne stepped sideways, trying to cut me off until London reached out. "Let them go. He knows where we are if he needs us."

But his woman spun around, anger burning in her stare. "And what about what she wants?"

He knew.

And none of it mattered.

My sister was Hell bent on our family's destruction and we were going to get answers as to why.

"Jude, Gabe." I called as I strode for the doorway with our sister in my arms.

I got the answers I needed to start. The only thing I didn't know was...where it was going to lead us.

"Owned." Angelica whispered in my arms.

"Yes." I murmured and strode out of the front door of London St. James mansion. "You most certainly are and I think it's about time you understood the full ramifications of that."

Chapter Seventeen

JUDE

I TOOK ONE LAST LOOK AROUND THE ROOM, THEN followed my brother out as he carried our sister to his car.

"You're in the back." Silas muttered when I reached him. "With her."

I knew without asking why. Gabe was barely two steps behind, lengthening his stride.

"What the Hell is happening here?" He barked as Silas opened the rear door, placing her inside as I climbed in on the opposite side.

"Get in the car, Gabriel." Silas muttered. "We'll discuss this at home."

I could feel the anger emanating from our little brother as I climbed in and closed the door behind me. He stood out there for a second, then yanked open the passenger's side and slumped in.

"Angelica?" I called and reached across, securing her seatbelt across her chest.

She never answered, just stared with that same glazed expression as Silas slipped behind the wheel and started the engine. We were backing out of the driveway in an instant, pulling away from London's home and headed for our own.

"I don't understand any of this." Gabe snarled and cast our brother an icy stare.

Silas said nothing, holding the same stoic, empty stare our father carried. He was so much like him...too much and look at where that led him? Murdered in cold blood in his own home.

My pulse sped and the thunder in my head grew louder as we turned into our own street. I'd never felt this kind of dangerous loyalty to my family before, but now...now it was all I felt. I glanced at our sister with her eyes closed and her head rolling backwards as we drove along the driveway and parked at the rear entrance.

Theo's car wasn't here and we hadn't been gone that long. Which told me he hadn't yet surfaced from whatever hole in the wall he'd crawled into. Our family was failing, growing more distant by the second and for once it fell on us to stop it.

"I'll get her." Silas killed the engine and climbed out before opening the rear door and pulled her into his arms.

"Silas?" She murmured, opening her eyes.

I climbed out, catching her words.

"What...what just happened?"

"Nothing." He said, his tone husky and strange. "Nothing for you to worry about."

I followed them inside with Gabe behind me as Silas carried her along the hallway and turn, pushing her bedroom door wider and entered her bedroom. The bed was unmade, sheets and comforter pushed aside.

A shiver coursed through me as I stopped at the doorway and watched them. I was waiting for whatever this spell was to break, and for Silas to lunge, grab her around the throat and scream in her face. This wasn't natural. It wasn't him. He didn't contain his emotions like this, not when it came to family.

No, when it came to blood my older brother was as dangerous as a goddamn viper, lashing out, striking whoever stood in his way...whether he wanted to or not. It was his nature. Maybe it was in all our natures?

"I don't know what's happening to me." Our sister murmured as Silas straightened his spine, standing above her. "And I can't seem to stop it."

He moved suddenly, reaching around to grab her by the back of her neck and stared into her eyes.

Her own widened, looking up at him. She was frightened of him, maybe even terrified and yet the longer they held that connection, the deeper her breaths became. It was almost like... almost like they—

I flinched.

No.

That's not happening.

One jerk of my gaze to Silas and I knew that gut reaction was telling me the cold, hard truth. My brother, our brother wanted her.

Heat soon replaced the icy chill of the truth, surging through my body until I felt flushed and fevered. My own body responded, replaying that night Silas forced her to his knees. Our lying, fucking sister. His cruel words resounded in my head.

Gabe cleared his throat behind me, shattering the moment making Silas jerk, then pull his hand away. "I'll bring you some food." He muttered, then turned and walked away.

I followed him as he headed for the kitchen, waiting for him to move around the counter, opening the refrigerator door and pulling out butter, cold meat and cheese before placing them on the counter.

"What the fuck are you doing here, Silas?" I asked. "Playing goddamn house, now?"

He never answered, grabbing the loaf of fresh sourdough bread and tossed it to the counter. He didn't want to hear it, but it needed saying.

"Goddamn *brainwashing* and a fucking *traitor*. You fucking saw what I saw and you heard what I heard. She's a liability just having her here. We need her gone, Silas and we need her gone now."

His fist clenched around the knife as he sawed it through the bread, carving one end so thin it fell apart.

"Gone where?" Gabe pushed past me. "You can't do this. She's *our* sister."

"No." I shook my head. "She's not."

Silas tried to butter the ruined slice, slamming the knife into the soft center over and over and over again, until it was a mangled mess.

"Enough!" He roared, grabbed the bread and spun, hurling it into the sink before turning back. "She's not going anywhere!"

"Are you fucking insane?" I barked. "Did you even hear what that guy said back there? She's been mind-fucked into laying a goddamn trap for all of us. For all we know she could be the one who killed our goddamn parents!"

Gabe unleashed a snarl and lunged, grabbing me by the shirt... and for once I didn't fight him. Instead I met the pain in his eyes. "Tell me you haven't once thought the same thing...both of you."

Gabe's fists trembled as he shook his head. He could fight his demons all he wanted, but the truth remained the same. We now lived with someone we couldn't trust.

"I am a liability," the whisper came from behind us. "And you should...you should send me away."

I spun around as Silas carved a new slice of bread. She stood in the middle of the doorway, staring at us with wide shimmering eyes. Her body curled in, arms wrapped around herself protectively.

"You heard?" Gabe pushed past, instantly going to her side... just like he always did.

"You're dangerous." I said.

She winced as though I slapped her. "Then do it...cast me aside. Put me somewhere you'll never have to see or hear from me again, then you'll all be safe."

Silas slowly lifted his gaze and looked at her, before slowly pushing the freshly made sandwich her way. "You're not going anywhere."

Then he just left, striding past without a glance my way. The only time he reacted was when he brushed past her. He looked down for a second, then left, his steps thudding back along the hall as he headed for his bedroom.

"Silas is right." Gabe cut me a glare. "You are not going anywhere, and I don't want to ever hear anything like that ever again, okay? You're our sister, your place is with us. Period."

But she didn't react with relief at hearing his words. Instead, she stared at that carving knife on the counter as though she wanted to snatch it free and plunge the blade deep inside herself, cutting out whatever black seed of deception had been buried inside. Guilt found me then, savaging that pulsing thing in the middle of my chest.

"Come on." Gabe strode to the counter, grabbed the sandwich our brother meticulously prepared and cut me a look of utter disgust before pulling her away.

Maybe I deserved it.

But someone had to say what we'd all been thinking.

Including Theo...wherever the fuck he was.

I grabbed my cell, swiped the screen and hit his number, listening to it ring before it went to voicemail.

"Hey, don't bother leaving a message. I won't ring you back."

"Where the fuck are you, Theo?" I hung up and lowered my cell. I needed him here. Hell, we all needed him here.

Chapter Eighteen

THEO

BEEP.

Beep.

Ding!

I surfaced. Barely. Crawling my way through dull agony for it to only

turn suffocating as I cracked open my eyes.

"Hey."

A soft jab came at my side. I slowly turned my head, wincing at the piercing overhead lights to find the rock hard surface at the base of my head.

"You need to leave." The guy at my side muttered. "We're about to open."

Open? The hazy room around me sharpened. "Where." The word was a hiss. I licked my lips and tried again. "The fuck am I?'

"Harley's on Fifteenth." The guy said.

The name meant nothing, but then again, not much did...

I lifted my head, twisted my body and slowly pushed, staring at the blue felt pool table underneath me. Jesus fucking Christ. I'd reached an all time low.

My head howled with the slightest movement, and my tongue felt thick and alien inside my mouth as I tried to ease the arid void in my mouth.

"You know I checked on you three times." He said, setting up the other pool tables and wiping down the gleaming wooden surface. "Thought for sure you were dead. You even looked dead."

It's how I felt. Dead.

I can't keep doing this.

"Yeah well." I pushed harder, then scooted forward, reaching the edge. "I'm clearly alive."

"For now. But I doubt that'll last long."

I scowled, anger flared fast, burning in me. The moment I lunged off the table something fell from inside my shirt and hit the floor with a splat. I squinted and focused on the small white baggie still half full of coke.

Clean your nose, Theo, your cocaine is showing.

My sister's fucking voice materialised. The bitch...the goddamn little bitch. I gripped the edge of the table and bent over, snatching what was left of last night's party from the floor and shoved it into my pocket. The guy moved off, flicking on lights before he stopped, turned and jerked his head to the side.

"There's a rear door in the back that'll take you out to the parking lot."

I glanced at the way he motioned.

"Don't come back." He said quietly, so quiet I could've mistaken it.

But I didn't. I knew I didn't.

Still, I turned and limped before I found my footing and walked out. The morning sun was blinding, unleashing a sledgehammer blow inside my head the moment I stepped out. I squinted, then scanned the carpark of the bar finding nothing more than a run down blue Toyota parked at the far corner of the lot.

My car's not here.

Then where the Hell was it?

I tried to think, but the punishing blows between my eyes grew more savage. If not here, then where did I leave it? The darkened parking lot filled my mind. Sander's club in the city, that's where. I started walking and patted my pockets, expecting to find nothing. But my wallet was there, secured in the back pocket of my trousers, and so was the Rolex attached to my wrist.

That's...unexpected.

I grabbed my wallet and headed for the road, lifting my hand to catch the attention of a cab driving past. The occupied light flicked on and he pulled over sharply to the curb in front of me.

"Sander's in the City," I muttered as I yanked open the door and slumped in.

The bitter stench of vomit hit me the moment I closed the door. I winced, resisting the urge to gag and yanked my belt across as the driver pulled the car back onto the street and accelerated.

Thought for sure you were dead.

Those words lingered as I stared out of the window, stealing me away until the cab turned into the parking lot of the downtown club and I saw my car right where I left it.

I pulled out a fifty dollar note. "Keep the change," and handed it over before clamouring out and closed the door behind me.

Fresh air plunged deep as I inhaled. The more I breathed, the clearer my head became. Tires crunched as the cab turned around and drove away. But I couldn't move.

I didn't want to go home.

And I sure as Hell didn't want to find the next party that I was sure was in full swing.

In fact the idea of it made me feel sick.

I thought you were dead.

No. Not home...but not anywhere else either. I strode forward, reached into my pockets and pulled out my keys before hitting the button and unlocking the doors.

Dad's apartment.

I climbed in and started the engine. I'd been there a few times. Once to crash after an all-nighter. Once more to find dad when I was hurting and in need. Agony plunged deep, leaving me to close my eyes and lean forward, unleashing a moan. He helped me, talked to me even though I expected anger and disgust. But there was none of that. Instead, he stayed up all night, listened while I wept and raged. He held me, one of the very few times in my life where he'd done that.

I needed that now.

I'd kill for that now.

But I couldn't, could I?

Because he was taken from me.

By her…

Pain turned to anger, then plunged all the way to rage. My hands clenched around the steering wheel. My jaw ground tight. Lying fucking cunt. I shoved the car into drive. The tires squealing as I peeled out of the parking lot and headed deeper for the city.

By the time I pulled into the underground parking I was shaking. I parked, climbed out, slamming the door behind me and strode to the automatic doors. I punched in the code that opened the elevator and stepped in. The lift gave a shudder then climbed before stopping at the top floor and the door opened.

It was just like I remembered. I punched in the code once more, expecting to find the place empty when I walked in. But it wasn't empty. In fact it was still the same.

The faint scent of my father's cologne still lingered in the air. I breathed in deep, that brutal ache moving deeper as I closed the door behind me and stepped inside. Serenity filled me as I made my way through the apartment. I walked through, searching empty rooms until I stopped at the main bedroom.

He could almost be here.

Almost.

I turned around and reached for the top button on my shirt, unbuttoning enough to pull it over my head. My shoes tumbled as I kicked them free, then unbuttoned my pants. Hot water hissed as I turned the tap and stepped in. Heat raced along my shoulders, and down the back of my neck. I dropped my head and groaned, standing there long enough until the ache in my head moved to the back before I washed, hit the taps and stepped out.

Dark eyes found me as I stepped into the mirror. I looked like Hell...no, worse than Hell. I looked like me every single day. I wrapped the towel around my waist and headed for my father's room, pulling on a pair of boxers before I climbed into bed.

Sleep came fast, dragging me down softly. I dreamed of him. His voice. His eyes. His...love. When I woke it wasn't so softly.

Theo, get out!

Dad's bellow was brutal, shattering the darkness and plunging me into the light. I jerked awake and opened my eyes to find the illuminated screen of my cell phone in my face. Five missed calls. Silas, Jude, more from Jude.

"Jesus," I rolled over and closed my eyes, willing the image away.

Beep.

"No." I squinted harder. "Go the fuck away."

But the damn thing haunted me. No matter how hard I tried to get back to that place of oblivion I couldn't. Instead she pushed in.

My stuck-up.

Lying.

Bitch of a sister.

The bane of my existence.

I hated her the day mom bought her home. I hated her cutting stare. Hated her pinched fucking nose. I hated the way mom was with her. Giving her a room under our roof, making her part of the family. Angelica gave mom something we couldn't and even though I'd seen what my mother had done I still couldn't hate her for it.

But I sure hated her.

I fucking hated her.

My sister.

I slowly opened my eyes as my breaths moved deeper. She filled my mind, every sneer she gave me with her turned up goddamn lip. A lip I wanted to bite until she winced. A lip I wanted to own, to make quiver, to part as she breathed hard. Just like I was breathing hard.

I couldn't stop it. My body reacted to her, just like it had that night Silas forced her to her knees. She'd been so different that night. So unlike herself. She was desperate, wasn't she? Needy, aching. I bet she was fucking wet too. I bet she was so fucking wet when she opened her mouth and traced the outline of my brother's hard cock under his jeans.

Was she like that when she fucked?

My cock grew hard. I bet she was. Legs spread, her eyes rolling back as she arched her back and rolled her hips, desperate for one more fucking inch of cock from that loser fucking boyfriend of hers. He was a goddamn loser.

I threw the covers aside, glanced over my shoulder at my cell laying there, then looked at the clock beside the bed. Six pm. Jesus, I must've been out of it. I yawned, then rose and made my way out of the bedroom and headed for the kitchen.

The fridge was bare except for bottles of water. The freezer held a full bottle of Grey Goose. One look at that and my gut rolled. No, Hell no. I closed the thing, cracked open the water and drank. The effects of the drugs still burned in my veins, making me ache and hunger. But it was all in my head. I knew that.

The drugs. The anger. The only thing that wasn't in my head was the fact my parents were dead and my family was a goddamn mess.

Theo, get out!

My father's voice still rang in my head. I winced and drank, letting the icy water hit the pit of my stomach. Hoping the shock of it would dull the goddamn nightmare still rolling around in my head. But it didn't.

Dad still stood in the middle of that goddamn thunderstorm. The sky was black...actually the entire world was black and yet, there he was. His white shirt drenched and stuck to his skin. The look of utter terror on his face.

I'd never seen him so scared. His eyes wide. The whites neon bright against the rolling, ravenous storm behind him. His fear haunted me.

Buzz!

I jerked, then wrenched my gaze to the door before I strode forward. A guy waited on the other side. Dressed in a nice suit James, Reception Manager.

"Yeah?" I muttered.

"Sorry to interrupt, Sir. My name is James, I'd just like to see if you were planning on staying for a while." He glanced into the apartment behind me. "I take it you're one of Mr. Ares son's?"

"You're correct."

One nod of his head and he shifted his focus back to me. "So if you require any services, please let me know."

"Thank you." I answered coldly. "But I'll be leaving."

"Oh?" His brow rose. "Where will you go?"

Where will I go? I took a step backwards, ignoring his question. He was too bold. Too fucking forward. It was none of his goddamn business where I was headed. I closed the door and ground my jaw as I strode toward the bedroom once more. There was only one place to go, wasn't there?

Home.

Chapter Nineteen

ANGELICA

On your knees, Angelica. Show me what a good girl you are.

I closed my eyes, trying to push away that voice in my head. But I couldn't. Instead I heard him clearer than ever before. Flickers of a memory rose up, stealing me away from the safety of my bedroom and plunging me back there, to that place where they...where they...used me.

"You don't have to be worried, he's not sending you away."

I lifted my head, finding Gabe standing in the open doorway of my bedroom. I didn't even see him open it, nor did I see him watching me. I was still held there, in that dream...and that place.

"For now.' I said quietly. "Until he changes his mind."

Gabe pushed off the doorframe and strode in. "And you think that's going to happen?"

Beep.

My cell chimed. "Maybe." I answered, then glanced at my cell.

Penn.

My chest tightened. I glanced at Gabe as my cheeks burned. She's a liability. Those words still howled. The worst thing was, Jude was right. They couldn't trust me. Hell, I couldn't even trust myself. Because I wasn't me...I was someone else. Someone who was still trapped in that place with a faceless man who used me.

My body tightened as my cell chimed again.

Penn: *If you don't answer me back right now, I'm coming over.*

Gabe bent down, snatching my cell from the comforter in front of me. He pressed the button and read the message. "Coming over, huh?" The corner of his lip tugged, baring his teeth for a second before handing it out. "Text him back, tell him everything's fine."

But it wasn't fine, was it?

And now Gabe seemed okay on invading my privacy, forcing me to do things I...I didn't want to do.

Only that's not true, was it?

You wanted to do anything they asked.

Especially if it meant you being naked or on your knees.

I flinched with the words. "No," I whispered. "That's not me."

"It is if you don't want him to meet a very pissed off Silas at the front door. You do know my brother carries a gun, right? There's no telling what he'd do."

That burn ignited in my cheeks once more. Silas would hurt Penn. In fact, I think he'd enjoy it. Just like he enjoys hurting me. I lifted my gaze to Gabe, to the sweet brother who had changed in the weeks since our parents' deaths. Who now looked at me like...like...that's the way, Angelica...do exactly as you're told. You're to listen and obey, then when we see each other again, you're to tell me everything. Do you understand? That faceless man commanded in my head. Do. You. Understand?

"Yes." I whispered and reached for my phone as Gabe held it out. "I understand."

I punched in the numbers, then replied to Penn telling him exactly what they wanted. I was fine. I didn't want him to come. We were still grieving as a family and he needed to respect that.

He would.

I knew he would.

"Good." Gabe reached out, brushing the hair from my face with hands that were far too big. "That's good, Angel."

Angel.

My body quivered with the name. Only mom called me Angel...her Angel. Now as I stared up at Gabe that name took on a whole new emotion.

"You're okay if I call you that, right?" He murmured, his voice deep and husky. Those big fingers brushed my cheek once more. "My Angel."

I swallowed hard and slowly nodded.

"Gabe." Silas called from the doorway. I glanced toward the sound. Silas stood there, watching his brother caress my face. "You're needed."

One nod and Gabe turned around and walked out, leaving me sitting there on the bed. Silas just watched, then glanced at the cell in my hands. I knew what he was going to do before he even moved. My hand clenched around the cell, then slowly lifted it in the air as he crossed the room and took it from me.

"You won't be needing this."

I could only nod. "Whatever you want."

Then without another word he turned and left, closing the door behind him. I was alone once more with that faceless monster in my head. A monster that programmed me to do whatever they wanted with barely a fight.

"I hate you." I whispered. "Almost as much as I hate myself."

I lay back down on the bed and stared up at the ceiling, my thoughts a muddled blur. But I remembered the doctor and the things he said to me. I was programmed and none of this was my fault. So if this wasn't of my own doing, then whose was it?

Promise me. Mom's desperate words resounded. I remember that moment clearly. Tires squealed as we tore out of the gate at that place, the Order. The look of desperation was terrifying on her face. *On your life, Angel. I need you to promise me. They can never know about this.*

I remembered the mismatched buttons on her blouse and the red marks on the side of her neck. Marks that looked like someone had gripped her. They used her like they used me. Fear rippled through me, the kind that chilled me to the bone. We were used as pawns, manipulated and controlled. Only I didn't know who did this. Who whispered in my head and tortured my mom.

I didn't know anything.

Fresh tears slipped down the side of my eyes as I willed sleep to come. One that would take me from this nightmare and plunge me back into my normal, boring life. One where my brothers ignored me...and my mom was my world.

Darkness slowly came, creeping in amongst the memories. Whispering words I couldn't understand...until I gave in...and fell.

"Fucking liar."

The bed dipped hard, shaking me. I slowly opened my eyes to a shadow looming over me.

"Need to be used, isn't that it, sister? That's what you want right? To be owned, used."

Cold air swept over me as the bedsheets were yanked aside.

Heavy breaths reeked of alcohol.

I knew instantly who it was.

"Theo."

"Just a cunt to be used." He slurred and drove his knee between my legs, forcing them apart.

"Theo, stop this." I said quietly...too quiet.

If he heard he didn't care. There was no stopping this as he yanked my nightdress higher exposing my panties. He stopped, then looked down, swaying above me. Those dark hazel eyes glinted in the moonlight that spilled from my bedroom window.

I couldn't move as he reached down and dragged his finger along my hard mound and along the crease between my legs. "That's what you want, isn't it?" He met my frozen stare. "To be used."

Heat followed the trail of his fingers as he pushed deeper, finding the ache in me.

"Jesus Christ I'm so fucking hard."

He winced and reached down, massaging the bulge of his cock. With a moan he straightened, working the button of his pants. In a rush the zipper gave way, and the thick, hard head pushed out. He was big and erect...and dangerous.

One hard shove inside my thigh and he pushed me wider.

"Theo, no." I whispered.

But that wasn't what howled inside my head. A low, delicious throb came from between my legs, one that only grew bolder as he gripped my hips and lifted, yanking me hard against him.

I cried out as warmth slammed against me. My teeth found the softness of my lip, biting down.

"Can't get it out of my fucking head." He grunted the words, his fingers bruising as they kneaded my thighs. "You on your knees for my goddamn brother. I hate you, you know that, right?"

He didn't even wait for me to answer. I don't think it mattered, still I answered. "Yes."

His hands pinched the soft flesh of my thigh, massaging my thighs wider as he slowly thrust his hips, driving against my pussy.

"Hated you the moment you came to us...and every day since. But especially now." The whites of his eyes shimmered as he met my stare. *"Especially now."*

That ache between my thighs grew more insistent. Pulsing and throbbing as the length of his cock pushed against me. The slip of thin cotton, the only barrier between us. Even that grew warm...and wet.

"Need to be used."

A moan escaped my lips with the friction. He was so hard, the blunt head driving against my core as his hands moved closer, his thumbs massaging along the edge of the elastic.

"Go on, little sister," he growled. "Moan and writhe and tell me you haven't thought of this."

I thrashed my head from side to side, the warmth between us growing damp. That slow glide of his cock burrowing.

"No." I whimpered. "I haven't thought of this."

"You fucking liar."

Strangled noises came from the back of my throat. He inhaled sharply and pushed his thumbs under the elastic driving the soft flesh of my lips together and rubbed.

"Look how fucking wet you are."

My eyes rolled back. My body clenched, throbbing against his fingers.

"You want to be used, don't you?"

I tried to shake my head, but my back arched, grinding my hips against him.

"Yeah, I see you now, little sister." He grunted, driving his cock along the length of my sodden panties. *"I. Fucking. See. You."*

My brain stopped working, short circuiting until sparks detonated behind my eyes. I couldn't stop it, couldn't stop the way my core clenched tight and unleashed a cry.

Theo lunged, bracing himself above me as he pumped and thrust. Shadows cut across his jaw, making him look chiseled and terrifying above me.

"I see you now." His lips curled back, baring his teeth as he pinned me to the bed. "And this..." tendons pulled taught along the sides of his neck as he grunted. "Is.. just...the... beginning."

He closed his eyes and threw his head backwards, slamming his hips against mine as an animalistic sound erupted deep from his chest. That warmth grew between my legs, sticky and slick. Silence followed. Chilling and deadly, leaving my skin to prickle.

This has gone too far.

Too far.

Theo slowly opened his eyes. That stare empty as he found mine. "You're mine now." There was no kindness in those words. "You get *that?* You're fucking mine."

The bed dipped once more as he pulled away and straightened, looking down at the mess between my legs. "Next time your panties won't stop me."

I couldn't move as he eased from the bed. I just lay there, legs spread, panting as Theo stood over me, fixing his pants before he slowly turned and stumbled for the door.

Oh, God...Oh, God. I slowly eased my legs together before dragging the comforter over my body. That just happened... that...just...happened.

Give them what they want, Angelica. That voice whispered in my head. *That's your sole purpose now. To be owned...used...it's only a matter of time before they tell you something I can turn against them. I will come for you when the time is right. Do you understand? Nod, so I know you're listening.*

Even here in my bed, my head dipped, nodding just like he wanted me to. Slowly warmth came back and I slipped my hand under the covers, inching down to where the sticky dampness welled between my thighs.

This was my purpose now.

I closed my eyes, but sleep never came.

Instead I lay there, desperately aching for more of the brother I loathed. The one who called me his.

Chapter Twenty

SILAS

Bang.

Bang.

Bang!

The faint sound woke me. I wanted to will it away, and sink back into the dreamless slumber but then faint raised voices followed and the heavy thudding steps of a guard grew closer.

"Silas."

"Go away."

"There's a Penn Hargreaves at the door, making threats and demanding to see your sister. Do you want me to hurt him?"

Hurt him.

I cracked one eye open, finding the blurred wall of my bedroom. Hurt him. It didn't even take me a second to find the answer. Yes. "No."

The answer I wanted wasn't the answer Penn Hargreaves wanted, nor was it the answer our family could afford. "Jesus fucking Christ."

I pushed upwards, blinked then dragged one foot out of bed and followed with the other.

"I demand to see her!" The high-pitched whine found its way into my room. "You can't keep me away! Do you hear me? You can't keep me away!"

I snatched a shirt from the back of my chair, dragging it over my head and followed the guard to the front door. Harsh morning light made me wince. My bare feet cold against the tiled floor as I headed to the open front door and my sister's pathetic boyfriend.

"You're-you're keeping her prisoner." Penn Hargreaves stuttered, his eyes were wide, amped up on adrenaline as he stared at me.

"And what makes you say that?" I muttered, narrowing in on this idiot.

I didn't like him. Not for any particular reason. In fact I didn't really know the guy. But that didn't stop me from being pissed off at his presence. I didn't want him here, not at my home...and sure as fuck not near my goddamn sister.

"I...I demand to see her." He straightened his spine, meeting my gaze. "And I'm not going anywhere until I do."

"Is that right?" I stepped closer, but his gaze shifted to something behind me. His eyes widened and a look of fear moved in.

"Yes," he whispered, looking at me once more. "That's right."

I didn't need to look behind me to see who it was. The stench of alcohol and regret told me all I needed to know. "Hargreaves, what the *fuck* do you want?"

Penn lifted the cell in his hand. "To see Angelica. Or the next call I make will be the police."

A twitch came at the corner of my eye. I didn't like threats, even empty ones.

I wanted to take that cell phone and ram it down his throat. Let's see him call the cops then.

Theo pushed in beside me. "What makes you think she wants to see you?"

"I'm her boyfriend."

My gut clenched with the word, even Theo snarled with the words. I wanted to throw this pathetic excuse for a man out of here. I clenched my fists. I ached for it. But one look in Hargreaves' eyes and I knew he wasn't bluffing. He'd call the cops, that I knew and right now, that was the last thing we needed.

"Fine." I answered.

"Fine?" Theo wrenched that furious glare my way.

I gave a shrug, then stepped aside. Rage rippled in my brother's glare as the kid stepped in, turning his body to the side as he skirted my brother and stepped inside our home.

"What's going on?" Gabe strode from the hallway, still dressed in cotton boxers, his chest bare. He took one look at Penn and froze. His eyes widened. "No, she told you not to come."

Did she just? And how did my little brother know that? Because he told her to say it. It was written all over his smitten goddamn face. I strode forward. "Looks like he didn't get the hint, did he, little brother?"

Gabe's eyes glinted with panic.

"You want to see our sister," I muttered. "Fine, I'll fucking take you."

But before I could lead him anywhere Theo grabbed my arm, stopping me cold. There wasn't just anger in Theo's stare now. There was fear, and now...desperation.

I'd seen that look far too many times to count.

It usually meant, he was in trouble...but what kind of trouble now? I slowly turned my head to the hallway and our sister's bedroom. Only one kind would prevent me from going into our sister's bedroom.

"Theo." I snarled and wrenched my focus on him, searching his eyes for the truth. *What the fuck have you done?*

But it was too late, Gabe was already heading toward the bedrooms...with Penn Hargreaves in tow.

"She's not leaving." Theo warned.

I yanked my arm free and headed after them. "No, she's not." Not if I had anything to do with it.

I caught up as they turned the corner and strode past Gabe's open door to Angelica's.

"*Angel.*" Gabe called and stopped at her door.

Angel? No one called her that...except for Mom.

That ache inside me only grew hungrier.

Angel.

The cold rush of air filled my lungs as Gabe turned the handle and pushed open her bedroom door. Hargreaves didn't waste a second, pushing into her bedroom and calling out. "Baby, where are you?"

"Here," she answered.

I stepped in, scanning the unmade bed and searched for anything out of place. Theo had something that I knew. But what?

I followed Hargreaves as he headed for a reading nook against the large bay window at the far end of her room. She was there, her feet curled up underneath herself, buried underneath an oversized caramel knitted throw that covered her body.

"Are you okay?" Hargreaves stopped, tilting her gaze to his.

I didn't like him touching her. Not like this.

"You don't answer my calls." The schmuck sounded desperate as he pulled the book from her hand, placing it beside her. "And now this text, telling me to stay away. That's not you."

He pulled her upwards, forcing her to stand to hug him. She did, but her gaze went to me. Her eyes were dull, lifeless... empty, just like she had been yesterday.

"Nothing." She answered, holding my stare. "There's nothing wrong at all. Everything is perfect."

"Perfect?" Hargreaves pulled her away, forcing her to focus on him. "Your parents have just been murdered. I don't think perfect is the word to describe you right now."

I turned and walked out, not wanting to see a second more. Rage rippled through me, enough to feel more dangerous than I should be.

"Silas." Gabe called as I turned along the hallway and headed for the kitchen. "Silas."

I stopped and turned. "What?"

"You're not just going to let him...be in there are you?"

"And what the fuck do you suggest I do, Gabe?" I hissed the words. "You seem to have some grand ideas on how to deal with...her." I glanced behind him. "So, speak the fuck up. What do you want me to do?"

Deal with her.

I knew exactly what I needed to do.

But that didn't mean they did...especially Gabe. He was too involved with her. Too...infatuated. I turned away and headed for the kitchen. One of us had to stay in control. One of us had to get to the bottom of this and it sure as Hell wasn't any of my brothers.

I strode into the kitchen, glancing at the dirty plate left on the sink from the sandwich I made her yesterday and set to work. Gabe lingered for a minute before he left, no doubt heading back to his room so he could listen to whatever was going on.

I pulled out a skillet, placed it on the stove and switched on the burner before adding butter and let it melt. My attention was divided, half focused on the doorway as I waited for Hargreaves to leave, the other part of my attention on the eggs I cracked into a bowl and whisked.

I rarely cooked for others, enjoying crafting a meal for myself. One that usually consisted of steak. But this was different. This was...purpose. Footsteps resounded. They were too light to be anyone who carried my genes, and they were too quick to be hers.

It was him.

Hargreaves scurried past as he headed for the front door. My fingers clenched against the bench as I stared at the pile of fluffy eggs on the plate in front of me. Goddamn lying bitch. I closed my eyes. Lying, fucking bitch with her goddamn boyfriend.

I didn't understand why she affected me like this and I didn't like it one little bit. Just keep to the plan, that's all I have to do. I stared at the plate in front of me, then grabbed it along with a fork and strode to her room. The door was still open when I stopped.

I knocked softly. "It's me."

She turned when I entered, her gaze moved to the plate.

"Thought you might be hungry."

She never spoke as I placed it on the desk along with the fork and straightened. But the way she looked at the food pissed me off. What, did she think I drugged it?

Movement came from the doorway behind me. Gabe's presence was a lingering pressure at the back of my head. Always there. Haunting me everywhere I turned.

But that wasn't true, was it?

No, he wasn't haunting me. He was haunting her. Our sister.

"Anyway," I muttered. "I'll leave you to it."

I turned and reached the doorway before she spoke.

"Thank you."

Her words were so soft. Still, I gave a nod and walked out, passing Gabe as I left and headed for my bedroom, closing the door behind me. Stick with the plan. I gripped the back of my chair and stared at my laptop. That's all I needed. I stick with the plan and this would all work out.

It had to.

There was no other way.

I pulled out the chair and logged into the server and sent a message to Sloane: *any word on our problem?*

I waited...but there was no reply.

What the fuck?

I typed again: *Sloane?*

Still, I waited and nothing.

I picked up the cell and called, listening to it ring and ring and ring.

This wasn't like him. He didn't not answer. I placed the phone down, staring at the empty screen. "Where the fuck are you?"

Cold air seeped in from somewhere, sending a shiver along my spine. The longer I stared at the silent cell, the more desperate I became. "First my parents, then my father fucks me with the will, and now this..."

IT WAS dark when I looked up from the laptop. I'd forced myself to work, going through the files of the Mexican Cartel of all things, trying to understand why someone broke into our goddamn system. All I found was records and records of just how fucking dangerous these men really were.

Murder for hire, guns and drugs...a lot of goddamn drugs.

There was no way around this.

I was fucked.

No.

Someone fucked me.

I picked up my cell, stared at the blank screen then slipped it into my pocket. It had to be all connected. My parents. This fucking Order...and her. Our lying sister. There was only one way to get the answers I needed. I had to become the bastard she thought I was. The unfeeling monster everyone saw. I had to become an Ares...a man created for war.

I pushed up from the chair and walked out, heading for her bedroom. The others were quiet, hiding in their rooms, or they were out partying. My thoughts turned to Theo as I turned and strode to her bedroom, turning the handle without knocking and pushed open the door.

She was in bed, staring at the wall with an unflinching stare. Open books lay scattered around her and yet it looked like she hadn't moved a muscle in a very long time.

"Angel." The cold, hard tone resounded in my chest...or was it her name?

The name only mom spoke.

Except now it was Gabe.

I took a step closer to the bed as the answer echoed back—long enough.

"Angel." She slowly turned her head toward me.

"I need you to come with me."

She didn't even hesitate, just pushed the bedding aside and slipped barefoot from the bed. Her breasts shifted under the satin top, long thighs reached forever, drawing my focus to the soft curve of her ass. Hunger surged inside me as the images of that video replayed in my head.

"Where are we going?" She asked.

I swallowed hard, my voice husky. "I just want to ask you some questions."

There was no, ask me here or, no, I don't trust you. Just a willingness to do anything I asked. That was the one thing I was counting on as I tore my gaze from her body and walked out.

Her bare feet were soundless as she followed me out and headed back to the den where we had our first encounter. One I couldn't stop reliving. I walked in, headed to a chair placed in the middle of the room and muttered. "Sit."

She did, looking up at me with those wide, consuming eyes.

"Why do you look at me like that?" I asked.

"How do you want me to look at you?"

"Not...not like you want to eat me alive." I reached inside that pit of desperation, grabbing hold of anything I could. My father's face filled my mind. Then it was my mom...and finally Lincoln's empty stare found me.

I closed my eyes, drew a breath then started. "I'm going to ask you one last time, Angel," I opened my eyes and grabbed a handful of her hair. The hard yank was brutal, making her eyes widen. "Then I'm going to do things I don't want to do. But I will and I will do them well." I pulled her hair harder, forcing her head backwards. "Do you understand what I'm saying?"

Her breaths turned panting.

"I want to know what happened on the night of my parent's deaths."

She shook her head. I knew she was going to do that, fighting me every step of the way. So I reached around, pulling my knife from my pocket. One hit of the button and the blade flicked out with a snap.

Her wide, unflinching stare was fixed on the blade.

"I will hurt you. I've hurt women before, so don't think I won't."

"D-don't..." she stuttered, staring at the weapon. "D-don't you mean our parents?"

I shook my head. "No." I whispered, shaking my head. "I don't." I pressed the steel against her cheek. "Tell me or I swear, I'll cut you so deep no surgeon alive could fix you."

She trembled, I felt it pressed against her. She was scared alright. But was she scared enough to tell me the truth?

"The night, Angel. Tell me about the night."

That shudder in her body only grew more violent. I looked down, watching her breasts tremble under her camisole. Hard nipples puckered against the fabric. I knew those breasts. I'd felt those breasts pressed against me, the softness of her perfect fucking nipples. The fucking scent of her skin.

I jerked my gaze up to her eyes and breathed deeper, drawing in that same intoxicating fucking scent into my lungs. .

Desire slammed into rage and my body responded, growing harder, more desperate. "Tell me." I forced the words through clenched teeth and pushed the blade against her soft cheek. "Or I will cut you."

She fought the need to shake her head, still the tip of the knife dug into the soft flesh below her eye, drawing a tiny bead of blood. My fist tightened in her hair. Her fear was so desperate, my howling need to pull the knife away was palpable...as was the overwhelming desire to kiss her.

The room swam all around me. Dazed and breathless, my body responded in ways I didn't understand. All I saw were her lips. Those lying, perfect fucking lips. A sound rumbled in the back of my throat as I stared at her mouth, fighting the intoxicating need to kiss her.

I unleashed that animalistic groan and tore my gaze away to stare at the wall. "You fucking push me..." I turned back to her. "You fucking push me to the ends of my limits. You don't want to see what's on the other side of those, little sister...believe me."

"What the fuck..."

My breath caught at the sound of Gabe behind me. I straightened, looking down and pulled the blade away.

"What the fuck are you doing?"

His voice rose in octaves as he flanked my side, staring at the knife in my hand. One panicked scan of her and anger rose in my baby brother's eyes.

"I knew it!" He drove his fist into my shoulder, driving me backwards. I stumbled, righting myself. He glared at the knife in my hand and shook his head. "I knew you were lying. You just wanted to use her, didn't you? You can't send her away, so you what...you plan on cutting her? Beating her, maybe. Is that the kind of animal you've become."

His words couldn't hurt me. "You have no idea of the things I've done for this family."

"I think I have a good fucking idea. What kind of man makes her food one minute, then holds a goddamn knife to her face the next?"

I wasn't going to...

I wasn't going to.

Hurt. Her.

But I couldn't say the words.

"Even after what the doctor said about her. She's been programmed, can't you see that?" Gabe threw his hand toward her as footsteps resounded.

"What the fuck is going on?" Theo grumbled.

Utter contempt is all I saw in my little brother's eyes as he answered. "Why don't you ask, Silas. I'm sure he has all the answers," he looked at the blade. "Or the means to get them no matter the consequences. Come on, Angel, you're sleeping in my room tonight. I'll sleep on the floor."

He grabbed her hand and pulled her from the chair in front of me before he dragged her along and headed for the door.

"Gabe." Theo took a step to block his way.

"You don't want to push me right now, Theo."

There was a dangerous edge in our brother. One which hadn't been there before. Theo looked at me, scowled, then stepped aside.

They left, Gabe pulling her with him as they made for his bedroom.

Theo stared at the knife in my hand, then lifted his gaze to mine. "What do we do with her?"

"I don't know." I lied, not wanting to admit to myself what I wanted to do.

Kiss her.

That need raged.

Fuck her.

Make her mine.

My hand clenched around the hilt of the knife, fighting every cell in my body.

Chapter Twenty-One

ANGELICA

"Let me take care of you." Gabe loomed over me. He looked down, his dark eyes shimmering in the muted light. The moment he touched the sting on my cheek from Silas's knife I pulled away. Pain flared, his brows pinched for a second before his stare hardened. That look...that hard, honey brown stare shimmered in my memory.

With it came a thunderous roar.

ANGEL...

ANGEL, PLEASE!

NOOO!

A blood choked bellow filled my head. Flickers came to life... the similar wide haunting eyes of our father returned in a moment of pure terror before...

BOOM!

Warmth splattered my arms. Bright red flecks smacked me in the eye. I turned my head...my mind blurring as in that vision a shadowed figure moved close.

That's it, Angelica. A low and hypnotic voice followed as the sharp bitter stench of gunpowder returned filling me. *That's a good girl. Let me take that now.*

There was a heaviness in my hand. I remember it now. I looked down as I sat on Gabe's bed and almost saw it. The cold steel in my grip, one splattered with blood.

"Angel."

I wrenched my gaze upwards as the vision started to blur. No... panic moved in. No, please no. "Are you okay?" Gabe asked, his jaw set hard.

Boom.

Boom.

Boom!

My pulse filled my head. But it was my ragged breaths which hurt the most tearing through my chest leaving a gaping hole behind. I lunged, throwing my arms around Gabe's neck and clung to him.

That vision faded.

That sick, terrifying vision.

What...the...Hell...was...that?

"That bastard." He wrapped his arms around my body as I shook and shuddered. "He's too rough with you. Too goddamn rough. I won't let him hurt you." He murmured in my ear. "Do you hear me? Never again. Never ever again."

My mind was a jumble. That shadowed figure loomed in my mind, until slowly the events of tonight came rushing back. Silas and the knife. A tremor tore through me as I pressed my fingers to my cheek. The tiny sting was sharp and instant, but it was nothing compared to the terror in my head.

It wasn't a memory. I closed my eyes. It can't be. That didn't happen. But the moment the words came they carried a weight that filled my heart.

"I should go back in there and put a goddamn knife against his face, let's see how he likes it."

I pulled away, staring into Gabe's dark stare and shook my head. "No," I croaked. "Don't do that. Don't ever do that."

"No?" His brow rose. "Give me one good goddamn reason? He fucking hurt you."

There was real anger in his voice. A hatred I'd never heard before. Gabe didn't hate. He comforted and loved. He was the quiet one. The loyal one. The longer I stared at him the more I realized that these last months changed us all. They made us lonely and afraid...and now, desperate. That's how I felt.

I felt desperate.

"You're staying in here tonight." Gabe said. "Don't bother arguing, I won't hear it. You can take the bed and I'll sleep on the goddamn floor, but I'm not letting you out of my sight."

I lifted my hand and caressed his cheek. "You can't keep me here forever. Silas needed..." I stopped. "He needed the truth."

ANGEL NO!

Those screams still lingered. Screams that'd never been there before. Silas wasn't the only one who needed answers.

We all did.

I swallowed a strangled noise in the back of my throat.

"I don't care what he needed. You're sleeping here."

Gabe moved, pulling down the comforter further on his unmade bed and jerked his head. "In."

"You can't sleep on the floor." I started.

"Then I'll sleep standing up."

There was a huskiness in those words, a need left unspoken. My pulse kicked as I slowly made my way toward him, meeting his stare.

"In," he urged.

I sank down and slid backwards, curling my feet up underneath me. The thick, musky scent of him enveloped me as I lay my head on his pillow. He towered over me, just as Silas had done before, only this time the bedding was pulled upwards, sliding over my feet and my legs to tuck high around my shoulders.

"Sleep, Angel." He said carefully. "I'll protect you."

A pang moved through my chest. I knew he would. There was no doubt about it now. He'd go to war with his brothers for me...and that hurt the most.

Brother against brother.

All because of the things I've done.

That's a good girl, let me take that now.

I closed my eyes and willed the memory away. It wasn't real. None of it. Not then and not now. I closed my eyes pretending to sleep, but I lay there listening to Gabe as he snarled. "You deserve better. Better than my goddamn brothers. I can't let him hurt you, not anymore. You need someone to protect you. Someone to take care of you. Someone to..."

He went quiet. I kept my breaths slow and quiet, tracking him in the dark as he moved away.

There was a shuffling of something on his desk before silence. If I opened my eyes would I find him looking at me in the dark? I knew I would. Something was changing between us, festering like rot, determined to take hold. That intoxicated rush rose, sending a flare of heat between my thighs. This was a rot between us. Silas. Theo and now Gabe and the only thing rotten here was me.

Filthy and foul, desperately clawing for a hold in this family.

ANGEL NO!

Those screams surfaced, turning that throb between my thighs into a sickening hunger.

"Angel." His voice was so quiet, as though he didn't really want me to answer. "Are you awake?"

I didn't move. Now even when the soft thud of his steps neared the bed.

The edge of the mattress dipped with his weight. I couldn't fight it anymore and opened my eyes, finding him bathed in the gloom.

"Let me take care of you." He murmured, reaching over his head to drag his shirt free. "I just need you to let me take care of you."

Sheets lifted, letting the rush of cold air in before it was gone once more.

The rough rub of his jeans pressed against my thigh and the warmth of his strong chest followed.

"I...love you." He murmured. His big fingers stroked my hair. "Christ, I love you."

My nipples puckered and that heady bloom of desire followed. This was wrong. I knew this was wrong...and still some sick part of me wanted it.

That's it, Angelica. That hollow voice of the monster in my head echoed. *This is exactly what you were made for...for them... and me.*

Gabe's fingers drifted lower, brushing my cheek until they disappeared and danced along the side of my breast. It was so sweet, so...careful. I squeezed my eyes tighter. The touch was completely opposite to Silas'.

My body came alive, flooding between my thighs with mindless warmth.

I turned my head, finding my younger brother in the dark. Still, he never stopped, brushing slow circles around my nipples.

"Will you do that? Will you let me take care of you?" He whispered.

I was helpless to do anything else but nod. "Yes." My words were raw and husky.

He wrapped his arm around my waist, pulling me hard against his body. "Thank you." He breathed into my hair. The desperate sound of his sincerity sent a pang across my chest.

The acid tang of guilt followed as Silas filled my head. His cruel hands. His vindictive glare. If I wanted the softness and kindness, then why was Silas in my head...and with him our hateful brother, Theo.

Warmth of Gabe's breath blew against my neck as the image of Theo was resurrected above me. Fucking liar. Theo's grunt only ignited that heat between my legs. I knew I was wet. I knew I was desperate. Need to be used, isn't that it, sister? That's what you want, right? To be owned. To be used. I swallowed hard as that ache in my pussy grew bolder. Just a cunt to be used.

The bed shifted against me, rocking...shifting. A hardness pressed against my thigh.

"I'm not like my brother's." Gabe grunted as he thrust against the side of my thigh, still fully clothed. "But I can't help myself."

I stared at the ceiling with the feel of Gabe humping against me and his brothers in my head, knowing no matter what they did to me was nothing compared to the things I'd done to them.

ANGEL...

ANGEL, PLEASE!

NOOO!

Those screams haunted me until I willed myself to the darkness of my mind and with it, sleep.

SUNLIGHT WOKE ME. Soft and filtered, leaving me to tilt my face to the warmth. It took me a second to realize I wasn't in my own bed. Then whose bed was it? I shoved upwards and looked around to see Gabe's things everywhere. In a rush last night came flooding back. Silas, Theo...and Gabe. Only everything else was a blur.

I stilled, my heart pounding as I remembered how angry Gabe was and then the events in this bed. I touched my cheek. He touched me, brushing my hair. The grunts of his desire rushed back to me.

But there was something else.

Something that hovered at the edges of my memory.

The door suddenly opened. Gabe walked in scowling. The moment he saw me sitting up in his bed, he stopped and the crease lines between his eyes eased.

"You're awake." There was an edge of nervousness in his tone.

"I am."

He shifted from one foot to the other. "Are you hungry?"

I wasn't, still I nodded. "I could eat."

"Good."

The empty hallway behind him called my attention. "The others?"

"Gone." He stepped closer. "You don't have to worry about them anymore. They won't be a problem."

The hard, dangerous way he said the words made me wonder what had gone down while I was asleep. But I couldn't think about that now. My stomach clenched as dread washed through me.

There was that sickening wave of terror. That knowing inside that something terrible had happened. Something far more terrible than anything my brothers had done.

"You're safe with me." Gabe moved closer. "I promise."

I gave a nod and slipped from the bed, grabbing my phone from the nightstand. "Let me shower and I'll meet you in the kitchen."

I didn't wait for him to answer, I just scurried around him and raced for the door and made for my bedroom. I grabbed my things, plucking a light caramel colored dress from the hanger in my wardrobe as well as matching underwear and headed for the bathroom.

I needed to shower and get my head right and I couldn't do that, not like this. I headed for the bathroom that Gabe and I used and closed the door behind me. The heady scent of his cologne still lingered. I hung my dress up and placed my underwear down before meeting my gaze in the mirror.

ANGEL, PLEASE!

NOOO!

I flinched with the faint terrified screams of my father. My eyes widened, my breaths were trapped. In the back of my head that terrified knowing came alive. Something happened. Something I remembered last night and now...now there was a gaping hole in my memories. One that threatened to swallow me whole.

I stepped backwards, yanking my shirt and pyjamas free before I stepped into the shower. The hot spray did little to quell the ice inside. I dipped my head backwards, shampooing my hair, taking my time as my thoughts returned to that moment. It was right there at the edge of my memory.

NO ANGEL!

PLEASE!

A bitter scent pinched my nose making my eyes sting. But it couldn't be, not while I was under the water. I knew that scent. Knew it in the pit off my stomach. I coughed and spluttered, lunging out of the spray until I spun and hit the taps, switching the water off.

My hands were shaking as I reached for the towel. Still, I grabbed one and hurried to dry myself. Normally I enjoyed taking my time, but not today. Today I dried and slipped on my underwear before grabbing the dress. Maybe this was a bad idea. Silas's baggy sweats and t-shirt felt more natural. Something I could hide in that wasn't me.

The thought of his scent around me made me rethink. I had no other option than to wear what I had. I tugged the dress on, smoothing it down my body and tugged the zipper along my side until it closed. I needed to get it together, and I needed to stop this fantasy in my head.

Because it wasn't real.

It couldn't be.

I grabbed my pajamas and wet towel, tossing them down the clothes chute before I dragged a brush through my wet hair, grabbed my phone and walked out. The smell of bacon wafted from the kitchen. Gabe said the others weren't here, still part of me didn't believe him, leaving me to step cautiously along the hallway toward the sounds of our sizzling breakfast.

But the moment I neared the front door a shadow shifted. Through the frosted thick panel of glass I saw a figure standing outside. For a second I thought it was Silas returning. I froze staring as whoever it was cupped his hands and pressed his face to the glass.

It wasn't Silas.

It was Lincoln.

How long had he been standing there?

Long enough to watch me walk down the hall.

He fixed his gaze on me and motioned me forward. That heady rush sent a chill through me. The doorbell was right there, still he didn't use it. He wanted me to open the door for him...and only me. I glanced toward the doorway of the kitchen and looked back.

Lincoln waited, watching me through the glass as I slowly took a step and then another. The lock gave a snap, but it was muffled as Gabe unleashed a curse and the door swung inwards.

"Angelica." Lincoln murmured.

His name was a whisper. "Lincoln."

One careful glance toward the kitchen and he stepped inside, moving closer to me in such a predatory way it made me freeze.

"I know your little secret, Angel." He murmured. "All that blood." He lifted his hand, brushing the wet strands of my hair as his eyes twinkled. "You were covered in it, weren't you?"

The foyer around me swayed.

ANGEL...

ANGEL, PLEASE!

NOOO!

BOOM!

My pulse stuttered.

My mouth went dry.

"Do you want to tell them?" Lincoln's mouth quirked as the clash of plates came from the kitchen. "Or me?"

No.

The image of that study came rushing back. Blood dripped from the bookcase and the wet warmth that was on my cheek cooled.

"So much blood." Lincoln murmured again, that tight curl at the corner of his mouth curling higher.

I forced myself to move, stepping backwards...before I turned around and ran.

Chapter Twenty-Two

I opened my eyes and stared at the ceiling. That beaded drop of blood on her cheek still burning neon fucking bright in my mind.

Sleep wasn't comforting tonight. It was hard and cruel, like a mistress who's touch left me wanting. Wanting and yet unable to have a goddamn thing.

Get the fuck off her!

Gabe's screams rang in my head as I shoved upwards and climbed out of bed, padding across the room to grab my cell and squinted at the time five a.m. "Jesus Christ."

But I didn't drop my phone back down. Instead I glanced at the unanswered messages from Sloane. He still hadn't responded, and he'd never not responded. One more look at my frantic messages and I looked over my shoulder to the mess of a bed. Sleep was gone with no hope of returning.

I was tired of waiting. Tired of being at the fucking whims of my father's brother and now my own employee. There was only one thing for it. I was going out to find him.

I strode into the shower, flicked on the light and hit the tap, starting the spray. Thoughts of our sister pushed into my head. I scrubbed, then rinsed, hitting the lever once again before I stepped out and grabbed a towel. The knife was too far. I knew that...and still some part of me didn't care that I hurt her.

Because the truth justified the means.

I stopped drying. But did it?

The answer was an empty void of nothingness that gave me no peace. I tossed the towel to the floor and strode out into my room, pulling on black jeans and a t-shirt before I grabbed my boots and my jacket.

By the time I walked out of the house, the sky was brightening along the horizon. I hit the button opening the garage and walked the Ducati out before I climbed on and pulled my helmet low. Everything fell away when I started the engine and pushed off, idling the sleek machine along the side of the house until I hit the street and accelerated.

I'd never been to Sloane's house. But as with all our employees it was a requirement to list their name and addresses and personal information in our database. My father always had trust issues, I guess now it was with good reason.

The GPS on the phone led me not far from where the offices were in the city. I slowed the bike, pulling in around the early commuters and pulled outside a darkened two-storey brownstone. My cell said it was the right address, but there was no car parked in the driveway.

I climbed off the bike and pulled my helmet free, running a hand through the still damp strands of my hair. One glance along the street on each side and I climbed free and headed for the front door. There were no lights on inside. No hint of anyone from the frosted glass panel of the door, which led me to skirt along the side against the fence to peer into the window.

The place was empty as in not a thing inside.

No furniture.

No photos.

I stepped back as rage rippled deep. I didn't know what I expected to find...but it wasn't this. I rounded to the rear, glancing along the long forgotten garden and stopped, picking up a heady rock and hauled it through rear door, listening to the glass shatter instantly.

Shards scratched my jacket as I reached in and unlocked the door from the inside before I pushed it open. Morning sunlight spilled through the windows as I made my way through the vacant house, heading to the stairs and climbed, taking them two at a time until I stopped at the landing. Bedroom doors were open on each side of me. I headed for the first one, stepping inside to an empty room.

The wardrobes were open and empty, leaving me to head across the hallway to the other room which was the same. The sonovabitch was gone...like really fucking gone. "Fuck!"

I shook my head and made my way downstairs and back to the kitchen...then I stopped staring at the item on the bench. "That gutless fucking bastard." One step and I snatched the ID and security tag from the bench. The same one we all had.

We gave him everything, and at the first sign of trouble the bastard turned tail and ran.

Rage seethed inside leaving me to clench my fists. He'd better run, because if I got hold of him. He was a dead man.

The heavy thud of music from outside pushed into my mind. I turned my head, slowly drawing myself away from the rage to focus on the thick, heavy beat and made my way to the front of the house. A car slowly rolled toward the house. The black, lowered Mustang stood out like a neon sign amongst the Toyotas and family wagons. The windows were down, what looked like Latino guys hanging their arms out of the windows.

Was it them?

The Cartel del Diablo?

I stiffened as fear replaced rage and that icy shiver of realization made me step backwards. Had Sloane run? Or had he been threatened? I glanced over my shoulder to the ID cards on the bench. Either way it told me one thing. I was on my own.

My phone vibrated in my pocket as the black Mustang disappeared. I pulled it free and glanced at the caller ID, then answered. "Yeah?"

"She's gone." Gabe's voice was frantic in my ear. "She's just gone, Silas! I don't know what to do. She was here one minute and then...and then I can't find her."

Everything else disappeared and all the desperation and rage came flooding back. I was focused now...so goddamn focused on her. "What the fuck happened?"

"I don't know. She was in the shower and I was making breakfast and then when I came out the front door was opened and she was gone."

"Her cell phone?"

"She had it with her."

"Her bags?"

"I don't know. I just don't know."

"Well, fucking LOOK!"

I was already striding for the rear of the house, leaving the abandoned ID cards on the counter behind. I didn't care about them now. She can't be gone. She can't run...not from *ME!* "Goddamn little fucking bitch."

Gabe's heavy steps thundered in the cell as my boots crunched on broken glass and I strode out, hearing around the side of the house once more.

"They...they're still here." He gasped. "They're all still here."

"So she can't be running fucking far, can she?"

"No." My little brother answered. "She can't."

"Then start looking. I'm on my way."

I strode out from the house and headed to where my bike was parked. There was no sign of the Mustang or anyone else for that matter. Right now the Cartel needed to wait. I pulled up my cell, scrolled through and hit the button as I climbed on my bike and pulled my helmet down.

"Silas." Kieran answered on the second ring. "Any word?"

"He's gone." I kicked the bike off the stand and into gear. "And he's not coming back."

"Jesus Christ. Did they get to him?"

"Who knows. All I do know is he's not coming back...not alive that's for sure."

Kieran was Sloane's team leader. The one who did every task set assigned to him, including the investigation into the breech and the Mexican Cartel. But when I called asking him where the fuck his boss was, the guy acted stunned. He had no idea Sloane was missing. He did now. Not only that it was his job to track his boss down.

But now I needed him for something else.

"I have another problem. One more close to home."

"Shoot."

"Angelica's gone missing. She has no bags, so she can't have gone far. I need you to track her cell."

"I'm on it. Was this planned, do you know?"

Her bags are here...

"No."

"Friends and family?"

That weedy, pathetic boyfriend. That's who set this up. The spineless coward wasn't going to see tomorrow. Not by the time I was done with him. "Her boyfriend, Penn Hargreaves."

"As in Sebastian Hargreaves's son?"

"Yeah." I throttled the bike and took the corner hard. "That's the one."

"Hang tight, Silas. I'll find her."

"I'm counting on it." I muttered and pressed the button, ending the call.

Something didn't feel right. She had plenty of opportunities to run before, so why now? And if she was so Hell bent on escaping us, why not take her bags with her? I pushed the bike harder, heading back home while I waited for Kieran to do his thing.

I pulled up out front and climbed off before heading to the front door. It opened before I got there, leaving me to stare at the frantic expression on my brother's face.

"Any word?" I stepped in, scanning the foyer.

"No." He shook his head, his eyes wide and terrified. "I don't know where she went."

I walked inside, heading to her bedroom. Only I didn't make it that far, stopping outside the open door to Gabe's room and stared at the messy bed and her t-shirt hanging on the edge. "She stayed in your room?" I turned to face him.

My little brother's cheeks reddened as he straightened his spine and looked me dead in the eye. "Yes."

Did you fuck her?

The question roared to the surface. I clenched my jaw, driving the words back down my throat and tried to get a hold of the unmerciful rage that seethed inside me. Gabriel was far too invested, and now it seemed so was I. "What did you... say to her?"

"Nothing." He shook his head. "I was in the kitchen making her breakfast when I thought I heard voices. When I came out the door was open...and she was gone."

It didn't make sense. None of it.

Beep.

I snatched my cell and lifted it.

Kieran: *The boyfriend is on the move, sending you his GPS tracking link now.*

A second later another message came through, this time with a link for me to click.

"What is it?"

I flinched and jerked my gaze up from the GPS location somewhere outside Benneton Park. For a second I'd forgotten about him...I'd forgotten about everything...except chasing her. "Nothing." I turned around and started walking, heading for my bedroom. "Keep me updated if you hear anything."

"Sure and you do the same." His words followed me as I walked out.

But would I?

Maybe before seeing the messed up comforter entangled with her t-shirt. But not now. No, now I was going to make our brother understand—our lying, betraying fucking sister was mine.

I stopped on my way out to my bedroom, grabbing my Sig from my safe and slipped it under the waistband of my jeans before making for my bike. The blinking light of the tracker called to me. If little Angel was going to run, hands down she'd run to this weasel.

She thought he could protect her from me...

She was wrong.

A heady gust of wind picked up from nowhere, leaving to duck my head as I pulled away and headed across the city past glistening moonlights of glass and steel where power-hungry titans pulled the city's strings and headed for their homes instead.

Nestled behind wrought iron gates and manicured hedges was a disgustingly opulent neighborhood dripping with obscene wealth. My family might've taken our money from men just as dangerous, but these men...these men were a whole new breed of bastards.

Not only did they lie and manipulate, they stole from the most vulnerable, bleeding them dry with predatory health funds created for one purpose and one purpose alone...to make every single one of them rich.

But they weren't content with siphoning cash from these people. Oh no, they had their claws deep into the drug companies too. The same vultures that inflates prices of life-saving medications, turning sickness into a lucrative and foul business. One they excelled at.

I slowed at the gates, eying the pristine, pot-hole free streets and towering monoliths in the distance. If our sister was running anywhere, I'd bet my fucking life it'd be here. I slowed the bike, the growl of the engine swallowed by the thick layer of trees that surrounded the perimeter. One scan of the gates and I aimed the bike for shadows between the gaps between the trees.

This cocoon of privilege wasn't a barrier...not to me.

It was a fucking challenge.

I nosed the bike into the thick of the forest and climbed off before pulling my helmet free. The gun scratched my back as I started walking, leaving the Ducati behind. I was betting this place was guarded by more than just locks, cameras and sensors. No doubt armed security patrolled every inch of this place. But all I needed was a few minutes, and a perfect blind spot leaving this cesspit of luxury wide open.

The wind howled between the trees overhead, almost driving me backwards. Thump. The sound came from up ahead. The closer I came, the more I saw the damage. Part of the fence swung free, no doubt from the storms we'd had recently, leaving nature to rip and tear, exacting her wrath.

I grabbed the section of iron fence as it swung outwards, pulling it wide enough for me to slip inside. Once I was in, I lowered my head and headed for the thick brushes of the nearest backyard and grabbed my cell. The red blinking light was up ahead, drawing me onward.

My focus shifted. The feel of the gun in my hand and the brutal strength of the wind howling in my face slipped away. All I saw was her in that recording, her eyes glazed with a look of pure fucking desire. One she gave to another man.

No, it wasn't slipping away...I was. Rage consumed me. Cold, bitter rage.

I clenched the gun and followed the beacon, stopping at one of the oldest houses in the estate. This wasn't just a house, it was a monument of old money, its grandeur unmistakable. I scanned darkened window after darkened window between the ivy-clad walls of weathered stone searching for any sign of life. But there was none. I headed to the rear of the house before I stopped halfway along.

There was a door open, one that entered some conservatory. I quickly glanced over my shoulder then stepped. Checkerboard polished marble tiles gleamed under soft overhead lights. The air was thick and pungent, each breath drawing in the earthy scent tinged with sweetness. Exotic orchids, delicate and vibrant, clung to mossy branches. I pushed past and headed inside.

I didn't give a fuck about their flowers, or their money. There was only one thing I was after and as I stepped out of the conservatory and into the house it felt like I moved between two worlds. Cold, serene grandeur greeted me. My steps echoed softly on the polished wooden floorboards, each board a deep, rich mahogany that gleamed under the light of a crystal chandelier that was switched on, even in the middle of the day.

Antique furniture was arranged with careful precision—wingback chairs upholstered in a rich brocade, sat around a black grand piano, its glossy surface reflecting the soft glow of the lights. The air was colder here, the scent of flowers replaced with the tang of wood polish. Every detail of this place spoke of history and wealth. The Hargreaves of this city didn't just come from money...they came from old money. The kind that didn't disappear in any goddamn lifetime.

The sound of voices drew my focus—a sound the clearest, one that sent a jolt of adrenaline surging my veins. My stepsister's name was like a spark igniting the smoldering rage I barely kept leashed. Every fiber of my being was focused on the one thing: finding her, getting her out and making sure the man who hid her paid for it.

I followed the voices, my hands clenched in fists, every step calculated and silent until I reached the second floor and stopped. The voices...now silent.

My pulse boomed as I tread slowly, step-by-step until I came to a closed bedroom door. Energy crackled inside. I didn't need to check the GPS beacon to know I was standing right over it. My fingers trembled as I reached out, grasped the handle and slowly turned, pushing it all the way in...and froze.

The bedroom was empty. The voices a faint echo bouncing off the cold, stoney walls of this place. I unleashed a curse under my breath, frustration fuelling the savage energy coiled tight within him.

He was here...I knew it, hiding somewhere, like the coward he is.

That meant Angel was here too.

Somewhere.

A creak came from behind me.

I whirled around, my instincts sharper than ever. In a heartbeat I was face to face with a shadowy figure...a man standing in the gloom of the hallway.

"Who are you?"

His eyes widened in recognition, not for who I was...but what I was capable of.

In the blink of an eye I lunged, crossing the space between us in an instant and grabbed the front of his shirt, yanking him hard against me. "Where the fuck is she? Where the fuck is my sister?"

Only there was no answer, just a choked hiss of a breath before he shook his head.

Still, it didn't matter.

It was far too late. Blood called to blood, only it didn't beg and plead...it howled my goddamn name.

With a savage snarl I drove him backwards, each step faster and faster until the guy slammed against that ornate balustrade and then over...until he was falling...end over end.

CRACK!

The sickening sound made me recoil.

Blood spilled out from the mangled body beside the stairs.

Blood that gleamed spilling across the polished boards.

WHAT THE FUCK HAVE YOU DONE? My conscience howled.

I stared at that mangled body with its leg crooked unnaturally and the wide, unblinking eyes of death on its face. That empty, disconnected feeling of rage moved in, smothering the howl of shock with a clenched, bloody fist.

Wrath was a vengeful mistress...and now she claimed me of my own.

My sister's face burned in my head as I turned away...her beautiful, haunting cunt of a face. I wanted to punch it. I wanted to hurt it. I flinched as I made my way quietly down the stairs. But more than anything I wanted to love it...and that feeling alone was the most disturbing of them all.

Chapter Twenty-Three

ANGELICA

I GRIPPED THE COLD WROUGHT IRON FENCE, STARING AT the towering dark brick mansion in the distance. Salvation. That's what I told myself. But even as I stood there, frozen in place, Penn's frantic messages waited on my phone, each one pleading with me to come to him.,

But he didn't understand.

I wasn't worthy of someone like Penn. I wasn't worthy of anyone. Not anymore.

Angelica. Lincoln's voice slithered through my thoughts, as clear and venomous as if he stood beside me. *Do you want to tell them, or me?*

I closed my eyes, but it was a mistake. The memories rushed in bright and brutal.

Blood.

So much blood.

The wrought iron fence creaked beneath my tightening grip, forcing my eyes to open. The gate began to shift, grinding along its tracks. A sleek midnight blue car rolled out of the driveway, its engine purring softly. Sunlight gleamed off the polished hood as it slowed near me. Through the windshield, a man—early twenties, sharp suit, indifferent expression—gripped the wheel with practised ease.

He didn't look at me.

Not once.

As he sped past, the wind carried the scent of leather and exhaust, tangling with the fading fragrance of Penn's cologne in my mind. For a moment I thought about stepping into his path.

"Ma'am?"

The voice jarred me, I whirled around to see a uniformed guard emerging from the trees, his expression sharp and suspicious.

"Are you supposed to be here?" He asked, his hand hovering too close to the gun on his belt.

I stumbled backward, the wrought iron fence scraping against my palm. My heart thundered, each beat punctuated by the echoes of screams in my mind.

"Well?" The guard stepped closer, his tone growing more aggressive. "This is private property. If you're not meant to be here, leave."

I nodded and took another step back. My throat was dry, but I managed to force out a whisper. "I'm sorry."

He didn't move until I turned and walked away, the weight of his gaze pressing against my back like a loaded gun.

I didn't know where I was going.

The streets blurred together, my footsteps pounding in time with the relentless voice in my head.

ANGEL, NO.

PLEASE!

BOOM!

I flinched at the phantom sounds, my breath shallow. The edges of my vision darkened as I stumbled into a park. Children laughed and played on swings, their carefree shrieks clashing with the chaos in my mind, mothers sat on benches, chatting and sipping coffee, oblivious to the girl who didn't belong.

I drifted toward the shadow of the bridge, my feet moving on autopilot. Beneath the cold concrete, the world felt heavier. The laughter of children faded, replaced by the low hum of passing cars.

Angel, you're mine now, Lincoln whispered in my head.

I dropped to my knees, leaning against the cool stone wall. My arms wrapped around my body, trembling as I fought to breathe. My mind clawed at the edges of a memory I didn't want to see but couldn't escape.

Gunpowder. Bitter and sharp. The metallic tang of blood. My father's scream.

Angel, NO!

And then...*silence.*

My hands flew to my ears, desperate to block out the phantom sounds. Tears burned hot trails down my cheeks as I rocked back and forth. The words Lincoln had whispered before he left me echoed louder, crueler.

All that blood, he whispered in my head and the world around me swayed. I closed my eyes as the scent filled my mind.

My fingers shook, dancing and trembling against my thigh until I wrapped my arms around my body and stumbled against the wall. No one could offer me salvation. Not Penn or his father. Not from what I'd done...and I had done that, hadn't I?

I murdered my parents.

I hit the hard concrete barrier and slowly slid to the ground. The squeals of children rang out, but the gleeful sound didn't linger in the darkness where I was. No, nothing did...but the memories of what I'd done. Tears came, blurring the cracked and weathered pillars before they slid down my cheeks and fell.

But I made no move to brush them away.

I couldn't...because I was back there.

In that room...

With that monster.

You've done so well, Angel. So well...now lay back and spread your legs, let's make a beautiful movie for Mommy dearest.

A sob tore free as I clung to myself. I dragged my knees upwards and lowered my head, desperately wanting to disappear. But I couldn't...could I? Because Silas just wouldn't let me go.

That's the way, Angel...you'll do exactly as I say, just like the good little whore you really are. I slowly rocked back and forth. A whore. That's what I was. A lying, murdering whore.

There was no salvation for someone like me. There couldn't be.

You don't need to worry about anything now. That cold bastard inside my head whispered. *Listen to the sound of my voice. What are you?*

Silence filled my head. A trembling, terrified silence.

Angelica, what are you?

"Owned." I whispered as I squeezed my eyes tight. "That's what I am...I'm owned."

That's right. Now, remember your training. Open your eyes... look at the screen.

Flashes filled my head.

OWNED.

DAUGHTER.

CONTROL.

That's the girl, he whispered and I was helpless to stop him. *Now open your mouth.*

The world seemed to melt away. There was no children's laughter from the playground. No darkness under the bridge. There was nothing but that whisper in my head. One I couldn't escape.

SIRENS CUT THROUGH THE HAZE. I flinched and jerked my gaze upwards as panic set in. How long had I been like that? A minute...an hour? I turned my head to darkened gloom outside and my pulse sped. A sickening, icy feeling washed through me. It'd been longer than an hour...a lot longer.

"Hey."

I jerked my gaze left and froze, in the gloom a homeless man sat hunched against the cold, crumbling wall, a shadow within shadows. The whites of his eyes were stark against the backdrop, neon white, etched with the bloodshot spidered veins.

"You alive?" He croaked, pushing his frail body upwards before he stumbled toward me.

Fear punched all the way into my stomach. I drove my hand down against the sharp edges of cracked concrete and drove myself away from him.

"Easy." He pleaded, his gaunt figure draped in layers of tattered, hole-ridden clothing.

I couldn't cope, not with this man in front of me, or this place. I didn't want to be here. I wanted to be with my friends, or my family. Tears blurred as I stumbled backwards. "I'm s-sorry." I stammered. "I'm really, really s-sorry."

I ran from that place and that man, plunging headlong into the darkening playground and kept on running. Cars flew past, some with headlights blazing, others just a blur.

Beep.

I stopped running, my panting breaths like swallowing lava as I grabbed my cell from my pocket and looked down.

Gabe: Please, Angel. I'm freaking the fuck out. Call me, tell me where you are?

I couldn't. I couldn't call him, couldn't tell him where I was. Couldn't call any of them. Because of him.

Beep.

I stared as another message filled the screen.

Silas: You'd better run, cause when I find you, Angelica, you'll wish you'd run faster.

My breath caught with the warning. I stared at the words until they blurred. He was looking for me. *He was looking for me. I* swung around, scanning the faces around me and pressed my spine against the enclave of a store.

I'll do things I don't want to do. But I will, little sister, and I'll do them well...

Silas' warning rang inside my head. Pain flared across my chest as I stared along the packed city street and tried to think. I needed to get out of here...and now.

I spun around and started walking, keeping my head down, avoiding any contact I could and searched for anything that was familiar. I knew this city, knew these people. Some of them at least. Daughters and sons of mom's friends, connected by wealth and social circles. They were creatures of habit, frequenting the same bars at the same time, ordering the same drinks and talking about the same boring events they always did.

I needed that now more than ever.

I pushed harder, searching the streets as the headlights of oncoming cars blurred and the ambient lights of bars I passed shone brighter. By the time my chest burned I caught sight of the Admiral, an old English style bar that Penn and his friends frequented.

My steps slowed as I scanned the Bentley's parked out front, the drivers waiting to take their pampered playboys any place they wanted to go. None were Penn's...nor were they anyone I knew. I stopped at the automatic doors, catching my breath at the rush of warm air as it hit me. Do I go in? Was there someone who could protect me?

I scanned the faces passing me, then slowly stepped inside.

Heads turned as I made my way toward the bar. I glanced around, finding nothing but cold, calculated stares and contempt.

"Can I help you, Miss?"

I jerked my gaze to a waiter beside the bar. He took one look at me and forced a smile. I knew that smile. It said this wasn't the place for me. I shook my head. "No, thank you," and walked back outside.

Cold night air was a slap in the face. I kept walking, heading to one of the bars we always stayed at.

Beep.

I lifted my phone.

Silas: You make it too easy for me, little sister.

I spun around, searching the cars...but he wouldn't have his car would he? No, Silas would be on his bike.

Single headlights became beacons of terror. I could almost hear the bike engine revving like a predator scenting its prey and my pulse raced in time with the sound.

The wind whipped my hair across my face, lashing my eyes until they watered. *Run...NOW.*

I lunged, driving myself forward. I didn't search for bars now. There was nowhere he wouldn't find me. No where I could disappear.

That's it, Angel. You'll do exactly what you've been taught to do, won't you? WON'T YOU?

That monster's voice echoed, relentless and cruel as I ran. My breaths came in short, ragged gasps, my chest burning with the effort. Panic clouded my vision, and I stumbled down side streets, unsure of where I was going, only knowing I had to keep moving.

The night around me was oppressive—shadows stretched across brick walls, the only sound the frantic rhythm of my own footsteps. But I knew better. I wasn't alone.

The low growl of a motorbike's engine cut through the air. It wasn't close, not yet, but it was getting louder. My stomach twisted into a knot of pure terror. I knew the sound of that motorbike's engine anywhere. I should...I heard it in my dreams.

I glanced over my shoulder, my vision blurring with tears. The headlights hadn't turned the corner yet, but the sound was unmistakable. *He's Here. He's here.*

I forced myself to move faster, ignoring the burn in my thighs and the stabbing pain in my side. Turning hard around a building, I barely registered the shape of a figure before I slammed into him—a wall of muscle and authority.

"What the fuck?"

The impact was so brutal my teeth gnashed together. My head spun as I stumbled backward, legs buckling beneath me. Strong hands caught me before I hit the ground, dragging me upright with a force that left me gasping.

"Why don't you look at where the fuck you're going?"

The voice was sharp, cutting, filled with irritation. But it wasn't his voice. I looked up, blinking through the haze of fear, and saw a man towering over me. A cop. His uniform gleamed in the dim light, his features carved with fury.

Relief hit me like a tidal wave, crashing over every cell in my body. I didn't think—I couldn't think. "Thank God," I choked, the words barely audible as I lunged forward.

I threw my arms around him, clinging like he was the only thing tethering me to the earthy. My entire body trembled as the adrenaline began to fade, leaving only the raw, overwhelming sense of survival behind.

"Hey, hey—" His voice softened, though his hands came up stiffly to pull me off him. Dark, piercing eyes locked onto mine, his expression caught somewhere between irritation and confusion. His gaze flicked down, taking in the dirt smeared on my arms, the wild look in my eyes and the ragged rise and fall of my chest.

That anger in his eyes faded, replaced by something colder. Controlled. He shifted, turning his head to scan the alley I'd just stumbled out of.

"Are you in trouble?"

The question hung in the air, cutting through the haze in my mind. I opened my mouth to speak, but nothing came out. The lump in my throat was too big, the relief too overwhelming.

Tears pricked the corners of my eyes as my knees finally gave way, and this time, he was ready.

He steadied me, one hand gripping my shoulder, the other hovering at his hip near the holster of his weapon. "Hey, look at me," he said, his tone low, steady. "Who's after you?"

I shook my head, there was no way I could say his name and no way this man would believe me.

The gunning of an engine echoed in the distance, closer now, and I flinched violently. He noticed, his body tensing as his gaze darted toward the sound.

"Stay here," he ordered, his voice sharp and commanding.

But as he moved, I reached out, gripping his arm like a lifeline. "Please," my voice husky. "Don't leave me."

For a moment, he hesitated, his dark eyes meeting mine again. Something in his expression shifted—resolve, maybe or understanding. His hand tightened on my shoulder.

"All right," he said, his voice softer now. "I won't."

The promise was enough to keep me upright, though the shaking didn't stop. Relief slammed into me, almost suffocating in its intensity. I wasn't alone...not anymore. And for the first time in what felt like forever, a flicker of hope surfaced, one that told me I might survive the night.

"Why don't you come with me?" He said. "The station's right around the corner. We can talk there, if you feel safe. You can tell me who's after you and I'll do my best to keep you safe."

Those tears came harder, silently sliding down my cheeks. I gave a nod, the words forced around the lump in my throat. "Thank you," I whispered. "Thank you so very much."

Chapter Twenty-Four

ANGELICA

THE FLUORESCENT LIGHTS OF THE SMALL POLICE STATION buzzed faintly above me, their harsh glare casting everything in sharp relief. I blinked against the brightness, my vision hazy, my head swimming. The cracked plastic chair beneath me creaked as I shifted, wrapping my arms tightly around myself. Goosebumps covered my skin, sweat slicked against my back despite the cold chill clinging to me..

"I need...help," I whispered, my voice barely audible, trembling with desperation.

ANGEL...ANGEL, PLEASE! NOOO! BOOM!

The memory hit me again, as sharp and as brutal as the first time. Mom's screams. The gunshot. The suffocating stillness that followed. My stomach twisted, my nails digging into my arms until the sting of pain brought me back to the present.

Even sitting here, under these cruel, sterile lights, I felt the weight of betrayal crushing me.

SWEAR TO ME. My mom's voice echoed in my head as she begged. *SWEAR TO ME ON YOUR LIFE. SWEAR IT. SWEAR IT!*

I closed my eyes, dragging in a shaking breath. I was breaking my promise just by being here, speaking to this stranger. But I had nowhere else to go.

"It's okay," the man across from me said, his voice steady and soothing, like he was trying to coax a frightened animal. Realisation dawned on me. I guess I was that animal, wasn't I? Sergeant Carter, his badge read. He sat on the edge of his desk, his tie loosened, the sleeves of his button-down rolled up. His face was tired but sharp, dark eyes studying me. Too intently.

"Take your time," he urged. "Just tell me what happened—from the beginning."

From the beginning.

How could I possibly tell him that? The truth about the blood on my hands, the gunshot that still haunted me? No...no I couldn't do that.

My voice came out brittle. "You wouldn't believe me."

"Try me," Carter said, his gaze steady. "You're safe here. That's all that matters right now."

Safe.

That word still tasted foreign on my tongue. I didn't believe it. I focused on the weathered police officer in front of me, searching those steady eyes for the truth—but I didn't have any other options, did I? Time was running out...and so were the lies.

"Someone's after me," I said finally, the words shaky but certain.

He nodded, grabbing a small notebook and pen. "Who?"

"My brother," I said, and the word felt like it weighed a thousand pounds. "Silas."

Carter's pen paused mid-air. "Your brother, Silas?" He asked, his tone dipping with something unreadable.

I nodded quickly, all of a sudden rushing to make him understand. "He's not normal. He's...dangerous. He'll find me. No matter what I do, and no matter where I go. He'll drag me back there, to that place."

A flicker of that room in the Order came rushing back.

"To what place?"

"Home," the word slipped out before I knew it as the memory of that stark room was replaced with another and the dim light of the den on our family home filled my mind. "He'll take me home."

Carter leaned forward slightly, his expression sharpening. "What do you mean by dangerous? Has he hurt you?"

I swallowed hard, looking down at my hands. My fingers twisted together, my nails biting into my palms as I tried to ground myself. The words felt stuck in my throat. How could I explain it? How could I describe the way Silas controlled everything around him, including me?

My lips parted, but no words came out. My mind flickered to the others—Theo's cruel smirk, Jude's cold stare, and Gabe's desperate broken gaze. They weren't just brothers. They were shadows I couldn't escape. And no matter how much I wanted to run from them, part of me still ached for their presence.

Carter's voice pulled me back. "Did he hurt you?" He asked again, his voice quieter this time, like he already knew the answer.

I slowly nodded, my voice barely breaking a whisper. "Not...the way you think."

His jaw tightened, but he didn't push. Instead, he learned back, tapping the pen against the notebook. "Then, why do you think he's after you?"

I hesitated. "Because I ran," that gnawing feeling twisting in my stomach. "And Silas doesn't let go of things that belong to him." Especially me.

Carter's eyes flicked up to mine at that, something unreadable flashed across his face. He didn't write anything down, just watched me with that same, unnerving intensity.

"He controls everything—my life, my choices. I can't breathe without him knowing about it. And if he finds me...I...I don't know what he'll do."

Yes, yes you do and that's what terrifies me the most.

Carter set the pen down, folding his hands over his knees. "You did the right thing coming here," he said, his voice calm and steady. "I can help you."

The words hit me like a lifeline, and for the first time in a long time, I felt a flicker of hope.

"I need to make a call," he slowly rose and pulled out his phone. "I'm going to bring in someone who can help you. Can you wait here a minute?"

I nodded without thinking. Too tired to question him.

Through the glass window, I watched as he stepped out of the room, his voice low as he spoke into his phone. He didn't seem hurried, didn't seem worried. He was helping me.

My body trembled with the thought as I watched him, the sound of the fluorescent lights buzzing in my ear. I waited for what felt like ages, staring at Carter's back as he stood there, talking until finally he pressed the button and ended the call.

But he didn't turn around, not for a while and when he did, he didn't meet my gaze.

My pulse skipped, then raced as he slowly turned and looked over his shoulder to where I waited. But there was a sureness about him, one I had to trust.

"Someone's coming," he said when he stepped back inside the room and headed for his desk. "They'll be able to help."

I glanced at the open door to the police station behind him. "Here?"

He gave a slow nod and moved closer, placing his hand on my shoulder once more. "You're going to get through this, you understand that right? You'll figure out what you have to do to be safe. You're a smart girl, Angelica. You're a very smart girl."

He slid his hand from my shoulder, grabbing the back of my seat instead.

The word help twisted in my chest, but I stood anyway, my legs weak and unsteady.

"Is this another police officer?" I asked as he guided me out of the station and into the cool night air once more.

"Something like that," Carter said as we left the spill of light outside the open door behind and stepped back into the darkness.

The street outside the station was quiet, lit only by the faint glow of a single street lamp.

"This way," he urged, steering me toward the alley beside the station.

A faint warning bell went off in the back of my mind. But I followed him, too desperate and too tired to resist. At the end of the alley, a sleek black Audi sat idling, its glossy surface reflecting the faint light. A figure leaned casually against the hood, a cigarette glowing faintly between his fingers.

Silas.

The blood drained from my face as that figure pushed off the car and slowly turned. Even in the darkness I knew him and as his eyes met mine. Cold. Sharp. Unyielding. I stopped walking.

Panic clawed at my throat. My head snapped to Carter, a primal scream of terror resounded inside my head, but all I could manage was. "You called him?"

Carter didn't meet my gaze. He just stepped backwards, putting distance between us and gave a hard shrug. "Sorry, kid," he said with little remorse.

Sorry, kid?

That's all he had?

That's all he was going to give *me?*

That hard lump in the back of my throat returned with a vengeance as Silas flicked the cigarette to the ground, grinding it out beneath his heel. He didn't say a word as he started toward me, his movements slowly and deliberate.

"Get in the car, Angel," he said, his voice calm, quiet, and utterly terrifying.

I stumbled back, shaking my head. "No," I whispered, my voice trembling. "I'm not going anywhere with you."

His lips curved into a faint, sadistic smile as he stopped in front of me and looked down, meeting my stare. "You don't have a choice, do you?"

My knees locked as he pushed closer, the suffocating weight of his presence bearing down on me. I glanced at Carter, but he was already walking away, his shoulders relaxed, as if this was just another day for him.

Tears burned down my cheeks.

"You can't keep running, Angel," Silas murmured, his voice like silk. "You belong to me, every foul, sick, twisted version of yourself. You always have."

And as his hand closed around my arm, dragging me toward the waiting car, I knew the truth.

There really was nowhere to run.

Nowhere to hide.

Not from him.

Not from any of them.

Chapter Twenty-Five

SILAS

She moved silently, heading to the passenger's door. Her steps were hesitant, measured, like she was bracing for something, an explosion, a punishment...or worse, me. I reached around her, opening it before she quietly slid inside, her head down, her long hair falling like a curtain between us. She said nothing. Not a single word. Just slipped into the seat, small and uncertain, leaving me to close the door behind her.

Carter was long gone by the time I turned back. The man was smart enough to know what to do and smarter still to keep his mouth shut. People like him didn't ask questions, they just disappeared when you paid them too. The call had been money well spent. My father's regular donations to a select section of the Police Department had more than earned back...especially when it came to *her*.

My sister.

I turned back toward the car, my hands gripping the edge of the door as I glanced through the glass at her. She was so small, her body pressed hard against the passenger-side door, as though trying to put as much distance as possible between us. Her knees were drawn up slightly, her arms wrapped around them like a shield. Even in the confined space, she looked lost—out of place.

Tiny. Breakable.

I climbed in, the door slamming shut louder than I intended, making her flinch. Her reaction was quick, almost instinctual, and it stabbed at something deep inside me—something I didn't want to acknowledge. I gritted my teeth, gripping the steering wheel tighter than I should, the leather creaking beneath my fingers.

Silence stretched out between us, suffocating and heavy, until it felt like the weight of it was pressing down on my chest. I reached forward and stabbed the button, bringing the car's engine to life with a growl. Still, I could feel her there beside me, her presence like a tangible thing, but she didn't move, didn't speak.

The air was thick with unspoken words as I shoved the Audi into gear and backed out, into the street, then drove forward.

She thought she could run. Thought she could get away.

She was wrong.

I punched the accelerator, throwing her back in her seat. Her shoulders stiffened as she gripped the edge of her seat. Still, she didn't look at me once.

"You know this was pointless, right?" My voice cut through the air, cold and sharp. So fucking sharp it could slice right through her. But I didn't turn my head as I spoke, keeping my eyes on the road ahead. "Running. Hiding. Did you honestly think I wouldn't find you?"

Her head turned just slightly, her profile barely visible in the dim light of the dashboard, every movement of her body calling me like a goddamn drug.

"You're quiet now?" My tone almost mocking. "Where's all that fight you had earlier?"

Her shoulders tensed, but she didn't respond. Her fingers tightened against the fabric of her pants, the small movement enough to betray the storm brewing beneath her calm exterior.

That fire in her was still there. I could feel it, simmering just below the surface. She wasn't broken, not entirely. But she would be.

"You're just damn lucky it was Carter who found you. Anyone else..." I glanced her way, forcing the words through clenched teeth. "Anyone else wouldn't have called me. They could've... they could've done whatever the fuck they wanted with you."

Her breath hitched, the faintest sound escaping her lips. She wasn't as unaffected as she wanted me to believe. I pressed harder, leaning back in the seat with one hand on the wheel. "You don't even realise how dangerous this little stunt of yours was, do you? How close you came to—"

"Stop," she whispered, her voice shaking.

I turned to her, studied every reaction until her gaze finally met mine, wide and glassy with something shimmering in them I couldn't quite place. Fear. Anger. Resolution. Please, for the love of God, let it be resolution. Because then she'd be...then she'd be mine.

That same sick need howled like a beast inside me. The same shrieks of torment which unleashed in me the moment I found out she was gone. My pulse raced, the sound pulsing from my temples like thunder in my head. I almost lost her.

Fuck, I almost lost her.

I focused on the road ahead, making our way back to the familiar streets and finally turned into our street. Her gaze shifted to our house before she swallowed hard. The car hit the driveway hard before I tapped the brakes, rolling to a stop at the front of the garage.

Shadows moved around me. Most of the armed men we had keeping an eye on the perimeter had been assigned elsewhere, leaving one or two behind. One of them headed my way as I climbed out.

"Sir, anything you need us to do tonight?"

I shook my head, my focus on the woman in my car. "Not tonight. You can leave."

One nod of the head was all it took. He turned around and disappeared. I waited for a moment until he was out of sight and then walked around to the passenger's door. She looked up at me and the past and the present collided. I saw her on her knees...wanting it so fucking bad it hurt.

My hand trembled when I gripped the handle and opened the door, stepping to the side. She didn't move at first, her body shivering until she had no choice but to step out. Her head hung as she walked past me, heading for the back door of the house. With every step behind her that ravenous beast inside me howled in delight.

She pushed in the code for the back door, yanking it open before slipping inside.

"Where do you think you're going?"

She stopped, then slowly turned. That movement alone triggering the animal inside me. I lunged, grabbing her arm and dragging her with me as I headed for the den. Her small frame struggled against my grip, fighting her pathetic fight, but she was no match for me. One hard shove of the door and it slammed backwards, bouncing as I shoved her inside.

"Sit," I ordered and pointed to the brown chesterfield sofa in the middle of the room.

She stumbled forward, giving me time to close the door behind us. There was that spark of defiance when she glared back at me, but I saw something else to—fear.

Good. She needed to be afraid.

"You think you can ever escape me?"

She didn't answer, her gaze fixed on the floor. Her silence only fueled that thing inside.

"Look at me!"

Her head snapped up, her eyes locking on mine.

"I told you, Angel," I held her stare, leaning down until my face was inches from hers. "You belong to us—*to me.*" I lashed out, grabbing a handful of her hair in my fist. "Now you're going to learn what happens when you forget that."

Her breath hitched, but she didn't look away. That stubbornness, that fire inside her eyes—it was maddening. I pushed in and sat, forcing her body to slide backwards, before I grabbed her thigh and pulled her against me in one swift motion. She had no other option than to be dragged onto my lap, her thighs straddling one of mine, her hands braced against my chest.

"Silas, don't," she fought, slamming her fists against me in a desperate need to escape.

Something inside me let her go.

My hold slipped and she scurried backwards, windmilling her arms before she caught her balance. Then turned and lunged for the door. This was what that animal inside me wanted. This was the trigger to act.

My entire body was wired tight. I lunged, driving myself forward and descended on her as she hit the door, grabbing her around the waist and lifted her feet from the floor.

"*LET ME GO!*" She howled, throwing her head backwards.

I jerked to the side, narrowly missing the blow and hauled her backwards, all but throwing her across the room toward the fireplace. She landed on her feet hard, then lunged once more, slamming right into my chest.

"You *THINK* you can escape *ME?*" I roared, sweeping my foot out to knock her off balance.

It worked, buckling her knees and taking her to the ground. She landed on the soft, plush rug in front of the cold hearth and scurried forward. But I was already dropping on top of her, grabbing her arms and jerking them high. She buckled under my weight, pinned in place with my hands around her wrists above her head.

Jesus fucking Christ she felt *good*.

Her muffled cries were swallowed by the rug. I couldn't hear them anyway over the roaring in my ears.

"Seems like you need a reminder of who exactly *is* in control here."

The words rose instantly in my head. Words uttered by the sick sonovabitch London called The Teacher.

"Owned." I growled against her ear. "That's what you are right? You're fucking owned by us…" I closed my eyes, my voice thick and husky. "You're owned by me."

The fight went out of her.

That alone did things to me I'd never felt before. I lowered my head, dragging in the frantic gasps of her breath and the scent of her skin.

"You ran," agony roared inside me. "Do you have any idea what that did to me?"

I was unhinged. Frantic. Tearing along the streets, thinking she was going back to that asshole boyfriend. I ground my hips against her, letting her feel how fucking hard I was. Let her know just how much she affected me.

"You drive me fucking insane, do you get that?" I growled against her ear. "I fucking hate you and yet I…I still can't let you go."

There was battling in her now, only the hard rise and fall of her chest. Still, I couldn't let her go. I was too far gone now, unable to stop this from happening even if I wanted to…and I didn't want to.

"Owned." I pulled backwards, looking down as she turned her

head, her lips parted. Fuck I wanted to taste those lips, to bite and lick and consume.

I'd never wanted anyone so fucking much in my entire life. I eased my hold on one hand and dragged my fingers along her arm, then down her body until I cupped her breast. My feet moved, driving between her legs, my thighs holding her still under me as I found her nipple with my fingers.

"You belong to me, do you get that?"

Deep down I knew what I was doing, that I was triggering whatever mindfuck she had inside her head. But I couldn't stop myself. I was out of my mind with desperation and rage...and driving all of that was this sick fucking desire for her.

The kind I'd never had before.

Not with anything.

I reached down, yanking her shirt upwards, but the fucking thing pulled tight, staying in place. With a growl I rose onto my knees, releasing her long enough to drive her shirt upwards, revealing the soft peach colored lace bra she wore. The kind that brought me undone.

I lowered my head, inhaling the scent of her.

"You didn't fucking think about the consequences," I groaned, inhaling deep. I couldn't get enough of her, her scent, her warmth—I lifted my gaze to hers—or that faraway look in her eyes. The one I'd seen back in that room at The Order. The same look I wanted to see now. "Did you? You didn't think how running was going to make me feel?"

She wasn't there, and yet somewhere deep down she was.

She was still the liar.

Still the betrayer.

Still the fucking sister who cut me a thousand ways and crawled under my skin.

"You will never run from me again, do you understand that?"

She stared at me blankly. I reached upwards, yanking on that soft lace cup until her bare breast slipped free. "Tell me you understand, Angel."

She tilted her head and looked down, watching as I lowered my mouth to her nipple. One hard lick and she shivered.

"Tell me...tell me you understand."

"I understand."

Her tone was empty, devoid of emotion. Yet that was all I needed. I lowered my head, dragging in that tightening peak into my mouth. My body roared with hunger. My cock so fucking hard it was driving me insane. I rubbed myself against her thigh as I moved, desperate to feel anything I could get from her.

She wasn't making any move to fight me, not anymore. So I released her other hand, dragging her shirt higher until it slipped over her head and was gone.

"What is it you understand exactly?" I eased upwards and looked down to where her nipple glistened with saliva.

My saliva.

She stared up at me. One hard look along her body and I eased backwards, my fingers reaching for the button of her black slacks. A twist of my fingers was all it took, leaving the clasp to spring free. My fingers moved to her zipper.

"Silas, no," she whispered.

I met that stare. "No?" I leaned down. "No, what little sister?"

Her eyes widened, yet her body betrayed her. Her nipples so fucking hard, her body quivering as I slid the zip low and looked down to the peach lace panties.

She lifted her hands to my chest as I gripped the edges of her pants. But she made no effort to push me away as I slid her pants low and cast them aside. They hit the floor behind me with a soft thud. That sound triggered her. She shoved backwards, driving the back of her heels against the floor.

I followed her as she shoved upwards, standing on trembling legs. "You want to run again, Angel?" I asked, reaching over my head and dragged my shirt over my head.

She stumbled toward the sofa.

But she didn't get far before I strode forward, grabbing her around the waist and pulled her with me. We fell, hitting the cold, leather seat. I shifted my leg, dragging her body against me in a way that made her moan and grip my bicep.

Her nails dug into my arm, and I couldn't tell if it was resistance or desperation.

"Stop," she whispered in a breathless plea.

But I didn't stop.

I had no fucking intention of stopping ever again.

"Do you feel that?" I demanded, forcing her to move against me. Her thighs clenched, her breath coming in quick, shallow bursts. "That's what happens when you disobey me. You lose control. Then, your body betrays you."

Her cheeks flushed with the words, her head shaking as she tried to fight me, but her hips moved despite herself. I saw her resistance crumbling, more than that I felt it, that line between defiance and surrender blurring with every slow thrust of her pussy against my thigh.

"You hate this, don't you?" I taunted, my voice rough. "Hate that you can't stop yourself."

Tears welled in her eyes, but she refused to let them fall. That fire in her—it wasn't extinguished yet. Part of me wanted to hold onto that, to fan those dying flames of desperation. I moved my ass, driving my thigh against her and allowed myself to get lost in the moment. Looking at her.

Really looking at her.

At the small, pathetic girl who slipped into our lives like a ghost, then haunted my goddamn world. The one I shouldn't be doing this with, and yet as I looked down, finding the sweet swell of her fucking pussy grinding against my leg I knew I didn't want to be with anyone else.

I reached up, placing my hands around her waist. "That's it, Angel," my voice deep and desperate. "Ride me."

She dropped her head forward, giving into the torment in her mind.

I knew she wanted to obey me.

To give in to that programming of that place.

To be used and hungered...and dangerous to us.

Because she was dangerous.

So fucking dangerous.

Like a viper, designed to draw you in right before it struck.

I was ready to be stuck by her.

"Fuck that's it."

She thrust and thrust, grinding her body on mine.

I tugged the cup of her bra, then dragged the strap down, leaving her breast to fall free. My hands were around her in an instant, sliding along her back to hold her against my chest. "Take what you need."

A low moan ripped from her.

Then another, only this time it was deep and husky...and male.

"What the fuck are you doing with him?"

I jerked my head upwards, finding my brother, Gabe standing in the doorway, his eyes fixed on our sister riding my knee.

But she couldn't stop. Oblivious to our little brother in the room she clung to me, climbing that wave of ecstasy.

Gabe strode forward, leaving the open door of the den behind and grabbed her arm, shaking her roughly. *"WHAT THE FUCK ARE YOU DOING WITH HIM?"*

Angelica froze, her body going rigid as the realisation dawned.

"No." I growled, stopping him cold.

He jerked those rage-filled eyes to mine. Those eyes that saw it all. All the sick, need inside us. The same need I saw in him.

"She needs to learn," I said, my voice devoid of emotion.

There was a scowl, then a tiny shake of his head as he understood.

"Learn?" Gabe looked sickened as he lifted a shaking finger at her. "You *think* this is teaching her anything? You're not teaching her anything other than the fact you're a cruel sadistic bastard who will do *anything* to get what *he* wants!"

He was right.

Because now I did have what I wanted.

It was her.

"This isn't who we are," there was a tremble in my brother's voice. He took a step backwards, jerking his stare to her, then back to me.

I slowly stood, the leather creaking beneath me as I rose to my full height. Gabe took another step backwards instinctively, his protective stance faltering for a moment.

"This," I looked at her standing there, trembling. "Is exactly *who* we are," I held my voice steady. "You're just too weak to admit it."

"She's *our* sister," He croaked and took a step toward her. *"Not* your fucking toy."

He reached for her, and she let him wrap his arms around her.

Not your toy.

Those words stayed with me as he pulled her against him and headed for the door. But there was a moment of hesitation before she stepped through. Those green emerald eyes flicked to mine. For a moment, I thought she might stay, that the part of her that craved this—the punishment, the control—would win out. Then she turned back and together with my brother they left the room.

But I saw that hunger in her eyes.

The same hunger that I knew she saw burning in mine.

Gabe was right.

She wasn't my toy.

She was all of ours.

And she *knew* it.

I let them leave, listening to my little brother's heavy steps as he guided her to his room.

He was just as desperate for her as I was.

He just fought it.

But if there was anything I knew now...he couldn't fight this need for her forever.

Sooner or later it'd win out.

And he'd be just as sick and fucking desperate as the rest of us.

Chapter Twenty-Six

ANGELICA

Gabe pulled me through the house, his grip too tight, too desperate, too much. My skin burned where Silas' had touched me, and I wanted to scream—wanted to tear myself open to get rid of the feeling.

But I didn't.

I let him drag me because I didn't trust my own legs to move. Silas had broken something inside me, and now I didn't know how to exist without him holding me in place.

Gabe's bedroom door was thrown open and I was shoved inside.

"I can't *fucking* believe this!" He roared and shoved the door closed with a *boom!*

I jerked with the sound, wrapping my arms around myself, feeling the coldness of my own skin as he started to pace.

"What the fuck was that, Angel? *What did he do to you?*"

My lips parted, but no words came.

I could still feel Silas. The heat of his thigh between my legs, the punishing grip of his hands. The way he dragged me over him until pleasure and ruin blurred into one.

And I'd let him.

My body responding in ways that both sickened and filled me with desire. Shame slithered through me, wrapping tight around my ribs to steal my breath.

I wanted it.

Even as I fought, even as I said no—my body craved him. His hands, his cruelty...his cock. I swallowed hard, my own desire still roaring inside me.

I needed it eased, anyway I could. I just wanted this torture to be over.

"Angel."

Gabe looked at me like I was something he could put back together. Like I wasn't already shattered.

"Talk to me," he pleaded.

I shook my head. *I couldn't.*

I didn't have words for the filth coating my skin, for the way my thighs still clenched like they missed Silas's grip.

For the way I ached.

I just wanted it gone.

I wanted it erased.

I stared at Gabe, at the warmth in his golden-brown eyes, the softness of his hands as he reached for me. I looked down to those long fingers and the way he touched me so tenderly, the total opposite to his brother.

He wasn't like Silas.

He wasn't cruel.

He wasn't a monster.

And that was the problem.

My mind drifted to Penn, to the way he barely had enough courage to hold my hand in public, even after a year of dating me. Even then when he did clutch my fingers it was only because his friends laughed and made fun of him.

But I wanted something else now.

Something darker.

Something *worse*.

I was ruined because of it.

But maybe...maybe if I focused on Gabe I'd get rid of it. Maybe if I clung to him like a life raft I could somehow wash some of this darkness away?

I lifted my gaze, then stepped closer, reaching for him before I stopped myself.

Gabe sucked in a sharp breath as my hands curled into his shirt. "Angel—"

I rose up on my feet, the warmth of his body against the coldness of mine was so entrancing.

I kissed him.

He froze against me, trapped between hesitation and hunger. But I needed this. Needed him to touch me, to make me feel different.

So I kissed him harder.

A low groan vibrated in Gabe's chest before his lips parted, giving in. His hands moved to cup my face, his touch so different from what I was used to. He kissed me like he'd been waiting forever.

I let him.

Let my fingers slide into his hair, let my body press against his, let his warmth seep into my frozen skin. His hands moved down, fingertips grazing my waist, hesitating. Like he was afraid to ruin me. Like he didn't already know I was beyond saving.

I shivered as his mouth trailed lower, brushing against my throat, soft and gentle—reverent.

"Angel," he murmured my name against my skin, like I was something precious.

Something worth loving.

His hands splayed across my hips, pulling me closer.

And suddenly—I couldn't breathe.

I froze.

The hands weren't his anymore. They were cold, rough, brutal.

A gun pressed to my lips.

You're owned.

That hateful voice whispered in my head.

NO!

I shoved him away so hard he stumbled.

"Angel, what—?"

I barely heard him.

Instead, I clawed at my own skin, raking my nails along my arms and lifted my hand, unleashing a blow against my cheek.

Slap!

Gabe's eyes widened, staring at me with a look of horror. Still, I couldn't stop the pain. It cut through me like a blade.

I couldn't breathe. I felt hands everywhere, too many hands, too many voices, too many fucking orders—

You are owned.

The words wrapped around my throat like a noose. I gasped, staggering backwards, my nails digging into my arms until the sting was all I felt.

Look at the screen, Angel.

That sick goddamn voice filled my head.

No. No, no, no.

I was back there.

In that same goddamn room at The Order.

Back in his hands.

My body wasn't mine.

It never had been.

"Angel?" Gabe sounded terrified now, stepping closer, reaching for me like he could somehow fix what'd been broken in me for years.

I recoiled.

"I'm poison," I choked out. "I ruin *everything*."

His expression cracked. There was a shake of his head. Still, those beautiful, sorrowful eyes held me transfixed and I knew I caused it.

I caused his pain and his torment.

If I could've only just died.

If I could've only had the strength to turn that gun on myself, then none of this would've happened.

I stepped backwards, my gaze moving to the door.

"Please, Angel. *Stay*."

I didn't let him finish. Instead I lunged for the door, yanked it open and stumbled out.

Darkness closed in around me. Cold, pressed in, leaving me shivering. I didn't know where I was going. All I knew was I needed out.

I sprinted down the hall, feet bare, breath ragged, head pounding with commands that weren't mine.

CONTROL.

SUBMISSION.

OWNED.

My vision blurred. My steps faltered. I wasn't in the house anymore.

I was at The Order.

Look at the screen. That vile voice whispered. *Look how fucking perfect you are when I fuck you.*

A cry ripped free as I ran, tearing around the corner. My body moved on its own. My mind screamed at me to go to my room, to lock myself away, but that wasn't the command I was following.

Instead, I stopped outside his door, watching the lights from inside spill under the door.

Silas.

He was the one I needed. The only one who could keep the beast inside my head at bay. The one who was even more savage than the monster who controlled my mind. Only this time...I wanted it.

I lifted my shaking hand.

But I didn't even have to knock.

The door swung open.

Silas stood there, still shirtless, the glow from his bedside lamp making shadows dance across the hard ridges of his stomach and the lines of his arms.

His dark hazel eyes devoured me.

I was a mess. Barefoot, breathless, still trembling. I wanted to run, but I knew I couldn't. Not from him. Not anymore.

His lips curled into a slow, victorious smirk.

I opened my mouth but only two words came out.

"Help me."

The smirk deepened as he stepped closer, gripping my chin, forcing my gaze to his. His fingers were warm, rough, possessive.

"I knew you'd come," he murmured, his voice thick with satisfaction.

His thumb skimmed my lower lip, slow and deliberate. Teasing.

My whole body went tight.

I hated how easily he pulled these reactions from me. How easily he controlled me. His thumb dragged lower, pressing against my pulse, feeling how wildly it beat for him.

I should've run.

I should've shoved him away, but instead I leaned in.

And Silas's smile deepened. Because he knew.

He had me.

And I wasn't going anywhere.

Chapter Twenty-Seven

THEO

THE BLARING SOUND OF A HEAVY BEAT THUNDERED IN THE side of my head, making me wince.

I didn't go home.

Even though I told myself I would, that I'd walk through the door and head straight to my room, and lock the world out. Instead, I found myself exactly where I always fucking ended up—somewhere dark, somewhere drowning in smoke and sweat, with a bottle in my hand and drugs crawling under my skin like goddamn ants.

The club was a haze of red and black, the music a pulsing throb inside my skull, loud enough to rattle my bones. Bodies moved around me, faceless, meaningless, women pressed against me, their hands trailing down my chest, over my belt. I barely felt them. I barely fucking saw them.

Because I only saw her.

My fucking sister.

Her name burned through me like acid, hot, destructive, corroding every rational thought I had left. She was in my head, under my skin, in my goddamn veins. Everything I did was about her, even when I was trying to get away from her.

Especially then.

I tugged out the small bag from the pocket of my trousers and pinched it open, pouring out enough to run along the back of my thumb before I lifted it to my nose.

Your cocaine is showing, Theo.

Her fucking voice resounded inside me. I inhaled sharply taking another hit, white power burned through my throat, numbing everything except the one thing I fucking needed— her.

I didn't want her. I fucking hated her. I hated her lies, her breath, the way she fucking existed.

And yet...she consumed me.

I was spiralling. Drowning.

The night spun sideways, colors bleeding at the edges, turning everything grey.

"Hey!" Someone yelled in my ear.

I turned my head, the ocean of people all around me nothing but a washed out haze. My pulse thundered, hard and erratic, thrumming through my skill like a war drum. The drugs were hitting harder than they should.

Fucking laced.

I knew it the second the last line burned through my system. Something else was in there, mixed with expensive cocaine.

Something that made the world too bright, too loud, too fucking surreal. My fingertips tingled, my skin burned, and my head felt like it was floating three feet above my body.

But I still felt her.

A hand on my chest, small but firm, pushing, steadying.

"*Whoa*, easy there, baby."

Her voice slithered over my skin like silk, soft and syrupy sweet, but it was fake—too fake. I blinked and tried to focus, her eyes and face nothing more than a haze. A mask, that's what she wore. One just like all the others. Warmth against my chest as she pressed against me. She smelled like cheap floral perfume and sweat, the scent clashing with the smoke and whiskey clinging to my clothes.

"You okay?" She ran her hands down my arms, her nails scraping just enough to feel deliberate. She was smiling—I could hear it in her voice, even if my vision was too fucked to focus on her face.

I blinked hard, trying to clear the static in my head, but everything lagged, the movement delayed, like I wasn't inside my own fucking body.

She took a step closer, pressing herself into me.

"Come on, let's get you to your car," she murmured, like she was doing me a favor. Like she was helping.

I let her.

I let her slide under my arm, let her guide me through the jostling bodies and between the tables to the darkness and the quiet. One hard shove and the cold, night air slammed into me.

Air so crisp it felt like I'd been under water this entire time. Maybe I was…maybe this was me drowning?

"Come on, baby," she crooned, pulling me with her.

I followed, my feet moving on their own as I stepped out of the club and into the night, my legs feeling like they weren't entirely mine. My head was a pressure cooker, the heat of the drugs pressing against the inside of my skull.

Bang.

I jerked hard with the sound of the door closing behind me. But her hands were there holding me in place as she dragged me deeper into the alley.

My vision tunneled.

I knew this game.

I knew this fucking game, and still I fucking walked into it.

Stupid fucking asshole!

"Just up here, baby," she drawled, pulling my attention toward her.

I tried to focus on her face, tried to gather the last few fucking cells inside my brain to try and keep me alive.

The alley was quiet, too quiet.

One stumble and my back hit the rough brick wall, before I could react shadows rushed toward me. Then came their hands.

Too many hands as they searched my pockets, yanking free my wallet.

"His keys," a man growled. "Don't forget his keys."

No.

I grabbed my pocket as the sound of tearing fabric came, clamping down on a hand inside it.

The first hit came fast. A fist to my ribs, hard and brutal, stealing my breath before I could even brace.

I grunted, my head snapping forward, body curling in reflex as pain splintered through my side. The fog cracked, the static buzzing in my head fading just enough to register what was happening.

A set up.

I lifted my head, the blur of the alley all too fucking real now. Two assholes stood in front of me. I winced, tried to breathe and scanned the alley. The girl was already gone.

Slap.

Something small hit the ground in the distance.

I caught a flash of her slipping past them, my cash in her hands, shoving it into her bra as she tucked the two remaining bags of cocaine in the pocket of her too-tight jeans.

Fucking bitch...

Movement came from the side, weight shifting, a fist cocked into the air. Still, I saw it far too goddamn late. His knuckles connected, sharp and heavy, snapping my head to the side. My body followed, slamming against the wall.

I unleashed a groan and spat blood, rolling my shoulders, my limbs feeling detached and foreign, like I was moving through someone else's body.

But the pain.

The goddamn pain was all mine.

My knees trembled, the hard wall was all that kept me upright. But even that wasn't enough at the end as my legs gave way underneath me. My palm dragged across the bricks as I slid down and hit the ground.

"Not so tough now, huh, pretty boy?"

Hard breaths came.

But so did something else.

Something that grew inside me

I lifted my head and smiled back at them. Blood-stained. Lethal.

And then I moved.

Fast.

I lunged forward, ducking with the next punch, my body reacting on pure instinct now, driving my hand down against the ground to push myself upwards.

One savage blow collided with his throat, right at the soft part above his collarbone. His eyes went wide as he choked, stumbling backwards, clawing at his neck.

You will be on your knees. Do you understand?

That fucking voice from the recording came back at me. And with came the sight of my fucking sister on her knees, looking up at him...or was she looking up at me?

"Fuck you!" I roared and made for the second guy.

I didn't give lying a chance to run, driving my body forward and dropped my shoulder. Muscles coiled and trembled along my body as I slammed into him, driving him against that brick wall.

"Hey!" The bitch from the nightclub screamed. "You're *hurting* him!"

I didn't stop as I wrenched my arms backwards and drove it into his stomach, watching the bastard double over. Hard, retching sounds followed as I swung again, this time connecting with his face.

Crunch.

Blood came...and so did the shadows as his buddy stumbled forward. I swung around and rushed forward, driving my elbow into his face, and felt the cartilage snap under my weight. He let out a strangled yell, clutching his nose and stumbled backwards, but I wasn't done.

I grabbed the back of his head and yanked down as I bought my knee up.

Bone met bone.

His body went limp before he even hit the ground.

The other guy was still coughing behind me as I turned around and set my sights on his once more. Somewhere in the alleyway that bitch screamed. But I didn't care about her now as I advanced slowly, then grabbed his collar and shoved him backwards, the back of his head slamming against the wall.

"You thought this was a good idea?" My voice was low, slurred at the edges, but my grip was steady as steel.

He gagged, clawing at my arm.

I tightened my grip.

"You ever steal from me again, I'll rip out your *fucking* throat."

His eyes bulged.

I shoved harder. "Do you hear me?"

He nodded, his eyes glassy with tears.

"My keys." I demanded.

"H-here." The bitch from the club stammered.

I jerked my gaze toward her, watching her advance with what was left of my wallet and my keys in her hand.

I let go of the asshole, watching in the corner of my eye as he dropped like a fucking ragdoll, gasping, clutching at his throat.

I stepped over him, spitting onto the pavement before rolling my shoulders, flexing my bruised knuckles.

Pain.

Good.

I fucking needed it.

I snatched my belongings from her, glaring at the greedy fucking whore as I walked past her and headed for the street.

My body was shaking by the time I slid into the driver's seat and yanked the door closed behind me.

It was late...really fucking late.

I blinked and leaned forward, holding my ribs and started the engine. Headlights blinded me as I pulled the car cut onto the street. The drive home nothing more than a neon blur. A red, pulsing haze of blood and rage and drugs.

You will be on your knees. Do you understand?

I couldn't get that fucking video out of my head even as I pulled into my street and headed for the driveway. A blur of movement came before headlights blinded me. Gabe's Jeep Wrangler shot forward, barely missing me as he took off out of the driveway. I unleashed something unholy and wrenched the wheel to the side, narrowly missing him. My brother's face was barely human, filled with rage before he was gone, leaving me pulling up in the parking space he left behind.

I barely remembered getting through the door, but I was there, shoving it closed behind me, pressing my back against it as I forced myself to breathe.

The house was too fucking quiet.

Too still.

I felt it before I saw it.

Her presence.

Angelica.

A shift in the air, a pull in my gut—like she was tethered to me, and I was too far fucking gone to fight it anymore.

I didn't even think about it.

I moved.

The hallway was dark, every creak ten times louder than it should be. A moan drifted out from my brother's room. Soft, desperate.

"You're so fucking desperate, aren't you, little sister?"

I froze standing outside his door, then I moved. My ribs no longer hurt. Nothing hurt because I couldn't feel my body at all.

I slowly turned the handle of my brother's door, breathing through the chaos inside me, through the drugs and the violence and the fucking aching need that wouldn't die.

I pushed it open.

And stepped inside, finding my brother standing in the middle of the room with our sister in his arms dressed in nothing more than her pretty fucking lace underwear.

He said nothing, unaware I was even in the room as he wrenched her hair backwards, extending her throat.

Her body stiffened, breath catching but it wasn't because of him. Her gaze fixed on me. Her eyes wide, too dark, reflecting the glow of moonlight through the curtains of my brother's room.

Fear.

Not full-blown panic—not yet—but close enough.

I stepped closer.

My brother felt me now. But he didn't turn around. Instead he let me come closer, flanking his side until I reached out, sliding my fingers through her hair and Silas let her go.

I didn't know what I wanted.

Not really.

But I needed to see her.

Needed to remind myself that I could have her if I wanted.

Even bleeding. Even high. Even when she cowered at the sight of me and tried to pull away.

I still fucking owned her.

A slow, crooked smile curled at my lips.

"Did you miss me, Angel?"

She shivered.

And fuck, that felt better than the drugs.

Silas leaned back, those dark eyes fixed on mine. "Took you long enough, brother."

I sucked in heavy breaths.

"I think our sister here needs a lesson on what happens when you try to leave our family, don't you?"

I jerked my gaze to his. She ran from him? No wonder he looked unhinged. I looked back at her. "You fucking ran from us?"

Mine.

That word resounded inside me, snatching away that desperate need. The drugs weren't helping anymore. Only the rage was there, smouldering, growing, becoming something monstrous and alive.

Angelica exhaled slowly, watching me, her wide, dark eyes reflecting the low light.

Not afraid.

Not defiant.

Just...*waiting.*

Waiting for me to lose it.

Waiting for me to hurt her the way she wanted to be hurt.

I clenched my fist and dragged her closer, forcing her to stumble out of my brother's arms and slam against my chest.

I looked down at her, at the woman I tried so fucking hard to hate. Her lips parted, a shallow breath hitching in her throat, and that single sound sent a bolt of pure hunger and rage crashing through me.

Silas didn't move.

Just watched as I leaned down and slammed my mouth on hers. I kissed her hard, making her spine bow under my need. My other hand went to her throat, grasping her jaw to hold her in place.

She wasn't going anywhere.

Not now.

Not ever.

I lifted my head, breaking the kiss.

She gasped, her lips red and bruising.

Still it wasn't enough.

"Get on the bed," Silas murmured.

Fuck.

My cock grew hard as I watched her stumble backwards, then drop down hard on the edge of the bed. Silas moved to her side, looking down and trailed his fingers lightly along her arm. Something about that made the fury inside me snap.

I reached forward, gripping her chin, the red marks of my fingers still there. "Do you even know what you fucking are?" I hissed.

Her lashes fluttered. "I—"

"You're *ours*." I tightened my grip, drinking in the way she trembled. "You belong to *us*."

Silas exhaled beside me, a quiet chuckle under his breath.

I ignored him.

Because she was looking at me the way I'd imagined a thousand times.

Broken. Desperate.

And knowing this was inevitable.

She wasn't running.

Not anymore.

I moved before I could think, lunging forward to drive her backwards on the bed. I was on top of her in an instant, her small body crushing the bedding under me. I leaned in, my mouth brushing her ear. "Tell me you don't want this, Angelica."

I waited.

She didn't say a word.

I pulled back, watching her face, watching the battle, and the slow agonising fall as she lost whatever was left of herself.

Silas moved around me, climbing up onto the bed, his palm sliding under her neck to turn her head toward him. A reminder. A claim.

Angelica shuddered between us.

Her hands clenched into fists.

And still, she didn't stop us.

Because there was nothing to stop.

I turned her face toward me again, leaning forward to brush my lips against her neck—not a kiss, just a breath, a whisper of what was about to come.

"You're ours," I murmured again.

And this time, she didn't deny it.

Chapter Twenty-Eight

ANGELICA

They were going to destroy me.

I knew it the moment I stepped into Silas's room, the air thick with something predatory, suffocating. My pulse hammered, that ache between my legs twisting into something darker, something I shouldn't want.

But I did.

God help me, I did.

Silas sat against the headboard waiting, watching. He always watched. Eyes like a hunter's, calculating, knowing. A touch came at my back, a heavy hand slid along my spine, dragging my panties over my hips. Behind me, Theo, all violence and hunger, those wide, pin-prick drug-soaked pupils pinned on me.

I was trapped between them.

I swallowed hard, forcing myself to think and feel the graze of those fingers. I still had a way out. One that made my pulse race. One I tried to fight, but I knew I couldn't anymore.

I still had... *sex.*

It was the only thing I had left.

If I gave them what they wanted, if I made them need me, crave me, maybe—maybe I could twist this to my advantage. The thought barely formed in my head before that voice slithered in.

Good girl, Angelica. Now you have them.

My stomach turned.

Not now.

Not him.

But that monster's voice from the Order had already sunk its claws into my brain, wrapping around my thoughts, whispering like poison.

That's right. You were made for this.

No.

Use it.

NO.

Silas leaned forward, dragging a lazy hand down his chest, his muscles tense, his smirk knowing. "You're thinking too much, Angel."

Theo's breath ghosted over the back of my neck. "She's always thinking. Always calculating. She's a liar after all, isn't she? A goddamn beautiful liar."

His fingers gripped my hair, yanking me back, exposing my throat. I let out a sharp gasp, but not from fear. Because my body—traitorous, filthy broken—responded to it.

Theo's chuckle was dark, knowing. "See? She likes it."

Silas's smirk deepened. "Of course she does."

They were toying with me. Playing with their prey.

But I was playing too, wasn't I?

I was destroying them more than they realised, picking apart the seams of this family until there is nothing but utter devastation left behind.

But I could use this.

I had to.

"Last chance, little liar." Silas murmured, his dark eyes sparkling. "You want out, wanna run again?"

Theo's fingers curled around the strands of my hair. I let him manhandle me, allowing my lips to part and an inhuman sound escape my chest. One that sounded like surrender.

"I thought so," Silas gripped my throat, driving my chin upwards until the tendons in my neck stretched taut. "You are a liar, Angelica. A cruel, fucking, beautiful liar."

My breath hitched. Something twisted in my chest, something dangerous.

He knew.

Not just about this. Not just about my games, my tricks, my body.

He knew what I was hiding.

The flash of memory hit me like a gunshot.

BOOM.

There was a gun in my hand and my father's blood on my skin, my mother screaming, no, not screaming—begging me.

NOOOO! What have you done, Angel? WHAT HAVE YOU DONE?

But then a flicker moved through my head and instead of the mother I loved in front of me, there was nothing but red and silence.

I shuddered, bile rising in my throat.

Theo felt it.

His grip tightened in my hair, yanking me back to him. "What was that, Angel?" His voice was too low, too knowing.

I shook my head.

Nothing.

I couldn't think about that.

Not now.

Not ever.

Silas slid his hand from my throat to knead the muscles of my thighs, not touching where I needed him to, just teasing, tormenting, making my body burn for him.

For them.

I hated them for it.

But I hated myself more.

"Tell us what you were thinking just now," Silas murmured.

I clenched my jaw, willing my body to stay still, to fight, to not break apart for them. But Theo yanked me back against his chest, his hand sliding around my throat, his teeth grazing my ear.

"Lying little bitch," he murmured, and I shivered.

Silas's fingers brushed higher, slipping between my thighs. I gasped, body jerking, betraying me.

He exhaled a mocking laugh, his fingers moving slowly, deliberately down the crease of my pussy, just enough to make my body tremble.

"I could make you beg, Angel."

Theo's grip tightened, his other hand trailing down my stomach as he moved forward, making me arch as he watched his brother's fingers trail up and down my crease. "She'll never admit it."

Silas hummed, his fingers ghosting lower, just enough to feel how wet I was for them.

Shame curled through me.

They knew.

They knew I wanted it.

They also knew I couldn't stop.

His fingers curled, driving deeper into my crease until my pussy clenched and my panties came away soaked. A shiver coursed through me as Theo's heavy breath came in my ear, watching what his brother was doing.

Silas's smirk sharpened. "Maybe she doesn't need to say it."

Theo's chuckle wasn't kind. "Then let's hear it another way." He shoved me forward onto the bed.

I gasped, hands clutching the sheets, but before I could even try to move Silas grabbed my wrist, yanking me into his lap. His thighs caged me, his chest, solid against mine, his hand curling around my throat.

A dark, wicked smirk.

"There you go," he murmured, his fingers flexing. "That's better."

I whimpered, shame burning my skin because my hips had already moved, driving his knee between my thighs. Silas's grip tightened just enough to make my pulse hammer.

Theo moved behind me, his hands hot, rough, yanking my bra strap down before he unhooked it from the back. Cool air kissed my bare skin and my nipples tightened.

I should have fought.

But I was too far gone.

Too consumed.

Theo's lip brushed my shoulder, his voice a low rasp. "Tell me you don't want this."

That monster's voice slithered into my head.

Good girl, Angelica. Just like you've been trained.

My throat closed.

My skin prickled.

Theo sank his teeth into my shoulder and I let out a choked moan.

"Fuck you sound good like that," Silas grunted, gripping my hips and yanking me upwards, until I rode his thigh.

Heat rushed through me, pooling in the base of my belly and flooded my core.

You have them now. That dark, demented urgency whispered. *I'm so proud of you, so very goddamn proud.*

"Her panties," Silas grunted. "They need to be gone."

Theo's warm blast of breath came at the side of my neck. "I never thought you'd ask."

Rough hands gripped the side of my panties. One hard yank and the lace fabric tore on one side, leaving the other to bite into my skin. The flimsy barrier between my body and Silas's was gone in an instant, leaving skin against skin.

Silas leaned closer, sliding his hands along my back, pulling me closer and dropped his mouth to my breast.

Theo grasped my ass, his cruel fingers probing, pushing along my crease until he hit my entrance.

"You feel that, Angel?" Theo grunted, his finger pushing inside. "This is us fucking owning you."

Owned.

Submission.

Control.

My body responded in ways that wasn't me, softening for Theo's probing fingers at the same time my nipples tightened in

Silas's mouth. Both men sucked and thrust, making me shudder.

"Fuck you feel good for a liar," Theo grunted.

Silas's teeth grazed my sensitive skin. Heat and hunger melding into a wet demanding pull that sent electric pulses straight to my core. One hard flick of his tongue came, teasing my sensitive bud before he sucked harder, drawing it deep, the pressure sharp and intoxicating.

Open yourself. Let them in.

I slammed my eyes closed, my spine arching. The scrape of Silas's teeth sending a violent shudder through me, pain and pleasure crashing in waves as he bit down, holding me there, his breath scalding against the wet sheen he left behind.

Your body is not yours. It belongs to them.

That voice murmured in the back of my head as Silas' lapped at my hardened peak, forcing me to look down. He swirled his tongue around my reddened stiff bud before sealing his lips tight and sucking with a force that stole my breath. Every pull was a claim, every flick of his tongue a silent demand for surrender.

The suction was relentless, a steady rhythm of pressure and release that sent need clawing through my veins. My nipples ached, swollen and raw, every tug a cruel, exquisite torment that left me gasping, my body bowing for more.

His gaze came up, rough fingers pinching the other nipple in perfect sync with his mouth, twisting just as he sucked, sending shockwaves of sensation through me, straight to the molten heat pooling between my thighs. *Oh, God.* I couldn't stand it and yet...I wanted more.

When he pulled away, my nipple was flushed and wet, glistening from his mouth, a raw aching point of sensitivity that throbbed in the wake of his teeth and tongue.

A moan ripped from the back of my throat as the panicked thoughts of escaping rose.

You don't need to run. That voice inside my head whispered. *You need to be used. You feel it, don't you? The truth? The truth of what you did to them...and what they want to do to you.*

Silas lifted his head, his dark eyes glinting as they met mine. I'd never seen such visceral hunger in a man before. But I saw it now...in my brother's stare.

Theo's fingers pressed harder against that tight ring of muscle, a slow, teasing pressure that made my body tense, breath locking in the back of my throat. That first push was agonising, stretching, a dark, forbidden invasion that had my nails biting into my palms.

"Relax," Theo murmured, his voice thick with hunger, but there was nothing gentle about the way he forced his finger in deeper, shoving past the resistance, stretching me wide. The burning licked up my spine, sharp and searing, pain twisted so deeply with pleasure I couldn't tell where one ended and the other began.

But he didn't give me time to adjust. His fingers drove in, deep and punishing, curling inside me, pressing against nerves I wasn't aware existed. A sob tore from my lips, still my body clenched around him, traitorous in its response.

He spread his fingers, pulling me apart from the inside, making me feel the full force of his possession. A slow thrust, then another, each movement claiming more of me, forcing my body to yield, to accept.

"Look at you," he grunted, dragging his teeth over my shoulder as his fingers twisted inside me. "Taking me so well. Just like you were made for it."

That's my girl. That hunger whispered. *They own you now. Just like I did.*

I felt every thick inch of him as he fucked me open with his fingers, pushing deeper, adding a third, stretching me even wider, until the pleasure turned brutal, unbearable.

My body betrayed me completely, hips rolling back, seeking more, the shame of my open need choking as my brother took me apart piece by piece.

The room breathed with heat. It wrapped around me, thick, oppressive, drowning out everything but them. Their scent. Their hands. Their mouths.

I couldn't think, couldn't breathe past the weight of Silas in front of me, Theo behind me.

I had nowhere to run.

And they knew it.

I twisted away, my lips trembling as I whispered. *"Please."*

Silas moved instantly. His fingers bit into my jaw, forcing my head up as his breath ghosted against my cheek. Rough, possessive, hungry.

"Please?" He growled. "Please what, Angel? Please let you go... please fuck you? You want to tell us the truth now? How about start with you telling us how much you hate us? Go on," his fingers clenched harder, driving the soft flesh of my cheek against my teeth. "Say you hate us."

Tears sprang to my eyes.

I wanted to.

I tried to.

But the words died on my tongue as Theo's finger pushed deeper into my ass, and he slid a finger of his other hand between my thighs, fingers gliding over slick heat.

"You can't run from this," Theo whispered, dark and cruel, his teeth grazing my pulse as his fingers slid lower, teasing my slick heat, his touch too slow, too precise—as if he was waiting for me to break.

"You still think you can keep lying to us?" Theo murmured, his voice laced with cruelty. "We know you, Angel. We see you."

I clenched my eyes shut as my body responded, heat licked deeper making me squirm.

"You wanted to run?" He whispered, his expert fingers dragging every shudder from between my thighs. "And yet—"

His fingers curled inside me, pressing deep, and my back arched in response.

"You let us catch you."

A mocking smile played on Silas's lips. His fingers eased, releasing their cruel hold.

"You didn't run, Angel," Silas's dark eyes glinted. "You came straight back."

Theo stroked...and stroked...and stroked. My thighs parted wider, hips rocking helplessly against his hand.

I hated them.

Hated them so much.

And yet I bit my lip and dropped my head, that desperate need climbing inside me.

Silas unleashed a groan, his hands sliding to my waist, rocking me as Theo's fingers drove inside.

"*This* is what she wanted," Theo's voice was husky and raw, dragging out his fingers only to drive them in deep again. "She just needed *us* to take it."

I clenched my eyes shut, that desperate urgency begging me to stop, to run...to do anything.

But I couldn't.

Because they knew...

How to break me.

Good girl, Angelica.

That voice whispered.

Now let go.

I opened my eyes and lifted my head. It was someone else who commanded me, taking control as I plunged deep into the depths of Silas's harrowing stare. A flicker of carnal desperation ignited in the depths before he moved, slamming his mouth against mine.

He kissed with the kind of passion I'd never known, hungry

and desperate. I opened my mouth for him, letting him take more as his brother took me higher and higher.

I felt burned alive between them, my skin flushed, my pulse hammering, my mind spiraling into a suffocating haze of control, heat, surrender as Theo pulled away. The slide of fabric against skin came before the slow slide of a zipper.

"Can't fucking stand it," Theo growled. "I'm not waiting."

Silas's mouth broke away, leaving my lips hot and slick as the bed dipped harder behind me and Theo's warm chest pressed against my back. His cock pressing against my inner thigh, hard, relentless, and Silas wasn't any better, his body coiled like a predator on the edge of losing himself.

I pushed back against Theo, my ass driving against his thigh as his cock rubbed me. I was a ticking time bomb.

And so were they.

"Tell us," Silas moved against me, his warm chest wedging me against his brother. "Tell us what you are."

I whimpered, desperate, the words clawing up my throat, a plea and a confession tangled on my tongue.

I tried to hold it in as Theo's cock slipped along my crease, the thick head searching for a way in.

God I wanted him.

I wanted both of them more than I'd ever wanted anyone in my life.

Silas looked down, parting my thighs with his strong hands, looking down as Theo teased, pushing in just enough to stretch me before pulling out.

"Tell us," my older brother demanded, lifting those incensed eyes to mine. "Tell us who you belong to."

"You," I gasped as Theo slipped back out, then plunged in.

I bucked with the invasion, my thighs slamming wider.

"I'm *all* yours."

Silas's growl was feral as he gripped my hips, driving my body down hard on his brother.

Theo cursed under his breath.

And I knew—I'd lost everything.

Now you belong to them, that voice whispered.

"Fuck," Theo grunted driving in harder. "I'm not going to last here."

"That's fine," Silas murmured, dropping his hand to the button of his jeans. "I'll do what needs to be done."

The slide of metal on metal came before Silas slid back off his bed, kicking his shoes off and pushed down his jeans.

Theo growled, his big hand on the middle of my back pushed me low. My ass was exposed for him, my pussy quivering and desperate as he thrust harder, slamming inside me over and over until with a hard grunt he stilled, deep inside me.

Warmth spilled.

My breaths were hard and hot, my chest heaving.

But Silas was there, grabbing me around my hips and pulled me free. The room blurred around me as I was spun around and pushed back against the soft bedding.

Silas was on top of me before I knew. Strong hands slid along my arms to capture my wrists. He rose above me, blocking out the glare of the overhead lights.

I whimpered, my body caught in an impossible war of terror and desire.

"You're ours, remember?" Silas growled, his cock pushing between my thighs, his eyes blazing with possession and something darker.

"Take her for fucks sake," Theo growled.

But as I stared into Silas's eyes I knew this was more than a fuck for him. He eased his body down against me, those thick thighs parting mine as his hands clenched around mine.

"Ours," Silas breathed and slid inside me.

This had nothing to do with possession.

This was a claiming on the deepest levels.

Look at you, giving in so perfectly. That whisper moved through me as Silas thrust deep. *You were never going to win, you get that right? You were always meant to be taken.*

"Mine," Silas growled, dropping his weight against me, his breath hot and heavy in my ear as he fucked me. "You get that, little sister? *You. Belong. To. Me.*"

Chapter Twenty-Nine

SILAS

SHE WAS STILL BENEATH ME, SKIN DAMP, BODY WRECKED from what Theo and I had done to her. I ran my fingers down the length of her spine, tracing the curve where I'd had my hands hours before, pressing her down, holding here there as we'd broken her completely. She trembled slightly, a phantom reaction, her body still lost somewhere using the space between ruin and surrender.

She belonged to us now.

No.

To me.

I knew it. Felt it. Deep inside, where logic should have ruled and instead, there was only hunger.

And that was the problem.

I wanted her again.

I hadn't even left the fucking bed, and my cock still ached for her.

Theo was gone, having had his fill, but I was still here. Still inside her world, still watching the slow rise and fall out her back as she lay against the sheets, her breath steady but shallow. She was spent, her body beyond used, but I knew—I fucking knew—if I touched her again, she'd take it. She'd let me. That mind control still lingered inside her, and while she thought she was fighting it, I knew better.

I curled a hand into the mess of her hair, tugging lightly, forcing her eyes open. She blinked at me, glassy and exhausted.

But I saw it.

That flicker of want.

"You're not fooling me, Angel." My voice was raw from using it too much, from growling in her ear, commanding her to break beneath me, watching her obey.

She shivered, pressing her thighs together as though she could hide the need still burning inside her. I smirked, foraging my fingers down to grip her chin, forcing her to look at me, to see the truth she was too afraid to admit.

She was still hungry for more.

"Stay in my bed," I murmured, brushing my thumb over her lower lip. "Be good. Be mine."

Her lips parted, her breath hitching, and for a moment, I thought she'd give in again. But then she swallowed, eyes flickering with something darker, something deeper, and that little spark of defiance burned its way back into place.

I fucking loved that about her.

And I'd love even more to break it. Again.

Bzzzt.

My phone vibrated, and I sighed, dragging my hand from her chin as I reached for the device on my nightstand.

Unknown number.

I sat up, tension tightening the back of my neck. My gut never ignored a call like this.

Angelica curled into the sheets behind me, her body nothing but warm temptation, but the second I answered, all of that burned away.

"Silas," a voice rasped. Kieran. The head of our security team. But his voice wasn't level—it was raw, panicked.

I tensed. "What?"

He exhaled hard through the receiver. Too hard. "You need to get here. Now."

I swing my legs off the bed. "Where?"

Silence, then—"Warehouse 14."

A sharp prickle ran down my spine. That was one of our primary sites, a location no one—not even the fucking cartel knew about.

"What happened?" I snapped, already moving, rising from the bed and grabbed my pants before yanking them on.

Another pause. Then Kieran muttered, voice grim, "We found Sloane."

My fingers froze at my zipper. I didn't need to ask if he was alive. I already knew.

Angelica sat up behind me, her voice hoarse. "What's wrong?"

I shot her a glare, but she didn't flinch. Not anymore.

I grabbed my shirt, yanking it on before I gritted out, "Stay here."

I didn't wait for her answer, already striding to the door...and was gone.

The cold night bit into my skin as I stepped out of the house, leaving behind the scent of sex, sweat, and my sister. The weight of what I'd just done—what we'd done—settled in my bones like a vice grip.

She was under my skin now.

There was no turning back.

But business never fucking waited.

My car waited in the driveway, the engine still warm from where I'd left it idling earlier, after Carter called me to get her. I slid inside, hands gripping the wheel, but my mind wasn't in the driver's seat—it was still inside that room, inside her.

With a low curse, I slammed my foot on the gas and reversed out of the driveway.

The city blurred past in streaks of dimly lit streets and neon reflections on wet pavement. The rain from earlier had dried, but the air still smelled damp—metallic, like iron. Like blood.

The warehouse wasn't far. It stood on the edge of the industrial district, tucked between abandoned factories and rusting cargo containers. A relic of the past—just like everything else in their world.

The weight of the Ares name had built a lot of this city. And now, it was it bleeding dry.

I pulled into the lot, the headlights slicing through the dark. Kieran's car was already there, parked at an angle, one door slightly ajar.

That wasn't right.

I killed the engine, my gut twisting with something close to dread. Kieran didn't leave his door open. Ever.

My boots hit the pavement with a dull thud as I stepped out. The air was thick with silence—wrong silence.

The kind that came before death.

I stalked forward, scanning the lot, my fingers twitching for my gun. Then I saw him. A shadow striding forward. My pulse thundered before he stepped out into the light and I exhaled a hard sigh of relief. Kieran headed toward me as my cell vibrated against my hip.

I pulled it free and stared at the screen. No caller ID. I lifted my gaze to Kieran. It wasn't him. I answered without a word, bringing the phone to my ear.

There was breathing on the other end. Slow. Deliberate. Measured.

Then a voice thick with Spanish and hoarse like rusted metal came. "Are you still feeling like a king, Silas Ares?"

I didn't blink. "Who the fuck is this?"

A chuckle, low and rasping. "You'll know soon enough. We left you something inside. A little gift."

A pause.

My pulse ticked like a bomb as the man exhaled. "And one for your girl. We'll see her soon."

Click.

The call went dead.

I was already moving before the sound cut off, striding past Kieran toward the shadows spilling across the single side door.

"What is it?" Kieran asked.

"Trouble." I answered and punched in the code on the locked pad outside the door and yanked it open.

The moment we stepped inside I knew something was wrong. The air was thick with the scent of oil and metal, but beneath it, something sharper lingered—coppery, pungent. Blood.

The warehouse loomed around us, its high metal rafters stretching into darkness. Expensive crates lined the floor, some marked with symbols of international luxury houses—Chanel, Patek Philippe, Rolls-Royce—art, antiques, high-end smuggled goods we used as a front to clean cartel money. On paper, this place was nothing more than an exclusive auction house, a place where the ultra-wealthy acquired the world's rarest treasures. In reality, it was a high-stakes pipeline for illegal goods and cash flow, a honey trap for those who needed to move money off the books.

Only now, something had ripped through the heart of it.

A shattered crate of Lalique crystal vases lay strewn across the concrete. A display table, once holding a sixteenth-century Venetian clock was overturned. The clock itself lay in pieces, its delicate gold-plated hands pointing nowhere.

"Kieran," I murmured, reaching around for the gun at my back. Someone was here...recently.

The second Kieran stepped ahead his body went rigid. "Fuck."

I rounded the side of a large shipping crate and stopped dead.

There, hanging from the steel beam above us, was Sloane.

Stripped to the waist, his arms were hooked behind him, wrists bound so tightly they cut into his skin. Blood—so much fucking blood—ran down his arms and chest, pooling onto the polished concrete below him.

They gutted him.

His abdomen was ripped open, a jagged canyon of flesh and ruin, his organs exposed—something raw and gaping in the harsh warehouse light. His head hung to the side, eyes glassy, mouth slack as if the last thing he tried to say had been stolen from him. There was a piece of paper stapled to his chest, the words smeared in his own blood.

I stepped close, ripping it free to read the crimson stained words.

A liar always bleeds. A traitor always dies.

Hand her over, or you'll all join him.

But underneath, lined red ink—one final sentence.

Angelica, we're coming.

My vision tunnelled. The room blurred into nothing but raw, pulsing fury. A scream ripped through the warehouse.

Not *mine.*

Kieran's gun was already swinging wide as shadows moved all around me and I caught the glint of steel far too late.

I barely had time to move, dodging the first swing—the knife missing my throat by inches, slicing through my jacket instead. Pain flared along my ribs, sharp and hot.

I caught the bastard's wrist before the knife could arc again, twisting my body and drove his own blade into the fucker's gut.

The man grunted, his breath turning wet.

I twisted the blade deeper, forcing it so far inside the glistening steel disappeared. Kieran grunted loud and brutal behind me, but I was transfixed by my attacker as his eyes went wide...wide enough to see the fear trapped inside.

Come for my fucking *FAMILY!*

Rage roared through my veins, humming louder than any thunderous pulse ever could. I twisted the knife deeper, then wrenched it free, spun and slammed the blade into the enforcer neck, pinning Kieran to the ground.

The asshole jerked upright, blood spurted from the gash the blade left behind before he gave a sickening gasp, choking on his own blood, then crumpled to the floor.

But it wasn't over.

A third attacker emerged from the dark with a machete raised high in his hand. I saw it far too late, the hatchet arced down, carving through the air before it bit deep into my shoulder, slicing through flesh and muscle. The pain was instant— blinding, electrifying.

He staggered, but his grip tightened around his own weapon. I lunged, ignoring the fire in my shoulder. The asshole grinned

—until I smashed the hilt of the blade into my hand into his face.

Bone cracked.

But I didn't stop, driving my attacker back against a crate, my fist colliding with his skull over...and over again.

A gurgled scream—then silence, before he slowly crumbled to the ground, his back sliding down the wooden pallet.

A gurgled scream followed—then silence.

I stood over him, my chest heaving, the warehouse spinning around me as I took in the fetid scent of blood and betrayal. Then a wounded sound, low...desperate.

I spun finding Kieran on the ground, barely conscious, blood soaking through his clothes.

Fuck.

My feet moved too slow, stumbling forward, before I dropped to the ground, grabbing Kieran's collar and dragged him up. "We're getting the fuck out of here."

By the time I shoved Kieran into the passenger's seat of my car, the world was tilting. Blood soaked through my shirt and dripped from my busted lip and the deep gash of my shoulder.

But it was Kieran I worried about. His breathing was shallow. His fingers twitched, as if trying to move. I reached into my pocket as I slammed the passenger's door closed and stumbled around the front of the car, all but falling into the driver's seat, pulling out my phone with blood-slicked fingers, then dialled a number.

No hospitals.

No fucking outsiders.

A voice answered, low and sharp. "Talk."

My grip tightened. "I need a clean fix. Fast. No questions."

Silence.

Then.

"How bad?"

I glanced at Kieran. His shirt was soaked through, his skin deathly pale. "Dying, but not dead yet."

Another pause. Then, "Same place as last time. Thirty minutes."

Click.

The call ended, leaving me to slump back against the seat, then press my hand against my bleeding shoulder, my eyes fixed on the warehouse straight ahead.

Fucking cartel.

They think I'm going to give her up?

I reached out, grasping the wheel before I stabbed the button for the engine...they thought wrong. My fingers tightened around the wheel, knuckles white, veins throbbing.

They'd learn who the fuck they were dealing with.

They'd fucking learn.

I took a sharp turn, my hold tight on the wheel despite the slick of blood that coated my hand. Kieran was dying next to me. I wasn't fucking losing him—not like this.

So I pushed the car harder taking the unmarked path deeper into the industrial outskirts of the city. The kind of place where bodies went to disappear—or, in Kieran's case, to be saved in silence.

I glanced at the slumped body in the passenger's seat and clenched my jaw, turning my focus back to the rundown auto shop looming up ahead. A single light flickered above the back entrance as I pulled hard into the space and laid on the horn twice.

A second later the back door cracked open. A lean man stepped out, his gray hoodie pulled low, cigarette dangling from his lips as he headed my way.

I shoved the car into park, killed the engine and climbed out. The headlights bounced against the dented roller door as I rounded the front of the car.

"Jesus Christ." The man exhaled smoke, eyes dropping to Kieran's limp form as I yanked open the passenger's door. "You look like hell."

"He's the one I'm here for." My voice was raw, my patience razor-thin.

The man, Dr. Alexi Novak, wasn't a real doctor—not anymore. His medical licence was stripped away years before for 'unethical procedures.'

Procedures I didn't ask about. When I called in the middle of the night, nor did he.

Novak flicked his cigarette away. "Bring him inside."

I barely managed to drag Kieran out of the car, his body a dead weight. Novak grabbed his other side, hauling him toward the dimly lit interior through the open door.

There was only silence from the man I'd known for the last ten years as we dragged him inside and toward a dented metal table stained with things I didn't care to identify sitting in the middle of the room.

We laid Kieran down and the Russian set to work, tearing Kieran's shirt open to gauge his wounds.

"He's lost too much blood." He snapped on latex gloves and ripped open a bag of IV fluids. "I'll stabilize him. You, on the other hand—"

"I'm fine," my words slurred as the room slowly tilted.

I stumbled backwards, slamming my hand on whatever I could find to stop from falling.

Novak arched a brow as he jerked that piercing glare my way. "You faint on me and I'm putting you on the table next to him."

That was the last thing I wanted.

One hard nod and I ground my jaw, holding onto whatever I had inside me...and it was her face I found.

Those big fucking eyes fixed on mine as she lay underneath me. The liar I called sister.

Novak worked fast, puncturing, squeezing, finally cleaning and stitching while he checked Kieran's pulse.

Finally he murmured. "He's here, barely, but he's here."

I swallowed hard, Angelica still raging inside my head...as well as the note impaled on Sloane's body in the warehouse.

Hand her over, or you'll all join him.

"Do you have this?" I croaked, my weak pulse growing louder.

"I got him."

I glanced once more at the pale body on the table and turned away. I had somewhere to be...someone to protect.

That need roared inside me as I stumbled from the auto shop and headed for my car once more. They were coming for my family.

No.

They were coming for her.

Bleeding or not, there was no way in hell anyone would touch her.

Not unless it was one of us.

I climbed back behind the wheel, started the car and punched the accelerator, spinning the wheels hard and headed for home.

Chapter Thirty

ANGELICA

Sleep came for me, leaving me to drift untethered in the darkness.

But when I woke, I woke alone.

The sheets were cold, the space beside me empty, but the scent of him still clung to the pillows, to the air, to me.

For a moment I lay there, disoriented, the silence pressing in from all sides.

Something felt wrong.

Off.

I could still feel him, the weight of his hands on my hips, the heat of his breath against my throat, the bruises he'd left in his wake.

But he was gone.

And I felt it.

A slow, curling unease slithered beneath my skin.

I sat up, pressing a hand against my chest, my pulse steady, but too sharp, too aware.

I didn't know where he was.

How long ago did he leave?

The emptiness should've been a relief. But it wasn't. Because without him—without the weight of them, the possessive press of their bodies around me—I felt...hollow.

Like something inside me had been carved out and left to ache.

I shifted, wincing at the soreness between my thighs, at the deep, bone-deep throb still pulsing through my body.

It was a good ache.

A delicious, bruising, possessive ache.

And that alone should've terrified me.

Something inside me had changed. I could feel it in my bones, in my blood. I wasn't the same woman who had fought them, who had tried to hold onto some version of herself they hadn't corrupted, claimed, used.

No.

Something inside me had snapped.

Cracked wide open.

And I wasn't sure if I wanted to put myself back together again.

I dragged in a breath, slow, unsteady.

The house was quiet.

Too quiet.

Like the silence itself was watching me.

Waiting.

Pressing.

I ran a trembling hand through my hair, exhaling softly and licked my dry lips, trying to work the moisture into the back of my throat.

I needed water.

Needed to get out of this bed, out of this feeling, out of the haunting weight of absence. I laid my legs over the edge of the mattress, my underwear lying discarded on the floor. I picked up my panties and slid them on before slowly rising and saw Silas's t-shirt tossed over the back of his chair.

My legs trembled, each step growing bolder before I grabbed the garment and pulled it on, ignoring the way the soft cotton brushed over my tender nipples. Still it did little to ease the discomfort in knowing what had happened in this room, my face and my body said it all.

I didn't need a mirror to know I was wrecked.

I could feel it.

And I wanted more.

The house was too quiet. The kind of quiet that wasn't natural —one that settled into the walls, thick with something unspoken, unfinished.

I moved through the darkened hallway, my bare feet whispering against the hardwood. Every step felt heavier than the last, like the silence itself was pressing down on me.

I hadn't meant to pay attention. To the way Silas had changed when the phone rang. To the way his body had gone still as he listened to whoever was on the other end. To the way his voice had dropped into something dark, something unreadable, something that made the air feel too thin. He had barely looked at me when he hung up. Barely breathed before grabbing his shirt from the floor, dragging it over his shoulders.

Stay in my bed. His command still echoed inside me, his voice final, demanding.

Like I was something that could be commanded, placed, owned.

Like I was something he wasn't willing to leave unguarded. I told myself it didn't mean anything. That I knew exactly what kind of man Silas was and me thinking I was anything more than a toy for him to use and discard was only going to destroy me in the end.

The air was cool, but my skin still burned, still thrummed with the remnants of what had been done to me.

The hunger was still there.

Low and simmering.

I should be sated and repulsed, all at the same time.

But I wasn't.

I was desperate and thirsty.

I stepped into the kitchen, exhaling softly as I reached for a glass, filling it from the tap. The first sip did nothing. The second barely touched the fire still twisting inside me. I pressed the glass against my lips, closing my eyes, trying to will away the feeling. But it didn't work. Because I wasn't just thirsty. I was starving.

For them.

For this thing they had created inside me, the thing that no longer belonged to me. My fingers tightened around the glass, my pulse thudding against my ribs. I should go back to bed—my bed. And pretend this ache will go away on its own.

I should—

The prickle of awareness slid over my skin, slow and heavy, curling down my spine like smoke.

My breath caught.

I turned.

And there he was.

Jude.

He leaned against the doorway, arms crossed over his chest, watching me.

Waiting.

Something deep inside me twisted, sharp and hungry.

Because I knew.

This was never just about water.

This was about him.

About of *all* them.

And *me.*

The moment stretched out between us, thick and weighted, pulling tight like a thread about to snap.

Jude didn't move.

Didn't speak.

But his eyes—God, his eyes.

There was something cold in them. Not detached, not indifferent, but something darker. Restrained. Calculated.

Something that said he wanted to destroy me, and hated himself for it. I swallowed, my throat suddenly too dry, too tight.

He wasn't like Silas.

Wasn't like Theo.

They took me with fire and obsession, with greed and possession.

But Jude?

Jude was fighting himself, and that battle terrified me.

Because I could feel how close he was to losing.

And I wanted him too.

I wanted him to fall the way I had already fallen.

"Do you even know what you look like right now?" His voice was low, almost quiet, but there was an edge to it. A sharpness.

I wet my lips, heart hammering.

His jaw tightened. His nostrils flared.

"Do you?" He repeated, the question softer this time.

I didn't answer.

Because I already knew.

Bruised, swollen, still aching from Silas, from Theo, from the way they had taken me, used me, fucked me.

And I was still here, standing in front of him, wearing Silas's t-shirt of all things, my panties still damp from my own desire.

Still hungry.

Still wanting.

Still having that sickening need inside my head howling like an animal into the wind.

Still theirs for the taking.

Jude let out a slow, sharp breath. His fingers curled into fists, the muscles in his forearms flexing as he fought himself, fought me, fought this thing between us.

"Use it on me," he said suddenly.

My stomach clenched. "What?"

His eyes flashed. Something unhinged, something raw.

"Your power," he said. "*Use it.* Make me want you more."

A shiver slid down my spine.

He was playing with fire.

And so was I.

I let that hunger slip out, a whisper of something forbidden, curling through the space between us, brushing against him like an unseen touch.

Jude inhaled sharply, his pupils blown wide, his body reacting instantly as he searched my gaze. His breath came faster, his shoulders rising and falling, his entire frame wired tight with tension.

But he didn't move.

Not yet.

Not until I whispered—

"Touch me."

The second the words left my lips, his hand shot out, grabbing my waist, pulling me against him.

I gasped, the impact jarring, my body melting into his without resistance. His grip was too tight, fingers pressing into my hips, his breathing uneven, shaky, wrecked.

"Fuck," he muttered, like he'd just lost. A battle he'd spent years trying to win.

Then his fingers slid lower, moving between my legs. Those thick fingers plucked the elastic of my panties and slid under. I didn't need to think, just react. My foot shifted, legs widening as he pushed into the flesh that was already swollen and tender.

I trembled, my body betraying me, opening for him, ready for him.

Jude let out a sharp, ragged breath.

"You're already wet for me," he murmured, almost like he hated it. Almost like it ruined him to know it. "Or are you thinking about my brothers instead?"

A tremble coursed through me. Heat flashed, twisting into something painful in its desperation.

Because I wanted to be ruined by him.

I wanted him to hate this.

Hate me.

And still give in anyway.

His fingers teased, brushed, dipping in and out of my body in slow, measured strokes.

My head fell back, a soft, broken moan spilling from my lips.

And Jude—Jude clenched his jaw so hard I thought it might break. Shadows carved lines down his strong jaw. He was so savage in this moment...so utterly savage.

"You're so fucking desperate," he murmured, almost to himself. "Still aching from them. And yet—"

His fingers pushed deeper, curling until I saw stars. Until a sob wrenched free. Jude reacted like I'd struck him, like the wrenched sound that came from me physically hurt him.

His grip on my hips tightened, hard, almost punishing.

I couldn't breathe.

I didn't want to.

Not if it meant he'd stop.

I rocked my hips forward, driving against his hand, trying to push him deeper, seeking more. But his hold tightened, forcing me still.

Forcing me to take exactly what he wanted to give me. No more. No less.

It was torture.

And exquisite.

"You *love* this," he whispered, his voice hoarse, breaking, fingers still slow, teasing, taunting.

I bit my lip, a sharp, desperate sound slipping out.

Jude groaned, deep in his chest.

And then—his control snapped.

His fingers slammed into me, deeper, harder, his pace no longer measured, no longer restrained.

My body shattered, my back arching as that heat flooded me. I was so close...so goddamn close.

Jude watched me falling apart, his own breathing ragged, uneven, pupils glistening with hunger. But there was something else too, something breaking inside.

He was fighting a losing battle as his head inched down until his lips came close to mine. His breath was hot, heavy, a blast of panic and hunger all mingled into one.

"Tell me you want this," he rasped.

"Yes," I moaned. "I want this."

"Tell me you want me to take you the way they do."

My pussy clenched around the invasion of his fingers, my body screaming for release.

"Just like that," I moaned, my voice desperate.

Jude let out a low, wrenched curse, like my words finally shattered what was left of his resistance. His fingers moved faster, hitting deeper and I felt myself spiralling, teetering on the edge of falling away completely.

Stars sparked in the back of my eyes, glinting with the oblivion I craved.

And then. *"Enough!"*

Gabe's voice was a blade, sharp and deadly, cutting through the haze of desperation like a gunshot in the dark.

Jude's fingers slipped free, jerking the edge of my panties before the elastic snapped back in place. I caught the slow, calculated smirk as though he knew Gabe was going to walk in.

I gasped, body jerking, throbbing as my pussy clenched around the loss, so goddamn close to breaking and now—

Now I was aching all over again.

Left starving for something ripped away from me.

Anger raged inside me as I turned my head—

Gabe was no longer standing in the doorway. He was moving toward us.

Fast.

Before I could react, he grabbed Jude by the collar and yanked him back, hard and punishing.

In this moment Gabe was no longer the baby brother. He breathed raw, terrifying rage. His shirt stuck against his skin, the sheen of sweat still glistening across his brow as he stood there still dressed in the clothes he wore to the gym.

I hadn't heard him leave, but he must have. Now he was back and desperate for an outlet for his anger.

Jude let out a sharp grunt as his back hit the counter, but Gabe wasn't looking at him.

He was looking at me.

His breath was fast, too fast.

His fists were clenched at his sides, his entire body tense. I swore I could feel the heat rolling off him.

His eyes.

His maddening eyes.

Dark.

Wild.

Desperate.

And I knew.

He had seen everything.

His chest heaved, his pulse a visible, violent throb at his throat. Then—before I could move, before I could speak, his hand shot out.

I barely had time to react before his fingers curled around my waist, yanking me against him, too hard, too desperate, too much.

I let out a sharp, shocked breath, my body crashing into his, my hands flattening against his chest.

He didn't move.

Didn't breathe.

And neither did I.

The heat between us roared, electric and unstoppable, re-igniting the desire between us from hours earlier. But this was different now, no longer silent, no longer able to be ignored.

His grip tightened, his fingers digging into my skin like he was trying to anchor himself to something real. But didn't he know by now, I wasn't real?

I was whatever they wanted me to be.

A liar.

A betrayer.

Something to use.

Anyway they wanted.

And then—he released Jude and tilted my chin up, forcing me to look at him.

I blinked, my lips parting, my breath shaking and uneven as he released his hold. His thumb dragged across my bottom lip.

A soft, slow stoke.

Like he was going to taste me.

Like he was going to take me.

Then, his voice—low and breaking.

"You want to be used, don't you?"

A sharp pulse of need shot through me and centred between my legs. My lips trembled, but I didn't speak.

I didn't have to.

Gabe glanced at his brother and then back at me, looking at me, really looking at me. My dishevelled hair. Silas's t-shirt I wore, then he lowered his gaze to between my legs.

Then he let me go.

Fast.

Abrupt.

Like he'd just realised what he'd done.

Like I had burned him.

His chest rose and fell, his breathing still uneven as he took a step back, and then another.

"This doesn't happen." His voice was low, raw, dangerous. "Not with me."

I didn't move.

Didn't breathe.

Because something had shifted.

No, not shifted.

Snapped.

Gabe wasn't untouched anymore. I could see it now. See how he was falling. Just like the rest of them.

And it was only a matter of time before he stopped fighting.

Before he stopped fighting me.

And that sick, darkness inside me chuckled with enjoyment.

That's my Angel.

You're doing so well.

Exactly as we'd planned.

A shudder ripped through me. Icy. Terrifying. Uncontrollable.

Chapter Thirty-One

GABE

I still felt her.

Even now, standing outside in the cold, early morning air pressing against my skin, I still feel the way she burned against me.

The way she looked at me with those big, doe eyes screaming with desperation and those swollen lips, parted with the promise of a plea. The way she ached for me...the way she ached for more.

And I almost took it from her.

I raked a hand through my hair, my jaw tight, my pulse a slow, steady drumbeat of violence beneath my skin. Violence I almost turned on my brother.

Get a fucking grip here.

They're your family.

But she was my family too, wasn't she? And that was the issue. She was my family too and yet I didn't see her like that—no—I saw her as something more.

My phone vibrated against my leg. I reached into my pocket, pressing the button instinctively and lifting it to my ear. Only one person would be calling me at this time of the night.

Before I could speak, Silas's voice exploded through the speaker. "Where the *fuck* are they? Theo's not answering his phone, and neither is Jude!"

I exhaled slowly, but it did nothing to cool the fire that rose inside me. Because I knew exactly what Jude had been doing the last time I saw him...our goddamn sister.

I closed my eyes as the image of that returned. The echoed sound of her grunting as she came apart against his fingers, the way she'd begged—

I shoved the memory down violently. Now wasn't the time.

"I have no idea where Theo is, asleep I imagine. His car's still here, but Jude...you could say he's been preoccupied."

Silas let out a sharp, ragged breath, filled with rage and something darker underneath it. "The warehouse is gone. Fucking destroyed and so is Sloane. They fucking tortured him."

An icy chill swept through me. "And you're only just calling?" A low, guttural sound came through the speaker. One filled with pain. "Silas? Are you hurt?"

"Nothing I can't handle, little brother," he moaned. "I'm heading back now. But you need to lock that house the fuck down. Call who you have to. I want every inch of that place under guard. They aren't done, Gabe. They aren't anywhere near fucking done."

That cold, realisation hit deeper. Because he wasn't done telling me everything.

"What else?" I demanded.

My eldest brother didn't answer right away. But it was the sound of his screeching tires and the sharp inhale through his nose. Then, finally, his voice came low, cold, and deadly. "They left us a fucking message."

I felt it then.

That slow, creeping sickness curling into my gut. "What kind of message?"

His voice was sharper this time. "Sloane's body hanging from the fucking rafters. Kieran and I walked right into an ambush."

My stomach dropped.

For a second, the world around me tilted, the words not making sense. I knew Sloane. He was one of our best guys...had been one of our best guys. Dad's right hand man, the only one he truly trusted. "Is he alive?"

Silence.

Too long.

Then—

"He's alive," Silas bit out. "For now at least."

Fuck.

The relief I should've felt never came. Because if they left Kieran and my brother alive, it sure as hell wasn't out of mercy.

"The note." I muttered. "What was it?"

"Fucking stabbed in the middle of his goddamn chest." Silas snarled, then there was a heartbeat of silence before— "They're coming for her. For our goddamn sister."

The world around me swayed. I lifted my gaze, scanning the shadows stretching out along the property, finding monsters when before there were none. "Coming for her, why?"

My brother didn't answer.

Not because he didn't want to.

But because he didn't need to.

We all knew. The lies trapped inside her head. The things she couldn't admit, even to herself. It was all there, every single lie she refused to admit...and every single desire that kept us tethered to her.

The moment I ended the call with Silas, a cold determination settled over me. The weight of our circumstances pressed heavily on my shoulders, but beneath it forbidden hunger gnawed at my resolve.

I dialed the head of our security team, my voice steady as it was answered on the second ring. "We have a situation unfolding here. We need a full lockdown protocol in place."

"Understood, sir," the slurred voice of Harley came through loud and clear.

I hung up the call, scanned the rustling trees at the edge of the property and turned, heading back inside.

"What the fuck?" Jude's voice drifted along the hall. "Silas, yeah...I just saw the messages. What's going—"

So now he wanted to be part of the family? I strode past him standing in the middle of the hallway with a stupid fucking look on his face and headed for Theo's room.

Movement came from the hallway of our rooms. She shifted like a shadow, her wide haunting eyes fixed on me. I could tell she'd been crying.

Fuck.

"Gabe?"

I winced at the sound of her voice, and kept on walking until I stopped at Theo's closed bedroom door, then shoved down the handle and barged in.

My brother lay sprawled across the bed, unconscious, his breathing deep and even. His phone lay discarded on the floor, the screen illuminated with multiple missed calls from Silas.

"Gabe, talk to me." Our sister's voice was barely above a whisper. "What's happening?"

My jaw tightened, no matter how hurt I was feeling, it needed to take a backseat—for now.

"Hey," I kicked the side of Theo's bed.

He responded with a heavy snore. That pissed me the fuck off. I strode closer, whipped my hand back and smacked him across the head. "I said, *hey!*"

Dark eyes cracked open, seething anger poured from between the slits. "Hit me like that again and you'll be eating through a straw for a fucking week."

"Oh yeah?" I grabbed a fist full of his hair and shoved his head to the side. "Don't answer your goddamn phone when our brother is fighting for his fucking life and you'll be the one eating through a goddamn straw."

He blinked, then pushed upwards, those dark eyes wider with the realisation. "What the fuck are you talking about?"

Then he looked down at his phone.

I saw the moment realisation hit. He scowled, reached out and snatched up his cell and stared at the missed calls from our brother.

"Don't bother calling back." I muttered and turned around. "I've already handled it."

Angelica stepped in front of me. The silence stretched between us, thick and suffocating. The air in Theo's room was stale, thick with sweat and sex, the weight of something unspoken that clawed its way to the surface.

I tore my gaze from her.

I had to.

Because seeing her like this—branded by my brothers—made something inside me twist too tight.

I forced a breath through my teeth and dragged a hand down my face.

"Someone wanna tell me what the fuck is going on?" Theo growled.

The slick sound of sheets shifted as he pulled himself upright.

"They hit the warehouse." Jude answered. "Sloane's... Sloane's—"

"Dead." I answered for him, staring at our sister. "Sloane is *dead* and our brother and Kieran were the *next* on the list."

"The goddamn cartel?" Theo stood, then stumbled forward.

Jude just stared at me. "That's what Silas is saying. But that's not all. There was a message...one left embedded in Sloane's chest."

"What fucking message?" Theo snarled.

There he was, the real brother. The one not buried under a mountain of cocaine and alcohol.

"Did you know?" The words slipped from my lips.

Her brow furrowed, confusion flared before panic set in.

I took a step closer, feeling the full weight of my brother's stares. "Did you...know?"

"Know what?" She whispered.

"That they were coming for you." I answered.

Silence.

A sharp, uneasy, deafening silence.

Angelica shook her head slowly. "No," she whispered. But something about the way she said it—too soft, too uncertain—made my stomach clench.

Theo stepped closer, glancing from me to her. "Jesus fucking Christ."

She shook her head, the confusion fading fast now, leaving only fear and terror behind. "I don't know what you're talking about."

I didn't believe her.

Neither did Theo.

Neither did Jude.

"Oh yeah?" Theo stepped closer, lashing out to grab the back of her neck and pulled her closer. "Maybe we don't believe you, little liar. Maybe we don't believe a goddamn word you say."

The sound of tires screeching against the gravel cut through the silence. It was barely a second later that headlights slashed across Theo's darkened window, white-hot and blinding, casting harsh, cutting shadows against the walls.

Silas.

He was home.

And if I thought the cartel was the biggest problem we had?

I was about to be very fucking wrong.

Chapter Thirty-Two

ANGELICA

Headlights cut through the dark like a knife. Dark shadows splashed across Theo's bedroom walls, but it was the haunted expression on Gabe's face that held me transfixed.

The second the engine was killed, the room fell into silence.

A thick, expectant kind of silence.

Silas was home.

And he knew.

The rear door of the house slammed open, the sound like a gunshot cracking through the air, rattling against the frame, shaking the walls, sending a ripple of tension through the house. Footsteps—heavy, deliberate, dragging.

Not slow, not cautious.

Angry.

The kind of rage that could level cities.

Theo exhaled sharply beside me, dragging a hand through his hair. Jude rocked back on his heels, rolling his shoulders like he was preparing for a fight.

And Gabe—

Gabe just looked at me like he'd already put something together that he wasn't ready to say out loud.

I turned away before I could see what was written on his face. Theo was the first to move, pushing past the rest of us and headed out of his room.

The others followed, leaving me behind. Panic set in, and that need to run surfaced once more. But I knew where that road led—right back to them.

Reluctantly I followed, my bare feet skimming the hardwood floors as I followed the sound of the others to the kitchen. The moment I stepped inside I felt him—even before I saw him.

But then I did and I couldn't move.

Silas stood beyond the doorframe, one shoulder braced against the wall, blood streaked down his arms and splattered across the base of his neck.

His breathing was shallow, controlled. Too controlled.

He looked at Theo first.

Not me.

Theo tensed. "Silas—"

But before he could finish, Silas was moving.

Too fast. Too unsteady.

He lunged, slamming Theo back against the wall, his forearm pining him in place.

"Where the *fuck* were you?" His voice was raw, torn open by something deeper than anger.

Theo winced, jaw tightening beneath the pressure. "I—"

"You weren't answering your phone," Silas's voice dropped into a snarl. "Did you even hear it? Or were you too busy fucking her?"

The last word hit like a slap.

Theo's fingers twitched at his sides. He didn't deny it. Instead his face turned red...which told me everything. He wasn't...but he wanted to.

Jude whistled low, shoving his hands into his pockets. "Well, that escalated."

Gabe cut him a savage glare.

Silas's breaths came out ragged, his body trembling from the effort of staying upright.

Theo clenched his teeth. "You don't—"

"I don't what?" Silas cut him off. "*Get* to be mad? *Get* to feel *this*." He slammed a fist into the middle of his chest, the *thud* sounding hard and heavy.

My own pulse skipped in response. What was he saying...that he was hurting at the idea of his brothers taking me? My mind raced trying to understand what that meant. But I didn't have time to explore that before Silas's weight faltered.

His knee buckled.

He caught himself before hitting the floor, but just barely.

A sick, cold feeling slid down my spine.

He was hurt.

Really hurt.

Theo made a move to grab him, to hold his brother steady as a look of anguish tore across his face. But that only incensed the rage in Silas. The fear and the thing he wouldn't say out loud.

His gaze flicked to me.

Dark, sharp. Wild.

And in them, I saw everything.

The things he wouldn't say.

The things he couldn't admit.

The way he wanted me.

And the way he hated that he did.

Silas shoved off Theo, stumbling slightly, but he didn't let himself fall. His hands clenched into fists. His breath left him in short, violent exhales.

"Do you have any idea," he rasped. "What they did to Sloane?"

Theo's expression tightened before he shook his head.

Silas's features twisted with pure rage. "They gutted him like a fucking animal!"

Theo winced.

Jude looked away.

But I was transfixed by the terror on Silas's face and the harrowing realisation that this could've been him. I swallowed hard—it could've been any of them.

I glanced to Gabe as agony ripped across my chest. It could've been him—Dear God, it could've been him.

"There was a note," Silas continued, his tone guttural and strained. "One stabbed into the middle of his chest."

"What note?" Theo muttered.

Silas' gaze found me. "They're coming...and they want her."

The entire room stilled. My breath caught. My brain misfired... her? Who? Then it hit me. Me.

Something cold and sick curled in my stomach.

"You already know," he took a step toward me. "Don't you?"

I shook my head. "I don't—"

"*Liar.*"

The word cracked across the room, hitting me like a slap. Jude's dark, cutting gaze settled on me, crawling under my skin.

Use it on me.

Jude's words still lingered in my head as Silas stalked toward me, like a wounded animal still looking for something to tear apart.

"You *always* fucking lie," he said quieter now, lower, rougher. His hand shot out as I dragged my fingers through my hair, grabbing my wrist.

Too tight.

Too desperate.

My breath hitched.

The blood on his fingers smudged on my skin.

Warm. Sticky. Real.

"You're been keeping things from us," he murmured. "And I'm *done* playing fucking games with you. I want to know what *it* is."

The air thickened.

His fingers tightened.

And in that moment, I felt the ache in him.

The hunger.

Not just for answers.

For me.

And it was killing him.

I didn't pull away. I should have. But I didn't. Because he was slipping. The mask was cracking. His breath came in short, uneven bursts against my skin. And then—

His body gave out.

It happened *fast*.

One second, he was looming over me, shaking with a rage that barely held itself together. The next—

His knees buckled.

He dropped.

I caught him before he hit the ground, my hands gripping his arms, lowering with him, feeling the heat radiating off his body. But beneath that heat was something else. Something just as volatile.

Pain.

Desperation.

He tried to push back up, tried to fight it, but this time, his body wouldn't let him.

His forehead pressed against my shoulder, his breath ragged and uneven.

There was too much blood.

Too much pain.

Theo moved beside me, reaching over the top of me, but before he could touch him, I felt Silas's fingers tighten in the fabric of his own T-shirt I wore.

"No." His voice was barely audible. "Don't."

I froze.

Because it wasn't an order.

Not a command.

It was something else.

Something raw. Something broken.

I exhaled slowly, carefully. "You're hurt," I whispered.

His fingers tightened again.

"I know," he admitted.

And that?

That broke me.

I swallowed hard, my hands gripping his arms. "Then stop fighting me."

His breath left him in a slow, shaky exhale.

His forehead still rested against my shoulder. His fingers were still cold, still pressing into me, as though he was desperately seeking the warmth my body gave.

And then—finally—

He let go.

Theo crouched beside me, his hand firm on Silas's shoulder. "Come on, man. Let's get you cleaned up."

Silas exhaled slowly, deeply. And for the first time that night— he didn't fight.

I helped him up, and Theo studied him as we moved him toward the rear bathroom. I felt his weight pressed into my side —his hard, ragged breaths shuddering against me—and all I wanted was to hold him, to touch him, to search his eyes for that desperate longing for me once more.

That's the way, that darkness whispered inside me...

Draw him into you.

Make him want you.

Gabe didn't move—not for a second—as I struggled to guide Silas out of the kitchen doorway and into the hall. I could feel the desperation emanating from him, see the absolute destruction unfolding inside him at that very moment. And there wasn't a thing I could do about it.

I tore my gaze away from Gabe, hating the way he looked at me —as if he were finally putting the pieces together. And for the first time, I realized—maybe they weren't the only ones breaking here. Maybe I was breaking too.

And when they finally figured out what I was hiding, what I had buried deep in my mind, stained with the blood of our parents all along—then none of us would survive. *But I will,* that deep, dark, haunting whisper echoed in my head.

I will always survive.

Chapter Thirty-Three

SILAS

The kitchen swayed, light bled into black as my grip on the counter faltered, fingers slipping against the slick surface as the room closed in. A sharp, lancing pain shot through my side, radiating outward in a sickening pulse.

Fuck.

The adrenaline that'd been keeping me upright—keeping me alive—was wearing off too fast. My knees buckled. The tiled floor rushed up to meet me.

"Silas!"

Theo's voice cut through the ringing in my ears. Hands grabbed me before I hit the ground. His strong hand clamped around my arm like a vice, stopping my fall at the last second. My body jerked against his hold, muscles seizing from the strain. The sudden movement ripped a new wave of pain through my side, and I sucked in a sharp breath, black spots dancing in my vision.

"No," my voice slurred.

I didn't fucking want this. Didn't want them helping me, didn't want to feel the weight of my own weakness pressing down.

But I couldn't fight it.

A second set of hands gripped me. Jude. His touch was firm, but careful, unlike Theo whose frustration was bleeding through every movement. They half-dragged me between them, their breathing rough with exertion as they hauled my useless, bleeding ass towards the hallway.

"Jesus," Jude pressed the back of his hand against my forehead. "He's burning up."

He wedged his shoulder against mine, taking more of my weight.

"You think?" Theo snapped. His grip tightened, fingers biting into my skin as he shifted to take more of the load. "He's been bleeding like a stuck pig for the past damn hour, and didn't say shit about it."

I gritted my teeth and lifted my head, forcing my gaze to his as I tried to move. My limbs felt like dead weight. I hated this—this fucking weakness, this dependence. My side was wet, the heat of fresh blood soaking into the waistband of my jeans.

Behind us, footsteps echoed.

Her footsteps.

I didn't need to see her to know she was there. Didn't need to hear her voice to feel the way she was watching me, her silence pressing like a phantom touch against my skin.

Angelica.

The only fucking thorn in my side...the liar, the betrayer...*our goddamn sister*.

Rage simmered beneath the pain flaring into something hotter, something viscous. I fisted my hands at my sides as they hauled my ass down the hallway to the bathroom at the rear of the house. But my ass was heavy, leaving Theo to stumble under the weight and slam his shoulder against the wall.

"Where the fuck is Gabe?" He barked.

"I'm here," Gabe's voice came from behind us...and behind her. My little brother's tone, low, flat...unreadable.

Jude reached inside the doorway, hitting the light switch.

Click.

The fact Gabe hadn't rushed in to help me spoke volumes.

The moment Jude wrestled me into the bathroom, dropping my ass onto the edge of the massive bath, I felt it.

The shift of attention, that crawling along my spine.

In that moment my pain took a backseat to something darker as she stepped toward me. I lifted my gaze to her, fixing on her tousled hair and wide, unblinking eyes. The same eyes that fixed on mine as I fucked her mere hours before.

Theo stormed to the sink, wrenching open the cabinet with so much force it nearly ripped the door off its hinges. The sharp snap of wood cracked through the room as he yanked out a bottle of antiseptic and a thick packet of gauze...he was going to need more than what we've got.

"You should've called," Gabe muttered, stepping inside the

doorway and pressed his back against the wall. "You don't have to be the hero all the goddamn time."

"Fuck *you*," I croaked as Theo grabbed the gauze and headed toward me.

They had no fucking idea what it meant to lead this family.

Not a goddamn clue.

"Fucking move." Theo snarled and pushed our sister aside.

I forced my head up, locking my gaze on her. The movement took too much effort, but I refused to show it. I refused to let her see how weak I was.

She looked like she was about to shatter.

Good.

I dragged in a slow, ragged breath.

"You're the one who did this," I rasped. "*So fix it.*"

The words landed like a slap.

Her lips parted, but no sound came.

Theo glanced from me to her, one brow rising as he took in the unspoken war that raged between us, then in an instant he lifted his hand, holding out the supplies to her.

I could see she was hurting, that lying brain of hers kicking into overdrive.

She knew.

She fucking knew.

Because she had to.

Our sister swallowed hard, stepped forward, grabbing the bottle of antiseptic then dropped to her knees in front of me.

And the real war began.

She was too close.

Too fucking close.

She knelt between my legs, the space so suffocatingly tight that every breath I took brought the scent of her in—floral and wrong, like it taunted me.

Her hands trembled as they hovered over my ribs, the torn fabric of my shirt barely clinging to my skin. I could feel the warmth of her breath, the soft hitch of air when she lifted what was left of the tattered mess and saw the deep gash from the machete underneath and stared.

The hesitation made my blood boil.

"Don't fucking think about it," I rasped. "Just do it."

Her lips pressed into a thin line, and she grabbed the shredded hem of my shirt. She hesitated for half a second too long.

Then she ripped it open.

A sharp sting raced across my skin as the fabric peeled away from the wound. I barely held back a hiss, biting down against the pain. Not in front of her. Not in front of them.

Angelica's breath hitched. She wasn't prepared for the sight of it.

I saw it in her wide, glassy eyes—the blood smeared across my ribs, the fresh, seeping gash, the damage she had indirectly caused.

She did this.

She fucking did this...

She fucking *ruined* me.

Her fingers ghosted over my skin, barely touching, but I felt them like a brand. I hated how my body reacted to it.

Hated that I wanted more.

I clenched my jaw as she poured antiseptic over the wound. The burn was sharp, eating through my nerves like fire, but I didn't make a sound. Not even when she turned, pushed to stand and moved silently to the cabinet.

We all watched her as she rifled through the drawers, pulling out a first aid kit and unclipped the latches, a staple gun was there, still sealed in the plastic. She tugged the edges, peeled it free before she came back to me.

One nervous glance and she eased to her knees once more. I fucking loved watching her kneel for me. I loved knowing it wasn't that haunting piece of fucking shit from that recording she kneeled for now.

Clack.

I winced, held my breath with the sting of pain, but I didn't move.

Clack.

Clack.

Clack.

Clack.

Each staple. Each breath. Each goddamn second stretched out in front of us until her touch jerked against my skin and she lowered the gun to the floor.

"Stop it," I said coldly.

Her head snapped up. "Stop what?"

"Shaking." My eyes burned into hers. "You don't get to be afraid right now."

Her throat bobbed. But she nodded. She pressed the cloth harder against the wound, whether out of defiance or punishment, I didn't know.

Jude crouched beside me, probing the wound, watching every move she made. "Looks like our sister is rattled," he muttered, voice unreadable. "She's not usually this rough."

Theo gave a snarl from the counter. "Guess we all have something to be pissed about tonight."

Angelica swallowed hard, but she didn't stop.

And I just sat there, hating her, hating myself, and wondering how much of me she had already ruined.

The silence stretched, suffocating.

Angelica's fingers tightened on the gauze as she pressed it against my wound. She was careful now, gentler than before, like she was trying to make up for something.

As if she fucking could.

How the fuck could she?

This was just another ambush right? Another fucking betrayal.

First, the recordings of my mother.

Then, the recordings of her...at that fucking place called the Order.

No matter how you looked at it—

It was her name stabbed right in the middle of it all.

All the way into my goddamn chest.

I let her do it. I let her hover over me, hands shaking, breath too fast. I let her pretend she was helping.

Then I grabbed her wrist.

Her breath hitched.

The entire room stilled.

I dragged her closer, her knees knocking against mine, her pulse leaping under my fingers.

"*Why* do they want *you?*" I said, voice like gravel. Low. Dangerous.

Her eyes snapped to mine.

"What the fuck are you hiding from us?"

Her lips parted, but nothing came out.

She froze, the guilt rolling off her in waves.

Jude straightened. Theo stopped pacing the damn bathroom. Gabe exhaled slowly.

But it was her, I was fixed on. Every goddamn reaction. Her body locked up, her fingers twitching like she wanted to rip herself out of my grip and run. But that's all she did right?

She fucking ran.

Not anymore.

I tightened my grip, even as I oozed fucking blood. I had the strength to pull her closer. "Tell me."

She swallowed hard. Her eyes wide and haunting. "I—"

"*Say it.*" Theo's voice snapped across the room, sharp and jagged.

She jumped. Her breath shuddering. Her body shook.

Jude's footsteps pounded against the floor as he stormed toward us. He grabbed the back of her neck, forcing her to look at me. *"Look at him! Tell him! TELL US!"*

She broke.

Her trembling lips barely parting as the words hissed out. "I...I can't."

Can't?

Or *fucking* won't?

Theo shoved her forward, standing over her. "You fucking can't? YOU FUCKING CAN'T? Our brother almost died tonight. You get that right? He almost died and we have a goddamn cartel coming for us. Now is not the time for can't, little sister. Now is the time for answers and they'd better come hard and fast."

He sucked in a hard breath. His eyes incensed and glinting, like he wanted to say something else. Something like.

Come hard and fast like you did, you lying fucking bitch.

She jerked and trembled, cowering as Theo's roar rebounded

against the tiles of the bathroom. My fucking heart was hammering, pounding against the confines of my chest.

"You...don't get out of this," Theo's rage simmered dark and savage. "You don't get to stutter and fucking shake. Answer his goddamn question. Answer it or I swear to God I'll unleash a hell on you that you won't be prepared for."

He lifted his gaze to Gabe.

"Family or fucking not."

She closed her eyes, squeezing them shut like any fucking moment she was about to wake up from this goddamn nightmare. One where she was forcing for once to tell the truth.

Gabe finally spoke.

"I'd start talking," he murmured, tone dangerously calm, like the one fucking brother she'd always had to protect her was slipping away.

She turned toward him like she might find some kind of salvation, but Gabe wasn't going to save her.

None of us were.

I felt it before I saw it—the way her body locked up, the way her fingers twitched, like she was fighting herself.

She wanted to keep lying.

She wanted to bury the truth all over again.

What the fuck kind of battle raged in her goddamn head? I needed to understand. To pry whatever sick motherfucker was in there out of her mind and erase his fucking touch from her memory.

"Tell him," Gabe snarled. "Tell all of us."

Angelica's breath was shaky, her shoulders trembling.

I watched it happen. The exact moment she broke.

She stopped fighting.

She sagged forward, as if the truth was a weight she couldn't hold anymore.

And when she finally spoke—when the words finally ripped from her throat—it felt like they tore the air from my lungs.

"I saw them die," she whispered. "Is that what you want to hear? *I. Saw. Our. Parents. Die.*"

The world stopped.

Her voice was thin, barely a sound, but it might as well have been a gunshot.

Theo stopped pacing.

Jude straightened.

And Gabe...

Gabe exhaled slowly, his jaw tightening just enough to show that it had hit him too.

I stared at her.

Stared through her.

I pushed from the edge of the bathtub, my body swaying. Pain ripped through my side, but it was nothing compared to the fire tearing through my chest.

I must've misheard her.

"You fucking what?"

The words were slow and deliberate, like my brain was trying to process them before they could destroy me.

Our sister wrapped her arms around herself. A pathetic attempt at protection. There was no protecting herself now.

"I was there that night," she said, voice barely more than a breath. "I saw them as they begged. As they fought. As they—" She squeezed her eyes shut. "As they were murdered."

The sound of Theo's fist slamming into the wall was deafening. He let out a sharp, jagged breath, his forehead dropping against his forearm. His entire body shook with something uncontainable.

Jude was motionless, his hands open at his sides, like he didn't know whether to lash out or collapse.

Gabe...

Gabe was staring at her like she was a puzzle he couldn't solve.

No one spoke.

No one fucking breathed.

I felt it creeping in—the cold realisation that nothing we thought we knew was real.

That she had been there all along.

That while we were searching for answers, losing our goddamn minds, spilling blood for revenge—she'd already known it all.

"You let us waste all this fucking time hunting ghosts," Jude said, voice hoarse. "You let us—"

His voice broke off.

He ran a hand down his face, then turned away so we couldn't see whatever expression had just flashed across it.

The things we'd done in the wake of their death. The fucking Hell we'd unleashed on anyone we even suspected had a hand in their death was fucking sickening.

"I didn't tell you because I—"

"Shut up."

My voice was quieter than I expected.

But it cut through her words like a knife.

Theo moved.

His entire body went rigid, his chest rising and falling with uneven, jagged breaths before he suddenly spun toward the counter. His hand swiped across it in one brutal motion, sending everything on top of it crashing to the floor.

Bottles of antiseptic shattered. The first aid kit burst open, gauze and needles scattering across the tiles.

The violence of it shook the air.

Angelica flinched, before she slowly pushed up from the floor.

Theo's hands braced against the counter, his shoulders heaving. His reflection in the cracked mirror was a fucking ghost, his face unreadable, except for the way his lips curled like he was fighting the urge to scream.

"You saw." His voice was low, wrecked, shaking with something I had never heard from him before. Something close to grief. "You fucking saw and said nothing."

Angelica didn't answer.

Theo turned his head just enough to look at her.

It wasn't the look of a man who wanted to hurt her.

It was worse.

It was the look of a man who had already lost too much, and now she had taken the last thing he had left—his fucking trust.

Jude's voice cut through the thick silence, sharper than a blade. "You saw our mother beg?"

Her brow pinched. Lips parted.

"You saw my father fight?"

Her throat bobbed.

I closed the space between us, as the image of that raged, my breath a razor against her skin. "And you did *nothing?*"

She shuddered.

I could feel it. The way her entire body reacted to those words.

Because she knew it too.

She'd destroyed us.

Gabe left.

No words.

No threats.

Just turned and walked out, his footsteps echoing down the hallway like the fucking death toll of what she'd done.

The silence he left behind was hallow and cruel.

Theo was still at the counter, his fingers breasted against the edge, his breathing harsh, like he was trying to swallow back something too fucking big to contain.

Jude just stood there.

Still. Staring.

And *me?*

I was right in front of her.

Her lips parted like she wanted to say something, but nothing came out.

Because what the fuck could she say?

How the fuck could she fix this?

"Say it," I demanded and took a step forward, making her retreat.

She swallowed hard.

"Say it." I didn't blink as I stepped again, forcing her against the wall. Didn't let her breathe without feeling it.

"I..." she choked. "I didn't want you to—"

I slammed my hand against the wall beside her head and pushed against her, feeling her warmth, smelling her goddamn scent. It crawled under my skin and took a savage bite out of my heart.

"You didn't want?" My voice was pure venom. "You didn't want us to know? You didn't want to tell us? You didn't want to stop it?"

Her chest pressed against mine as it rose and fell.

She was fraying at the edges, unravelling against me like a fucking thread I could rip apart with my bare hands.

"Jesus fucking Christ," Jude grunted. "You let us fucking suffer?"

Theo let out a dark, bitter laugh.

"I thought—"

Her voice broke.

She didn't finish.

She didn't have to.

"You thought?" Theo's voice was quieter than before, but the way it curled around the words made my skin crawl. "You fucking thought?"

I sensed the movement as he stepped toward us, coming up against her side. It was the two of us and her all over again.

"Tell me, Angel, what exactly you thought?"

She took a breath, but it was shaky, uneven, destroyed. "I...I thought I was protecting you."

The words landed soft.

Too soft for how loud the answer inside me had grown.

I let out a hiss of air.

Theo unleashed a sound somewhere between a curse and a growl. Jude shook his head. I eased backwards, taking a step as I watched her.

None of us believed her.

Because it wasn't fucking true.

She didn't do this for us.

She did it for herself.

"Get *out*," Theo muttered, his voice strained.

Angelica stiffened as Jude turned and followed Gabe out of the bathroom, disappearing down the hall.

Theo lingered for a second longer, like he was tearing himself apart on the inside, before he exhaled sharply, and stormed after them.

And just like that—

We were alone.

She didn't move.

Just stood there, watching me like she wasn't sure what the fuck I was going to do next.

I wasn't sure either.

My chest wasn't my own anymore.

My body wasn't my own anymore.

It belonged to the rage seeping through my gut. The devastating poisoning my fucking lungs.

It belonged to her.

I lifted my hand.

She didn't flinch.

She should have.

My fingers brushed her jaw.

Her breath hitched.

She was so close.

So fucking close.

I traced my thumb over the soft skin of her cheek, feeling the way she trembled beneath my touch.

I hated her.

Hated her so much I could taste it.

But I wanted to *ruin* her more.

I leaned in, just enough for my breath to ghost over her lips.

Her eyes fluttered closed, like she thought I might actually kiss her.

Like she thought I might still want her.

Maybe I did.

And that was the worst part.

"You will be the end of us," I murmured.

Her whole body shuddered.

She knew it, too.

She knew there was no coming back from this.

She had destroyed us.

And still, we couldn't stop.

Chapter Thirty-Four

ANGELICA

You're going to be the end of us.

Silas's words were still warm on my lips, his breath a cruel caress over my skin as his grip on my chin tightened—then loosened.

He let me go.

And the moment he did, I stumbled back.

The air in the bathroom was too thick, too hot, too suffocating. I could still feel him against me, his voice coiling through my veins, sinking into my bones.

I was going to be the end of them.

Just as they were going to be the end of me.

I shook my head, stepping back faster now, my body trembling.

The words wouldn't leave my head. They clung to my skin, seeped into my blood, whispering through the cracks in my mind where that haunting voice didn't reach. There wasn't anything left of me, not from him...or them.

I needed to get away from him.

From his eyes.

From the truth.

I turned and ran to my room, slamming the door behind me, locking it, pressing my back against it as I tried to catch my breath.

It didn't work.

Because that whisper was still there.

Your brothers will never forgive you.

I squeezed my eyes shut, but it was useless that sickening hiss resounded in my skull.

How long until you kill them too?

"No," the cry ripped free.

The memories were pushing through, forcing their way in.

The warmth of a gun in my hand.

The smell of blood.

The *thump* as my father's body hit the floor.

I clapped my hands over my ears, shaking my head, whispering. "No, no, no," under my breath—but it wasn't enough.

It was never enough.

Because I hadn't just been there the night our parents died.

I'd pulled the trigger.

And this voice—this unmerciful goddamn voice—*made me do it.*

I staggered to the dresser, gripping the edge, my nails biting into the wood. I wanted to tear my head apart. I wanted to dig my fingers into my skull and pull this thing out.

I wanted to pull him out.

The man.

The shadowed, faceless man who haunted me.

"Show me," I moaned. "Show me who the hell you are so I can *kill you!*"

The low, guttural chuckle that followed made me sick to my stomach. I grabbed the first thing I could reach—a heavy glass perfume bottle—and squeezed it in my hand, my knuckles turning white.

"Shut up, shut up, shut up—"

I swung it at my head.

Crack.

The force slammed into my skull, a sharp explosion of pain, but it wasn't enough.

The whispers were still there.

The memories still crawling around my thoughts. Biting like thousand ants.

I swung again.

Crack.

And again.

Crack!

White sparks ignited behind my eyes. Pain stung at the side of my face and warmth trickled down. My hand trembled and somewhere in the house, a door slammed. *BOOM.*

Heavy footsteps followed.

A voice—deep, dark, filled with fire. "Where the fuck is she?"

Theo.

I froze.

The perfume bottle slipped from my fingers, shattering against the floor. The footsteps came closer.

"ANGEL!"

I took a step back, my breath coming too fast, too shallow.

He wasn't just looking for me. He was hunting me. If he found me like this—blood dripping down the side of my face, the evidence of what I'd done still fresh on my skin—I didn't know what he'd do.

So I did the only thing I could.

I ran.

Not to escape him.

Not to get away.

But because I had to tear it out of me before it destroyed everything.

The whispers were relentless now, rising like a storm inside my head, a thousand voices speaking over each other, layering, twisting, growing louder.

You killed them, Angel.

Your brothers will never forgive you for this.

You didn't just let them die, did you?

It was your hand around the gun.

Your finger on the trigger.

Your name your parents screamed.

You.

You.

YOU.

.

.

.

Run.

My bare feet slammed against the floor, the hallway stretching before me like an endless voice. The walls blurred, my vision tunneling, the edges of the world twisting.

I wasn't in the house anymore.

I was there that night.

The smell of blood, wood smoke, and gunpowder choked me. My hands were slick, wet, my fingers twitching around the phantom weight of a gun.

Steady now, little doll. You know what to do.

NO.

I clawed at my head, gasping as the pressure built, as the voices slammed into me from all sides.

Pull the trigger, Angel.

They don't need to suffer. Just do it. Just finish it. Get what we want and we'll end this for good.

My blows were useless, still I slammed my knuckles against my head over and over...and over again.

What did your father whisper to you before he died?

An animal sound escaped my lips

Before you looked him in the eyes and pulled the trigger. What was it Angelica? Did he tell you he loved you? Or was it hate?

I sobbed, the sound ripped from my throat like an open wound, but my body kept running, slamming through the rear door and out into the first rays of the morning light.

I had to get away.

Get away from it.

From them.

Behind me, a door slammed open so hard the walls rattled. Theo's roar of fury cut through the night, a violent, jagged sound that sent a shudder through my entire body.

"Where the *fuck* is *our sister?!*"

My breath hitched. My pulse skipped, then lunged. His voice wasn't just rage now—it was desperation.

I stumbled around the corner, my body moving on instinct, my vision swimming with memories and shadows.

"ANGEL!"

I pressed a hand to my chest, holding in my heart as it slammed against my ribs like it wanted to escape me. But I had to keep moving.

The whispers grew louder.

Tell them the truth, Angel.

Tell them what you did.

Tears pricked at my eyes as I ran, blurring the thick brush that surrounded the compound of our house. I crashed through the branches, my breath raw in my throat.

Pick it up, Angel. You know how to use it.

The gun. The *goddamn* gun. It sat there, waiting on the edge of the desk, gleaming beneath the dim light.

Behind it, my father and mother—bound. Gagged. Pleading.

I tried to fight then, just as I tried to fight now.

Pick it up.

The dark whisper slid inside my skull, curling around my mind like a lover's fingers. My breath came in quick, shattered gasps.

Pick. It. Up.

I let out a shaking breath, my body convulsing as I tore through the brush, desperate to disappear. Desperate to become nothing.

The harder I ran, the colder the night air became. But it wasn't enough. The whispers didn't stop. The memories didn't stop.

Blood streamed down my father's face. His wide, desperate eyes locked onto mine, his head shaking violently as he pleaded with me, his screams trapped behind the gag.

The gun was in my hand before I even knew it. Heavy. Cold. Unfeeling.

Just like I was.

You know what to do.

That voice wasn't just a whisper anymore. It was a command, a kiss against my ear soaked in sin.

You know exactly what to do.

The past and the present blurred, twisting into a single moment of terror.

And then, he screamed.

Please, remember!

Dante Ares. My father. The ruthless man who built an empire. The man who never pleaded for anything in his life—except this.

My mother didn't scream.

She didn't cry. Didn't fight.

She was motionless, her dead eyes already fixed on me.

As if she knew.

As if she'd always known.

Pull the trigger, Angel.

The dark whisper kissed against my ear, venom and silk.

Kill your father. End it before it ends you.

The voice wasn't a whisper now. It was a command.

I choked on a sob as my knees buckled.

I hit the brush hard, the impact slamming pain through my body—knees skinned raw, hands scraped and bleeding.

And then my fingers curled around something cold and heavy.

A stone.

I lifted it with a shaking grip, my chest heaving, and for one agonizing second, I knew.

I was going to smash in my own goddamn skull.

Before I could move, a snarl cut through the night, sharp and lethal.

Then something massive slammed into me.

The world collapsed around me as Theo tackled me to the ground, his weight crushing me into the dirt. His grip unforgiving, punishing. My hands were wrenched away from the stone as it clattered into the darkness.

His rough hands grabbed my wrists, pinning them down, caging me beneath the sheer, suffocating force of him.

"You think you can *fucking* leave?" His voice was a raw, guttural sound, so thick with rage it coiled through my veins like poison.

I screamed, bucking, fighting, but he was fucking relentless, his strength unyielding. My mind snapped between reality and the past, between the ghosts in my head and the beast pinning me down.

His fingers fisted in my hair, yanking my head back with brutal possession.

"LOOK AT ME!" Theo bellowed.

My breath hitched. Something cracked inside me.

The whispers screeched in protest, but the moment I locked eyes with him, everything stilled.

Not because I was afraid.

Because I wasn't.

Theo's pupils were blown wide, his chest heaving, his entire body tense, shaking with rage.

And I felt it. All of it.

The darkness. The hunger. The uncontrollable need to own, to claim, to ruin.

My lips parted, a breathless, shuddering whimper spilling from them.

Something flickered across Theo's face. Realization.

You like this.

You fucking love this.

Before I could take another breath, I was hauled over his shoulder, his grip punishing, his breath ragged, hard, like he was on the edge of losing control.

"Fucking done with this," he snarled. "You wanna run from me? Run inside."

I screamed, kicked, but it didn't matter.

He dragged me back through the trees, through the compound, up the steps and into the house, straight into his room.

The door slammed behind us.

I barely had time to breathe before he shoved me against it, his massive frame caging me in, his breath burning against my lips.

"Tell me," he rasped. "Tell me you don't want this."

I couldn't.

Because I did.

I always had.

His fingers tangled in my hair, yanking my head back, exposing my throat. His teeth grazed my pulse.

"Fucking say it," he demanded.

My nails bit into his shoulders, my entire body trembling with the force of everything I'd spent years denying.

"You can't fight it," he growled. "You were made for this."

And he was right. I was.

I was programmed to be whatever they wanted me to be.

Liar.

Lover.

Sister.

Everything...

The moment his mouth crashed into mine, I shattered.

There was no hesitation. No softness.

This was brutal, desperate, possessive—the kind of kiss that consumed, that took, that destroyed. My lips were crushed against my teeth, bruising and hurting until I couldn't breathe.

His hands were rough, punishing, leaving bruises in their wake as he gripped my hips, lifted me, pinned me against the door.

I moaned into his mouth, nails dragging down his back, my body aching, needing.

I yanked his shirt, nails digging into his skin.

His hand wrapped around my throat.

"Say it," he growled. "Say you're mine."

My throat worked, the words tangled somewhere deep inside me.

His grip tightened, forcing me to feel the sheer power of him, the absolute truth in his touch.

And when I whispered, "Yes," it wasn't surrender. "I'm yours."

It was a revelation.

Because I'd known it all along.

I belonged to them.

And he was never letting me go.

I was still trapped in the whispers.

They coiled around me, sliding inside my mind, threading through my veins.

There is no escape, Angel. No escape from us. No escape from what you are.

I stopped fighting.

Theo didn't notice.

His grip on my wrists was iron, his breath ragged and scorching against my skin. His body pinned me down, his hands branding me as his fucking possession.

"This is what you fucking wanted, isn't it?" Theo growled, his voice thick with something raw and violent.

My lips parted, but I didn't speak.

I didn't need to.

Because he already knew.

He reached down, yanking Silas's t-shirt up and pulled my panties aside, not even stopping to pull them off before he lifted his hips, rearing backwards. The second he slammed inside me, my body arched, my breath ripped from my lungs.

Theo didn't move slow. He didn't tease, didn't wait.

This was brutal. Desperate. A war he was fighting with himself as he thrust inside me over and over.

Every brutal blow was punishment, but not for me—for him.

Because I'd run.

Because I had almost left him.

Because no matter how much he owned me, I would always belong to something else first.

And then, my lips moved.

Soft.

Reverent.

A whisper that wasn't mine to give.

Las Almas Perdidas.

The words came from nowhere.

But it wasn't from that dark, foul whisper in my head. It came from nowhere, blooming from the back of my mind.

Theo stilled.

Just for a second. Just enough for the whisper to slip between us like a blade to the throat.

And then, the door slammed open, wrenching my gaze toward the spill of light from the hallway.

Silas.

His ragged breath filled the silence.

He saw everything.

His eyes dragged over the room, over my wrecked body, over Theo's shaking frame still locked against mine.

And then, they settled on my lips.

Those words came again, slipping free from the depths of my mind.

"Las Almas Perdidas."

Silas took a step forward. But it wasn't because of what Theo was doing...he was fixed on me. Enraged by me. His expression shifting into something lethal.

"What did you just say?"

Theo's head snapped toward him, his muscles still tight, his possessive rage not entirely gone.

Angelica. His.

But I wasn't his.

Not fully. Not yet.

I turned my head, my pulse thrumming, my body still trembling from what Theo had done to me.

I licked my lips, tasting blood, sweat, and something deeper. Something broken.

And then I laughed.

Soft.

Haunting.

A sound that *didn't* belong to me alone.

Silas' jaw clenched. "Angelica, where the fuck did you hear that name?"

Theo finally focused, his grip tightening on my hips, like he could physically anchor me back to him.

But it was too late.

The whispers were too deep.

"You already know," I murmured. "Don't you? You. Already. Know."

And that's when everything changed.

Chapter Thirty-Five

SILAS

I didn't want to be here.

I told myself I wouldn't step foot in this room again, that I'd let the dust settle, let the ghosts have it. But now standing in the doorway, I knew the ghosts had never left.

They were waiting.

They were waiting for me.

The study still smelled the same. Leather and whiskey. Smoke clinging to the walls like a lingering threat. It was untouched, frozen in time—apart from the gaps in the book shelves where there were once blood-splattered books and the Persian rug stained with their blood that was now a pile of ash.

The last time I'd seen my father alive, it was in this room. Behind that desk. A glass in his hand, brows furrowed in focus. Unbreakable. Untouchable.

And then he wasn't.

I couldn't help but glance down. The blood had been scrubbed from the floor, but still I saw it. The splatter from where my mom had stood, begging...pleading.

Bile rose in the back of my throat.

And now I knew she'd been here.

Our lying goddamn sister.

Angelica.

My fingers curled into fists. My lungs burned, my breath caught between rage and disbelief. She'd stood in this goddamn room. She'd been here when they died, watching it as it happened.

My stomach twisted, a sickness curling deep in my gut. How much did she see exactly? And why the fuck didn't she fight whoever did this?

I exhaled sharply, forcing the memory down. I wasn't here for the past. I was here for the truth. But as I stepped deeper into the room, the weight of everything pressed in.

Maybe I wasn't ready for the truth after all?

I should've never stepped into this room.

I knew it the second I crossed the threshold. The second the door clicked shut behind me, sealing me into the past.

But I wasn't a kid anymore.

I wasn't thirteen, standing in this same fucking room, asking the wrong goddamn question like the naive fool I'd been.

Las Almas Perdidas.

The memory hit me like gunshot to the chest—sharp, sudden, inescapable.

I'd only said the words once.

Standing right here, just a kid who didn't know better. My father was at his desk, reviewing something in one of his ledgers, and I—like the arrogant little shit I was—had spoken without thinking.

"What does Las Almas Perdidas mean?"

The shift was instant.

One second, he was flipping through pages. The next, he'd gone completely still. The kind of stillness that made my stomach drop, that made my instincts scream at me to take it back.

I'd never seen my father freeze like that.

Never seen his fingers tighten around a pen like he wanted to break it in half. The silence stretched too long. Long enough for dread to settle deep in my bones.

Then, suddenly—*movement*.

He slammed the ledger shut. Hard. The sound ricocheted off the walls like a gunshot. Before I could react, before I could breathe, he was grabbing me.

One second, I was standing. The next—my back hit the bookshelves. Pain exploded up my spine. The breath punched out of my lungs as books toppled to the floor beside me.

I sucked in a sharp breath, my ribs aching. "Dad—"

"Where the fuck did you hear that?"

His voice was razor-sharp, all steel and rage.

I stared up at him, wide-eyes, my thirteen-year-old brain trying to catch up. Trying to understand why the man who'd taught me how to shoot, how to fight, how to survive—was looking at me like I was already dead.

I didn't answer fast enough. His fingers tightened around the collar of my shirt, twisting the fabric against my throat.

"You don't speak those words." His voice was low, cutting. Final. "You don't ask. You don't fucking know."

I forced myself to swallow past the fear clawing up my throat.

And that's when I saw it.

Not just the rage. Not just the fury.

Fear.

It was buried deep in his eyes, but it was there.

Dante Ares didn't fear anything.

But this?

This scared the shit out of him.

I should've backed down. Should've dropped it, let it go. But I was a kid, and I was too damn stubborn to know when to shut up.

"I just heard you say it." My voice came out steadier than I felt. "I didn't know it was a—"

"Forget it, Silas."

His grip tightened one last time. Then just as suddenly, he let go.

I hit the floor with a sharp inhale, sucking in air like I'd been drowning. My father turned away, adjusting his tie like nothing had fucking happened. Like he hadn't just slammed his son against a bookshelf for asking the wrong question.

He sat down at his desk, picked up his drink, and took a slow sip.

Like the conversation had never happened.

Like I'd never heard the name at all.

But I had.

And I never forgot it.

The memory of that moment ripped through me, clawing at my ribs, leaving something raw and uncontrollable in its wake.

A growl built in my chest, burning hot and violent. I turned toward the desk. The same desk he'd sat behind when he ordered men to live and die. The same desk where he'd...lied to me.

Rage took over before I could stop it.

I slammed my hands down on the wood hard. The force rattled through me, but it wasn't enough. Not fucking near enough.

With a snarl I grabbed the edge of the desk, lifting the heavy wood until my muscles strained with the effort. The more I lifted the more my rage took over until the tipping point hit, and the desk flew backwards with a crash.

The heavy mahogany beast crashed onto its side, papers exploded into the air, cascading down like pieces of a shattered past. My breathing was harsh, uneven, my pulse roaring in my ears.

And then—something caught my eye.

Beneath the wreckage, near the splintered wood where the desk had been, something small and torn peeked out.

A single fragment of paper. My gut twisted. I crouched down, ignoring the sting in my side, and reached for it.

The edges were rough, jagged—ripped violently from something bigger. A ledger.

My father's ledger.

I pulled the torn remnant closer. The rest of the room blurring as I focused on what was in my hand. The ink was faded, smudged with time, but the words weren't completely lost.

And when I read them, my entire fucking world tilted.

It was never meant for him.

The air felt too thick. The walls too close.

I clenched the paper in my fist.

Who?

What?

It wasn't a full sentence. It wasn't enough to mean anything. But it meant something.

Something my father had hidden.

Something I wasn't supposed to find.

My fingers tightened around the scrap, the paper crumpling in my grip. I should've shown Theo. Should've told Gabe or Jude.

But I didn't.

Instead, I slid it into my pocket.

No one had to know.

Not yet.

Not until I figured out what the fuck this meant.

And why the hell Angelica knew something I didn't...

The torn fragment of paper burned in my pocket, but I didn't look at it again. I clenched my jaw, pushing down the pain twisting in my ribs. My body fucking hurt, worse now after slamming the desk, after tearing through my father's study like a feral animal. But none of it mattered. Not the goddamn wound in my chest, or the deep ache in my head that made my vision flicker.

What mattered was the knock at the door.

Three sharp raps.

I turned toward the entrance of the study, my pulse still hammering against my chest.

The door creaked open slightly, and one of our men—Marco— stepped halfway in. His expression was tight, unreadable.

"Boss, we've got a problem."

I exhaled sharply, flexing my fingers before curling them into fists. "Of course we did."

I slid the page deeper into my pocket, making sure it was secure. Then, without another glance at the wreckage of my father's past, I stepped forward. My hand landed on the edge of the door, and before I crossed the threshold, I pulled it shut behind me.

A coffin sealed. A grave left behind.

The moment I stepped into the hall, the weight of every set of eyes landed on me.

Theo.

Gabe.

Angelica.

They were all there, standing in the dim lighting, watching as I passed. My sister stood there, hair dishevelled from being fucked by my brother, looking like she wanted to speak. Like she wanted to ask what the fuck I had been doing in the study —and what I'd found.

Wouldn't she like to know.

I didn't stop.

Didn't slow.

I walked past her.

Her gaze burned into the side of my face, but I didn't acknowledge it. Not when my body still ached with the desperate need to put my fucking hands on her for lying to us.

I kept moving.

The sharp pain in my side made my vision blur for half a second. Fuck. My stitches were screaming, the damage from the fight, from the staples she put into me, from the chaos—it was adding up.

But I couldn't stop.

Not when I caught the look on Marco's face as he led me outside.

Because one of our men had stopped answering his radio.

I stepped into the open air, the night pressing in. Our men were positioned as usual, walking the perimeter, but there was tension in the way they stood, the way they looked at me.

I scanned them quickly, counting, even through the growing headache pounding behind my eyes.

And then, the sinking feeling in my gut turned cold.

"Rigo's the one not answering?" I asked flatly.

Marco's jaw clenched. He pointed toward the far perimeter, past the line of vehicles.

"We've been calling him for the last twenty minutes. But he hasn't checked in."

That wasn't like him at all.

Rigo was one of dad's best men. Loyal to a goddamn fault. There was no way he wouldn't answer.

I didn't say anything. I just started walking.

Each step was agony, fire burning through my side, but I forced my body to move.

The further we went, the quieter it became.

The closer I got to something wrong.

I saw the car first.

The shadow of it, half-covered by the darkness.

Then I saw the body.

Slumped against the tire, his head tilted at an unnatural angle.

His radio was still clipped to his vest, the light blinking like he had tried to call for help but never made it.

His throat was slit.

One clean cut. No struggle. No noise.

Just dead.

"Jesus fucking Christ." Marco's growl came from behind me.

My stomach twisted as I crouched down, pain screaming in my ribs, but I ignored it. I reached out, my fingers pressing against the blood on his collar. Still warm.

I stared at the wound, at the dark pool of blood spreading like ink across the pavement.

Whoever did this was still close.

The night air felt too thick, pressing in from all sides.

I pushed myself upright, my body protesting the movement, my vision flickering at the edges.

I didn't care.

I turned to Marco, my voice dangerously low.

"The house isn't safe. We need to get out of here. Get the men together. We need to leave now."

"And go where?" Marco stared at me, hanging on my every word.

I felt the weight of this moment.

The concrete blocks pulling me down...pulling all of us down.

Something was coming.

And we were already too late.

404

Chapter Thirty-Six

ANGELICA

THE WAREHOUSE SMELLED LIKE OIL AND STEEL, THE AIR thick with tension and something darker—something unspoken. The men moved around me, their voices clipped, their steps quick, but they never looked at me for too long.

Not Silas.

Not Theo.

Not Jude.

I was invisible to them now, except for the moments they needed to remind me I wasn't one of them anymore. Silas leaned against a rusted metal table, a cigarette burning between his fingers. His other hand rested against his ribs, the place where I had stapled his wound shut, but if it still hurt, he wouldn't show it. His eyes flickered between the men giving reports, his mind elsewhere—distant, calculating, dangerous.

Not once did those dark, haunting stares ever drift to me. It was almost like he'd convinced himself I no longer breathed the same air he did...almost like I wasn't the one he wanted.

Or cared about.

Theo was worse. He barely even acknowledged me. I still smelled of him. Still, felt his savagery on my body.

And Jude... Jude just watched. Too careful. Too controlled.

I crossed my arms, pressing my back against the cold steel of a storage container. My stomach twisted as the weight of their distrust settled deeper into my bones. I had spent my whole life fighting to be a part of them. And now? Now I was just watching them move around me like I didn't belong.

Maybe I didn't? Maybe I was just a ghost in their life. A problem they never truly wanted and now they've finally made up their minds, I wasn't worth a second of their attention at all. It sure felt like it.

I pushed off the wall and started walking, heading deeper into the darkness.

One of the men stalked in from outside, his radio crackling. His expression was sharp with unease. "We're still missing three guys. No contact."

I stopped, then slowly turned around.

Silas didn't move. He just inhaled slowly, the cherry of his cigarette burning bright. "They're dead."

The words hit like a slap, flat and final.

Theo cursed under his breath and pushed off the crate he had been leaning against. "How the fuck did we not see this coming?"

No one answered.

Because there wasn't an answer.

Jude exhaled sharply, rubbing his hand over his jaw, but his gaze flickered in my direction—just for a second.

I swallowed past the knot in my throat, feeling the weight of that glance like a silent accusation.

Because that's what they all thought, wasn't it?

That this had started with me.

Maybe they were right.

The radio crackled again, and this time, the voice on the other end was different—strangled, barely above a whisper.

"We've got bodies," the man murmured. "Three. Could be more."

The tension in the warehouse cracked like ice.

I barely had time to process the words before Theo slammed his fist against the side of a steel shelving unit with a boom! The metal rattling from the impact. "How the fuck did they get this close?"

Still, no one had an answer.

Gabe stepped forward, slow, deliberate. "They're testing us."

The words sent a sharp chill through my spine.

Testing us.

Pushing, inching closer, waiting for us to break.

An icy chill slithered down my spine.

Jude stopped pacing. His gaze flicked toward the warehouse entrance, then back toward me. There was something there—something unreadable in his eyes—but before I could place it, he looked away.

I swallowed against the dryness in my throat. My pulse was too loud in my ears, the weight of everything pressing down harder, suffocating.

Silas had said we needed to move. That the house wasn't safe. But was anywhere?

The radio crackled again, this time with something quieter. More urgent.

I couldn't hear the exact words, but I saw the way Gabe's expression changed.

Saw the way Theo went still.

Saw the way Jude's fingers flexed at his sides.

And then Gabe turned toward me, his expression grim, his voice edged with something cold.

"They took someone."

Took. Someone?

What did that even mean?

The moment I asked myself the question, images of blood and terror surfaced.

The world tilted.

I stepped forward, my stomach twisting. "Who?"

His gaze met mine, sharp as a blade.

"Penn Hargreaves."

Penn?

As in *my* Penn?

"What?" I didn't understand. My mind struggled to keep up.

Silence settled over the warehouse like a storm about to break.

Penn was gone.

The words still hung in the air, suspended between us, crackling with something thick and wrong.

Theo was the first to react. His body jerked like a live wire, rage sharpening his every movement. "The fuck do you mean they took him? The Cartel?"

No one answered right away. Gabe was staring at the ground, jaw tight, and Jude had gone still. Too still.

Silas barely moved. His face was unreadable, but I could see it—the way his fingers curled slightly, the way his breathing slowed like he was working through the pieces of a puzzle he didn't like the shape of.

"They don't just take people," Theo snapped, turning sharply toward Silas. "Why the fuck would they take him?"

Jude exhaled sharply, rubbing a hand over his mouth, his brows drawn together in something close to frustration. "It doesn't make sense."

I shifted, my stomach twisting. He was right. None of this made sense.

The Cartel didn't take people alive. They killed them. Quickly, brutally, without hesitation. A bullet to the head. A knife to the throat.

But they had taken Penn. Alive.

Gabe moved first, his voice low and careful. "Unless he saw something."

Silas' head snapped up. "What?"

Gabe's expression darkened. "What if all this wasn't about him?"

A sharp silence fell over the group.

My pulse spiked, my hands curling into fists as I forced myself to breathe evenly.

Silas' gaze narrowed, his thoughts running too fast for the rest of us to keep up.

Gabe kept going, his voice controlled but deliberate. "What if they took him because he saw something he wasn't supposed to?"

A heavy pause.

Something shifted in the room, something dangerous.

Theo let out a slow, measured breath. "If that's true, then what the fuck did he see?"

No one had an answer.

The weight of the realization pressed down, suffocating. It wasn't just that Penn was gone—it was why he was gone.

This wasn't a demand.

This wasn't about leverage.

This was a message.

I glanced around the warehouse, to the men armed with guns and a savage look of survival. And suddenly, it was obvious.

They hadn't taken Penn because they wanted him.

They had taken him because they wanted us to know they could.

"We should contact London St. James." Jude murmured.

There was a beat of silence.

I turned toward Jude, barely suppressing my surprise. He'd always been the least vocal of the brothers, but when he spoke, everyone listened.

Even Silas.

Especially Silas.

Theo let out a sharp laugh. "You can't be serious."

Jude arched a brow. "We need resources. Manpower. Someone who knows how to move outside the Cartel's reach." He shrugged. "We're running out of options."

A slow, creeping unease settled in my stomach.

Because he wasn't wrong. London St. James—the man who destroyed the Order, moved in circles of power even beyond our family's reach—could help us.

And yet...

There was something about the way Jude suggested it. Something in the way his fingers flexed at his sides. Excitement.

I saw it. Felt it.

And so did Silas.

"No," Silas said, his voice cutting through the room. "We handle this ourselves."

Jude's jaw tensed. It was subtle. So goddamn subtle. But it was there.

For the first time, I saw it. The shift. The crack beneath the surface.

Once I saw it…I couldn't look away.

Silas' fingers flexed at his sides. The tension in his body was unreadable, but I felt it in my bones.

"We need to move." Theo murmured, glancing from one brother to the other.

Silas nodded once, sharp, decisive. "Yeah we do…and now."

The finality in his voice sent a chill through me.

Whatever had started tonight—we were already too late to stop it.

The warehouse pulsed with tension, thick and suffocating. The men moved with precision, setting up a perimeter, reinforcing exits, checking their weapons. Orders were issued, plans solidified, but I wasn't a part of any of it.

I was watching. Always watching.

Like an outsider looking in.

I stood near the edge of the room, arms wrapped around myself, my breath slow and measured as I tried to block out the weight of their distrust pressing against my skin.

Jude had vanished outside, his suggestion about London St. James still lingering in the air. I had seen the way Silas had shut him down. The way his shoulders had gone stiff, the way his fingers twitched at his sides before he masked it under his usual calm.

Jude didn't usually react like that.

And that meant something.

Theo was still fuming, pacing near the back of the warehouse, barking orders at the men like he was barely holding himself together.

Silas was silent, watching everything, his eyes dark and unreadable.

And then there was Gabe.

He wasn't standing with the others. He was closer to me, near the stacks of crates, running a hand over his face like he was trying to shake off the weight pressing down on all of us.

I swallowed, shifting slightly, my boots scraping against the floor.

His head turned. His gaze landed on me.

And for a moment, we just stood there.

He was the only one who wasn't treating me like I was poison, the only one who hadn't let his anger consume him completely. Maybe it was because he had always been different from the others—softer in ways the rest of them weren't.

Or maybe I was just desperate for any kind of warmth.

I took a hesitant step toward him. Then another.

He didn't move, didn't back away, but his jaw tightened slightly, a flicker of something in his expression that I couldn't quite read.

I stopped a breath away from him. Close enough to feel the heat of him, close enough to see the tension in his shoulders.

"I don't know how to fix this," I admitted, my voice barely above a whisper.

He exhaled slowly, tilting his head slightly, watching me with something unreadable in his gaze. "Maybe you can't."

The words hit harder than I expected, but I didn't pull away. I reached out instead, my fingers brushing against his wrist, feeling the warmth of his skin beneath my touch.

His breath hitched. Just slightly.

I looked up at him, my pulse pounding, and for a split second, I saw it.

The hesitation. The war inside him. The way his gaze dropped to my lips before snapping back up.

He wanted this.

He didn't want to want it.

But he did.

I took another step closer, my chest brushing against his. "Gabe..."

His hand twitched like he was about to grab me. Like he wanted to pull me in, like he wanted to break the space between us.

But then—

"Shouldn't you be with the others?"

Jude's voice cut through the air, sharp and knowing.

I pulled back immediately, my stomach twisting. Gabe's entire body went rigid.

Jude stood near the entrance, watching us with that same unreadable expression. The flickering light above cast shadows across his face, and for a second, I could have sworn I saw something almost smug in his eyes.

Gabe took a slow step back, putting distance between us.

The moment shattered.

Jude didn't move, didn't react, just waited.

I turned and walked away before either of them could see the way my hands were shaking.

The air inside the warehouse felt thicker—like the walls were closing in, like something was crawling beneath my skin. The silence stretched, tight and suffocating.

And then—

Gunfire.

The first shot cracked through the air, shattering the uneasy quiet. Then another. And another. The warehouse exploded into chaos as bullets slammed into the walls, into the steel crates, ricocheting with deafening force.

A cry ripped from my lips.

Someone shouted—Gabe or Theo or maybe Silas—but I didn't hear the words. I was already moving, throwing myself behind a stack of crates as the gunfire ripped through the warehouse like a storm.

Screams.

The sickening crunch of bodies hitting the ground.

The sharp, acrid scent of blood and gunpowder filled my nose.

I peeked around the edge of the crates, my heart pounding. The cartel wasn't holding back this time. They moved in from the open bay doors—fast, ruthless, brutal.

One of our men went down, a bullet tearing through his throat. He dropped without a sound, his blood splattering across the concrete floor. Another staggered back, clutching his stomach, eyes wide with shock before his legs gave out.

We were losing men too fast.

Silas was already on his feet, his body protesting but his fury keeping him upright. He raised his gun, his movements sharp despite the bloodstains on his shirt. He fired—two clean shots.

A cartel man collapsed. Another stumbled before Theo finished him with a ruthless blow.

But there were more. Too many.

I pressed my back against the crate, forcing myself to breathe. Gabe was near the loading dock, his knife flashing in the dim light as he buried it into a man's chest. He ripped it free, blood arcing through the air before he turned to the next.

Another gunshot rang out—close. *Too close.*

I twisted just in time to see a man lunging for me. My pulse spiked. I barely managed to duck, his blade slicing the air where my throat had been a second before. I scrambled back, hands slipping against the bloodstained floor, panic surging in my veins.

He was on me in an instant, grabbing my wrist, dragging me forward. I fought, kicking, twisting, but his grip was ironclad.

And then—a gunshot.

The cartel man's head snapped back. Blood sprayed, hot and sickening, across my arm.

I gasped as his body dropped.

Silas stood behind him, gun still raised, his expression dark with fury.

"Move," he snapped, his voice cutting through the chaos.

I pushed up on shaking legs, but the moment I stepped forward —I saw it

The cartel men weren't advancing anymore.

The bodies on the ground—their own men—hadn't mattered to them.

Because this attack wasn't about winning.

No... it felt more than that.

Like the attack wasn't their purpose at all. I sucked in the fetid, terror-stained air and tried to think. Not an attack...then what was it? A distraction.

The realization struck like ice through my veins. My breath stilled.

Silas knew it too. I saw it in the way his eyes darkened, in the way his fingers curled tighter around his gun.

And then he turned sharply, his voice deadly quiet beneath the ringing silence.

"We're not safe," he said. "We need to get out of here. Now."

Marco hesitated. "And go where?"

Silas exhaled slowly, his jaw tightening.

The weight of the moment settled over all of us, pressing down, squeezing, suffocating.

And deep down, I knew—we were exactly where they wanted us to be.

Chapter Thirty-Seven

ANGELICA

SMOKE STILL CLUNG TO MY SKIN, TO MY CLOTHES, TO THE air we breathed as we fled the warehouse. My boots pounded across the blood-slicked pavement, the sharp burn of adrenaline clawing up my throat.

Behind us, the bodies were still warm. The cartel had come fast and hard, but they hadn't meant to kill us. We all knew it now.

This was never a fight.

But what was it?

"Move!" Silas's voice rang out, hoarse and ragged, but full of command.

He should have still been down. He could barely stand. But somehow, he was ahead of us, limping with fury and precision as he led us out the back.

Theo was beside him, covering their flank, his jaw tight and his movements sharp. Jude moved with a kind of eerie calm behind them.

Gabe was at my side, his hand on my elbow, guiding me through the shadows like he didn't trust me to keep up.

Maybe I didn't.

The warehouse disappeared behind us, swallowed by darkness and smoke. I didn't look back. I couldn't.

The street was cold and wide and empty. Too empty. Every sound felt too loud. Every breath, every step, every click of a weapon being reloaded—it all felt like it was leading us somewhere we weren't prepared to go.

Ahead, three black SUVs waited—silent, menacing. Marco stood at the farthest one, his expression grim. Our surviving men were there too, scanning the street, ready for another wave that hadn't come.

Silas stopped hard, his breath ragged. "We split up," he said.

Theo turned on him. "We don't even know what direction they're coming from."

"We'll find out soon enough." Silas didn't raise his voice. He didn't have to.

There was something in the way he stood, in the way he watched the shadows, that made my blood run cold.

"Take her," Theo barked at Gabe, jerking his chin toward me. "Get her in the car."

I wanted to object. To scream that I wasn't the problem here. That I wasn't their burden to protect or control. But Gabe was already at my side, ushering me toward the SUV.

I looked back once, just in time to catch Jude slipping into the back seat of the vehicle with Theo. His eyes met mine through the open door.

He didn't blink. Didn't look away.

Then the door closed, and that was it.

I slid into the back seat beside Gabe as Marco started the engine.

My heart was still pounding, my hands trembling in my lap. Something was wrong. Something was always wrong.

We were running.

But it didn't feel like we were getting away.

The SUV jolted forward, the engine growling as Marco floored it down the empty street. Gabe sat beside me in the backseat, silent, jaw clenched, one hand braced on the door like he couldn't fully relax.

I stared out the window, trying to ignore the tremble still working its way through my limbs. The warehouse was gone now, swallowed by distance and shadow. But the feeling of being watched—that crawling sensation across the back of my neck—hadn't left.

Something was wrong. I could feel it in my chest. In the way Gabe kept checking the rearview mirror. In the way Marco didn't speak, his eyes flicking to every alley, every parked car.

"Where are we going?" I finally asked, my voice low.

"Safe house," Marco answered without looking back. "One of ours, off-grid."

Gabe's gaze didn't leave the road behind us. "We rotate through it every few months. No one should know it exists."

Should.

The word hit harder than it should have.

I leaned back, heart pounding, my fingers curling into the fabric of my jeans. The silence between us stretched, heavy and taut.

"I don't get it," I murmured, mostly to myself. "Why split up?"

Gabe didn't answer immediately. When he did, his voice was tight."Because if they can hit us like that, we can't risk staying together. We're better spread out."

"But that makes us easier to pick off."

His jaw tightened. "Not if we move fast."

We passed a row of shuttered shops, their windows covered in metal grates. The world outside felt abandoned. Like we were driving through the bones of a city already lost.

I looked down at my hands. The blood under my nails wasn't mine, but it might as well have been.

"I didn't see Penn," I said suddenly. "At the end."

Gabe looked at me then, really looked. His eyes were tired. Angry. But under that, something softer. Sadder.

"They took him and he messaged me. Did you know that?" I lifted my gaze meeting Gabe's stare. "He messaged me days ago and I never responded. This is..." my pulse thundered in my ears. "This is all my fault."

"No." Gabe shook his head. "It's not. You don't need a fault. You carry the Ares name. That was *always* more than enough."

"But they took him, Gabe," my throat tightened, choking the words. "Why him?"

He shook his head. "I don't think it was about him at all."

I swallowed hard. The car turned sharply, tires screeching as Marco took a side street. We were moving fast now, too fast. I could feel the tension ramping up again, the sense that we were being chased even if no one was there.

I glanced behind us. Empty road. Nothing.

And yet...

"Something doesn't feel right," I whispered.

Gabe didn't argue. He just nodded once. "I know."

Up ahead, the city fell away into a stretch of overgrown industrial land—forgotten buildings and cracked pavement swallowed by weeds. It looked empty. Dead. But so had the warehouse.

We were running.

But I still didn't know if we were getting away.

We didn't speak for the next five minutes. The silence in the car wasn't just heavy—it was strangling. My gaze flicked between Marco's eyes in the mirror and Gabe's rigid profile beside me.

We were driving deeper into nowhere. The city had long since given way to industrial sprawl, and even that had bled out into long stretches of cracked concrete and rusted fencing. There was nothing here but silence and shadows.

And yet—

My heart wouldn't stop pounding.

"Something's off," I said.

Gabe looked over at me, a flash of surprise in his eyes like he hadn't expected me to speak. But then it shifted, and I realized he'd been thinking the same thing.

"I know," he said. "But we're too exposed to change routes now."

I sat forward slightly, eyes scanning the road. The headlights barely cut through the darkness ahead. I tried to ignore the way my gut twisted tighter with every mile.

This was supposed to be safer. Splitting up, moving fast, staying low.

So why did it feel like a trap?

"I feel like we're being led somewhere," I whispered.

Marco tensed at the wheel, just for a second. Gabe caught it. I did too.

"Then we're not stopping," Gabe said. "We get in, we lock it down. Nobody gets in or out until we clear this."

I nodded slowly, but the feeling didn't ease.

Because I wasn't afraid of who was following us.

I was afraid that someone had already been here.

That this wasn't just a relocation.

It was a setup.

Gabe shifted, pulling his phone from his pocket, trying to ping the others. Static crackled through the line—no service. No signal.

And still, we kept driving.

"I don't like this," I said again, my voice harder this time. "It's too quiet. Too clean."

Marco didn't reply. Gabe just looked out the window like he could feel it now too.

Whatever this place was, it wasn't a safe house anymore.

It was something else.

We pulled off the road just past a rusted chain-link fence, the tires crunching over gravel and glass. The safe house loomed ahead—if you could even call it that. It looked abandoned. Faded paint peeled from the siding, a sagging porch half swallowed by weeds.

"Here?" I asked, the word catching in my throat.

Marco cut the engine. "It's secure."

Gabe opened his door first, scanning the shadows before he moved. I followed him, but every step felt heavier. My boots crunched down, too loud in the silence.

Something was wrong.

Not just off. Not just uneasy.

Wrong.

Marco disappeared around the side of the building to sweep the perimeter. Gabe led me toward the front steps, his hand tight on my arm even though he didn't say a word.

We stepped inside.

The air was stale. Cold.

Dust floated in thin streams through the moonlight slicing in from broken windows. Furniture was covered with sheets, and the walls looked like they hadn't seen life in years.

Gabe moved through the rooms like a soldier on a mission, checking corners, clearing sight lines, peering through narrow windows. I stayed near the front, staring at the warped floorboards, at the shapes beneath the covered furniture.

Something in the air crackled. Like static. Like electricity waiting to bite.

I turned slowly, the back of my neck tingling.

Gabe reappeared. "It's clear."

"Is it?" I asked, barely recognizing my own voice. "Because it doesn't feel like it."

He didn't argue. He looked at me the same way he had in the warehouse—like he was seeing something he wasn't ready to believe.

"I need to check in with Silas," he said. "We're blind out here. No signal. We'll try from the second floor."

I nodded slowly, not trusting myself to speak.

Gabe turned and disappeared up the stairs. Marco hadn't come back in. The creak of the boards above me faded.

And I was alone.

Alone in a place that didn't feel abandoned.

It felt like it was waiting.

I backed toward the front door and pressed my hand against it. Not opening it. Just touching it. Like if I kept one part of myself close to escape, I'd be okay.

But deep down, I knew.

We weren't safe.

We'd never been safe.

Not with me—the liar—at the centre of it all.

Chapter Thirty-Eight

SILAS

THE SILENCE WAS LOUDER THAN THE GUNFIRE.

Echoing.

Haunting.

Blood still clung to my hands, sticky and warm, but my fingers didn't shake. I'd bled so much I could barely feel the wound now. I should've been flat on my back, unconscious. Instead, I stood at the edge of the street outside the warehouse, every muscle locked in place, watching the shadows stretch across the concrete like they were waiting to swallow us whole.

The others were scrambling—repositioning, regrouping, trying to make sense of the mess. I didn't speak. I couldn't. My ears rang with more than just the aftermath of gunshots.

I replayed it again.

The attack.

The timing.

The retreat.

Too fast. Too clean. *Too simple.*

But my brain wouldn't stop—wouldn't let it settle as just that. I saw it all unfolding again, not like a memory, but like I was still inside it.

The moment the first shot rang out, slicing the silence like a scream.

The way Lucas' body jerked.

The way blood hit the wall—sprayed across it like someone had painted with him.

The way one of our men dropped without a sound, just a sudden thud and nothing else, like someone pulled his plug.

I remembered the way Angelica had screamed—not out loud, but with her eyes. Like she knew this wasn't chaos. Like she recognized it.

That was what stuck with me most.

Not the bullets. Not the fire.

Her expression.

That flicker of realization just before the floor split open beneath us.

Too fast.

Too damn clean.

I'd seen war.

I'd led hits.

I knew what real violence looked like—and this wasn't it. This was a fucking illusion. A show.

A performance designed to drown out the truth.

And I'd fallen for it like a fucking amateur.

I clenched my jaw, my mind moving faster than my body could keep up.

The cartel had come in like a storm—but they hadn't stayed, had they?

They took Penn, then hit us hard and vanished. No demand. No message. Just noise.

A fucking distraction. Calculated from the very beginning.

The thought sank its teeth in deep.

We weren't the targets. Not tonight.

I turned slowly, pain flaring in my ribs as I scanned the bodies littering the concrete. Most of them weren't ours. A few were. But there were no reinforcements coming. No second wave. Just corpses and smoke.

We'd won.

Bodies littered the ground like discarded warnings. Smoke still hung in the air, sharp and bitter.

And yet—

So why the hell did it feel like we'd lost?

I shifted my weight, pain burning along my ribs as blood soaked back through my shirt. The world around me had gone quiet, but not in the right way. Not in the relieved way.

In the way that comes before another hit.

Theo stalked past me, barking orders into his comms, jaw tight, gun still drawn like he didn't believe it was over.

Jude was further back, speaking with what remained of our crew, coordinating cleanup—but his eyes kept flicking to me. Like he was waiting for something I hadn't said yet.

Gabe had taken Angelica. Marco was driving.

That choice—at the time, it had felt tactical. Clean.

But now?

Now it felt too clean. Too easy. Too fucking neat.

Like someone had offered us an escape route just so we'd take the bait.

My stomach twisted.

I glanced down, watching my blood drip to the pavement. The staples in my side were tugging apart. I could feel the warmth spreading again, soaking through the makeshift dressing.

"Silas!" Theo's voice cracked through the silence. "You need to sit down, brother. You look like hell."

I didn't answer. Couldn't. Every part of me was hyper-focused —ears pricked for a sound, a movement, anything to explain what we'd missed.

Think.

THINK.

This wasn't just an attack.

This was the beginning of something else.

Something worse.

The world tilted sideways.

The concrete beneath my boots blurred for a moment—just a second—but it was enough. Enough to send a ripple of something cold through my gut.

I staggered back from the body, blood soaking into the gravel, my breath shallow and burning. My hand brushed my side— sticky warmth already leaking again through the staples. But that wasn't what stopped me.

It was the weight in my pocket. Something I didn't remember putting there.

My fingers closed around it—paper. Brittle. Torn.

And then I wasn't in the warehouse anymore.

I was thirteen again.

Back in the study.

Back in that goddamn room with the smell of cigar smoke and whiskey.

Back in the place where my father shoved me against the wall and spat the words never say that name again with a kind of terror I didn't understand.

Not then.

But I did now.

My hand trembled as I pulled the scrap free. It was stained at the corner, the ink faded but still legible.

"Silas?"

I barely heard Theo behind me, boots crunching as he crossed the warehouse floor. My throat was dry. My chest hollow.

"What is that?" he asked.

I didn't answer. I couldn't. I just stared at it—those same four words.

It was never meant for him.

Theo stepped forward and snatched it from my hand, his expression tight with confusion. But as he read it, something shifted in him—something subtle and dangerous.

His brows pulled together. His mouth opened, then closed again.

And I knew.

He recognized the handwriting.

"Where did you get this?" he said, voice low, eyes never leaving the paper.

"The desk," I rasped. "From the study."

Theo shook his head slowly, something brewing behind his eyes. "That's dad's writing."

I said nothing.

And that said it all.

"What does it mean?"

I closed my eyes, the washed out grey world fading. "Nothing."

"Don't nothing me, Silas." He leaned closer until all I could see was him. "What the fuck does it mean?"

His confusion.

His pain.

"Las Almas Perdidas."

There. It was.

The words I'd fought so hard to unhear. But here they were again, worming their way under my skin.

"I asked him once about it," I said quietly, the memory scraping against my voice. "I was just a kid. Thirteen, maybe. I saw the name scribbled in one of the ledgers. Didn't know what it meant, only that it felt wrong. Twisted."

Theo didn't speak, but the silence between us sharpened.

"He reacted like a man possessed," I continued. "Grabbed me by the collar, slammed me into the wall. He was shouting —never say that name again. He looked at me like I'd cracked open something he'd spent his whole life trying to bury."

Theo's expression darkened. "You think this..." He waved his hand toward the bloodied warehouse. "All this is because of some fucking words?"

I shook my head. "Not just words, Theo. Not. Just. Words."

"What the fuck does it mean?"

Theo's silence stretched.

I...

Don't...

Know.

And then he said, barely above a whisper, "First our parents... now this."

I didn't move.

He wasn't asking for comfort. He was asking for the world to make sense again.

"It doesn't add up," he muttered. "Our mother. Our father—ripped apart like a goddamn warning. The fucking videos and the goddamn Order—" His voice cracked. "And now this? This fucking name she shouldn't even know?"

I said nothing. Because what the fuck was I supposed to say?

That I felt it too?

That all of it—the blood, the lies, the secrets—it felt like it was circling one person?

"I'm not saying she's guilty," Theo said, eyes burning. "But don't ask me to believe this is coincidence anymore."

I didn't.

Because something bigger was moving under the surface.

Something that started long before she ever came into our lives.

Something that ended in our parents' blood... and started again the second she said those words.

My phone buzzed.

Not a contact. No name. Just a number I didn't recognize.

I stared at the screen, the air thick and unmoving around me. The silence after Theo's words still hung heavy.

And then I answered.

Nothing.

No sound. No breath. Just dead space.

Until a voice slipped through the line. Deep. Rough. Dark Mexican accent.

"You should've left us alone…"

My spine stiffened.

"…should've rolled over like the dog you are, Ares."

Theo moved beside me, sensing it. Watching.

The voice dropped lower. Slower. A murmur soaked in threat.

"She always belonged to them."

Then a sound—quiet, stifled. A breath caught in panic.

Sharp. Fragile. Real.

Angelica.

The line went dead.

I didn't move. Didn't breathe. The phone was still in my hand, but it might as well have been a live grenade.

The silence that followed wasn't empty.

It was waiting.

Theo's voice snapped through it, hard and sharp. "What the fuck was that?"

I didn't answer right away. I couldn't. My throat felt sanded raw. My pulse was a slow, relentless hammer.

"We've got a problem," I said finally, and the words felt like gravel.

Jude turned toward me, tension winding through his frame. "Where's Angelica?"

I blinked. The question hit harder than it should have.

Not because I didn't know.

But because I suddenly realized—I hadn't seen her since the smoke cleared.

"With Gabe," I muttered, and as soon as the words left my mouth, that sickening wave of dread curled its fist around my spine.

Theo's expression cracked. "And where the fuck is Gabe?"

No one spoke.

No one moved.

Time didn't just slow—it stopped.

"Call him," I said, already stepping back, already reaching for my weapon. "Now."

Jude fumbled for his comms. "Gabe? Come in. Do you copy? This is base—check in. Report."

Static.

Theo cursed and punched the wall.

My heart was thundering now. My ribs throbbed where I'd bled through my shirt again. But none of that mattered.

We were too late.

Or close enough to it that the difference didn't matter.

We'd been looking in the wrong direction. Fighting the wrong war.

And now the only person who could unravel all of it was already slipping away.

Chapter Thirty-Nine

ANGELICA

It was too quiet.

That was the first thing I noticed.

The air felt wrong—too still, too clean, like the silence itself had teeth. Gabe stood a few feet ahead, his hand resting on the side of the SUV as he scanned the tree line. Marco hadn't come back yet. He'd gone to check the perimeter ten minutes ago. Maybe more.

Something scratched at the back of my skull, a whisper that wasn't a voice, but felt like one.

Move.

"Gabe," I said, my voice tight, "we shouldn't be here."

He looked back at me, brow furrowed. "We're safe. Just until backup comes."

But I knew better.

I stepped closer to him, my boots crunching over gravel. The warehouse was long gone. The road behind us was empty. The isolation wasn't safety—it was separation.

And then I heard it.

The low purr of a high-end engine. Smooth. Expensive. Deadly.

Gabe turned toward it as it crested the rise—sleek, black, windows tinted like obsidian. It didn't belong here.

It didn't belong anywhere near us.

"That's not one of ours," I whispered.

The car slowed. Stopped.

The rear door opened.

And the world dropped out from under me.

Shadows poured from the vehicle like smoke. Two men stepped out—faces obscured, movements precise. Not Cartel. Not at all. These men didn't swagger. They didn't shout.

They owned the silence.

Gabe stepped in front of me. His voice wasn't loud—but it didn't need to be.

"Angel...baby. Run."

It wasn't a suggestion. It wasn't a plea.

It was an order. A final act.

There was something in his voice I hadn't heard before. Steel. Rage. The quiet heartbreak of a boy who'd grown up too fast— and knew this might be the last thing he ever did.

I froze.

For a split second—less than a breath—I couldn't move.

Not because I didn't want to.

But because this was the moment. The line between before and after. Between being the girl in the shadows... and the one they were hunting in the light.

The terror hadn't reached my bones yet. The mind control hadn't sparked.

I just stood there.

Staring at the brother I had only just begun to understand—and knew, deep in some shattered part of my soul, that he was about to be taken from me.

That second—

That single, agonizing second—was the last moment I was just me.

And then survival kicked in.

The heartbeat of instinct. The ripple of fight.

I turned and—lunged.

I got five steps before something sharp exploded at the base of my skull.

I hit the ground hard. Gravel tore into my palms. Sharp. Burning.

My elbows cracked against stone.

The air punched out of my lungs before I could scream.

Hands—rough, cold—clamped around my ankles. My wrists.

Dragging.

Dust filled my mouth. The sting of blood.

NO!

The scream rose too late.

I kicked. Hard. Fighting like an animal.

My boot connected with flesh. A grunt.

I twisted. Bit down. Screaming.

The taste of sweat. Salt. Skin.

A curse—sharp and furious—in Spanish.

Then a crack across my cheek.

My head whipped to the side.

Strands of hair lashed my cheek before the burn came.

Searing.

Scorching.

White light.

My vision dazed.

But I didn't stop.

Couldn't.

Wouldn't.

Not until I saw him.

A sound broke through.

Faint. Distant.

Gabe.

His voice—shredded with fury. My name torn from his throat like it was the only thing keeping him alive.

"Angel!"

The scream cracked the silence like shattering glass.

I flinched, my body seizing. My head snapped toward the sound.

My vision blurred—tears, blood, the sting of the hit.

But I saw him.

For one breathless second—I saw him still fighting.

Still reaching.

Then—

Nothing.

Hands clamped around my arms again.

Rough. Heavy.

Fingers like steel digging into the flesh of my biceps.

I screamed, thrashed, my boots scraping against gravel as they dragged me backward—toward the car.

The sleek black blur of it loomed closer. The rear door yawning open like a mouth.

"No—no, let me go!"

My heel caught on the edge of the pavement. I kicked back—caught one of them in the shin.

A grunt. Another curse.

The second man grabbed my legs. Lifted.

I was weightless for a moment—fighting air, panic clawing its way up my throat.

Then they slammed me down.

My spine hit leather.

The door slammed shut behind me.

Dark.

Hot.

Hands still on me. The press of bodies. The stench of sweat and smoke.

And then—

The voice.

A whisper, low and velvet-smooth against my ear.

"Hello, Angel..."

They shoved me inside the car like I weighed nothing.

The leather seat was hard underneath me, knees scraping the edge, my body collapsing sideways. The door slammed shut behind me with a sound that felt final—like a lid sealing a coffin.

Darkness pressed in. Not just the absence of light, but something heavier. Thicker. Breathing.

Then I saw him.

Penn.

He was seated across from me, spine straight but hollowed out like something vital had been scooped from his chest. His lip was split, one eye swelling shut.

He didn't speak.

Didn't move.

And when his gaze finally met mine—it wasn't relief or guilt.

It was shame.

Shame so deep it made my stomach twist.

"Sorry, Angelica," he said, voice rough. "They made me do it."

The words sliced through me.

No.

No.

I scrambled back, my foot catching on the floor mat as panic crushed my ribs from the inside. I reached for the door handle, blind with terror—

A hand caught me from behind.

Cold. Dry. Iron.

It slammed over my mouth as the scream built inside, killing the sound cold.

And then I felt him.

Behind me. Around me.

Him.

The monster in my head. He was real.

He was here.

His breath brushed my ear. Slow. Intimate. Poison.

"Go still, little flame..."

The words didn't just touch me. They pierced me.

My muscles froze. My heart thundered once—twice—then slowed to something dull and dragging.

I could hear the blood moving in my veins. Could feel the shift behind my eyes.

The command dug in. Burrowed deep.

My body betrayed me.

My arms fell limp. My mouth went slack beneath the hand that still held me in place.

Tears leaked from the corners of my eyes, but I didn't blink.

Couldn't.

And through the rear window—blurred and smeared with blood—I saw Gabe.

Fighting.

Bleeding.

Ripping through one of the masked men like a fucking wolf.

Trying to get to *me.*

Screaming *my* name.

Another man came up behind him and slammed something against his skull. Gabe dropped. Hard.

Everything in me shattered.

But I couldn't move. I couldn't speak.

I was a passenger in my own skin.

The monster's hand slid from my mouth to my throat, holding me like something precious. Something owned.

"You were always ours," he whispered.

And in that moment, I knew—this wasn't just fear.

It was annihilation.

My body was still. But inside—inside, I was on fire.

I wanted to scream. To claw. To bite.

But the command still gripped me like iron.

I felt him behind me—closer now. The monster. The one whose voice lived in my nightmares. His presence filled the car, pressed against my skin like heat, like pressure, like something that would never leave.

His hand moved slowly down my arm, the backs of his fingers grazing from my shoulder to the inside of my elbow.

My skin crawled. Every inch of me recoiled, but I couldn't move. Couldn't cry.

Couldn't even blink.

"You're doing so well," he whispered.

I shook inside. Silent and screaming.

Then I felt it.

A pinch. Barely more than a prick behind my knee.

Something cold sliding into my blood.

The drug hit slow. Creeping tendrils of warmth curled through my limbs like smoke. My heartbeat stuttered, then slowed. My fingers twitched, then sagged.

But the fire in me—it wasn't out. Not yet.

I saw Gabe in my mind again. His face. The blood. The sound of my name as he screamed for me.

My heart bucked against the stillness. Just once.

The man behind me didn't speak again. He didn't have to.

The programming did the rest.

I could feel the darkness rising to swallow me whole.

Then—

A voice.

Crackling. Distant. Male.

"...Silas. We have her."

And then, through the haze of my failing consciousness—I heard his voice.

Silas.

Feral. Furious. Unhinged.

"Who the fuck is this?"

But I couldn't answer.

My body had already given in.

The monster leaned in, his mouth at my ear.

"You were always ours."

The last thing I felt was his breath against my skin—cold and calm and final.

And then nothing.

Chapter Forty

SILAS

The moment the line went dead, I knew.

Not just that we were too late.

But that whatever had taken her—wasn't coming to negotiate.

It was coming to finish what it started.

Blood. Smoke. Silence.

Then the storm broke.

I didn't need confirmation. I didn't need coordinates or names or witnesses.

They had her.

Deep down in my gut I knew they had Gabe.

They had to.

A wave of guilt hit me.

It tore through me like shrapnel. Images I didn't want—Angelica's face, the look in Gabe's eyes, blood, the sound of the call—ripped through my skull.

But guilt wasn't going to get me what I needed.

No.

Rage was.

And we were going to bury them for it.

"Get in the car," I snapped.

Jude didn't speak. He moved. Theo was already behind the wheel, the engine roaring to life before the doors even shut.

I barely got the door closed before he peeled out—tires screaming, gravel spraying behind us like gunfire.

The warehouse blurred in the rearview.

So did the blood.

Jude loaded another clip into his gun with steady hands, his jaw tight. "We track them to the safehouse, we hit hard. No questions. No survivors."

"They went after them, didn't they?" Theo growled, eyes locked on the road. "They laid a fucking trap, Silas and we—"

"I know."

"What are we going to do, Sil? What. Are we...going to do?" His voice cracked as he turned to me, and he was that desperate, pleading kid all over again. The one I fought and the one I protected.

I didn't answer.

I couldn't.

Because if I opened my mouth, I wasn't sure what would come out.

The headlights cut through the dark, carving a path toward the safehouse. My heart beat in time with the engine—hard, fast, too loud.

Every mile between us and them felt like an insult.

I wanted to be there already. I wanted to pull them from the walls. I wanted to make them bleed.

Theo's knuckles were white on the wheel. "What if we're too late?"

"We're not."

"But if we are—"

"We're not," I snapped.

The silence that followed was sharp. Heavy.

Jude looked back at me. "And if they hurt her?"

I looked out the window. My reflection stared back. Hollow. Vicious.

"Then we burn the world down."

We didn't slow when we reached the perimeter.

Didn't wait.

Theo skidded the car as he punched the brakes. Gravel crunched beneath the tires as we skidded to a halt.

Doors slammed. Boots hit dirt.

Rage hit harder.

Jude was already moving.

His coat flared behind him, knife gleaming in one hand, gun heavy in the other.

There was no hesitation in him. No fear.

Just that calm, coiled rage that lived in his bones—a kind of quiet, righteous fury carved out of blood and purpose.

His face looked carved from stone. Cold. Beautiful. Biblical.

Like a weapon forged in silence.

Theo was fire beside him. No finesse. No subtlety. Just rage and raw muscle.

He moved to the side of the building where we'd seen one of the cartel bastards run. Boots pounding over gravel, shoulder slamming into the door hard enough to split the frame.

It exploded inward.

The scream that followed didn't belong to him.

It was high. Sharp.

Wet.

The sound of someone learning, too late, that they'd chosen the wrong side.

Theo didn't stop.

The gunfire that followed wasn't even frantic—it was methodical. Angry. Precise.

By the time I reached the threshold, the blood was already on the walls.

I kicked the first bastard I saw straight in the throat. He dropped, choking, and I didn't wait. My gun barked twice—once into his leg, once into the floor beside his head.

"Where is she?"

He muttered something in Spanish. I grabbed a handful of his hair and slammed his face into the wall.

"Wrong answer."

The next man came out swinging. I caught the blade with my forearm—white fire across my skin. It didn't slow me. I hit him with the butt of my gun, teeth flying, blood spraying.

Jude covered the back. Theo had the stairwell.

The house was screaming now—men shouting, gunfire echoing off cement walls, the sound of bones breaking like percussion.

We fought like men with nothing left to lose.

Because we didn't.

Gabe was gone.

Our baby brother.

The one we raised. The one we bled for. The one I swore—*I swore*—I'd protect with every breath in my body.

Angelica—

No.

I couldn't think about her.

If I thought about her, I'd break.

I couldn't afford to break.

We cleared the building room by room. Blood on the walls. Blood on our boots.

And still no sign of them.

I found a phone. Drove my heel through the goddamn thing. Smashing it.

I found a radio. Interference only.

Then I found a man hiding in a supply closet, praying in rapid Spanish. I yanked him out by the collar and slammed him into the concrete.

"Who took them?"

"I don't know!"

"Wrong answer."

I pressed the muzzle against his kneecap.

"I'll ask one more time."

His voice cracked. "They weren't cartel! They weren't ours! They came in separate. Black suits. Clean. Quiet. They weren't supposed to take the girl. They just... did."

"Who gave the order?"

His eyes flicked toward the door. "He left. Right before the attack. Said he was going to 'finish it.'"

I dragged him to his feet. "Give me a name."

He didn't.

Not fast enough.

Theo was already behind him. One shot to the head. Blood sprayed.

The body hit the ground like punctuation.

I turned to Jude. "Status."

"Back's clear. No signs of either vehicle. They're gone, Silas."

No.

They couldn't be.

I clenched my fists until blood welled around the cuts in my palms.

Theo was breathing hard. Jude's eyes were glassy. They looked to me. Always to me.

But for once, I had nothing to give.

Just the fury.

Just the fire.

They'd taken our blood.

They'd broken their last vow.

Now we were going to break them.

All of them.

Chapter Forty-One

ANGELICA

DARKNESS WASN'T SILENT.

It whispered.

"You're such a good girl."

Soft. Slithering. Sickening.

"Such a good little liar... *for us.*"

The words coiled around my spine, dragging something ancient to the surface. Not a memory. A truth.

I had been lying for so long, I didn't know where the truth ended anymore.

And now I was back.

Back in Hell.

But this Hell I knew right? This Hell I'd survived before.

Only this time, it felt different.

Not like punishment.

Like purpose.

Cold air fought for purchase in my aching chest, dragged deeper with each breath. The tiles beneath me slick. Somewhere distant, a voice hummed. Another recited something that sounded like prayer. My body was still. Stolen.

But inside me—something stirred.

A name.

Silas.

A knife in the dark.

Theo.

A drug I couldn't kick.

Jude.

A bruise that never healed.

And then—

And then.

Gabe—

My eyes fluttered open.

The man from my mind—the shadowed monster—stood over me.

Real. Solid. Close.

Run.

It was the last word Gabe said to me. Screamed at me.

The old me would have.

But I didn't run this time.

My lips moved. Sluggish. Dry. Curling as I formed the sound. "F..."

The monster tilted his head. Watching. Waiting.

"F-fuck... you."

Confusion flickered in his face. Only for a second. A breath.

But it was enough.

Every touch my brothers ever gave me roared back.

Every flicker of desire. Every scream of rage.

Every broken thing they loved in me.

And I used it.

A shiver tore through me.

He felt it.

"Are you fighting us, little flame?" he asked, crouching closer. Voice like poison honey. "Are you fighting my hold on you?"

Yes.

Yes, I was.

Not for me.

For them.

A smile cut across his mouth. Slow. Cruel.

"It doesn't matter."

His voice was a needle beneath my skin.

"You won't be alone for long. You wanted them so badly..."

He leaned in. Whispered against my mouth.

"I bought one for us to keep."

To keep.

A pinch came at my side.

Movement before I realised.

Then I knew what they'd done.

"No," I shook my head, fighting the drug that was coming.

A low, guttural moan came from somewhere in the dark in front of me.

Deep and masculine.

Raw and pain-filled.

The tortured sound came again.

And this time.

This time I knew.

I knew what they'd done.

Gabe.

The monster in front of me smiled.

That smiled blurred, then slipped.

Maybe it was me that slipped?

The darkness didn't take me this time.

I fell into it.

But before I hit the bottom I heard one whisper.

A whisper from a brother I loved.

"Where is she?"

She knelt for him.

And I watched it happen.

I let it happen.

Now I can't breathe without tasting her shame.

She thinks I hate her for it.

But hate would mean I've stopped wanting her.

I haven't.

I dream of her on her knees.

But this time—it's for me.

I told myself I'd protect her.

That I'd save her from the monsters who broke her.

I didn't.

I was one of them.

And now?

She doesn't need saving.

She needs to be claimed.

No more lies.

No more masks.

No more soft touches and whispered names.

If she wants to survive this, she'll learn one thing:

Crawling isn't weakness.

It's worship.

And I want to see her worship *me*.